Paper Swans

Also by Jessica Thompson

This is a Love Story
Three Little Words

Jessica Thompson

Paper Swans

CORONET

First published in Great Britain in 2014 by Coronet
An imprint of Hodder & Stoughton
An Hachette UK company

First published in paperback in 2014

1

A CIP catalogue record for this title is available from the British Library

ISBN 978 1 444 77652 2
ISBN Export Edition 978 1 444 77653 9

Typeset in Sabon MT by Palimpsest Book Production Limited,
Falkirk, Stirlingshire
Printed and bound by CPI Group (UK) Ltd, Croydon, CR0 4YY

Hodder & Stoughton policy is to use papers that are natural, renewable and
recyclable products and made from wood grown in sustainable forests. The
logging and manufacturing processes are expected to conform to the
environmental regulations of the country of origin.

Hodder & Stoughton Ltd
338 Euston Road
London NW1 3BH

www.hodder.co.uk

For Andrew*

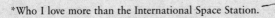

*Who I love more than the International Space Station.

One

Elation and desperation
– it all felt the same

Thursday 19 June 2014
Canary Wharf, London

Ben Lawrence sat in the quiet of his office, hovering his mouse over the subject line of an email that had arrived just seconds before. The new message had landed above thousands of others; collectively, they became a din of tiny imaginary voices, all screaming requests for things to be done, deadlines to be met, and promises to be fulfilled. But the only real sounds that could be heard were the gentle buzz of the workplace beyond his door, the feverish hum of phones ringing and the odd trill of soft, female laughter. Ben read the subject line once more: 'Oil Campaign'.

His stomach flipped and sweat materialised on the surface of his palms. It filled the tiny creases of skin like miniature streams, connecting to each other to form a damp and tangible network of human fear.

He reached out and grabbed the plastic cup of water on

his desk, taking a few cold gulps to calm himself down. It had the tinny taste that confirmed it had come from the water cooler in the modest staff kitchen, never really used because the building was surrounded with buzzing restaurants and wine bars.

Come on, Ben! Everything's going to be OK . . . he told himself, breathing in deeply through his nose. It was his mantra, the words he needed in a career where so much was perched on his shoulders, and so much could be destroyed with just a simple mistake.

The email was from Dermot Frances. His boss was sixty years old and a loud, frightening PR veteran who had more money than he could possibly spend – even in a lavish lifetime. Dermot had a slight frame, possessing what one would imagine was a gnarled, rickety spine. His ageing body was draped upon it like a creased Burberry mackintosh, waiting to be flogged on eBay. But despite all this, and a swiftly receding hairline that he often tried to disguise with clever combing techniques and designer hats, he was still quite a presence, commandeering any room he entered. This probably accounted for why he was so successful. Ben had considered this on many a tense morning after the Board had slipped away from the main meeting room, loosening their collars and mopping small beads of sweat from their brows with the backs of their hands. Dermot's fluctuating moods were felt across the building. He came down hard on failure and showered success with champagne. His employees left his office in tears or varying shades of elation – legs trembling like Bambi's either way. He was whispered about most frequently during those idle water-cooler conversations. What made success? What made such a man – the kind of bloke you wouldn't look twice at in a coffee shop or huddled under a bus shelter on a rainy London morning – so powerful?

Ossa PR was a pioneering beacon in the industry of saving face and glossing over detail, within a towering central London office that lovingly kissed the clouds and glittered proudly in the city sunshine. All the magic happened on two floors within a twisting glass and metal structure that held some of the greatest minds in public relations.

Many considered Ben the greatest young mind yet. He'd earned a name for himself and was reaping the benefits. Executives from other firms frequently discussed him over magnums of champagne in upmarket restaurants. He was a talking point, he had a reputation; he had the kind of career and life people envied.

From the outside everything was just perfect. His salary kept him dressed in designer labels, and had paid for his three-bedroom Dalston flat with its unintelligible modern art and fancy coffee maker. Yes, from the outside, Ben's life was the ideal, and sometimes people resented him for it. He was a strikingly handsome man, a city slicker, young and free. Women lusted over him, licking their bottom lips while wondering what it would be like to kiss him. Men either despised him or sucked up to him.

But today was a big day. Today epitomised the real pressures in his life. The things that people didn't see, or couldn't imagine that he had to deal with.

Mr Frances's office was down the corridor of a floor that felt very much like a rabbit warren thanks to the recent installation of numerous tall, brightly coloured space dividers. They had managed to disorientate even the company's longest serving staff, who found themselves suddenly lost and irritable within their own stamping ground.

'The campaign, shit, the campaign . . .' Ben muttered,

his heart thumping solidly beneath his crisp blue shirt. He bit his lip and ran a hand through his dark brown hair. It needed a cut. He was sporting a thick fringe comparable to a wave, and it was threatening to crash over his face. As his hair slowly fell back into place, Ben took another deep, cavernous breath.

This campaign had been his biggest yet. At just twenty-eight years of age, he'd achieved such unexpected success in his career that the demands placed on him only seemed to rise and rise – but even he had been fazed by this one.

It had been a difficult decision to take it on at all. An ailing oil company, found responsible for one of the twenty-first century's most appalling environmental disasters, had come to his employer for a reputation salvation: a short-term plan that would turn the whole business on its head and see it out of the gutter and earning big money again.

It was a huge contract for Ossa PR. It was worth millions. The kind of project that landed unexpectedly as an initial query and was followed only minutes later by a meeting of red-faced executives in suits and braces, clucking over the scale of it all. Due to his exceptional creative talent, Ben had been selected as the light to lead Ropek Oil out of the dark tunnel it was currently stuck in: he'd been ordered to transform the company's muddied reputation in just twelve months.

His mother, however, had been far from thrilled. She'd been to his flat for lunch the weekend after he accepted the brief, and berated him for his decision. As she'd violently pulled apart a langoustine – as if the crustacean were her own son, lying there defenceless on a thin bed of salad leaves and garlic oil, waiting for its grizzly end – Ben had winced. She'd been very clear about how she considered his taking the project was both immoral and unethical; she

4

felt that the oil company had been so incompetent it didn't deserve another chance. His father Michael had been busy playing golf that day, but Ben had been assured he was also 'pissed off' about his son's decision. Even if he was choosing to be so on the eighteenth hole of the village golf club.

Claire Lawrence was proud of Ben for all he'd achieved, but she wanted him to be 'happy'. While his material success had been undoubtedly spectacular, she dreamt of the day he'd marry, live in the countryside with a family, and exist in a state of what she considered to be true contentment. She didn't understand his life. There was nothing about it she could relate to, especially considering her working years, spent running an art gallery near Ashdown Forest, at the heart of a tight-knit community. She didn't know how constant drinking and partying *truly* made him happy; she couldn't comprehend how real joy could be found behind the dull eyes of the expensive modern portraits he purchased in heated auctions at Sotheby's. 'You need to start thinking about your future, Ben . . . you know what I mean, don't you?' she had said one Saturday afternoon a year or two ago, grimacing a little with the awkwardness of it all. Ben had sighed in response. 'I'm sorry, darling, I just worry that one day all of this' – she had gestured at his flat – 'won't be enough for you . . .' He needed *love* – that was her opinion anyway. She wondered aloud whether his city-slicker life where everything was disposable would suddenly not suit him any more. She worried about what the future held. She worried about how much he drank, how stressed he was, how much he smoked, how he went through women as if there were no value in their feelings. She just . . . worried.

Ben had tilted his head to one side and screwed up his

5

face in confusion as he watched her furiously disconnect another prawn's head from its body, her brow furrowed in anger. 'But that's what PR is, Mum . . . I can't just pick and choose . . . The company has accepted its role in the whole thing, they've been fined a huge amount of money, they've paid for what they did and they need to move on from that now. It's not my business . . . I just have to do my job,' he said gently, smiling at his mother as he fluffed up a halloumi salad with a large pair of wooden spoons. When he smiled, the left side of his mouth always rose a little faster than the right, making him smirk a little. He was very aware of it, because people sometimes pointed it out, rather fondly.

'You *can* choose, Ben. That fire killed hundreds of people, and injured plenty more, and you will be part of the machine that just wipes over that now and actually gives them the chance to start earning big money again . . . By doing this, you are a part of it, and you're going to have to live with that.'

Ben couldn't really understand where she was coming from. She just didn't get it. He had closed the conversation by taking some plates over to the sink, and talking about his latest date. He'd exaggerated just how much he liked her, because he knew his mother was keen for him to meet someone. He knew it would distract her. In reality, he hadn't been at all bothered by the glittery-eyed woman who had sat before him in an East London bar just a couple of nights before, twisting a thick lock of hair round her finger and throwing her head back as she laughed. Still, they had swerved any kind of romantic tension by clattering back to his in a drunken frenzy and covering his flat in their clothes. He'd never heard from her again after that and it suited him just fine.

But here, back in his London office, the results were in. The culmination of months of hard work and strategising; the fruit of dozens of late nights that ended in him falling asleep on his keyboard clutching an espresso.

'Come to my office now, please, Ben.'

That was it. Short and demanding. Very Dermot.

Oh shit, oh shit, oh shit, Ben thought, staring at the words for a few moments, the black lettering almost swallowed whole by the brilliant whiteness of the screen. He blinked hard, but the characters were burned into his eyes.

He pictured, for a moment, packing the meagre possessions that lined his desk – a stress toy shaped like a telephone, a copy of the Frank Ocean album, and a tiny radio with a broken handle – into a brown box and having to make his way out of the building, his eyes to the ground.

Ben got up from his chair and turned restlessly on the spot, as if in a strange bid to prepare himself for what was about to come. He smiled widely and chuckled to himself a little, like he often did when he felt a little out of control – there was a hint of madness to it all. He placed his hands behind his head and took a brief, panning view of the office – on floor forty-five of Tower 100.

Behind his desk was a huge window, looking out over the whole city from a breathtaking height. He'd discovered that if he stood against the window, face pressed to the glass, looked ahead to the Gherkin, and held out his arms, it felt like he might fall. He'd stared down at that scene in many moments of elation and desperation – it all felt the same.

He'd grown to learn that the more he accrued in life, the

7

more frightened he became of losing it all: worry did not deplete as the noughts in his bank account multiplied.

He noticed the sound of his own heartbeat in his ears, but he was still smiling. He thrived on this stuff, this feeling. What was about to happen next would be a huge gauge of his future. If he had failed, things would be hard for him at work; if he'd succeeded, he would be trusted with more projects, bigger projects; and he would climb the ladder even further than he already had.

He composed himself, grabbed his suit jacket from a hook on the wall, slung it over his broad shoulders and marched out into the corridor. He donned his best 'I'm cool' face.

He was good at this. At pretending.

He had to be.

'Ben! Hi, buddy, do you want to go for lunch later?' his colleague David asked, pointing at Ben with both hands and shimmying a little as he walked. His cheeky grin and the nature of his movements implied that this wouldn't be a quick ploughman's and an OJ in the pub next door.

'Not now, mate,' Ben said, charging past him, looking ahead.

People moved out of his way. Everything was just noise. David said something in response, but Ben couldn't hear properly for the blood thudding in his ears.

He reached his boss's door, his name engraved in straight, gold lettering: D E R M O T   F R A N C E S

Ben knocked but, just as he did so, the door was opened suddenly from the inside, causing him to knock on air for the last attempt. He was left hanging for a moment, a limp half-gesture dangling in the space between him and Dermot.

As usual, Dermot had made him feel small before the meeting had even started.

Ben quickly put his hand down and smiled.

'Ahh, Mr Lawrence, just the man with whom I wanted to speak. Come the hell in,' Dermot said. He gave nothing away in the tone of his voice, which was as flat as if it had been measured by spirit level. The expression on his face also failed to reveal the big result. He was very good at that. Hiding stuff.

This was PR, after all.

'Take a seat,' Dermot ordered, as he walked round to the other side of his huge, wooden desk. It was an old-fashioned thing, a weighty-looking table with a green leather surface nailed into the wood with giant gold studs. The room reeked of *Mad Men*. In fact, now that Ben came to think about it, the whole company did. There were hardly any women working in executive roles there: even though Ossa PR was a pioneering, new-age business, some of its values were lagging behind. Ben was sure that Dermot was the reason for that.

As Ben sat opposite his fearsome boss, he noted again how he was surprisingly small for his personality. Speaking to him on the phone conjured images of a large-built bloke, surrounded by a haze of steely strength; in reality, he was a rather stringy chap, just about clinging on to his last strands of wispy grey hair, which looked as if they would float away in a strong wind. But his build was certainly no barrier to his authority: he had the whole thing sharpened to a point.

Ben sat back in his chair – also leather – and shuffled his feet a little to hide his nervous energy.

'So, Benjamin. As you know, I've had the results through today for the oil campaign . . .'

There was a pregnant pause, interrupted suddenly by a large bird flying directly into the window behind Dermot.

9

There was no sound from the impact because the glass was so thick, but Ben clocked the look of shock across its beaky features as it face-planted the surface. He flinched a little and watched in horror as the creature bashfully peeled itself away from the building and began what he could only assume was a dizzy, jerky descent to an almost certain, painful end. He blinked.

'Ben. Something bothering you, is it?' Dermot asked, looking irritated and turning around to see what Ben was looking at.

Of course there was nothing left but a small, greasy smudge.

'No, no . . . sorry. Please continue,' Ben muttered.

'I will,' said his boss, crisply. 'So . . . the results. The results . . . are what we are here . . . to talk about,' he said, his deep voice dropping a couple of octaves to denote the discussion of a very serious subject. He was drawing out each word like chewing gum, creating huge pauses between sections of sentences in the infuriating way adults do when talking to children and trying to do something else at the same time.

Come on, come on . . . Stop bloody well stringing this out! Ben thought to himself, an expression of false confidence plastered across his face. He made a mental note to bill his boss in advance for the nervous breakdown he would inevitably have in five years time, thanks to his position at the dizzy heights of Ossa PR.

Silence.

Dermot leant back in his chair, his face still holding secrets like a series of playing cards fanned out neatly in the frontal lobe of his brain. There wasn't even a glimmer of something in his eyes. Ben wondered for a moment if he was a robot – a heart made of tin and battery acid for blood.

There was a knock at the door, which disturbed their strange stare-off.

First the bloody bird, now this! Ben thought.

'DON'T come in!' Dermot shouted furiously, the added volume on the word 'don't' quite deafening. But the poor fool on the other side must have had selective hearing because the door slowly creaked open.

It was Gavin from IT. The only man who was stupid enough to call Dermot 'Guv' on a daily basis.

'Hi, Guv, I just came in about the network issue,' he said, fiddling nervously with his left earlobe.

'I said DON'T come in, Gavin! There's a massive difference, am I right?' Dermot said calmly, his hands placed over his stomach in mock patience.

'Oh, sorry. Right! I will, err, well, I'll disappear then,' Gavin stuttered, before swiftly extracting himself from the room like a snail retreating into its shell at a sign of danger.

'Fucking moron,' Dermot said, turning back to Ben, who was now feeling distinctly unwell.

Dermot seemed particularly vicious today, akin to an irritable bear, poked from a distance with a large stick, wound up to the very final point of snapping.

It wasn't a brilliant sign.

'Not very talkative today, are we, Benjamin?' Dermot asked, drumming his spindly fingers on the desktop. They resembled the legs of an evil little spider.

'Say less, mean more,' Ben said, surprising himself with his outward calm. But he knew he was a smart talker: he always remained ice-cold on the surface.

'Very wise.' His boss looked at him, narrowing his eyes slightly. 'Well, as I said before, the results are in and we do need to have a chat about this,' Dermot went on, reaching down to something beneath his desk.

Ben gulped as time seemed to slow down into a thick, gloopy liquid. Ben wondered what his boss was reaching for, and pictured for a split second a revolver, or perhaps more realistically, Ben's P45 . . .

TWO

'It's all thanks to you and that brain of yours'

There were a few more seconds of silence before Dermot decided to put Ben out of his misery. 'Well, of course you absolutely bloody smashed it, didn't you?' Dermot exclaimed, as if it were the most obvious and logical thing in the world. His face relaxed suddenly as he pulled out a giant bottle of Moët & Chandon from under his desk.

Just for a moment Ben felt a flicker of irritation at being kept in suspense for so long. *How typical*, he thought, suddenly noticing a feeling of relief weave through his veins until it tickled at the tips of his fingers. He realised at that very moment that his boss was an actor, and that the company was his stage. He loved every minute of it – the drama, the sweat, the tears. He played people in an almost pantomime way most of the time, and he knew exactly how to do it.

'Your campaign has got that company well on course for a complete turn-around, and the directors at Ropek

Oil are, naturally, very, very happy. We've earned more on this contract than initially expected, and it's all thanks to you and that brain of yours,' Dermot said, placing the bottle down on the table with a gentle thump.

'Thank you,' Ben replied, with a confident grin. He tried his hardest to give off the impression that he had whole-heartedly expected this result.

'And here is an additional bonus for you . . . I will also be giving the members of your team a reward,' Dermot gushed, pushing a thick white envelope across the surface of his desk. Ben half suspected it would be a few John Lewis vouchers. That was the usual thing.

'Well, gosh. Thank you, that's – that's brilliant. I'm so glad to he—' Ben started, but was suddenly interrupted.

'Stop bumbling, Ben. I will send you the response so you can see it for yourself and then I would like you to piss off with the boys for lunch and celebrate your success,' Dermot said, still smiling, but clearly keen to summon the next pawn in his giant game of chess.

'Now leave, please, and, well, don't come back until tomorrow. I don't want you lot coming back here, smelling of booze and cigarettes and pretending to work, thank you very much,' Dermot said, with a sly wink.

'Right, er, OK . . . Thanks very much. I'll see you tomorrow, then,' Ben replied, grabbing the bottle and leaving the office.

He closed the door behind him, and leant his back against the gateway to Dermot's hellish lair for a moment or two, his heart rate slowing and relaxing into a pool of wasted adrenalin. Ben wondered briefly where all that nervous energy went – he reckoned he could help out the National Grid with all of his . . .

David materialised in the corridor again, his small

paunch folding over the top of a pair of black suit trousers, failing to be concealed by his jacket. 'Ben! What a legend! Contract went well, I see?' he said, eyeing the bottle of bubbly, then pulling Ben in for a man-hug and slapping him on the back so hard that Ben wondered if he would cough up a lung.

'Yes, yes, it did, thank you. Does that lunch still sound good?' Ben asked, choking slightly and smiling, but looking forward to celebrating his success.

'Absolutely,' David replied, as he continued on down the corridor.

Ben went back to his office, and en route several people high-fived him. Word travelled fast in his workplace.

He felt like a king as he shut the door of his office gently behind him, beautiful London sprawled out in the distance.

He sat at his desk and opened the envelope, the thick paper tearing loudly.

£40,000.

'Jesus,' he whispered to himself.

Friday 20 June 2014
Dalston, London

'Don't go, please,' Marina said. Ben slid his arm a little tighter around her waist in response, a half-hearted gesture of reassurance. He could feel the soft hairs at the small of her back. The early morning sunshine was pouring through the tiny gaps in the blind, lighting up her features.

On waking, Ben had wondered for a second what on earth she was doing in his bed, stark naked, with him. Then his hangover had kicked in, like an off-tune brass band clunking away in his head, and he had felt sick, with a vile metallic taste in his mouth.

Guilt was also starting to creep in.

Ben had been out with his colleagues to celebrate the oil contract. The night was a blur: words and memories all smudged at the edges like a tea-stained novel. Inevitably it had ended in a midnight booty call, as his nights so often did. It had become as habitual to him as brushing his teeth. Marina had arrived at the softly lit doorstep to his flat at 1.30 a.m., tottering around on her heels like a newborn giraffe, equally pissed and full of laughter and soft kisses. Her curves had been wrapped in a black halter-neck dress, and Ben had felt that familiar animalistic wave of desire rush through him as her perfume drifted past his nose. She'd pushed him back gently against the door and traced her finger over his bottom lip, and Ben had felt as if he might melt into a puddle on the floor. He knew she would be his, entirely – well, for a few hours, anyway . . .

Now, Ben wanted to blur out the dull thump in the front of his skull by getting up and having a coffee and a couple of painkillers. He traced his mouth across the back of her neck, noticing again how impossibly soft her skin was. She giggled, and shuffled around until she was facing him, her eyes a limpid blue.

'I've got to go to work soon . . .' Ben said.

'Oh, come on! You swagger in at ten thirty all the time, don't you . . .' she whispered, tracing her index finger down Ben's nose and smiling.

He kissed her fingertip softly, as soon as it met his mouth. There wasn't much he could say to that. She was right.

He studied her in the half-light, her thick brown hair splayed out across the pillow, a few burnished strands across her face. She was perfect, for now. For then. For those exciting city nights and those naked mornings they would spend together before she would become as much of a stranger to Ben as the people who pushed past him to catch the Victoria line in the morning rush-hour.

'Very true.' He sighed, theatrically. 'But don't you have to start soon? Save some lives or something?' he joked, kissing her gently. He was sure she'd dashed off and brushed her teeth before he woke up: she was suspiciously fresh for the morning; a gentle hint of minty toothpaste tingeing her breath.

Ben was someone who managed to meet lots of women, despite his busy work schedule. He worked hard and played hard. Usually it happened when he was out drinking with friends. After several pints/glasses of wine/shots (deleted as applicable, according to the day of the week and nature of the drinking occasion), he would find himself propping up the bar in a fug of drunken glee, and that's when he would spot her, whoever she was, usually coyly glancing at him over the top of a cocktail glass. Ben didn't really have trouble attracting the attention of women; his looks did all the hard work for him. It both irritated and wowed his friends in equal measure.

He and Marina had bumped into each other in a Holborn bar six months previously, and met up occasionally for no-strings fun. Ben had spotted her immediately, dancing with a group of girlfriends with her arms up in the air and a wiggle in her hips. She had made him smile when she danced – she was his type: slim but not a rake, Continental-looking, and utterly mischievous.

He and Marina certainly got on well, but Ben was not in this for commitment. He didn't feel ready, or able, to give anyone that much. Not Marina, not anyone. He always figured that some people were just like that, and as long as people were honest about their intentions then that was OK. Ben strongly believed that he had the right to desire

17

independence as much as another had the right to desire commitment; it all just hung on honesty. But, unfortunately, things did not always run this smoothly, as he'd come to learn.

Lately there was something different in her eyes. He'd seen this before. Probably too many times. The subtle agreements had been made – that there would be nothing serious – but then, inevitably, feelings would change, someone would want more and suddenly there would be expectation, and with expectation came disappointment, and ultimately anger.

Ben had realised that it usually ended in tears, with one member of the party (always the woman in his case), hurriedly shoving on their underwear, usually back to front and inside out, and leaving the flat, the door slamming hard in its frame. Ben was no stranger to this and it looked like Marina would be the next to desert him, leaving him in a room full of crumpled bed sheets and a strange twinge of loss that would last for a week or so, maximum, before it just became another part of the patchwork of his strange and slightly dysfunctional love life.

Ben did not have the ability to love like these girls did. There was too much happening in his life. His career was too demanding. He worked ridiculously late and couldn't cope with someone placing their needs on him in that way, and it would be unfair to let a woman think that he ever could. Plus there was other stuff . . .

'Ben,' Marina said, her voice turning serious. She bunched her eyebrows together in the way she did when she was angry.

Ben felt a little twinge of dread in his stomach: he knew for certain now that she'd misread him, despite what he'd said to her about wanting something casual. *I don't know why so many people take it as a challenge*, he thought, as he studied the light flickering across her face.

He had thought Marina would be different. She had always come across as fiercely independent, so he'd thought the situation would work perfectly for her. Marina had told Ben her story on their second date, at a funky burger place in Chelsea. He'd loved how she'd ordered more food than he had. She was cool, but certainly had a bit of an axe to grind, he'd considered, as she blurted out her story between not-so-dainty mouthfuls of burger and lettuce, her arms gesticulating wildly as she animated her words with confident body language. But he liked that grit about her. Marina was originally from Italy, and had found herself in England after the umpteenth row with her teenage sweetheart forced her to do something dramatic. Because she was a dramatic kind of woman, she had felt that booking an off-the-cuff one-way flight to London at the age of nineteen seemed appropriate. She'd never gone back. Now, at twenty-six, she was a senior nurse at London Bridge Hospital, working all the hours in the day. And now, when she miraculously seemed to find more, she wanted to spend them with Ben.

'Yes?' Ben replied, kissing her again, hoping he could distract her. She ran her fingers through his thick hair and took a deep breath; he felt little shivers down his spine. Marina was bewitching, and enchanting, but that still didn't change Ben.

'What's happening?' she asked.

'What with?'

'Us,' she said, pressing her lips against his nose. Her body language was that of adoration; he suddenly realised she was wrapped around him like ivy.

He feigned ignorance which, a small voice told him,

might prove to be a mistake. 'I don't know what you mean,' he replied, staring at a tiny mole just below her left eye.

He knew exactly what she meant.

Marina took a deep breath. 'Listen, I know, I know . . . that this was supposed to be just for fun, Ben. But it's been going on for a while now. I'm starting to feel . . . well . . . differently about you,' she said, the sunshine lighting up her face as the blind wobbled a little in the breeze coming from the open window. *Here we go*, Ben thought, kissing her on the cheek softly.

'Well,' he replied, carefully, 'I love spending time with you, we have so much fun, obviously . . . But I'm just not . . . you know . . . in that place . . .' Ben felt a coldness swamp his stomach. It was uncomfortable. He hated this part, he genuinely did. But when it came to love, something inside him was dead – it wasn't there . . . it didn't *exist*.

He'd always quietly hoped his inability to love would be resolved when he met the right person, and he just hadn't spotted that person yet, sipping a Long Island Ice Tea and looking over in his direction every few minutes.

Marina looked down at Ben's chest and traced a mani-cured finger over his collarbone. It tickled a little.

'Why is it so hard to be close to you, Benjy? Not like this, but actually close to you,' she muttered, just a whisper away from his lips.

He knew why. Of course he did.

'I'm sorry,' Ben said quietly, kissing her again. He could offer no solution.

She sighed and pulled him closer to her, if that was even possible. Ben knew that this would be the last time he would be with her like this. He was trying to make the most of it. Even if she decided to continue things after this conversation, Ben wouldn't allow it. He'd clearly become a person she could imagine loving wholeheartedly one day; maybe even one day soon. And he felt she deserved more than him, more than someone who was unable to love her.

'I can't carry on like this, you do understand that, right?' she said, tracing her fingers down his back.

He knew he was going to miss her, of course, but it wouldn't be fair to continue. She'd already made a vow to herself to remain composed; Ben could see it in her expression. It was in the language of her eyes, the way the laughter lines were creased at the sides; it was in her mouth, slightly turned down at the edges, but the stiff upper lip was there all right.

Like a lot of disappointed people, she would allow herself a cry in the toilet at work, and then that would be it. Maybe there would be another female colleague by her side, rubbing her back and making all the right noises. Then she would pad the tears away with a fistful of crumpled Blue Roll and she would move on. Which was, in his opinion, exactly what she should do, because a woman like Marina deserved nothing less than someone who would do anything for her. Ben tried to make himself feel better about it all, and thought back to her story. She'd survived this crazy city at the tender age of nineteen; she could survive this – it was just another bump in the road and he was fully aware of that.

Ben Lawrence was just another bump in the road.

'Of course, I totally understand. I'll be sad not to see you any more, but if it's making you unhappy—'

'I've got to go,' she said, abruptly. As she spoke, Ben noticed her eyes already filling with tears and he felt like an absolute bastard, yet again.

Despite the fact that he'd always been honest with her.

She kissed him softly on the cheek. For the last time.

As she dressed, Ben sat up in bed, fiddling with his hair, which was sticking out and pointing in all directions. His headache was entering a whole new territory. He wondered what he should do. He couldn't make promises he couldn't follow through . . .

'Bye, Ben, look after yourself,' Marina said, looking at him and fake-smiling.

Ben thought in actual fact she probably hoped he'd be hit by a bus.

He got up to see her out, but she pushed him gently back onto his bed, one hand on his chest. 'Don't. Please,' she whispered, her eyes brimming with tears.

Three

He hadn't the
concentration for films

Saturday 21 June 2014
Crouch End, North London
'I just think you're, well, amazing!' the girl said, sighing a little and pushing a pair of thick, round glasses a little further up her snub nose.

There was an awkward silence as the girl stared and sniffed a little, admiration tinting her vision a rose pink. It was a typical Saturday morning in North London. The pair had decided to meet in the Vintage Tea Rooms near Crouch End. Their conversation would be played out to a backdrop of delicately decorated teacups, knitted creatures with one leg longer than the other and legions of quirky paintings.

'Well, gosh, thank you,' Effy Jones said, shuffling a little awkwardly in her seat and taking an unnecessary sip of her coffee just to fill the space with something – anything.

Effy was never very good at accepting compliments. In addition to this, she found the overused adjectives too difficult to live up to: the *amazing*s, the *inspirational*s, the *I've told my granddaughter all about you*s. It made her nervous. She just felt like a mess, really.

The girl, a twenty-one-year-old tattooed graduate called Lily, was still gazing at Effy Jones and her freckled face, long, thick eyelashes and shock of vibrant red curls that trickled down her shoulders like a waterfall.

A girl crush had happened.

'So, tell me a little more about yourself,' Effy said, clearing her throat, shuffling some papers and firing up her temperamental laptop. She felt dizzy and tired from the day before, spent almost solidly in front of the computer from 5 a.m. to 2.30 a.m. the following morning. Plus they could barely hear themselves above the hubbub of the small café after a group of mothers and toddlers had suddenly bundled in through the door for a weekend catch-up. Effy's tiredness made it seem as if they'd all arrived at the doorway at the same time, and she'd been amazed at how the tangle of prams, limbs and expensive clothing had made it through in one piece. Within seconds the children had been tearing around the tiny space, banging cups, crying and smearing snot all over their sleeves. The mothers, seemingly oblivious, talked about karate classes, third birthday parties, business trips and Spanx. They added to the now buzzing atmosphere of the café, which was lovely despite the chaos. It was an award-winning venue; handsome waiters dashed around, ensuring everyone was full to the brim with delicious coffee and slabs of dense, moist cake. Fairy lights twinkled around the windows all year. Effy often came here to work if she needed to get away from home.

She tried to pull her attention back to the young, fresh-faced girl before her. She was that kind of untamed pretty. She had a thick, unruly bob of wiry black hair and a pair of dazzlingly blue eyes that seemed to have the same effect as car headlights. Her tattoos snaked out from beneath the sleeves of her cardigan: thick black lines and grey shading. From what Effy could see, they followed an English countryside theme, with poppies, roses and bumblebees.

They're beautiful, Effy thought, suddenly wishing she had been a bit more daring in her youth. She recalled a time when she was just about to be tattooed: the artist, needle in hand, had been slightly shocked when she had suddenly jumped up and run from the studio at breakneck speed, too embarrassed to go back and retrieve her cardigan.

'Well, basically, I've just, like, graduated from uni with a first in International Development. I had a good time but I worked, kind of, really hard, you know? It was all worth it. I can't believe I got a first. That was, like, a fucking shock. I had a boyfriend but he was a distraction so I dumped him, ha. God, that sounds mean. Sorry! But, anyway . . . yah, I want to work for your charity. I've heard so much about it – it's, like, amazing, isn't it? I just think it's incredible that Dafina Kampala will be supporting some of the most vulnerable and sick children in Uganda, taking a holistic approach too, and helping their families. How old are you, Effy? You look too young to have achieved all you have. Sorry, I shouldn't ask that. I know I will be extremely valuable to your charity. I will work really hard, I'm never late, and I'm really flexible . . . I . . . I'm sorry, are we doing this bit, yet?'

The girl spoke at one hundred and ten miles an hour, but seemed to come to a grinding halt as she realised how hysterical she sounded. There was a slight tinge of panic in her eyes as she had clearly listened to herself and decided she didn't like what she was hearing.

Effy had been forced to squint a little to keep up with her, cocking her head to one side to take it all in. All the ambition, wanting, dreams and hopes of youth were opposite her, covered in chunky knitwear, ironic spectacles and hours of intricate ink work. The world seemed limitless. There were no corners, no edges and no boundaries. Anything and everything could be achieved; it was lovely, if a little fast . . .

Effy remembered when she, too, had been like that: a twenty-one-year-old woman fresh out of university and ready to take the fashion world by storm. She would never have dreamt she'd end up doing what she did now – she often questioned if life had some kind of pre-determined element to it, wondering if there was a path for everyone and you actually had very little control over where that went.

As wild and unkempt as this girl was, Effy was glad they had met. She had reminded her not to get jaded; to keep her eye on the ball, on the possibilities . . . it was too easy to become tired, worn and negative. Effy knew that if this energy could be disciplined, and channelled in the right direction, it could be very helpful.

'I'm twenty-eight, Lily. Probably not as young as you think,' Effy whispered, starting to giggle to herself.

'Hey! Don't be sad. That's so young, like, really young!' Lily protested, as she struggled to pull a file out of her leather satchel, her eyebrows wiggling as she spoke.

'I'm not sad . . . it's OK,' Effy said, quietly amused by this girl, and accepting the bundle of dog-eared papers that had been pushed across the wooden table.

Effy scanned the CV. Her presentation wasn't exactly there yet, but Lily had done a lot . . . she was impressed. There was fundraising experience, strategy, social media planning, budgeting, resource management and a lot of placements with charities ranging from small to large, local to international. It was a good start.

26

'I like this, Lily. How many days a week can you help? You know I can't pay you, don't you? The charity is very young and I just don't have the funding yet,' Effy said, glancing out of the window and hoping the day would arrive soon when she could have paid staff supporting her. She dreamt of her own office with five or six staff members, nice new computers donated by a local shop and motivational posters . . . But this was just the beginning. A small seed had been planted and she hoped that one day soon it would grow into a mighty tree.

'I know, Effy, that's fine. I just want to work for Dafina Kampala. I want to help sick children get better, yah? I can do three days a week. Is that OK?'

Effy gulped a little. *This could be really helpful*, she thought, adjusting the skirt of her green Grecian-style wrap dress. 'That's fantastic, Lily! I very much look forward to working with you.'

'Yesss!' Lily yelped like a puppy, getting up from her chair and doing a strange kind of glory dance. Effy grimaced a little, but started to laugh again. This girl made her cringe in the loveliest way.

Her new recruit froze self-consciously on the spot before bursting into more bubbles of excitement. 'You won't regret this, Effy! We're going to make mountains, I mean climb mountains – whatever Trevor, we'll smash this!!' she yelled, a smile on her face so big Effy couldn't help but smile too.

Sunday 22 June 2014
London
'Start with a perfectly square piece of paper. A special kind of paper for origami can be found at most craft stores . . .'
Effy thought to herself, looking down at a baby-blue sheet of paper, a darker blue shade on its reverse.

She could remember the instructions she had learned at her aunt's house, when she was living in Africa, word for word. There was something soothing about the order of it all.

Effy made paper swans a lot. She did it to make herself calm in times of stress, which had multiplied recently. The swans were everywhere, crumpled up in the bottom of her never-ending handbag, on window ledges, stuffed into envelopes with cards for her friends and family. They were like a signature.

'*Begin by folding one edge to meet the other . . .*' She replayed the instructions word for word in her mind as she carefully ran her finger over the new edge she had created.

Effy was in the kitchen, having spent the previous three hours bent over her laptop and scratching the side of her head with a biro, trying to make sense of the thirteenth page of the latest charity grant application form she was working on.

Her boyfriend, Frank, was lying in their huge double bed, as he often did nowadays, probably staring at the ceiling and twiddling his thumbs.

She was taking a break, so had decided to make yet another paper swan to join the pile that sat Jenga-like on top of the paperwork, just to give her some thinking space.

'*Now, fold the paper diagonally. Make sure you line it up corner to corner . . .*' Effy continued folding and fiddling with the paper, until her latest swan had a body and the start of its all-important wings. As she did so, she thought back to where everything had begun . . .

Effy was in her early twenties and was still working in the fashion industry when she had visited her aunt in Uganda. Her aunt had been out there for business, and that summer had changed Effy's life: it had led her to set up her own charity. She made her paper swans now to remind her of this. To remind her of the reasons why she worked so hard. What the purpose of it all was. It kept her going.

'*With the open end towards the left, fold in one flap so that the edge lines up with the centre line . . .*'

Effy was interrupted by the sound of Frank sighing loudly – so loudly that it floated down the corridor of her Muswell Hill flat, crept up to her left ear and whispered into it, a little reminder of his misery and discontent.

She wondered if he'd sighed so loudly on purpose. She wished he'd spend less time in bed and more time in the outside world, doing stuff, whatever it was – stuff for him, she didn't care what.

She would have preferred that to him slinking around the flat like a fart without an escape route.

'*Forming the head is easy. Just invert fold one of the upper tips like this . . .*'

It was 12.30 a.m. and Effy guessed that he couldn't sleep again. She sometimes wondered if he was depressed: he'd changed so much lately that she found it hard to believe it was all down to her new job. He hadn't the concentration for films. The images on their huge flat-screen were 'repetitive and boring' he'd said, like a kid rejecting a really cool birthday present for the sake of rebellion. Frank had told Effy over dinner once that high-definition technology made those fictional lives that should have stayed and ended behind the glass too real. *But he's always been different*, she reflected. He was painfully cool, and with that came the resentment of stuff like brand-new TVs where you could see every wrinkle of an actor's skin, or the peach fuzz on a woman's cheeks – she wondered if this was to do with his fear of getting old. It just wasn't 'acceptable' for Frank to like many things any more, and Effy quietly despised him for that. She was beginning to loathe his rigidity and inflexibility, and the way he couldn't just chill out with a few beers and watch a good film on a bloody good screen for an hour or two while she was trying to work.

When Effy had first met him, she had found this quite attractive, but it hadn't gone so far then – he had just been really keen on recycling, and watching old movies on projector screens. It was OK then, because she had fallen madly in love with him and had lost herself in a rosy haze of infatuation that had gilded him in heady perfection. Now, Effy felt like he was becoming a different man.

Frank had got into books. Lots of them. Old ones that smelt of charity shops; new ones that carried the familiar fragrance of sweet sawdust . . . but he told her that the words all seemed to jumble together. He found himself rereading the same chapter, over and over again. He was uncomfortable. Worried. Frustrated. Effy knew this, but she was working harder and harder, unable to give him the time he needed. She often wondered if it was her fault, or had they just lost touch with each other?

He had recently bought a new mattress because Effy had complained of a stiff neck. It was a lovely gesture, but now he was lying on it, alone – yet again.

But Effy knew she had to turn in this application the next day. There was nothing she could do. People depended on it. Lives depended on it. There was a lot of work to complete, and it all came down to her. It frightened her.

Frank had noticed that, for some months, she had been swallowing Nurofen with gusto and grabbing at the back of her skull while on one of the many frantic phone calls she made. The phone calls were 'never ending', he had complained. He did have a point – they came at any time, day or night. Given the nature of her charity, she had to be available to talk to people when it was their working day. She wasn't always talking to people in Africa, where the time difference was only a couple of hours – her research and enquiries had led her to speak to people all over the world who had expertise in various areas.

Effy had, she admitted to herself in quiet moments, taken on a little too much, but it wouldn't be forever. She had hoped Frank would be proud of her; she had never expected things to go so wrong all because of a little hard work. Effy blamed her neck-ache on the old mattress; he blamed it on her working life. They had rowed about it for all of four minutes on a Tuesday evening over a fortnight ago, Frank saying he felt like that was all the time she ever had for him any more. *Four minutes* . . .

Frank had lost the argument, and that was when he had traipsed to Westfield to order a new mattress. Even though he knew what her neck pain was really down to, he'd forked out £2,000 on a very good one, hoping that maybe it could fix them . . . somehow, because she'd see that he was trying. That perhaps if they had some amazing mattress made in a factory in heaven they would find themselves rolling around on it, locked in lust, like the good old days. Frank also hoped that maybe if Effy saw how much money he'd just whacked on their joint credit card – way above their budget – Effy would start paying some attention to him. It was a passive aggressive approach.

Effy sighed now, unable to shake off the thoughts of their relationship and the god-awful mess it was in as, once again, she started typing into the boxes on the screen before her, his sigh still running circles around her in the kitchen.

She missed how Frank had been before, during the first few years of their relationship. He'd been amazing, and now she wondered if she was just hanging on desperately to the love they once had, hoping it might just come back one day . . .

At first she had just known him as 'Mr Rhodes', because he was 'kind of a big deal' as *Anchorman*'s Ron Burgundy would have put it. The kind of person you didn't call by their first name the first time you met them, or even the second or third, unless you interested them enough to be noticed, let alone spoken to.

Effy had been in her early twenties, working in the fashion industry, dealing with designer samples and accessories for shoots and the like, when they met. He had been twenty-nine, a famous model who had built up such a name for himself in the industry that he was constantly called upon for consulting roles: the world's biggest designers wanted his opinion for the latest shoots and so, naturally, she had bumped into him every now and then in the course of her work.

Effy hadn't, however, been too fussed about him at the time. She respected him, but resented the way all the staff tripped over themselves if he wanted so much as a toothpick. He later told her that was what he liked about her, because she didn't turn into a puddle of uselessness whenever he walked into a room.

When he had paid her some attention at a shoot in a Hackney warehouse for *Cosmopolitan* magazine, she couldn't quite believe it, and when he had wanted to see her at the weekend, she had been bowled over. Effy's colleagues – who she had thought were friends – were filthy jealous about the situation and had started turning their back on her in that way that only envy allows for. She was no longer invited to drinks, or birthdays, and it was painful.

But it was a flourishing love story – Effy had fallen hard and fast in love with him, like a backpacker jumping into a lagoon without knowing what lies in its murky depths. She was so enchanted by him that she had felt she could handle any darkness that came their way; but she had never dreamt things would be so bad just a few years on.

Frank was still a very good-looking man; he only seemed to improve with age, too. In the real world, of course, he was still young, but the warped world of fashion said otherwise. He had always been a little beardy, but now he had a full mop about his face – curling into an almost pretentious handlebar moustache – but it suited him. Effy often thought that he'd matured in the way that Ryan Gosling did in *The Notebook* – as if he had grown into himself – and it all worked better the more he grew. He was beautiful. He dressed well still, at least – but she always thought it wasn't too hard when designers were still sending him umpteen packages in the post in the hope he would get on board with their latest collections.

Frank still worked, but not very much. He did the odd shoot here and there, but increasingly he was being replaced by younger men with what he described angrily one morning while buttering a slice of toast as, 'better cheekbones, sharper eyes and perkier arses'. Effy had always seen this as an inevitable development in his future and assumed he had, too. She accepted it, and knew that life moved on. She felt previous endeavours should be replaced by new pleasures, greater joys that extended deeper than having a face entirely free of wrinkles, and oodles of so-called friends at the touch of a mobile-phone button . . .

On the rare occasion they would go out for dinner or to the supermarket, people often still noticed him. She could see the nudges between those seated at tables around them; the discussions when strangers recognised him but couldn't quite work out from where; or the 'subtle' taking of photographs on camera phones. Sometimes people came over and asked for his autograph – but she'd see a little twitch in his jaw as he scribbled on whatever they had handy at the time (he was once asked to sign a plaster-cast). Effy thought it was all too painful for him as he failed to accept the changes in life which inevitably awaited him – the fact that he couldn't be forever young and vibrant.

Frank didn't work many hours in the average week, and sometimes went two or three weeks without a job, but he was paid handsomely for the ones he did and was obviously not short of cash. The rest of time he spent idly wandering around London coffee shops and libraries if he was in the right frame of mind (which he often wasn't), or, if he remained where he was, as tonight, in bed, feeling low.

And while Effy felt guilty, she resented him for this. She really did.

She was trying to work, but her mind kept drifting into their bedroom, away from the boxes and the figures and the spreadsheets on the screen before her. She had wondered if they should talk openly and honestly about their love story that had now turned so sour, but she supposed the truth was that she didn't want to lose him because things *used to be so good*. She knew that talking openly and honestly could be the end for them, and she had loved 'them'.

She was ashamed to admit it, but she secretly hoped that maybe he *was* suffering from depression or something. Not because she wished such an affliction on him, but because she wanted there to be some reason for his misery and apathy, other than the truth she feared – that this had all been caused by her, self-centredly chasing her own dreams and career to the detriment of the man she loved.

Effy carried on typing, trying to push these horrible thoughts out of her mind, but then heard another sigh as he turned over in bed. And then, 'Fucking hell,' he said to himself, the flat so quiet that the words came skipping down the corridor, holding hands, until they reached her.

To Effy, these sighs were his invisible cries of 'Love me . . . please, just love me!' and her stomach folded over with guilt. She put down her pen, closed her notebook and shut the laptop lid, rising slowly from her chair and looking around at their kitchen, which had fast become her office. There was paperwork littered between pans, mugs filled with biros and paperclips, and the clock had run out of batteries three weeks ago. There was no point of time in her world, she realised – the working day didn't start or end at any tangible point, there was no boss encouraging her to go home and have fun; there was just her, and this job, and it never ended.

The room, a large open-plan one that had once been home to parties, the sound of laughter and the clacking shoes of the fashion elite, was a shadow of its former self. It needed a lick of paint, just like Effy Jones' relationship with Frank Rhodes, but she wondered if it was too late to repair the damage.

Effy walked quietly down the darkened hallway and into their even darker bedroom. The moon was full, a soft light trickling though the curtains.

There he was, curled up in a little ball, staring out of the window.

'Frank?' she asked quietly, already feeling tears prick at

her eyes. It was a strange way to start the conversation, because she knew he was there. It wasn't really a question . . . or was it? Thoughts started rushing through her mind: the fifty/fifty split between anger at him and her own crushing guilt.

Was this all her fault? Had she done this? Why didn't he support her? Why couldn't he fill his life with new ambitions, too?

Frank rolled over and stared at her, his eyes only just glittering in the low light from the moon. He said nothing, but pursed his lips together sulkily.

Effy went over to the bed and sat next to him. The mattress made an uncomfortable crunching sound because, well, it was shit, despite how much it had cost.

'I think we need to talk,' Effy said, taking his hand in hers and squeezing it. He didn't squeeze back, and it just sat, warm and useless between her fingers, like play dough. She squeezed again, but there was no response.

'Yeah, I'd say we do,' he replied, finally, despondence in his tone.

Effy looked down at his naked chest. There had been a time when they were virtually unable to keep their hands off each other, constantly late for dinners and drinks because they'd failed to control themselves even before they left the house. She was still hugely attracted to him, but there was something in the way now. It all seemed like such an effort. *Mutual resentment*, she guessed.

She gathered all her strength and just asked him: 'Are you depressed, Frank? Do you think that's what's happened?' He sighed again, and it struck Effy that she was growing mightily tired of that sound. 'Because if you are, I will help you, I will support you. We can get some help. It isn't the same any more . . . I know that men sometimes struggle to talk about that stuff, but there isn't the same taboo ab—'

'No, Effy, no. I'm not depressed, not in that way,' he interrupted sharply, sitting up a little on his elbows.

Effy quickly switched into silence, taking in the smell of the room. It was a warm smell, a little musty perhaps, but tinged with his familiar spicy aftershave and fresh linen. For a second, she realised how much she would miss it if they broke up. She felt even more tearful.

'I just don't know what to do about us. Nothing is the same since you started that charity,' he growled.

There was so much anger in his voice, and she flinched at the use of the word 'that' put so dismissively before something she'd poured her heart, soul and every inch of her being into.

'I know I'm working a lot, but what are *you* doing? I don't feel that you're being at all supportive; in fact, you're making things difficult for me. This won't be forever, things will calm down a bit, but I feel guilty all the time—'

'Well, maybe you feel guilty because you should be.'

It hurt. Those words made her feel sick. She wanted to lash out at him, but she couldn't, there was no energy left.

He was saying everything she'd feared he would.

'The truth is I miss you and how you were before all this. You used to finish work at a reasonable time, and then you were mine, and we did so much cool stuff. Don't you remember, or miss that? When was the last time we went on a proper date together, Eff? When?' He was growing frantic as he spoke, his own voice wobbling.

Effy scanned her mind's catalogue of memories and struggled to answer his question.

'See? You don't know, do you? I can tell you now, it was

37

nine months ago, Effy – your twenty-seventh birthday. And do you know what happened?'

She stayed silent. He was shouting now, and the memories were crawling back to her on their hands and knees.

'You were *late*, Effy. You were an hour and a fucking half *late*. And then you had to leave *early* because you needed to call some funder in the US, for fuck's sake!'

Stunned, Effy started to pick at the seam at the edge of the mattress, revealed by the rucked-up undersheet. She'd long since let his hand go. 'But you always knew I had an idea to do this, Frank. Did you think I was lying on our first date when I talked about my experiences in Africa when I went to see my aunt?'

'No, of course I didn't, but I never imagined it would swallow you up to such a degree. It's too much work for you – you've no life, and our relationship is going down the pan.'

Fat tears built up in Effy's eyes and spilt over her eyelids; she felt them race each other down her cheeks, curl over her chin and run down her neck.

Frank continued his attack, sharp words like knives in the darkness. 'You know, I've thought about this, on the bus the other day on my way to that stupid fucking job for Rapture in Archway. I thought about what I would have to do to get you to notice me. Would you notice if I accidentally set myself on fire in the kitchen one day, while cooking spaghetti Bolognese? Would you turn away from your goddamn computer if you heard the sound of me frantically trying to put myself out with a damp tea towel? What if I were hit by a milk float one morning and the hospital tried to call you – would you bother answering? What if I fell down an open manhole and was forced to live for thirty days and thirty nights on a pack of chewing gum and a sodding Nutri-Grain bar? What would you do if one day, I just, well . . . disappeared?'

He was really shouting now, and Effy was losing patience. She could just about make out in the dim moonlight the veins that were popping up on his neck and forehead. And then she snapped.

'Oh, for fuck's sake, Frank, you're a grown man, not a child! Stop being so bloody melodramatic. I think you are being selfish, I really do. Where's *your* life? Why can't you focus on something for you for once?'

When he didn't answer her question, and just carried on, she knew then, deep down, that they were probably both to blame for this disaster. Regret filled her heart.

'I miss the old Effy – my *fashion girl*, that was what I liked to call you, before everything changed. Do you remember that? Do you remember how things were?' he yelled. There was an aching silence, but it wasn't long before he continued his verbal assault.

Effy cringed internally at the term 'fashion girl'. At the time she'd loved it, but now it reeked of misogyny. It was patronising, and she feared he hated the fact that she was no longer his to control, not really.

'Once, Effy, ages ago, you were young and stupid enough to wrap your arms around me in front of St Paul's Cathedral and ask if we'd ever get married. It was early on in our relationship and you scared the shit out of me by saying that, but I didn't run away, and that's how I eventually knew you were the one . . . because before, I'd always run away. I remember that very moment, above all the fear and the boyish resistance, thinking at that second in time that I might just be the luckiest man in the world . . . I love you, I can see a future with you, but not like this.'

And, finally, here was some understandable emotion

39

from him, Effy realised, as she stared into the inky blackness in a far corner of the room. This was all she had wanted – some honesty and some truth that wasn't laden with his own grizzly comedic ends. Here it was, pouring from his heart in the stuffy room of their flat in North London. That very moment, she held a flicker of hope that they might be able to understand each other again.

She never did finish that swan.

Four

'I'm proud of you, though, Ben . . . for everything . . .'

Saturday 19 July 2014
Kensington, London

Ben met his sister, Gina, for lunch in a swanky restaurant off Gloucester Road, but he guessed his choice of venue was probably a mistake. He loved treating her to nice meals when they met every couple of months or so, but forgot that she got a little bewildered when faced with the sort of places he booked: she always fiddled awkwardly with tufts of her hair and looked around the room with a kind of startled trepidation. When she first arrived to meet him, wherever it was, her face would usually be fixed in an expression akin to the one a cat has when it falls off a fence or a radiator – utter panic. It was almost as if she'd never eaten out.

Today, she had moaned about the 'spiky cutlery' and whinged over the 'teeny-tiny portions that would barely satisfy a slug on the Atkins diet'. He had reacted in the usual way, which was to roll his eyes and ignore her.

When the bill came, she joked that she wouldn't even be able to afford even a quarter of the fishcake starter, but of course he was always going to pay. Ben thought it was nice for her to get away from her stressful job and family life in the village by the sea where she lived, and enjoy herself for once.

Ben's relationship with his sister was good, although their lives couldn't have been much further apart. He was twenty-eight, single, living alone, and working in PR in London. She was thirty-four, a married mother of two, and a veterinary nurse at a remote but busy practice.

When he took her out it was all white tablecloths and well-turned-out waiters; when she treated Ben to dinner, it was normally some grotty central London burger joint or noodle bar with one member of staff. But that was fine with Ben. He liked to think that he wasn't a snob, despite his circumstances; he just liked hanging out with her every now and then. He had made a mental note that day, though, that the slightly OTT eateries in Kensington and Chelsea were just not her cup of tea.

'How's that bloody silly car of yours?' Gina had asked, taking a little sip from a china cup of peppermint tea and raising an eyebrow at him. She'd recently cut her long blonde hair into a pixie-esque bob, and it rather suited her. Being her little brother, Ben couldn't bring himself to actually be nice to her and admit that, so had instead likened her to Boris Johnson. They had always had that kind of relationship: there was a sort of gold-standard benchmark of piss-taking and sibling cruelty that neither of them was keen to stray from. Whenever they were together, they reverted to their childlike selves and took the mickey out of each other relentlessly, until the insults no longer meant a thing.

'It's great, thanks,' Ben had replied, matter-of-factly, not keen on telling her that he'd managed to burn out the clutch already and that it was actually sitting in the garage being tinkered with by a guy with three stomachs hanging over his blue overalls and a fag fused behind his left ear.

'I still can't stop laughing over the fact that you couldn't drive it properly when you first bought it, and probably still can't now. Oh, the sight of you skidding away from our house with the sunroof hanging off in front of that horsey girl you were trying to impress . . . You really did look like a knobber, Ben!' she replied, giggling to herself.

'Do you still have to do that strange magic dance to get your Ford Fiesta going?' he replied quizzically. 'How does it go again?' he probed, starting to flail his arms around and nearly knocking over his glass of wine.

'Yes, I do actually, and it keeps me fit, which is more than I can say for you. Do you actually walk anywhere now, or is it a Segway these days?' she responded crisply, smiling widely and revealing her big, square teeth that looked as if they belonged in an advert for Colgate. She was tremendously healthy, Ben thought, always feeling slightly ashamed of himself after an hour in her company, having heard the latest stories about what food was likely to kill you, even though you had always thought it was harmless.

'So, how have you been? How's Horse Girl?' Gina asked a little more seriously to change the subject, as she sat across from him behind the smooth cream tablecloth.

She'd made an effort today, Ben realised, and had ditched the usual dowdy dresses spattered liberally with baby sick and hamster bedding. He thought she looked really lovely.

'Horse Girl, who, if you remember, has a name – Felicity –

is someone I catch up with now and again, and she's fine, thanks. And I'm OK, Gina. You know, the usual stuff going on. And what have you been up to when you haven't had your hand wedged up a cow's backside?'

'Oh, well, when I'm not doing that, which is most of the time, I'm loving being with Dan and my beautiful children. You should try it some time—'

'What, getting a husband?' Ben replied quickly.

'No, you silly idiot, although of course that wouldn't be a problem. You know what I mean . . .' she continued, grinning to herself.

Gina was a very smiley woman, and Ben liked that. And they were genuine smiles, too; they came from somewhere deep inside and weren't plastered on, like lots of the people in London who were actually on the edge of a nervous breakdown but who just kept grinning wildly to hide it.

Ben knew that, in all honesty, Gina thought he was very silly really, and he understood why. His big sister led what he felt was a 'meaningful life', if they were comparing things on that level. Her job involved doing good things for animals, even if it did mean decongesting constipated rodents and fishing satsuma nets from the stomachs of Golden Retrievers. She was married to a great guy, and had two healthy, happy kids. OK, they were pretty broke because Dan was out of work, but essentially he knew she was blissfully happy, which was all he could want for her.

Ben knew his sister had always been a little baffled by the way things had worked out, though. She had been very studious at school, and had initially wanted to be a lawyer. She had always been holed up in her bedroom, her brace-clad teeth aching dully in her mouth and her face wedged in a book, while Ben was the one running around town with his 'chavvy' friends, as she used to call them. While

44

she had been trying to distract herself from the pain of her orthodontic treatment with sweet knowledge, he had been smoking weed, stealing DVDs and coming home only to puke violently all over the living-room carpet, having spent nights downing neat vodka in abandoned barns. Ben realised that everyone was quite baffled that he had managed to survive his teenage years, let alone grow into a young man who could not only support himself, but flourish, too. In addition to that, he had somehow survived the tragedy of his youth. *That day* . . .

But despite people's opinions of him, and the lavish lifestyle he enjoyed, Ben knew that money didn't bring real happiness . . . Sure, it helped, but it kind of just glossed over the surface. Everything beneath was always there: it didn't change the past; the things that had happened. Regrets. Mistakes. Would he trade with Gina if he had the chance? He didn't know, really . . . But he knew for sure that she wouldn't trade with him, which probably told him all he needed to know.

She loved him, though, in spite of it all. Ben knew his sister would never normally associate with him if he weren't her brother. She had made it clear to Ben that she found his lifestyle excruciatingly excessive, and that she thought his attitude towards relationships was dysfunctional. In addition to this, she often lectured him about that fact that he drank too much, smoked too much and failed to take enough exercise.

Maybe he was a little dysfunctional, but Ben felt he was OK as he was and, anyhow, he couldn't properly love someone at the moment even if he tried . . .

'Have you spoken to Mum and Dad recently?' Ben asked, realising he hadn't so much as called them for several weeks, which instantly filled him with guilt. Ben's mother had been doing her usual thing of posting him the occasional envelope stuffed with carefully cut out 'relevant' articles she'd found in the paper as not-so-subtle hints that she still worried about him. He read them, of course, but there were only so many carefully highlighted extracts from the *Guardian* about healthy eating and how to look after your teeth a man could endure at the age of twenty-eight.

'Yeah, I spoke to them this morning. They send their love. Sounds like Dad's at war with that bloke at the golf club who let the air out of his tyres the other week, but I think he quite enjoys the drama really . . . He says he may have to resort to trashing his nine-iron ahead of some competition coming up, which I advised him against, but he didn't want to listen.' She rolled her eyes.

'God, I hope they don't murder each other . . .' Ben trailed off, suddenly imagining this petty feud escalating wildly out of control.

Gina snorted derisively through her nostrils and Ben suddenly felt glad that he had extracted himself so dramatically from his old life. He felt their hometown – or village, rather – was toxic in many ways, and he detested how people in small communities knew everything about each other and felt entitled to know everything too, like it was their God-given right. Plus, he'd had something to run away from; a reason to throw his small collection of books and clothes into the boot of his first car (a green Nissan Micra) and keep driving towards London and never return.

'You look good, though, Ben,' Gina said, slightly shocking him. He didn't really know how to reply, and wondered if she was feeling a little unwell. 'I'm not sure when you learned to dress and present yourself like that, because when you were a teenager you were a disaster area, all Global Hypercolor, BO and tracksuit bottoms . . . I'm proud of you, though, Ben . . . For everything . . . Well, apart from that oil contract.'

Oh, God, here we go, Ben thought, bracing himself for another lecture. The pair had been momentarily disturbed by some fuss caused by a woman enthusiastically tripping over another diner's handbag – a Hermès Birkin, according to Gina – before they were back on the subject again.

Ben still couldn't understand all the fuss his family was creating about this contract with Ropek Oil. He was just doing his job, a high-pressure task he had been designated and trusted with, which he felt should actually be something to celebrate, surely? He worked in PR and couldn't just say no to stuff like this; he hated how they failed to understand his position, but knew he had to just write it off as one of those things. Plus, he had too much else on his mind.

'Well, I know you don't agree with it, but my work on the contract has been a success and I may well be promoted again, which is good news, I reckon. Probably time for a glass of bubbly to celebrate?' Ben had asked, trying to shed some positivity on the matter and warm up the cooling atmosphere with some expensive alcohol.

'No, I'm good, thanks, Benjy.' She grimaced. 'I have to be up early for a horse show tomorrow.'

Horse shows. Ben couldn't imagine anywhere he'd like to be less on a Sunday morning, apart from maybe a dog show, which must be infinitely more boring, he considered, zoning out briefly. Sunday mornings for him were all about hangovers, sex, the *Observer* – oh, and filter coffee.

There were a few quiet moments between them as he sipped his wine thoughtfully. While Ben loved seeing his sister it was always a little difficult when, looking realistically at it, the inadequacies of their own lives were so greatly high-lighted by each other's mere presence: his lack of family or love life; her constant fight to pay the bills each month. It made for a tricky atmosphere sometimes.

'So, is there really no sign of a nice girl on the scene? You're a real catch, Ben, even if you can't drive for shit,' Gina said, lightening the mood. A hint of hope danced in her green eyes, enhanced by the soft lighting of the rest-aurant, which was set to a default super-wealthy glow.

'No, I'm afraid not, Gina. I'm just not in the right place for anything serious at the moment,' Ben said, fiddling with his serviette. He felt uncomfortable, yet there seemed to be no release in the delicate pattern of the thick fabric nestled between his fingers.

'OK, well, that's fair enough. As long as you're happy . . . That's all that matters,' Gina said, greedily mopping up some garlic sauce from her plate with a fat, fluffy piece of bread and chewing with her mouth open.

Ben had blown out his cheeks at her in a 'fat' face, and she had thrown her napkin at him.

Phew, interrogation averted, Ben had thought.

Five

'Your brilliance makes me small'

Friday 25 July 2014
Muswell Hill, London

Effy angrily cracked an egg into a pan, watching intently as the clear gunk slid around and filled the surface. It sizzled loudly, flecks of searing hot oil jumping into the air and stinging her fingers.

Over the course of the day, Effy had reached boiling point, too.

'You see the thing is . . . Frank . . . the thing is . . .' she started, surprised at the words coming out of her mouth, but still unable to tear her eyes away from the egg. She was starting to get double vision.

She was trying to get her feelings out in some kind of understandable form, but it was proving very difficult. Effy was aware of Frank's presence. He was sitting at the kitchen 'table' – better known as the 'paperwork dumping ground'.

He had been polishing an apple on his jeans the last time she'd glanced over at him.

Their recent late-night chat had failed to quell her concerns about their relationship, and she feared she was about to break up with the man she loved, while cooking an egg.

Effy hadn't planned to do this when she'd woken up next to him that morning. She'd taken a few moments to watch him while he slept, his chest moving up and down, his lovely profile dark against the early morning sunshine. She had ached inside with sadness when she imagined him moving on and falling in love with another woman; there was so much of her that didn't want to end it. She asked herself if she still loved him and decided the answer to that question was yes. Then she asked herself if he was in her future: could she picture him waiting for her at the front of a church? Holding their child? Being there forever? And the answer was no.

That was when she'd known.

All she could imagine was more distance growing between them. She had committed wholeheartedly to her charity work now, it was her primary focus, and she knew for this she must take a large chunk of responsibility for the loss of him. But, equally, Effy didn't feel supported by him at all, only resented, and – she hated to even think it – he was jealous. Jealous in the same way a child might tug at his mother's trousers because she's busy doing something other than tending to his every beck and call.

Yes, the end of their relationship had been hiding under the bed among the dust and discarded shoes like a furry little critter, counting down the days until it would be brought out to wreak the chaos and destruction it craved.

Effy glanced around again from her 'cooking'. Frank was now inspecting his apple-polishing in the light of a single candle's flame. It was wedged haphazardly into a holder in the middle of the office chaos – a few drips of wax slapped onto an invoice, drying almost immediately. The place where they used to eat together had been suffocated by her career, and Effy felt bad about that.

She had been feeling bad a lot recently.

Frank pursed his lips and squinted a little, proud of his handiwork and inspecting himself in its reflection. It was so typically Frank, Effy wondered if he'd become a parody of himself.

He was only half listening to her. 'The thing is what?' he asked calmly, bringing the crisp, red fruit down towards his left knee.

Thoughts were spinning around so busily in her head that she wondered if his was empty, and she was doing the thinking for both of them. She doubted either of them imagined that night would be the night it would happen, but, at the same time, it was so clearly coming. *Maybe, like an injured dog, he'll be put out of his misery*, she thought. The misery of a love, without, well . . . *love*.

They had agreed to make the effort to go to the cinema the next day but Effy suddenly just wanted to draw a line under everything. It felt like a now-or-never kind of scenario, and if she didn't take the step, they would be stuck in this place for a very long time. She was tired of Frank, this solid, constant thing, the eye of the storm in her crazy life, while she just twirled madly around him. She was tired of feeling guilty, and his apathy was sapping every last bit of her energy.

'Well, it's clearly not working out, is it?' she cried.

As she did so, the temperamental extractor fan over the

hob turned itself off, leaving them in an awkward quiet, interrupted only by the gentle fizzling sound coming from the pan.

There. She'd said it now. It was too late to take it back. The words were published there, in the middle of the kitchen, like the alphabet magnets on the fridge, and no amount of scrambling them around or swapping the letters would lessen their impact.

Frank looked up from the apple on his knee and stared at his girlfriend, a kind of blankness washing over his features until Effy no longer recognised him.

She turned around again and pretended to cook, despite the fact that it was she who'd just dropped the bombshell. Her long, grey maxi dress was twisting round her ankles and skimming the tiled floor – even her own clothes were irritating her. She was glad that her curls were tumbling over her slender shoulders, hiding the side of her face.

The egg was now a bright white, with tiny bubbles of air rising to the surface and the yolk standing proud inside its translucent dome. *Just look at the egg – focus on the egg*, Effy told herself, feeling tears come to her eyes. Suddenly, she felt like she couldn't stomach a bite.

'Pardon?' Frank asked quietly, setting the apple down gently on the only paper-free space on the red-checked tablecloth. He must have known this was coming, but Effy felt as if he was feigning ignorance to punish her, to make this harder.

'Us, Frank,' Effy said, turning off the heat and abandoning the pan. It was useless trying to continue the farce of cooking while she was ending their three-year relationship so casually on a Friday night. So randomly. And in the minutes prior to this moment, there had been nothing but calm chatter between them, which actually had made it a pretty 'good' day in their relationship, because they had actually spoken to each other about the mundane events of everyday life, rather than grunting at each other and one of them shuffling to another room.

Frank's brown eyes almost instantly pricked with tears: Effy could see it from two metres away, and she felt an instant flash of regret. Was she making a mistake? Was she so embroiled in the situation she couldn't see straight?

'But who will look after the goldfish?' Frank asked, trying to chuckle a little, somehow finding humour in the shitty situation.

Effy looked over at the tank and noticed that Biscuit's little pink, glittery castle had fallen over, and felt guilty again.

'Maybe joint custody would be an option. You can have him during the week and me at weekends?' Effy replied flatly, feeling like she might crumple into tears at any moment.

How strange that it was the goldfish that made her feel that way.

'Well, you're right, Miss Jones. Things aren't working out,' Frank said dryly. He had used to call her 'Miss Jones' in the old days; there was just defeat in his tone now. He was looking down at his feet, placed neatly side by side on the wooden flooring. He was no longer home.

Effy knew that Frank had a decision to make, and he had just seconds to make it. She assumed he knew that he could fight this like a soldier, until he was covered in gaping wounds and cuts. But she imagined that he also knew there was no hope. Pinning her down at the moment would be like trying to catch a cloud in a butterfly net.

'You don't understand the demands of my life any more – what I have to do to achieve my dreams. You don't

53

accommodate that,' Effy started, her back against the ledge of the sink. She ran her hand through her hair, before letting it drop gently down to her side. Two solid silver bangles around her forearm jangled against each other as she did so, and she felt the sudden urge to clean out Biscuit's tank before he died from neglect. Effy didn't think she would be able to cope if that happened. Poor little bastard.

Even so, Effy looked into Frank's eyes and wondered if he'd try to fight for her. If there was any fight left within him.

'But Eff, how can I sit back and be your boyfriend, partner, whatever I might be, and have to put up with you being away for weeks, sometimes months on end? It's not fair on me,' he said, making an effort to try to speak evenly.

Effy nodded to herself. Frank was still unable to really connect with her – the woman he said he'd fallen in love with at a shoot. He'd strolled over to her so confidently and slipped her a piece of paper with his number on and Effy had felt like the luckiest girl in the world. It was impulsive, something he later said he had to do at that very moment, and he wasn't intrinsically an impulsive man . . . She was lost in a daydream right there and then in the kitchen, going back to the start when it looked as if they were right at the end.

Effy had a sudden flashback to their ninth or tenth date, when he'd stopped playing it cool and leaving three-hour gaps between text messages and told her how he really felt about her. They had been in a little rum bar near Old Street, tucked away in a dark corner, unable to stop kissing each other. Effy remembered feeling her heart melt. 'You were instantly beautiful to me, Effy. That face of yours set against *that* hair. I love your dirty green eyes,' she recalled him saying in an alcohol-fuelled haze, and as cheesy as it was, she had looked up at him and smiled with glee. No one had ever described her as having dirty eyes. He had made her feel attractive and sexy back then . . .

She snapped out of her reverie suddenly, aware that they were supposed to be having a conversation. 'You? But you've always known this was what I wanted to do. I warned you that I would be spending time in Africa one day. What did you think would happen? That I'd fall in love with you and just roll over?'

He'd always known what she wanted. She'd never lied to him, and that was the only redeeming part of the situation for her.

Frank took a deep breath and told the truth. 'I just assumed you wouldn't be able to handle it, Effy, to be totally honest. You were this fluffy fashion girl who dealt in accessories and vintage garments, for God's sake! You just seemed like a little girl with a dream, a kid pining for her very own unicorn with a sparkling silver mane.' As he said this, he laughed a little to himself, looking at Effy as if he was proud of her for the first time ever.

His words made her cringe.

'And how you surprised me, Effy, with your hard work and dedication. The hours and hours you put into research. All the incredible things you've achieved in such a short time. How you didn't get pissed when you finally got a charity number, but just carried on working while I put the champagne back in the fridge . . . You are amazing, Effy.'

Effy suddenly felt frightened and tearful. She didn't think she was 'amazing'. Amazing was a label she couldn't possibly live up to. Amazing wasn't fair – it was absolutely bloody terrifying. *No one is amazing*, she thought, *because we are all human and full of mistakes and flaws, trying*

to muddle our way through this strange, complicated life.
Effy felt like someone who had taken on too much and was just plain scared. Would she fail without him around, even if he were just hovering in the distance? Was he, in some way, the grumpiest, most miserable lucky charm she'd ever had?

'Did you know I actually felt jealous? Jealous of the nights you spent holed up in your "office", launching Dafina Kampala, trying to make Skype calls to an aid worker in Uganda with a shit internet connection. And every time you go away I feel jealous and I hate it.'

Effy had started to feel light-headed as she listened to him speaking.

'Before I met you, I was never jealous. Never needy. Now I am both of those things.'

And *that* was why he wasn't fighting tooth and nail for her, she realised.

'Your brilliance makes me small, and I simply never feel good enough. I never thought you'd just roll over, Eff,' he said, rising to his feet now and walking towards her slowly. She could suddenly feel soapy washing-up water seeping into the back of her dress from where she'd rinsed some mugs earlier.

'I just need you around more . . . I'm sorry about that. I don't want to put you under any more pressure, so I'm just going to leave.'

Tears filled her eyes until it was like watching him through the other side of Biscuit's tank and, for a moment, the world seemed so unjust. She knew what 'unfair' was: her time in Africa had proved that, with the things that she'd witnessed. But this all seemed so blindingly *unfair* . . .

Life isn't fair, she considered, looking at Frank's handsome face and wishing he could be a stronger man. She loved Frank, she really did, but she was born to do what she was doing in Africa. She was sure of it. But why couldn't she have love *and* her dream? Why did it always feel like one or the other?

Effy watched Frank carefully as he moved past her, a fat tear rolling down her cheek and settling at the top of her lips, waiting to spill over.

And, as he got close to her, he rushed in at the last minute – *catching a cloud*. It was as if he was scared he might lose his last opportunity to kiss her. He settled his lips on hers. They didn't really kiss, but merely stood there for a while, face to face. All Effy could think about was trying to take a mental photograph to remember what it felt like.

'I love you, Frank, I really do. But I have to do this,' she whispered, still against his mouth.

Effy never did eat that egg. It was still there in the morning, sitting in the pan, while Frank dragged his last bag out of the front door and shut it quietly behind him.

Click.

Six

'But you've heard it before'

Tuesday 26 August 2014
Sloane Square, London

The waiting room. Decked out in magnolia. Peppered with wishy-washy watercolours. The pictures. The paintings. There were a lot of them. Dyspeptic-looking tortoises clawing miserably at a pile of greens. Drab seaside scenes with no people. Overweight seagulls that couldn't muster the energy to move, let alone steal anyone's chips. Calm imagery for the troubled mind.

Ben sat on the same wooden chair he always chose, and undid the top button of his shirt. He didn't know why he always sat in this one, but he noted that clearly people were creatures of habit and there was comfort to be found in his own groove, wherever that happened to be.

It had been a sizzling day in London and Ben's shirt was damp with sweat at the small of his back. The heat was oppressive; it pushed down on the forehead and smothered the mouth. It was only exaggerating his state of mind, stringing out his fears in front of the commuting world, making them drip in a sticky glaze.

Ben was a mess. The suffocating heat, anxiety and fear were clawing at his throat, gathering everything tighter and tighter until it became hard to breathe. *It* had come back to get him, when he least expected it. He needed to unload some things because *it* had all been building up again. He wished he could be spread out like a pack of cards, shuffled around and put back in some kind of order so it *hurt less*.

He had decided he was going to have to go back to see his therapist. He should have been on a date right now, but had cancelled and booked an appointment instead. He was struggling to sleep again. It was urgent.

It had been a while since Ben had sat in this waiting room. He thought things had got better in recent months following an intensive course of therapy, but somehow *it* always came back, seeping through the darkness and into his heart. Stalking him in the shadows of the night.

'Mr Lawrence?'

Tula, the receptionist, was leaning over the high glass counter at which she worked and was calling Ben in what he could only describe to himself as her kind of quiet scream. A large chunk of her thick black hair had freed itself from a messy bun and curled seductively at the side of her face.

Ben nodded and rose from his chair slowly, and Tula winked at him as he walked past before turning back to her computer and typing violently. Ben couldn't help but feel this was a little unprofessional, but it made him smile in spite of himself.

He padded across the room, looking at all the people

gathered there as he went, barely noticing his legs moving, feeling as if he were floating. The faces, so drawn and tired. He wondered what his colleagues would think if they knew he had to go to this place. He would be so embarrassed if they knew all the things he battled with in private. 'Ah, Benjamin, there you are,' said Sally Whittaker, as he quietly stepped around her door and into her consulting room. Ben had noticed that she always sounded surprised that he was there, which he thought was amusing. She was good, expensive, reputable, and therefore in very high demand.

Sally was sitting behind an old oak table with the classic banker-style green lamp casting a warm glow on all the paperwork in front of her. She was a blonde, attractive woman in her fifties, who had to listen to what must feel like the whole of wealthy London's most inflated concerns. Everything about her was floaty and gentle – the perfect effect for someone who waded amongst frayed nerves for a living.

'Hi, Sally,' Ben said cheerily, making his way over to the huge chair near her desk. He always feigned a kind of upbeat demeanour whenever he went to see her, but he knew it was futile because within minutes it usually melted into the kind of honesty he genuinely could not express anywhere else: not to his friends, not to his colleagues, not even really to his family. He was too proud to admit that he was scared. And his honesty in this room did not take him to a happy place, so it seemed a little silly to be so chirpy upon arrival. Ben looked up at the clock. He was aware that he only had forty-five minutes to try and feel just a little better. To get through a few nights with some kind of quality sleep.

He had started seeing Sally more than a year ago after suffering two 'bad' months on the trot. He had felt it coming. That familiar feeling of dread. *It* found him and wouldn't let him go – the dog's teeth had a firm grip on him, biting and shaking until it felt like his soul was limp.

They had spoken about *that day* the very first time he had gone to see her, and Ben had handed over £250 for 50 minutes of her precious time in some kind of hope that she could heal him.

For the first time ever, he'd spoken with a stranger about the events of that dreadful day. It had felt like he was living it all over again as the words started to pour from his mouth, but by the end of his first session it was like a tiny weight had lifted, and every time he went back he felt lighter. Sometimes by only a tiny little bit, but it always did. Sally made Ben explain it all from scratch. Every moment of it, from the second he woke up that morning to the last memories he had of that night. His friends didn't know about it, only his family, and now Sally of course.

'So, how are you feeling?' she asked now, the soft wrinkles creasing at the sides of her eyes as she gave him a warm smile. Ben thought that she must have had a haircut recently because her hair was shaped into a thick bob, which wobbled a little in the way that only freshly trimmed hair does.

'Well, that's an interesting question. I really thought I'd made progress, but it's coming back . . . And I'm surprised it is, too,' Ben said quietly. As he did, he glanced out of the window and noticed how the blisteringly hot day had suddenly melted into stormy skies. Raindrops were gathering on the glass. It was somewhat indicative of his mood.

'OK, well, that does happen of course. I have visits from a lot of my clients months and sometimes years after their initial intensive therapy, just to keep things on track. There is no set time when this will get better for you, Ben, so it's fine that you're back here. You are always welcome,' she said, reassuringly.

A loud clap of thunder interrupted them briefly. Ben took a deep breath as he suddenly felt panic wash over him. The imagery came flooding back. The huge white feathers. The water. The screaming. He swallowed hard, feeling sick.

Ben wished he could outrun the demons. Become strong enough to hare through the woods and lose them at every twist and turn, down holes and amongst thick bracken and that, one day, he would emerge at the other side into the sunshine and never be troubled by them again. He had tried antidepressants prescribed by his GP, but they had made him nauseous and yawn a lot. He'd thrown them in the bin and made a vow to stay away from them. Ben had never told his doctor the real reason behind his pain, or much about the problems he experienced – he'd just said he felt anxious and within twenty minutes he'd left clutching a prescription for escitalopram. He wondered if he shouldn't go back and ask for more, give them another try . . . ride out the side effects perhaps. Sally couldn't help with this stuff because she was a therapist, rather than a doctor or a psychiatrist.

'Well, I felt it was important to come back. All the usual feelings have returned.'

Sally got up and closed the window softly because rain-drops were blowing in and splattering a pile of books on the sill. Then the room was deathly quiet.

She spoke calmly as she walked back to her desk. 'So, the last time, we identified some elements of what you have been feeling, and we routed it back to where it came from and I believe that from your feedback, this was how you felt better . . .'

'Correct,' Ben said, leaning back in the chair a little and trying to take deep breaths. He looked down at his suit. It had cost £2,000. Nausea. Confusion. He always felt he might throw up when this conversation started, like his whole being was frightened of it.

'So, which feelings have come back, would you say?' she asked, putting her hands together on the table and intertwining her fingers.

'Guilt.'

'OK, I want you to just speak about that.'

'But you've heard it before, we've gone over this again and again . . .' Ben responded, his voice tinged with panic. He could feel his nose crinkling slightly at the bridge. He didn't want to be dragged back to that place, but he knew he had to go. He always felt like they were dredging up old ground and he was frightened that if this never got better, he might not be able to live with these feelings any more.

'That's OK. I want to know about it again. Now. If you feel you can talk about it . . . ?'

Therapy was never aggressive. Sally Whittaker tended to coax him in the right direction, and he was intelligent enough to realise the methods she used: the long silences that forced him to fill in the gaps with words and sentences, as if he had been presented with a white sheet of paper and a marker pen. *Fill it.* She herded his feelings together until they were gathered in one place, where they could be dealt with somehow. He knew how this worked. *Maybe that's why it didn't really fix anything*, he thought. But maybe it was a matter of accepting that the past could not be 'fixed', or erased, or re-written, and that he merely had to learn to live with it. Ben wished he could.

'All right, I'll say it once more. I guess when it all comes back to haunt me, I feel like I am intrinsically a bad person because of that day . . . It's kind of at the core of me, or like a smudged finger mark all over me . . .' Ben had started. As he spoke, the swan came back into his mind. The huge bird with its breathtaking wingspan, and the way it had looked on so nonchalantly as their lives smashed into a million pieces. Then he could hear water. Splashing. Bubbling. His heart began to race. A strange, tingly feeling flooded his fingers and his legs, a feeling that he might lose control washing over him. He'd had dreams about that bird, on business trips or holidays, when he thought he was doing OK, and then he'd drift off to sleep again and there would be water and whiteness, and he would find himself sitting up in bed suddenly, grabbing on to unfamiliar sheets, ones that made his skin itch, having to light a cigarette and paw through the pages of a tatty old novel to calm himself town.

He carried on. 'And so, therefore, I feel guilty about the achievements I make in my career, guilty about the loving family I have and feel I don't deserve, and guilty when I get close to anyone who comes into my life . . .'

'Because you don't feel you have the right to any of the privileges that come with your wonderful life – and don't you think it is a wonderful life, Ben, despite what happened?' Sally said, calmly.

'Yes.'

'And you also fear that you will hurt someone. Because of your past, you no longer trust yourself in the future,' she added.

'Well, yes . . . Plus, I don't know why I keep being blessed with the things I am blessed with. I don't know why things go so well at work. I was given a bonus, a fucking *bonus* . . . a cheque for £40,000 the other day, and it felt dirty in my hands. I feel like I shouldn't be on this earth, let alone achieving the things I do.' He paused. 'I don't deserve it. I don't even deserve to be here.'

'But we know that is an irrational inner voice speaking to you, don't we, Ben? We established that before, didn't we?' Sally said, her fingers still locked together, a single diamond ring sparkling in the light.

There was a flash of lightning followed by a dull thud of thunder, masked effectively by the triple glazing.

'Yes, apparently so, but when it comes, when I feel like that, I can't shake it off.'

The rain was coming down hard now. Big drops raced each other down the glass and onto the windowsill. Flowers in the window box outside were thrown left and right as they were battered by the angry rain.

'Do you remember how we spoke about these things, these blessings, and even you said yourself that most of them don't just come to you, but that you earn them?'

'Yes,' Ben muttered shamefully. He thought about the oil company. About life, and about death. Sally had tried to point out that the great relationships he had with family and friends, and these pay cheques, were a result of his hard work, attitude and empathy, and that he in fact deserved everything he enjoyed because he made it happen – all of it. And that he should stop seeing these things as random gifts that he didn't deserve. It had struck a comforting chord at the time, but then of course his mind had shelved some of the most helpful elements of his therapy, letting his fears take control again.

'It's becoming particularly difficult now, on a personal level. I meet women. I date women. Things move on, we get closer, but as soon as I can see that things might get serious, the fear comes.'

'How does it feel?'

'My heart races. So fast I feel I might die, and I feel light-headed, and I want to run. It's fight or flight. I suppose I try to kid myself that I'm just built that way, that I'm not a relationship person, but I know deep down that's not why.'

'What is the fear that underpins it? Why does it frighten you to be really close to a woman?' she asked, her look sharpening. Ben had the impression that Sally Whittaker thought she might be about to strike gold. To gain the information she needed to really help him.

'Because then I will have to tell them what happened, and I might hurt them, and I never want to hurt anyone, and I'm scared because this is what happens in life . . .' Ben's emotions surged and he suddenly felt as though he might cry.

'And what do you think would happen? If you met a woman, and you fell in love, and you told her about that day . . . What do you fear might happen?'

There was a long moment of silence.

Ben's breath had quickened in his lungs, and his mouth felt as if it were packed with cotton wool.

'I know she would disappear,' he said.

Seven

'So, you might be wondering how this affects you'

Wednesday 27 August 2014
Canary Wharf, London

'Lawrence. My office. Now.'

Ben jumped in his seat at Dermot's presence, his heart fluttering suddenly. He was hung-over and this always made him tired and anxious. His spindly, spider-like boss had somehow opened the door to his office with such speed that Ben had not even had the time to hide his phone and pretend that he was working.

He was surprised that Dermot had actually bothered to walk down the corridor – he normally opted to send one of his snivelling, bumbling minions, or press the '5' button on his phone, which was Ben's number on speed dial, because he was too impatient even to use the four-digit extension.

'Oh, right, of course. What, sorry, right now?' Ben muttered, as he slowly put his phone on his desk, hoping the fact that he was sending filthy messages to a woman wasn't written all over his face. The vague flush of horniness that he'd been basking in had suddenly disappeared and had been replaced by a kind of cold, yet sweaty, humiliation.

Dermot always made Ben confused. It was a particular type of bewilderment that he often experienced when dealing with people who were so frightening and direct that it became difficult to listen to and digest even the most basic instructions. Normally he was very switched on. Ben always quietly cursed himself for not being more together in these situations.

'Yes. Now. Follow me,' Dermot said, turning around suddenly and marching back out into the corridor. Ben almost tripped over his satchel on the way out, eventually catching up with his boss who was, by now, almost halfway to his thick and imposing, gold-lettered office door. A few people glanced at Ben as the pair made their way across the office.

'Is everything OK?' Ben asked, a little out of breath, running a hand through the front of his hair as he walked. They were moving so fast that the front of his blazer flapped a little in the air.

'No, of course everything isn't bloody OK, Ben. It's never OK! What fucking planet do you live on?' Dermot sneered, opening the door for Ben and letting him through.

'Right, of course, yeah,' Ben said, wishing he hadn't asked and taking a seat, the thick leather squeaking under his weight as he sat down.

Dermot darted to his own chair and sank into it, crossing his knobbly knees and linking his fingers together in front of his chest. 'It's charity partnership time again, Ben,' Dermot said, raising an eyebrow and pushing himself back a little in his seat.

'Oh, right. That's nice,' Ben said flatly. He wondered how this affected him. Charity was one of many subjects that never crossed his mind, like home improvements, baking and parish councils. It just wasn't on his radar. He wasn't against it, of course, he just wasn't really interested.

'The charity board has chosen the organisation Ossa PR wants to help. I think it's a pretty sterling decision.'

Ben started to glance out of the window behind Dermot's pale face as he droned on about the charity, which he'd never heard of, and explained what it did. It was a brilliantly sunny day, and Ben couldn't help but notice that London seemed to be basking in the glory of it all. He wished he'd not had that fifth whisky and Coke last night after his therapy session. *Drinking alone, too. That's dodgy*, he thought. He started to think about the dry cleaning that he needed to pick up, the fact that he'd forgotten to put the bin out, and whether or not he would buy a fragrance from Jo Malone for his mother's impending birthday, or whether a coffee machine would be a better choice. And if he got a coffee machine, which make should he get? *Frother or no frother?* And then the neighbours had been noisy recently. They weren't normally. What if they started doing it all the time? Would he go for the polite-knock-on-the-door approach, or the passive-aggressive handwritten note? He'd hardly had any sleep. God, he was tired.

'Back in the room, please,' Dermot yelled suddenly, clicking the fingers of his right hand sharply. Ben was startled again. He hadn't thought he was being obvious in his zoning out but, yet again, his boss had seen right through him. It was unnerving.

'Sorry, Dermot. The charity sounds great, what an amazing cause,' Ben said quickly, hoping Dermot wouldn't ask him any specific questions about what he had just said.

He felt a wave of panic when he realised he couldn't even recall the name of the charity.

'So, you might be wondering how this affects you . . .' Dermot muttered, pursing his lips at the end of his sentence.

'I am a little, yes,' Ben responded, shuffling uncomfortably in his seat. He had a horrible feeling he knew where this was going.

'I want you to be the charity contact for this year's corporate partnership.'

Bollocks, Ben thought. This was a disaster.

Each year some unfortunate soul was given the title of 'Charity Champion'. This meant managing the relationship between Ossa PR and the non-profit organisation it was choosing to help through a mixture of free PR services and fundraising.

The dreaded task was always passed around the building from year to year, like a game of Pass the Parcel, except this time, nobody wanted it to land on them. The sheer mention of it could clear a room, with people suddenly needing to go and make a phone call, or urgently sort out something stuck under their contact lens. The reasons for this were unclear, but it involved a lot of hearsay and, Ben suspected, exaggeration. The job was rumoured to be difficult to manage on top of everyday work, and often involved lots of random and irritating tasks like chasing forgetful colleagues for their sponsorship money and organising coffee mornings and the like. That said, whoever took it on was always adored by Dermot (if it had gone well) for at least three minutes, which was pretty good going. It was also one of those tasks that people always felt glad they had done afterwards, so it probably wasn't all bad . . .

Due to a collective reluctance to take on the job, Dermot

had now opted for randomly choosing members of staff. It could be anyone: the receptionist had done it last year, and the in-house legal advisor the year before. No one was safe.

'Up for it?' Dermot asked, as if it were a choice.

'Of course I am, you know me. I love this kind of stuff,' Ben said, with a mock enthusiasm that even he was impressed by.

'Good lad. You'll need to ring them in the next couple of days to tell them the happy news – I'll send you the contact details in a minute. Do a bit of research as well, will you? It would be beneficial if you knew what the fuck you were talking about, and you certainly weren't listening to me for the past God knows how long. Anyway, I think your client will be quite happy about it all,' Dermot said with a smirk that signalled their meeting was over.

'Sure, of course. I'll check it out,' Ben said, standing up.

He could feel his heart sinking as he made his way back to his office. How was he going to manage all this on top of everything else? He could always pass a lot of it on to an intern or something . . . that was generally allowed. He felt bad for thinking this, but he just couldn't cope with it all on top of everything else. And what was this research Dermot was talking about? And why would his client be happy about it? He had back-to-back meetings for the rest of the day, and a corporate networking event later on that night. The rest of his week was blocked out with meetings. It just wasn't realistic.

'Fuck the research. It'll be fine . . . I'll wing it,' he whispered under his breath. He got back to his desk to find twenty-eight new emails had materialised since he had left the room.

Eight
Effy imagined a city guy

Thursday 28 August 2014
Muswell Hill, London
Effy pulled the duvet over her head. It was 3.30 p.m. on a weekday but she couldn't face life. *It's strange how grief, or shock, hides away for a while, and then returns a little later to tap you on the shoulder, desperate for a chat*, she thought.

'I'm not feeling good, Rosa,' she whispered down the phone to her best friend, feeling her own breath hot against her face in the microclimate she'd created under the sheets.

'Have you brushed your teeth yet?'

'No.'

Effy was pretty sure her breath would be capable of tranquilising a rhino from quite a distance. It had been over a month since Frank Rhodes had left their flat as the sun rose on a new summer's day, and things had been more difficult than she'd expected. She missed him more than she had imagined she would, even though she knew it had been the right thing to do. She had thrown herself into work to

72

try and block out the reality of what had happened but, instead, she'd just delayed her tears. Effy thought she was doing OK, but those difficult emotions had come to find her a few days ago and she'd been flailing around in bed ever since, wavering between panic, regret and anger.

Everything had been stunted; she felt like she was losing control. She felt guilty, but exhausted. Emails were piling up and the phone kept ringing. She only had the energy to answer calls from friends and family members. *Everything else will have to wait*, she thought. Her work had slipped badly in the past forty-eight hours, but luckily her new volunteer, Lily, was keeping things afloat, even though this also made her feel guilty . . .

Meanwhile, Effy's mother, Alison, had been very understanding, spending hours on the phone from her villa in southern France, making all the right noises from beyond a nice glass of sauvignon blanc, but nothing seemed to help. Her father, Alan, had been passed the phone at various points – Effy assumed this was when her mother needed to fill up her glass of wine – and, in his deep, booming voice, he'd shared 'helpful' observations such as: 'The guy is a moron' and 'I knew he was trouble because of that useless handshake of his. You can always tell the substance of a man by his handshake . . .' in a bid to try and make her feel better. She'd appreciated their efforts, nonetheless.

'It was always going to be hard, Effy . . . It's totally normal that you're upset. But it will get better, you know – hearts mend,' Rosa said at the other end of the line, with that warm, honey tone she possessed.

She was always so comforting. She was a friend who always put things in beautiful perspective, and untangled even the most complex of knots. Effy was glad she had her in her life.

73

'I just wake up in the night and I expect him to be there, but he isn't, of course. And that's when it hits me. What if I've made the wrong decision?' She gulped, her eyes welling up with tears. Her curly hair was unkempt and tangled. It was splayed all over the pillow beneath her head, and Effy wondered distractedly if she'd ever be able to make sense of it all. As she spoke, she swished her legs around restlessly in the twisted bed linen. She missed his legs. His ankles. His chest. The way his hair always grew too long around the back of his neck. Effy missed the moles on his arm that looked like a cluster of stars – Ursula Major. She was forgetting all the bad things, and only their most beautiful moments were coming back to her in her rose-tinted rut. Why hadn't he fought for her? That was the most shocking part of it all . . . The least Effy had expected had been a little bit of a battle: for him to tell her how much he loved her, and how sorry he was for being a brat, and that he would change. She'd pictured roses. Lots of them. Flowing through the letterbox and splashing up the walls like a great wave of soft, pink petals. This was the biggest disappointment of all for her. But he'd just seemed to give up. Just like that. Secretly, she'd hoped they would be able to sort things out, somehow.

'You haven't. He's not enough for you, Effy. I'm sorry to say it, but you need someone who has big ambitions and big dreams, too. You've always been like that, it's never going to change. You need someone who can not only handle that, but someone who is proud of you. Someone who supports you,' Rosa said through a line that broke up occasionally, severing some of the words. But they were still understandable.

'Do you think I'm a selfish cow? This is all my fault, isn't it?' she cried.

'No, Effy. Of course not!'

Effy knew what she had to do. She had to get out of bed, put on some clothes, go for a walk or a run, cook a meal, look after herself. She had to move on. As she started to say something along those lines, her phone made a beeping noise. She pulled it away from her ear. There was a call coming in from a landline she didn't recognise.

'One moment, Rosa, sorry. Someone's calling me.'

Effy's stomach flooded with butterflies. She was sure it would be Frank, calling her and saying he would change, and that he missed her and loved her, and that he'd decided to come home and be more supportive of her dreams. Effy hoped he'd breathlessly promise to actually do the washing up, help around the house sometimes, and not sulk in their room while she worked late nights. Effy hoped they could have their happily ever after.

She pressed a button and was put through to her unknown caller.

'Hi, is this Effy Jones?'

It was a pleasant male voice. A polite one, she noticed. Effy imagined a city guy, all suave and cool, someone who looked a little like Hugh Grant, sitting casually on a huge leather chair and generally being sexy and posh.

It wasn't Frank, though . . . Her stomach sank, and a little wave of frustration washed over her. 'Yeah, hi. Who is this?' she asked, noticing that she sounded distinctly uninterested. It was also getting hot under the covers, so she had to emerge for air.

Effy looked around at her tip of a bedroom. The sweet smell of Frank had long gone, replaced by the sour odour of heartbreak. She was being ambushed by the obvious wreckage of a break-up. An empty ice cream tub, three empty Doritos bags and a selection of weepy films with the DVDs in the wrong cases were glowering at her threateningly. Frank would have hated that; he always liked things in the right place, in the right order. Effy wondered if she was doing it in some kind of attempt to rebel against him, but he'd never see it anyway, so it was pointless. She was just creating her own personal health hazard.

'This is Ben Lawrence. I'm calling from a PR firm in the city, Ossa PR. I have some good news for you.'

'Oh, right,' Effy said flatly, pretty sure this would be some kind of annoying promotional call where she would try unsuccessfully to wean the clinger-on off the line, before getting irritated and hanging up. She wondered if she should just cut the crap and do it now. She'd heard of Ossa PR. They were massive. There was no way they would be of any real use to her; they probably thought her charity was much bigger and were touting for contracts.

Effy's finger hovered over the red button. She could just end this now.

'Erm, OK. Miss Jones, is this a good time to talk? You sound busy,' the caller said, his voice becoming somewhat sterner. It was also mixed with disappointment, she noted, which caught her attention.

Effy sat up in bed and swung her legs out into the not-so-fresh air, realising that she was going to have to cut the attitude. She blushed.

'Sorry. My apologies. I was busy, but I'm not now. You have my full attention.'

'Great.' The voice on the other end of the line brightened. 'Well, every year we choose a charity to be the organisation we support for twelve whole months of fundraising fun—'

'Corporate partnership!' she whispered quickly to herself, intrigued, and a little embarrassed that she'd automatically

76

said it down the line with such hunger. Effy needed a corporate partnership. Badly. She'd contacted dozens of companies. If she were lucky, the receptionist would pass a message on, or at least do a great job of pretending to. But there hadn't been a shred of interest. She wondered if Lily had put the application in for this one – so much had happened that she couldn't remember the details any more. They were constantly applying for money because funding was the missing piece of the puzzle. The lack of it was the only thing holding them back.

'Yes, absolutely. Anyway, our board has chosen your charity,' the voice said.

The voice had a smile to it. Effy could hear that. And then a smile was plastered all over her own face.

'Really? Dafina Kampala? We've made it to the first round?' she shrieked, feeling her heart fluttering a little beneath her musty pyjamas.

The man laughed softly. He sounded attractive, she realised, quickly telling herself off for being so shallow. Effy generally hated PR people, with what she considered were their flashy ways. But she had to play ball.

'Well, it's better than that, Effy. We chose you and that's it, really. We've been working for charities like this for many, many years. Are you keen to go ahead? We raised £100,000 for The Desert Rhino Trust last year . . . We can't obviously guarantee a figure like that, but we hope for it to be similar—'

'Pardon?'

'Sorry?' the man asked, confused.

Effy raised her free hand to her mouth and tried to calm herself down a little. She imagined Uganda and its dusty roads, the chaos, the cows and the chickens. She thought about the children, their faces, all the problems they had to overcome. She thought about £100,000 and what she could do with that. The lives she could change.

'No, nothing. That's incredible news. Thank you so, so much,' she responded, getting to her feet and doing a little dance, before stubbing her toe on the corner of her dresser. It hurt, unbearably, the kind of pain that made her want to punch inanimate objects. Her eyes instantly watered due to the searing agony running through her foot, but it was not the time for swear words to slip through gritted teeth.

'Great, that's fantastic. We would love to invite you to the office to celebrate. It would be great to meet you, as we'll be working fairly closely for the next twelve months or so. Does next week sound good?' he asked.

'Yes, yes,' she sighed, now sitting on the edge of the bed and squeezing her foot in a vice-like grip with her free hand. She had to catch her breath. 'Next week sounds perfect,' she added, falling onto her back and smiling at the ceiling.

'Oh my goodness Lily I could actually hug you right now . . .' Effy had gushed down the line, with tears in her eyes.

'Say what?' Lily responded, sounding completely perturbed by this sudden elated phone call from her boss, who had been in hiding recently.

'Ossa, Ossa PR, as in Ossa bloody PR have chosen *Dafina Kampala* as a new charity partner . . .'

The line went quiet, Effy could hear Lily's breathing. It had sped up a little.

Excitable chatter, the clinking of mugs and the grinding of coffee beans could be heard in the background. She pictured Lily in some cramped London café, wearing something strange (probably thrown together from a vintage shop's bargain bin). She imagined her, hunched over a laptop with a hand over her mouth, the other resting gently on the keys. Black nail varnish and statement rings.

More silence.

'Lily? Is the line OK? I can't, I can't . . . hear you?'

'Are you shitting me, Effy? Are you being seriously serious?' Lily eventually asked.

'Yes, I am being the most seriously serious I have ever been in my whole history of being serious. How on earth did you do it? I didn't even know you were applying, in fact. God I'm sorry, I feel bad. I've been so preoccupied lately with all this stuff with Frank . . . Do you even realise how unlikely it is that we should have been picked by someone like Ossa?'

'I'm so made up about this!' Lily said, sounding a little emotional.

'I promise I will be back on top of things as soon as possible, Lily . . . I'm so, so sorry. You're doing a fantastic job . . .' Effy trailed off, feeling extremely guilty now.

'It's fine . . . Seriously. I'm taking care of business just fine, and you need a break anyway . . . I'll contact you if anything urgent comes up, but for now all is well. Read old books, watch your favourite films, cook some chicken, just do what you need to do for you . . . Just feel better, yah?' Lily said, with confidence. Effy chuckled a little. She couldn't help but smile at the things this girl said.

'You're amazing. Thank you, thank you, thank you. I can't really thank you enough. I've got to go to Ossa PR's offices soon, to meet them, and speak to them about it all. I'm so bloody nervous already, it's ridiculous . . . I'm not in a good place at the moment, what if I screw it up?' Effy said down the line, feeling sick at the thought of it all.

'You'll blow them away . . .' You've got nothing to fear.

You are a unicorn,' Lily said kindly, before blowing her nose and sniffing a couple of times.

'Are you OK. Lily?' Effy asked softly.

'Yeah, yeah, sorry. I'm just so happy . . .' Lily said, with a smile in her voice.

Nine

Where are all the women?

Thursday 4 September 2014
Canary Wharf, London

Effy stared at her reflection in the mirrored walls of the lift. It was a long way up to Ossa PR and time seemed to blur in the seemingly airtight box as it ascended the inside of the building, powered by hydraulics. In reality it was probably only a few seconds. '*I love your nose . . .*' She heard his voice in her head as if he were in the lift with her. She raised her left eyebrow and felt shivers up and down her spine. It was startling, Frank's deep tones, materialising in her ears like this. The ghost of a past relationship was taking a ride with her to the forty-fifth floor of Tower 100. She felt like she was going crazy. Frank had said it to her in the middle of the night on many occasions. It was his favourite part of Effy, and he always told her so. He'd look down at her as she lay on his chest, the brilliant white moonlight filtering through the blinds. He'd told her it was the first thing that came to his mind as he traced his finger gently from her forehead to the tip of her nose.

He had made her feel beautiful, but now, as she looked at it, it didn't seem so spectacular. Nothing really did, any more. Even this meeting. Despite her initial joy, she was now quietly dreading it. Languishing in bed, heartbroken, even the thought of being outdoors had seemed overwhelming to her.

The mirrored glass was darkened, and her reflection was an almost charcoal version of herself, the usual pink glow of her cheeks turned down like a light had gone out inside her soul. She thought she looked awful – she certainly felt awful – and she was terrified her heartbreak would show. She was afraid her attitude would jeopardise things.

Effy told herself that she had to focus. This was a big day, and could mean a huge amount to Dafina Kampala. *This isn't all about you, Effy*, she mouthed at herself. She dabbed on some lip balm and took a deep breath. She'd left her curly hair down and had concealed several sleepless nights and the smattering of freckles she hated with expensive make-up given to her by her high-flying lawyer sister, Hannah, after a recent shopping trip.

The doors opened and she stepped out into a busy office, full of noise, energy, clean lines and expensive-looking fittings. Effy looked down at her white Converse trainers and suddenly felt they might be unsuitable for an office like this. What had she been thinking when she got ready this morning? At least she was wearing them with a nice lace dress from French Connection in navy blue, making her look a little bit smarter than her shoes would vouch for.

Ossa PR. *It could be the answer to all my prayers*, she told herself, smoothing down her dress and walking towards the reception desk, though she didn't really feel ready for the meeting. She'd looked briefly through their website: their clients mainly consisted of major brands, from fashion and make-up to electronics companies. In fact, there were so many listed she'd given up halfway down the page because they were clearly a big deal, and it was a no-brainer to be working with them. All she could think about was the money to be raised – she was already considering how it could be spent within her project.

As she reached the desk, a young, dark-haired girl seated behind it was frantically answering calls, typing and sorting through mail at the same time. It was a mind-boggling sight, a whirlwind of paperwork and manicured nails.

After a moment or two, the woman seemed to have a window for her visitor. 'And you are?' she asked, super-directly.

It made Effy pull her chin up sharply, and she felt that angry beast in her stomach raise its head and start to roar. Effy had always had a thing for manners. It had been drummed into her since she could remember by her slightly quirky mother, who had struggled to understand so much of the modern world, its digital egg timers and 3D movies, and hung on to good, old-fashioned values. 'It costs nothing to be polite,' she'd told her little girl for the umpteenth time while she held her tiny hand in her own and took her into yet another charity shop in the Yorkshire town where she had grown up. *God I miss the North*, she thought, thinking of her parents and how far away they were now, having fled to rural France in their retirement.

'Yes, OK, I'm Effy Jones,' she said.

'Seat. They won't be long,' the receptionist said abruptly, before answering another call.

Effy tried not to be rude, hiding the contempt that she feared would be written all over her face, and turned around to sit on a chair that looked like it belonged on the set of *Teletubbies*. But before she had the chance to sit down properly, there was a voice behind her.

'Miss Jones?' It was the same voice from the phone call that first day. That attractive male voice, with all its politeness and suave confidence. For a split second her mind ran through all the lovely voices she'd heard before, and how sometimes, when she met the people at the other end of the line, her image of them was shattered. She remembered a particular instance when a man who had sounded like Jude Law on the phone had turned out to be a tubby, elderly guy with breath like a blocked drain.

Steeling herself, Effy turned around. On this occasion, she was surprised by what she saw: the voice certainly matched the man before her.

Ben Lawrence was standing with both hands in his pockets and a smile on his face, leaning back a little on his heels, exuding confidence. The stance of the self-assured. *He's rather handsome*, she thought, fleetingly, *though perhaps a little sure of himself* . . . He was wearing a navy suit. It was simple, but it fitted him perfectly. It must have been very expensive, she realised. He looked like he would cough and money would come out: spitting coins; sneezing notes. He had a little stubble – just the right amount, she considered, totally unable to speak because she had seemingly left all her social skills behind in her mouldy bed. Ben was tall and had the sharpest, bluest eyes. He wore a smile that curled up a little more on one side than the other, and made him look mischievous. There was a kind of perma-smirk going on, too, but it suited him. He had dimples, and a perfectly straight nose. Effy was fused to the spot.

'Effy? It is Effy, right?' he repeated, pronouncing the 't' at the end of 'right' with such clarity, putting his hand out into the void to shake hers, while looking a little concerned that he was talking to a corpse. A touch of confusion blurred his face momentarily. It was awkward.

'Shit. I mean, sorry! Am I Effy. I mean, ha ha, I'm Effy,' she replied, baffled at her total inability to speak properly. Her face had turned a violent crimson. She started to laugh. And then she snorted. Like a little pig.

Silence.

'Er. Right, OK . . . do you want to come with me? We have a celebration organised to mark our exciting new partnership with Dafina Kampala,' Ben said, moving away from the moment, a slight waver in his voice. Instead of being cool about it, or making light of her social faux pas, he looked as if he thought she was weird. She picked that up in his expression and it riled her.

Now Effy felt even more on edge than she had before she arrived, a kaleidoscope of butterflies exploding in her stomach as she hurried down the thickly carpeted hallway after him. As she followed, she thought about the very few times in life she had snorted whilst laughing – three, four at the most. Five now. And she wondered why the hell it had happened just then.

They reached a door marked 'Meeting Room C', and Ben turned to face her again. 'So, Effy, I would like you to meet some of the team here at Ossa PR. They are all very keen to say hi,' he said, smiling enthusiastically, but it all looked a little fake, like he was putting it on and wanted to be somewhere else . . .

With that, he flung open the door, revealing a room full of balloons, streamers, party food (mainly sausage rolls) and champagne. A bunch of equally well-dressed men in various shapes and sizes were lined up around the meeting space and cheered flatly as she came in.

It was all a little awkward, but the right sentiment was there, she quickly decided.

'Wow! Gosh, hi everyone!' she gasped, still slightly taken aback by the effort that had gone into the meeting, and once more finding herself flung into a situation where she would need to be socially adept – rather than her recent communication attempts, which had simply involved muffled grunts beneath a thick duvet and the gentle, face-masking nature of email.

Effy eyed the champagne, feeling a little concerned. It had been a long while since she'd had much to drink, and she worried it might go straight to her head. Images of her on a desk singing 'I Will Survive' into a stapler before pulling the nearest man popped into her mind. Work had been so hectic for the last few months, she'd been trying to keep herself on the straight and narrow as much as possible – long gone were the days when she used to stumble out of the Hoxton Pony at 2 a.m. before heading home to lovingly embrace the toilet. She was out of practice, while these guys looked dedicated to it all, already halfway through their own drinks, the smell of stale cigarettes in the air from where they had been nipping out onto a nearby fire escape for a nicotine fix.

A slight man with a few wispy hairs on his head approached her, vigour in his walk. He was like a miniature cannonball and he was headed her way. 'Hi, Effy, it's really nice to meet you. I'm Dermot and I run this hellhole,' he said, deadpan.

Effy wasn't sure if she had heard him properly, but was so overwhelmed by everything she could hardly address it. He spoke quickly. She shook his hand while Ben darted away like he couldn't escape her fast enough and mingled with some of his colleagues. *Bollocks to him. Where are all the women?* she thought, wondering fleetingly if the business was stuck in the fifties.

'We are so excited to be working with you and Dafina Kampala, Effy,' Dermot said, smiling to reveal a toothy grin. Effy uttered her gratitude over and over again.

'Your application was outstanding, and you were up against some really big organisations Effy. Everyone who voted for the charity we would be working with felt so emotionally drawn to the work you are planning. I know your charity is quite small and you're just starting out, but your plans are inspirational and solid. We all just wanted to give the little guy a chance for once – you know, really make this money go somewhere . . .' Dermot told her. Effy made a mental note to reward Lily for her work; what she had achieved was quite phenomenal.

Within ten minutes, the room was full of noise and riotous laughter. It was so loud, Effy's ears were ringing. It was starting to make her feel even more irritated, her introverted side begging her to leave, go somewhere quiet and leaf through a newspaper. It was such a different world to hers – this expensive, high-powered environment was so far away from her workspace, her messy but well-loved home for, well . . . one.

Swallowing determinedly, Effy spoke to Dermot for a while and continued to thank him, managing to dodge the flecks of spit that flew from his mouth with his machine-gun talk and threatened to land on her face. He was very good at talking.

Throughout it all, Effy noticed the belly laughs coming from the executives. There was something aggressive about them. *They're like a pack of wolves*, she thought, exactly the kind of people she would avoid in bars and restaurants because they would rile her. She glanced over and saw Ben, tuning out Dermot for a while as he continued to passionately yak at her about the developing world. Ben looked like the life and soul of the party. Brash, wild, intimidating even, standing confidently in the middle of his captivated subjects as they watched him gabbing away, his hands flapping as he spoke. At one point he even broke into some strange comedy dance; she had no idea what he was telling them.

Suddenly, Effy was sure he was an idiot. Ben was shouting and swearing a lot, he came across like a bit of a knob, immature and cocky. He reminded her of the silly young men she had gone to university with, and all their 'top lad' hijinks. The kind of guys who treated women like shit and thought it was cool to mix eggs, vodka and orange juice and down them until someone threw up. The kind of guys who emerged from their time there with this horrible kind of arrogance . . . He suddenly melted back into the image of the PR suits she'd known in previous encounters, rather than the sparklingly handsome man she'd just met. There was something quite, well, just *idiotic* about him. *God, I'm becoming so cynical and bitter*, she thought. *Perhaps it's my hormones?*

Effy looked back to Dermot. His mouth was moving, but she still couldn't really focus on anything properly. She hoped he couldn't tell that she'd only taken in a maximum of 4 per cent of whatever he'd been talking about for the preceding few minutes.

'So, Effy, can I interest you in a glass of the finest champagne we could get our hands on?' he said, already holding out a tall, elegant flute.

She reached out and took it, feeling it would be rude to

say no, tucking a huge wave of curls behind one of her ears as she did so. Effy felt small. Intimidated. Out of place. Despite all the niceness on display for her, she was a fish out of water.

Just then, an attractive woman in a tight suit walked into the room and hovered near the back. Now there was a kind of leery vibe coming from the men. No one had said anything, but it was thick in the air, and Effy caught the animalistic glints in their eyes, their collective gaze flickering across her cleavage. The licking of lips. The sniggering. The woman was so quiet. So nervous looking.

Effy smiled at her, and the woman smiled back, shyly. Ever the closet feminist, Effy felt quietly riled by it all, the way the men seemed to just rule the place. She tried to dismiss her feelings today as a result of her own bad experiences lately. She was in a foul mood. Perhaps she was so down she just couldn't see the good in things right now . . .

'So, Ben, when are we next going out on the piss? You've been a boring shit lately, haven't you?' she heard a short, tubby man say to her new contact at Ossa PR. 'Last time we went out, you went home early for a quick shag with that nurse bird. We can't be having you sneaking off all the time, even if it is for a fit bird,' the man continued, leaning back and letting out a booming laugh.

That nurse bird . . . Effy thought, wanting to dive across the table and grab the guy at the throat by his tie. But, £100,000, *Effy*, £100,000, she reminded herself.

Ben looked over at her and suddenly seemed sheepish. 'Don't be silly, mate, we can go out soon,' he responded quietly, looking at the bottom of his champagne flute – which had very quickly emptied – and turning a salmon pink.

'Tonight?' his colleague pushed.

'No, not tonight,' Ben replied, swiftly glancing over in Effy's direction again, which she thought was odd.

'Seeing the nurse again, mate? Time for a check-up, is it, pal?' His friend continued to tease, violent laughter erupting from his mouth again.

'Shut up, David,' Ben said tightly, staring at the floor.

The hysteria broke down a little at that, until all that was left were a few awkward coughs before the group dispersed to get more alcohol.

Effy suddenly wondered what it was she had got herself – and Dafina Kampala – into. *It'll be fine*, she told herself. *Things are just difficult right now . . .*

Ten

Reality was starting to wear thin

Friday 5 September 2014
Canary Wharf, London

Theo walked towards Ben, clutching two pints and a tray of shots with the kind of skill only perfected by dedicated drinkers. But it all went horribly wrong as he approached their table, crashing into it with his 6' 4" rugby-player frame.

'Here you go, Ben. The weekend starts here!' he yelled as he sloppily thumped the drinks down, rocking the table violently under his force.

For a split second Ben feared a full-on disaster involving shards of broken glass, applause and screams of, 'You muppet!' *It wouldn't have been the first time*, he thought, scanning back through a mental catalogue of other, noteworthy disasters.

'Woah there, careful mate,' he said, just about steadying his own pint glass, which was wobbling precariously in a pool of spilt beer. The others seemed to steady by themselves in their own puddles of boozy slop.

Ben looked at Theo, who was also decked out in a nice suit. *Probably Armani*, he considered, *and new season, too*. Theo had a wide grin on his face, and he looked thirsty for trouble.

Ben cracked a wide, sizzling smile. It was Friday, and all the suited city boys were out to play. They were rammed into every corner of every bar, shouting and jeering against a backdrop of modern furniture and low lighting. And when they weren't in the bar, they were hovering around outside like fireflies, smoking cigarettes and yelling into the night like a pack of wolves. Old Jamiroquai tracks were playing in this particular joint, taking most of the clientele back to a time when they had been significantly younger, and more successful with the opposite sex.

Theo Ryland, forty, worked at another corporation in the Canary Wharf area. He was a good, but unlikely, friend of Ben's. They'd met at a networking event five years ago, and had been great mates ever since. Theo had a mop of thick, brown curls and a face full of character and wisdom. He was one of Ben's most down-to-earth friends – yes, to a degree he was like all the rest of the lads, but he was funny. Devilishly so. He didn't take himself quite so seriously, and Ben loved nothing more than a great sense of humour. Theo was also someone he could confide in, about anything – well, almost . . .

'Bloody good week it's been, Ben,' Theo said, settling into his seat, a giant red winged affair with cavernous depths. He ran both hands through his hair and took a deep breath, as if he'd been running a marathon all day and this was the first chance he'd had to actually stop.

Ben grinned and looked at him beyond the rim of his

glass. He was exhausted from another mad week at Ossa PR, and was grateful for the booze that was trickling into his legs and arms, rebooting him into relaxation. 'Glad to hear it. Why?'

'Well, work's bloody good for once. That fucker Smith Cartland lost the contract battle, so I'm obviously very happy about that, but actually my smiles are mostly lady-related,' Theo yelled over the din, his face lighting up.

He'd been talking about the Smith Cartland affair for months, but Ben had failed to listen properly, and was now too lost in the plot to ask any educated questions. But the woman part . . . that was interesting. Theo was always like an excitable puppy when it came to the ladies. Despite his age, he still behaved like a teenager. He was romantic, and wore his heart on his sleeve, and he wasn't ashamed to admit that he was desperate to fall in love and settle down. He reminded Ben of his teenage self, when he used to steal flowers from neighbours' gardens as soon as it turned dark, and then turn up on his first girlfriend's doorstep, sweaty and out of breath, clutching the floral gesture, with muddy stems trailing scruffily from his fist.

Ben felt a twinge in his stomach. He liked Theo for this, because he wasn't afraid to be different. He liked him for the time he fell off a boat into the mucky Thames while drunkenly declaring his love to a girl from his office. He liked him for the time he accidentally posted his wallet, instead of a hand-penned love letter, and had had to sit next to the box in the rain for five hours to get it back.

For everyone else it seemed to be about playing the field, and it was almost embarrassing to admit that anything other than casual sex was going on. Theo, however, had this brazen desire to be a modern-day Romeo, no matter how much trouble he got himself into in the process.

'Oh, right. Sophie, is it?' Ben asked, placing his glass carefully on the surface again and suddenly thinking that he just wanted to go to bed. Early. And then wake up and go for a run, rather than rising with a filthy hangover like he did almost every Saturday. *Maybe one day*, he thought – if he could stop this never-ending carousel of binge drinking – *I could do something constructive at the weekend.* He imagined long walks along the beach and actual fresh air that hadn't been churned 150 times through an air conditioning unit. There was a type of man that Ben really quite fancied being: the guy who exercised a lot; took part in events like Tough Mudder, and went to the Lake District for walking holidays. He had toned, hairy legs and an intricate knowledge of outdoor survival techniques. But he knew he'd never be that guy – the guy who knew how to make fire from sticks. He'd never be able to wrestle an angry deer, catch and prepare a salmon, or lie beneath the moon and know which star was which.

'Yeah, Sophie,' Theo said, snapping Ben out of his reverie. 'The poor girl seems to actually want to get involved in something serious with me, which I'm glad about, as you can imagine.' Theo looked like the cat that had got the cream. He'd been chasing after Sophie for several months after she left the company where he worked. She'd come to a few drinks dos on Theo's arm, looking oh-so-uninterested, rooting around in her Mulberry bag for her phone, which she had then stared at longingly as if it might teleport her from the awful event she'd attended.

Ben was a little surprised things were working out. She'd seemed so aloof before, if not actually rude. But he decided not to raise this while Theo's face was so nicely lathered in bubbles of loved-up joy. 'What did you do?' Ben asked, starting to laugh.

'I don't know, mate. Persevered, I guess. Either that or she's panicking and has decided to settle with me out of pure, unadulterated fear,' Theo said, with a raised eyebrow.

Ben coughed a little on his recent sip of beer. 'Oh, don't be silly. That's brilliant news. I'd like to meet her again. Could you bring her along to the next gathering, maybe?' he asked.

My friends are dropping like flies, Ben thought, smiling to himself. Each time he met up with them they seemed to have big news: they were falling in love; or getting married; or, even worse, pregnant. His pool of night-out contacts was drying up, and he was no closer to being able to let a woman into his life in any kind of meaningful way, let alone actually meet his friends or, God forbid, his family . . . Ben was happy for them, but it was becoming increasingly clear that his time window to 'get better' and deal with his issues was narrowing.

Therapy still wasn't getting him closer to resolving this issue of his. This fear of intimacy of the heart rather than just between the sheets, because he was so damn scared of hurting someone. It was easy, he had thought, to sleep with a woman and not 'mean it'. For him, the most frightening thing was holding a woman's hand as they walked through the streets, being there to talk about problems and issues, living together – all that kind of thing. And for someone to get to know him, to get to know about that day, what he did, all those years ago, when his life was torn in two. For someone to allow him to get close enough that he could genuinely break their heart, because he felt like he'd already done enough damage in his relatively short time on Earth.

'So, Benjy. Still seeing that nurse?' Theo asked now, with a little hope in his puppy-dog eyes, pulling Ben away from his thoughts again.

'No, no, that ended ages ago,' he replied, shaking his head gently. 'I told you a couple of Fridays ago, in Cargo. Don't you remember?' Ben asked, suddenly filled with the image of himself drunkenly screaming into Theo's left ear, while he stood there, wobbling backwards and forwards in a haze of tequila-fuelled disorientation. Theo simply shrugged, clueless. 'I don't remember anything from that night. Literally, nothing,' he said flatly.

A little panic coursed through Ben's veins. He had started to feel a shift: a kind of dawning realisation had hit him in recent weeks. A realisation that maybe his mother was, after all, right. That possibly his life was becoming an empty rat-run of big cheques, booze and women. It had sounded like the stuff of dreams, but the reality was starting to wear thin. Ben didn't even know what had prompted this whole thought process, but it had been creeping up on him slowly. A little bit like regret, with its gnarled claws that stuck in his back and hung on for the ride.

A big moment had come just the day before, when Effy Jones had walked into Ben Lawrence's workplace, and, for some strange reason, he had felt instantly embarrassed and ashamed of who he was. He didn't know this woman, but she had made him feel elated and shit at the same time. She had just come swanning into his office with her auburn curls, and tiny waist, and those beautifully sharp green eyes . . . She was frightening to him. Not because of the laughter snort . . . *That was cute*, he thought, almost wanting to laugh himself just thinking of it.

She had scared him because she was good, he could tell. He knew this not only because of her work – it was something that kind of radiated from her every movement. It was on her skin, running through her veins, it seeped from her pores. She was so unusual to him.

Ben had felt awful about himself when she was in the room, especially during the conversation with David. *She must have heard that*, he thought. David and his fat, flaccid mouth and all the guff that constantly came from it. Ben shuddered inside.

'Ahh, don't worry about it. You're only a pup, anyway. Anyone new?' Theo asked, looking crestfallen for his friend, who was clearly embroiled in some kind of inner turmoil: it was written all over Ben's face. But Theo didn't feel he had the skills to start delving.

'No,' Ben responded, the image of Effy suddenly entering his mind again. It made him feel very uncomfortable.

It got to 9.25 p.m. and Theo made his excuses to go and walk the cat, or whatever reason he had cooked up that night, leaving Ben alone in the bar with a warm half-pint left in his glass.

He thought about returning to his flat. He pictured his place and all its fancy artwork and posh furniture, but he didn't want to be there alone, watching old Bond films and stuffing his face with Kettle Chips. *Plus, it's too early to go home*, Ben thought, his isolation-avoiding excuse marching all over his previous wish for an early night.

He people-watched for a few minutes. The bar was heaving. Well-dressed women shimmied around in frighteningly high heels, often grabbed around the waist by various men pretending to be charming. But these guys were actually just talking to the women's chests, Ben noticed, and holding them for far too long. There was so much ego, so much crap . . . Ben felt suddenly, again, like he was seeing the world from a totally different angle; as if his eyes had been replaced with someone else's and he had this whole new way of looking at things. Everything was kind of . . . *ugly*. He would never normally have noticed this kind of things before. *In fact, I'm probably part of it*, he thought, with dismay.

Suddenly, Ben wanted something more, something greater than this life he only vaguely 'lived'. But right then and there, he needed to fill the void. He needed something. He knew that the sexual adventure he was about to chase did nothing to break the monotony of his life; it did nothing to stare change in the face and embrace it in any kind of way. It was the cowardly way out, because it was the easiest thing for him to do.

Ben sank the remains of his beer and picked up his phone. As he walked out of the bar, he found the number of Lisa, a twenty-nine-year-old wine merchant he'd had a brief fling with some months back. The daughter of a banker, she had enough money to fill a large swimming pool. She was also one of the rare women who accepted their 'situation' for what it was, and seemed to have no more interest in falling in love with him than she did in cleaning her own house. She was a stylish, attractive diva, and she always loved to have a good time. Ben could no longer count the number of times he'd stumbled away from her driveway on a Saturday morning with a skull-thumping hangover and a head full of blurred memories of pleasure.

As Ben walked out into the evening air, he pressed the call button.

She answered almost immediately. 'Ben, how lovely to hear from you. How are you?' she asked, in her clipped accent.

'Great, Lisa, thank you. I was wondering . . . what are you doing tonight? Do you want to do something?' he asked, pausing for a moment by a bus stop and running a hand over his stubbly chin. He had been hopeful, perhaps desperate even, for a woman who could make his night less lonely. She seemed like the perfect answer. He couldn't hurt her, because she didn't really care about him. He knew this.

'I'm alone in the house, Ben. Well, not in the house as such – I'm currently in the hot tub with a cigar,' she said softly.

It almost seemed too clichéd, but Ben knew exactly what Lisa was like. She was a walking cliché. She revelled in luxury. It was her way of life. His mind suddenly filled with images of her naked body in the soft light of her candlelit garden. He said a little prayer to himself, realising he was now partially wrapped around a bus timetable sign. *'Please say yes, please say yes,'* he prayed to a nearby lamppost.

'Right, well, that sounds like fun . . .' he said, flashing a cheeky smile as he spoke into the phone.

'Come round, Ben, and bring a bottle of Moët,' Lisa replied, before hanging up the phone.

Eleven

The broken creature before her

Tuesday 9 September 2014
Sloane Square, London

'What happens if you fall in love?'

The clock ticked loudly. Ben thought about everything that was happening in the world as the second hand patiently made its way round the white, circular board it was mounted on – like it always did, day in, day out. It didn't need cheering on. It didn't need an audience. It didn't need encouraging. *Time just gets on with it*, Ben thought.

He considered each sharp movement denoting one sixtieth of a minute, and what had happened within each tiny slice of time every time it ticked. How many people had died? How many had been born? How many had got married? How many had divorced? How many people were smiling? And how many were mopping tears from their faces? Ben thought about the whole world, from the orange, dusty villages of Africa to the dry, gnarled countryside of southern France. His mind took him from the lush, green Amazon to the quiet backstreets of London. *Time is eternal and I am tiny. I mean nothing in the grand scheme of existence.*

Tick.

Tock.

Ben always got lost in this room. Totally lost in the wilderness of his mind, and no one seemed to be able to provide a map to make any sense of it.

'I don't know what it is . . .' he said, sliding his hands over the material of his light blue shirt and across his chest. He could feel his heart beneath it, thumping hard. He didn't even feel he deserved a heartbeat. *Why is it still going?* he asked himself . . .

The consulting room was warm and Ben guessed that Sally Whittaker had opened the window just a few minutes before he had arrived. This time there was no rain, just the arse-end of a delayed city summer that made people fan themselves on the tube with newspapers and swear under their breath.

'Have you ever been in love?' Sally's voice was gentle.

He thought about all the women. All their faces. They way they kissed him, in the sunshine and the rain. He would know if he had loved a woman in his adult life, surely? He would remember it.

'No, I don't think I have, not since I was young. I don't allow it, but you know that,' Ben muttered.

It is how I will pay for what I did. He'd decided this long ago. The images started to come back to him yet again. The swan and its callous black eyes. Those feathers. The wings unfurled slowly in his brain, metres of feathery whiteness. Death. The end of something that should never have come to a close so soon. And the swan just watching.

I don't deserve to be here, Ben thought.

The voice had returned, and the flashbacks, too. It was his, and only he could hear it. *You deserve nothing. Nothing.*

'So will you go through life never letting this happen to you – one of the greatest pleasures of human existence – because you feel too bad about yourself for something that wasn't your fault? Does that sound logical, Ben?'

It was interesting what she was saying, he realised. Love – one of the greatest pleasures of human existence. Something altogether spiritually elevated. Something so far above the 'meaningless' romps he'd enjoyed for the past few years.

It seemed that everyone was obsessed with love. Ben had long realised that all music was essentially about love. Guitars trying to encapsulate it until strings broke, drummers trying to beat it into a rhythm people could understand, singers screaming it into a rusty microphone. And when he walked around the streets of London it was everywhere. It floated around, from the young couples holding hands and walking along the South Bank, to the elderly couples sharing sandwiches and memories of the past in the park at Alexandra Palace. Women cried about it in the toilets of bars while friends cooed over them. Guys tried to wash away the pain with beer, whisky and thoughts of leaving town.

Everyone was talking about it, thinking of it. Lamenting love lost, chasing love desired, imagining an unknown encounter . . . but Ben felt like it was all so bloody hopeless. The human species was collectively obsessed with that four-letter word, and Ben, at the age of twenty-eight, didn't even know how it felt any more. He hadn't even come close since his first love and those heady days of stealing flowers and fashioning the words 'I love you' in giant letters on a field in freshly trimmed grass cuttings.

'Tell me again what you did wrong,' Sally said, looking across her desk at Ben, the broken creature before her. She'd asked this time and time again, trying to get him to re-route his thinking.

'I was responsible for it all,' Ben said simply. 'I didn't do enough. It is my fault, and somehow I have to live with that.'

'Do you not think that, sometimes, people just make mistakes? That you were a very different person, and you didn't know how to handle it. That, maybe, looked at simply, it was a horrific thing to happen to a person?' she asked.

Ben nodded, wearily. 'People do make mistakes . . . but not like this. I couldn't have fucked things up any more, really. A mistake is forgetting to pick up the dry cleaning, throwing a cricket ball through someone's window, or dropping a plate on the floor. This was far more serious. And I could have turned that day around . . .'

Sally pursed her lips and moved her head a little: Ben guessed that she did this a lot when she was thinking about what to say next – probably doing a little scan in her mind from her many years at university, studying the craft of fixing broken people.

'How often do you think about it, Ben?'

Ben wondered how honest he should be. It was destroying his life. Sometimes, when tubes screamed into the platform, he looked at the tracks and wondered if it would be easier to just disappear.

How could he express this? How could he put the demons into words? The slavering creatures that chased after him wherever he went, baring their sharp, grey teeth. The ghosts

103

that lurked in every corner of his flat, screaming in his ears while he lay in the bath.

In the water. Bubbles. Thick water. Even just having a shower brought on the flashbacks, a recurring horror film behind his eyelids.

Ben turned to face his therapist, and looked her in the eye. 'Every day. And not just every day – it's the first thing that crosses my mind when I wake up. The last thing at night. It colours everything I do. It's a feeling and it's always there.'

'I think, Ben, it has become a way of life for you, hasn't it? I don't believe you know any different. I'm concerned about you . . .'

He tried now to remember life before that day. It was a blur of childhood memories, snagged sharply by the events that had ruined his world. A blue bike he had been given for his fourth birthday. A teddy bear with a broken ear, which dangled from just two threads of light pink cotton. Hugs with his mother. Watching his father polish a set of golf clubs. A simple time before he knew of real pain. Of course it had become a way of life . . . it had happened so long ago that it was hard to know what a normal life was.

Ben suddenly felt his breath quicken in his chest. Panic was returning. He was with one of the best therapists money could buy but this wasn't getting better. It had been too long. He started to sweat. He needed to get out. He had to take flight.

'Ben, how about if you—' Sally started, but was interrupted.

'I hate myself . . . I really fucking do . . . I'm sorry, I have to go. I can't be helped,' Ben spat suddenly, rising to his feet and feeling as if he was no longer in control, was just watching himself from a place beyond his body.

He could feel a glaze of sweat on his brow. His chest was rising up and down, and fight or flight instincts had kicked in, his sense of smell and vision totally sharp. He had tears in his eyes.

'Ben, wait,' Sally said, rising to her feet. But it was too late.

Ben picked up his bag and stormed out of the room, through the stuffy waiting room and into the muggy night air.

Twelve

'Where are you, Ben?'

Wednesday 10 September 2014
Canary Wharf, London

Ben was mortified as he sat in the office, clutching his skull with one hand and his phone with the other, hoping he could avoid his upcoming meeting with Dermot.

He had been an hour late for work because he felt so ill – he'd had to get off the tube three times to take deep breaths in case he threw up over some poor fellow passenger. He'd almost considered ringing in sick but, as always, there was a lot of work to do with his name on it. He couldn't trust anyone else to take it on. *What a disgrace*, he thought. Getting so ridiculously drunk on a weeknight was the kind of behaviour his twenty-two-year-old intern should be indulging in, not him . . .

Ben had decided, in his infinite wisdom, to call his sister at 11.45 last night after another evening on the sauce. Of course, it hadn't been the result of a good social gathering, oh no. It had been a sad, boozy night, fuelled mainly by his total panic just hours before, in Sally Whittaker's office.

He felt guilty today firstly because, in his opinion, city time worked differently to country time. For city dwellers, 11.45 p.m. just wasn't that late – you could quite reasonably start another film at that time on a weeknight, and just tough it out the next day at work. It would be quite reasonable to pop out for bread and milk at 11.45 p.m. Hell, if you tried hard enough, you could probably find somewhere to get your hair cut. It just wasn't particularly late. It was different in the countryside, though. Where Gina lived, it was just a village draped in silence and darkness at 11.45 p.m. Everyone and everything was sleeping. Now, Ben could only imagine she had probably just drifted off when the call came, having battled to find a dreamy escape after an hour or two lying there listening to her husband's famous snoring. *God, I'm a selfish bastard*, he thought, opening up his emails and squinting at the screen. Nausea playfully danced around his body. It was all coming back to him now . . .

'Sister Sledge!' he had shouted the moment she answered, slurring the words in true drunken fashion. At the time he had thought it was a perfectly normal way to address someone on the phone: Ben's drunkometer was at 'wedding', and as he'd been to enough of the sodding things, he knew only too well where that was on the slider scale. Unfortunately, he hadn't been wasted enough to find himself with short-term memory loss today, so he could recall pretty much all of it.

He cringed to himself as he squeezed a stress toy and gritted his teeth together.

'Sister from another mister,' he had continued, laughing to himself down the line, while he heard Gina speaking groggily, probably trying to make sense of which utter fool could be babbling that rubbish down the phone at her at such a strange hour. 'We are family!' he had then started singing.

At the time, Ben had been absolutely convinced that he was a shit-hot singer in the same league as John Legend and that everyone must hear his wonderful vocal range. Then he had nearly got hit by a car – well, a black cab, if he remembered correctly – the driver of which was forced to swerve quite violently in a bid to avoid him. Naturally, said driver had been rather angry – as drivers in London so often are, by default.

Ben had taken a brief pause from the call to shout abuse at him, and the driver had shouted back. Ben recalled his chubby face, cheeks red-hot with rage as he had had a showdown with yet another silly, drunken suit.

'Oh, fuck you, arsehole!' he had screamed, or something similar, and accidentally directly down the phone to his sister, before the taxi driver had decided it wasn't worth getting out and punching him in the jaw, and had proceeded to drive off.

'Ben, Ben, get away from the road!' his sister had demanded, suddenly sounding a lot more awake, her mind probably filled with images of her brother walking wildly in and out of the flow of traffic.

It made him shudder.

'Ben, are you away from the road?' she had asked as Ben was bent over, laughing to himself at his near-death experience.

Because of course nearly being run over is so bloody funny, isn't it?

'Yes, yes, I am. Lighten up, Gina,' Ben now recalled snarling, straightening himself out again, looking down and realising that his suit jacket was all crumpled.

'What's wrong?' she had asked and, at that moment, Ben remembered the hint of disappointment in her voice.

'Ev-ev-everything is wronggg, Gee Gee,' he'd said

breathlessly and matter-of-factly, sinking back into his drunken sadness. By this point he'd managed to wander into some dirty alley that smelt of wee and was littered with discarded kebab, which he now knew had been distinctly unwise.

'Where are you, Ben?'

'In an alleyway,' he had tried to say, as if it were the most normal thing in the world. Way too many vowels were coming out of his mouth, rendering his sentences almost unintelligible. He had the latest iPhone pinned to his ear; in retrospect, everything about him had screamed 'MUG ME!'

It made Ben shudder anew to think about it. He put the stress toy down on the wooden surface of his desk and span his chair round, looking at the city and wishing he could just pull himself together.

'Good God, get out of there, Ben! Get on the bus or something, but keep talking to me,' his sister had demanded, sounding a little breathless if he recalled it accurately.

'Yeah, all right then, I will get the bus,' Ben had responded nonchalantly, probably breathing heavily down the line as he started to run towards one, nearly knocking a man over in the process and mumbling some kind of half-hearted apology.

'So, why is everything wrong?' his sister had asked, speaking more loudly now, having probably moved from the comfort of her bed to the kitchen downstairs.

'I just, I guess, Gina . . . I don't feel like I can cope with what happened,' he'd half whispered, getting on a bus and stumbling through to get a seat at the back, thumping his shoulder on a pole on the way.

She hadn't needed to ask him what he was talking about. He was talking about *that day*. Gina was one of the very few people in Ben's life who knew about it, though they hardly ever discussed it. He expected she was probably quite surprised it had come up again.

'Does it still haunt you?' she'd asked seriously. Ben had heard her pouring some boiling water into what he assumed was a large mug – probably making one of those raspberry and strawberry teas she loved. He imagined now, in his hung-over state, the water hitting the bottom of the cup, the tea bag twisting playfully round and round, blood redness seeping from it and tainting the liquid.

'Yeah, it really does . . . and I don't know if I will ever recover,' he had spat melodramatically, trying – even when drunken – to take the piss out of the situation.

'Can't you get some help? Professional help, maybe?'

'I am. Well, I wasss . . .' he had slurred in reply.

His sister had then said she was struggling to understand him. He'd descended into typical drunk talk, as if his words were socks in the washing machine and they'd come out all tangled up in each other and missing their matching counterparts.

'I told her to forget about it. Today, I told her I did . . .' he had replied.

'What do you mean?' his sister had said, sounding as if she was a little frustrated with him.

'I just, I told her . . . that I can't be helped,' Ben had replied, trying to be quiet on the bus, but probably failing miserably, he imagined. He could remember hearing the automated voice in the background saying which stop was next, and where the bus was headed. He had been desperately trying to ensure that, in his inebriated state, he would be able to get off at the right stop and somehow he managed it.

'Ben. You can be helped. Listen, I'm coming round tomorrow, OK? Go home, go to bed, and get some sleep.

Take the day off work tomorrow and I will come up to London. You don't sound like you're in a good way at all. We need to talk,' she had demanded.

'But, Giinaaa,' Ben had protested, instantly realising that he would not want to talk about it in the cold, sober light of day.

'No, Ben, seriously. You have to do as I say now,' Gina had told him, and he could hear the panic in her voice.

'OK, OK!' Ben had capitulated, probably sounding like a child being dragged around a department store by his grandmother.

'I'll call you in the morning. And text me when you get home,' Gina had said, before hanging up on him, probably sick and tired of his tequila-based gibberish.

And he had got home all right, although he did spend at least seven minutes trying to get the keys in the front door, and then dropping them, over and over again.

When he'd woken up at seven this morning, he had been aware of an agonising headache, and then remembered the drama of the evening. He'd instantly regretted it. His sister couldn't come round. He didn't want to talk to her about it.

He had composed a text message:

Hi, Gina. My apologies for last night. Please ignore it, I'm fine. Off to work now. Will speak to you soon. B

Thirteen
Broken memories and biscuit crumbs

Wednesday 17 September 2014
South Bank, London

Effy was feeling better. So much better. It felt incredible . . . a new lease of life. She didn't feel guilty about not being around enough for Frank; she didn't feel worried that he may be curled up in bed being miserable. She had energy again; she had more time, and oodles of enthusiasm. She smiled at check-out assistants, and told them that she hoped they would have a great day. She gave the strong, carefully considered advice that Beyoncé would be likely to dish out to mascara-smeared women sobbing in bar and train station toilets, rather than grabbing a tissue and joining them. She could actually get herself ready in the morning and look like a proper, functioning part of society. It was amazing, and she was loving every moment of it. She had even stuck the mattress on Freecyle, because it was uncomfortable as hell. It was symbolic. Effy Jones was back.

Effy now truly and wholeheartedly believed that Frank and she ending was the best thing that could have happened. Granted, it had taken her a bit of time to reach this place, but not as long as she had first imagined when she was lying under the sheets, wallowing in a pool of despair, broken memories and biscuit crumbs. She still missed him, of course – she still thought about him and remembered everything, but after enough moping and crying she had gained some clarity, and could now see what life really should be like.

No more sitting in her room for hours making paper swans to comfort herself.

There was something strange about break-ups, Effy realised. She'd felt this before: she could be lost in this aching chasm of sadness and then, one day, she would just wake up and feel better. Not only better, but also free. And that's how she felt as she made her way to meet Rosa on a sunny September evening, the promise of hope dancing in the air.

Effy was off to celebrate this new beginning with her best friend and a bottle of sparkling wine in one of her favourite places: the South Bank. It was a warm night, so she and Rosa scoured M&S for some treats, grabbed the wine, and made their way down to a crowded pathway near the river. It was about a ten-minute walk from the vicinity of Waterloo Station to the best part of the strip.

It was busy. They made their way through the usual groups of kids, who were spread out across the pavement, throwing sweets into each other's mouths and laughing; the elderly who tottered along, wrapped up warm despite the temperature; and her least favourite, the tourists, who would stop suddenly to stare around them, making it near-impossible to overtake them.

Rosa was not usually a fan of this part of London: she

felt it was too commercialised, and preferred funky East London bars decorated with stuffed birds, graffiti and discarded car parts. But Rosa had come here this time because a) this was Effy's night, and b) Effy had promised her there would be a beautiful sunset from one of the bridges – the bridges that looked as if they were part of an architectural model when viewed fondly from a distance.

The direction they were headed hid the sunset Effy had guaranteed, and Effy had asked Rosa not to look behind her as they walked, so it would have even more of an impact.

'Oh, but I really want to see!' Rosa said now, angling her face towards the long, sprawling carpet of paving stones that would lead them to one of the most beautiful places Effy knew of.

Rosa was smiling widely and clutching the wine in her left hand. Her long, brown hair was piled into a messy bun, revealing the several ear piercings she'd had done as a teenager. They really suited her still, and she could certainly carry them off at twenty-nine. She even managed to do this at work – the reception of a local GP surgery – alongside two female colleagues in their mid fifties who always wore sensible shoes and skirt suits in various shades of pastel. She had that kind of look. Alternative. Kooky. It worked.

'I know you so desperately want to see it right now, but this is the best way to do it, trust me,' Effy said. She had suddenly realised that her father had taken her there for the first time when she was a child, and now said to Rosa exactly what he had said to her then: 'Don't look yet, little one. It's a surprise.' Rosa smiled widely.

And it certainly was beautiful, Effy had thought, standing a couple of feet shorter than her father at seven years old and wondering how many people were in the city at that very moment. She had asked her dad, in her piping, child-like tones, if 'a million billion fafillion' people lived in the city. He had said 'not quite', but that she was 'pretty close' and this had made her smile.

The cityscape had obviously changed since then. There were new buildings, new additions to her favourite place in the whole wide world. The Shard being one of them.

When the pair had finally made it up the two flights of stairs to the bridge, Effy held Rosa's shoulders and gently turned her around.

'Oh my goodness,' Rosa said, sighing, looking out at the panorama before them. London was draped in a fading display of striking shades that marked the end of a warm day: pinks, purples and yellows. She dramatically flung open her arms, still holding on to the bottle, her blue silk vest top fluttering softly in the breeze.

'Amazing, isn't it?' Effy breathed, totally taken by it, like she always was, and slightly smug that she'd managed to drag her best friend away from the cool haunts of East London and into some different territory for once.

The sun was starting to slide down the sky, chased in slow motion by the cloak of night-time.

'It's amazing! What a great place! I know there are lots of annoying people around, but you're right, this is pretty damn cool . . .' Rosa said enthusiastically, winking a little.

They opened the wine and poured it into plastic glasses, still in love with the view. It made Effy want to travel, while Rosa remarked that it reminded her of the time she had spent backpacking at the age of nineteen. Effy thought about how city dwellers could be so lost in the world of tube trains and coffee shops, totally forgetting about the wonders around them. Some of which were never too far away. The bridge was a place that made you think about life.

I don't need a man, Effy thought, the cool breeze flapping through her corkscrew curls. She was totally dedicated to her work now. If that, the love thing, if that happened, well, it would be nice of course, but one of the most comforting things she'd discovered recently was to just be happy alone, and it was so liberating. Everything else on top of that was a bonus.

She was so glad to be there with Rosa. They had known each other since they were three years old, and had so many shared memories. Making camps out of chairs and sheets, hunting for the witches of their Roald Dahl books, and pretending to be lions in the playground. Now they were apparently all grown up, but they still shared everything.

'It's amazing you got that support from Ossa PR,' Rosa said, out of the blue.

'Yeah, it's incredible. It's worth so much money,' Effy agreed quietly, still disbelieving. She ran her hands over her arms, which were crossed, the hairs standing to attention as the evening started to cool down. She'd expected to have to fundraise for years to get that kind of money. The way it had come about, she felt like someone was watching over her. Lily's success in the charity partnership application was almost unbelievable. For such a small charity to succeed against other major national or international charities was a minor miracle . . . Effy guessed it was that youthful confidence that had shone through in Lily's writing, and had won the hearts of the Ossa board. At that very moment, Effy, who wasn't particularly religious, had thanked God that Lily had walked into her life, with all her ink and second-hand cashmere.

'What are you going to do with it?' Rosa asked, before taking a small sip from her glass.

Effy started rooting around in one of the bags, pulling out olives, humus and some chorizo salad, and balancing them precariously on a wide section of the bridge's handrail. 'Well, I'm actually probably going to buy a centre out in Kampala with it. It should pay for a fairly large building.'

Rosa nodded, the strap of her cami sliding down her shoulder as she bent down and pulled a huge fluffy jumper from her bag and slid it over her head. 'That's great, Eff, amazing,' she said, as her forehead emerged from its confines.

'We can kit it out too, with everything. It will effectively be like a hospital, but with more long-term care and full family support.' Effy was thinking aloud now, imagining all the amazing things that could be achieved with the money.

It would be hard to get the cash to fully set up the centre, as her charity was in its very early stages, but it was incredible for her to be able to see it happening so soon. She couldn't even begin to imagine how good it would be to treat injured children from all over the country and have them stay for a little while to recover properly, while providing grants to their families to support them. Their home lives were often difficult and medical facilities in Uganda were limited – living with such little money meant that many children worked whenever they could, looked after their siblings while their parents worked, or helped out at home – and it made it difficult for injuries and illness to be treated for the long term. This was Effy's dream, and it was looking much more achievable now, thanks to this support from a PR company that had arrived so unexpectedly.

'I'm flying out to Uganda soon, for a while. I'll be leaving in a couple of months and I may be gone for six months or so,' Effy said, looking at her best friend.

To her surprise, Rosa looked down at the deep, murky waters of the Thames below them and forced a smile. She started playing with a ring on her right hand. Effy had noted that she'd always done that since she was little, but only when she was sad. Whether it was the delicate, silver band she wore nowadays, or the spiky, gothic-style thing she used to wear at university, she always did it to express a certain type of sad – the kind of sad a person can feel, but is never really able to express.

The sadness that comes with setting someone free.

'I'm so happy for you. I'm going to miss you, though, of course,' Rosa said, looking up. Her eyes were watery.

'What's wrong, Rosa?' Effy asked, surprised and not a little concerned by how emotional her friend was.

'It's just . . . sorry, this is really embarrassing,' Rosa said, wiping two huge tears from her cheeks.

The crowds and the people around them felt as if they'd disappeared. It wasn't like Rosa to cry. She was always the tough girl: the first to get tattooed in a North London inking studio; the first to buy the shots, the first to drink them; the girl who would plunge into the sea before anyone else, while others stood, watching and whispering until she emerged from the deep, breathless and laughing.

'It's OK.'

'I'm just so proud of you. I was concerned when you started this charity, Effy, I really was. It's a huge thing . . . And, honestly, I wasn't sure how you'd cope – in the nicest way possible, of course.'

Effy felt a little sting at hearing these words. The honesty of a good friend was not always easy to swallow – and Rosa was always honest – but Effy knew where she was coming from: until that call had come from Ossa PR, she hadn't fully known how she was going to do it. She had been, genuinely, quite frightened.

'You were this kind of fluffy, slightly naive girl – you know? A bit dippy actually, and I loved you for that, I really did, but you've proved how you have so much more inside, and you're doing it, actually *doing* it . . . People change . . .' Rosa said, her tears stopping now, the tough girl coming back. She bit her bottom lip a little as she stared at the sunset, which was now a rich pink, streaked with slips of silver cloud.

Effy was reminded again of how much she loved her friend's voice – she had a real London Lily Allen twang to her. She was just, well . . . *cool*.

Skaters tore past them in the background, spinning their boards as they soared in the air, making businessmen flinch as they walked past, their eyes to the ground, gripping onto briefcases full of problems – this was quite the juxtaposition. Effy and Rosa could just about make out the clatter of wheels on wood as they landed clumsily, not quite perfecting their skills.

'This is a toast to you, Effy,' Rosa said, raising her glass to the fading sun. The big wheel stood before the friends, proud, tall and beautiful.

'Thank you,' Effy replied, gently touching her friend's plastic glass with her own.

Suddenly, they were interrupted by the sound of a man shouting in the distance, on the bridge, but just beyond a huge metal pole in the middle. The part Effy assumed held it all together.

'Arghh, Jesus! You fucking idiots!' came the voice, only just audible.

Effy squinted a little, her attention caught. Rosa tried

to carry on talking, but her friend wasn't listening, so she craned round, too.

They could see a man lying on the boarded floor of the bridge, with what looked like a skateboard beneath him. There was another one right by his feet. It was far enough away to make it difficult to work out what was happening, but it looked like the man was pummelling his fists on the ground in sheer anger. A group of five or six teenagers were gathered around him, trying not to laugh; one of them had failed miserably, and was bent, weeping in hysteria, over his own board.

'Why aren't you more careful, for fuck's sake! You shouldn't just leave them lying around like that!' came the voice again. It sounded like the man was genuinely in rather a lot of pain, and also very, very angry.

Effy and Rosa could merely make him out – his face was hard to see due to its angle to the ground – but something piqued Effy's interest. She recognised the voice, and her heart started to race. *Surely not . . . It couldn't be*, she thought.

There was garbled chatter, and more people rushed towards trains and bus stops over the bridge, making it more difficult to see what was unfolding.

'It's not my bloody fault! I was just walking along and this little bastard—' came the voice again.

It's definitely him, she thought, taking two steps in the direction of the chaos. That distinctive posh accent, the way he pronounced his 't's so carefully.

'Effy, what's up? Don't worry about it. Someone's just fallen over a skateboard. Looks like a pissed-off businessman – his own bloody fault probably . . . they never look where they're going . . . Pah, serves him right,' Rosa said, grabbing her friend's hand and trying to pull her back.

'No . . . no, hold on a minute. I know him,' Effy said in disbelief, squinting in the direction of the kerfuffle.

The South Bank was a popular place, Effy knew, but the odds of he and she being there at the same time were low . . .

She had to check, she had to see.

'I'll be back in a minute,' she said, starting to run across the bridge, leaving her baffled friend alone with the Thames for company, a few unidentified objects bobbing on top of the water.

The sunshine was still warm on the top of Effy's head as she thumped across the wood, weaving in and out of the people. By now a large group had gathered around the scene.

'I need your phone number, young man. Your mother needs to know about this! That bloody skateboard!' the man yelled through the crowd. The teenagers had started to walk away, tutting and laughing. One of the boys aggressively pulled his skateboard from beneath the crumpled frame of the suited man; another grabbed the one by his feet, and sloped off with his mates.

'You can't just bloody walk away! I might DIE!' he screamed now, exasperated, still lying on the bridge where his walk had met an unfortunate end.

And as Effy fought her way through the band of people, there he was, just as she suspected. Ben Lawrence, lying on his front, telling everyone standing around him to piss off.

His face switched the moment he saw Effy emerging from between the rubberneckers, in the same way it had at the Ossa PR meeting when his colleagues were ridiculing him. He quickly stopped shouting, a crimson blush spreading across his cheeks.

She was interested in how transparent he was. *Ha!* Effy thought, quietly pleased he'd been brought down a peg or two after seeing him act like such a show-off at the partnership celebration.

'Well, hello there, Effy!' he said, as jovially as if they'd bumped into each other at a check-out in Waitrose; as if his lying face down on a bridge was the most normal thing in the world. He even seemed to have perfected the art of looking delighted but also very embarrassed at the same time. He tried to get up, but suddenly screamed out in agony before sinking down onto the wooden decking again.

'Shit, I can't really get up. Something feels broken . . . well, a few things feel broken,' he muttered, softly dropping his head onto the wooden boards in humiliation before looking up again, half hopeless, half worried.

'Hi,' Effy said shyly, her cheeks betraying her as she flushed a brilliant red at the awkwardness of the situation. She knelt down beside him. *He looks rather handsome,* she thought, *even when he is on the boards of this bridge, yelling and carrying on like a bit of an idiot.* She wondered why she'd rushed down to see him like this. She didn't know him well at all, and she could have easily got away with pretending she'd not heard anything, and he would never have known. It would have saved all the embarrassment of stumbling upon him in the middle of the South Bank as he lay on the ground and shouted at the world.

'I take it you saw all that, did you?' Ben asked, a further shade of humiliation and amusement on his face.

'What? The fall? No, I missed that. I just heard the aftermath. You're quite the noisy one, aren't you? Skateboard, was it?' she questioned flatly, raising an eyebrow and crossing her arms. The decking was hurting her knees already.

'Yeah. Well, two, actually. The one I stepped on and the one I landed on. It's a pretty unusual accident, isn't it? I was texting when I was walking so it was probably a little bit my fault, of course, but I'm going to go with the sob story of being cruelly injured by a gang of reckless skateboarders. Not really sure what to do, though,' he said, starting to laugh.

At least he can laugh at himself, she thought.

'What hurts?' she asked now, leaning a little closer to him, awkwardness all over her face . . Effy wanted to laugh at him. But she knew that sounded mean, particularly when her day job involved helping the injured.

'Well, most things at the moment. My chest particularly, and my knees,' he muttered.

'Are you bleeding?' Effy asked, just checking that this wasn't more serious than she'd first imagined.

Ben tried to lift himself up a little one more time, and she instantly spotted some blood coming through his crisp, white shirt. Effy felt a wave of nausea run through her; she was pretty squeamish, in truth.

'I think you need an ambulance,' she spluttered, pulling out her phone.

'Oh, heavens, no. No need for that, it's just a scratch! I'll get up in just a minute and—' he said, his tone almost begging her to leave it.

'—take your sorry, bleeding self to the bus stop?' Effy questioned softly.

'Well, yes. I guess I will do that, or a taxi or something.'

She had found him so . . . so brash and irritating when she saw him at that 'party', he was just the kind of guy she loathed, but when he wasn't around his colleagues it was as if he were a different person. She'd noticed it when

123

he came to pick her up from reception, and she noticed it now.

Effy remembered that she had left Rosa to play a very lonely game of 'Name the unidentified object in the Thames' and felt bad. She turned around quickly and saw that Rosa had packed up their belongings in a bag, and was now marching towards them, a look of amusement on her face.

'Oh God, who's that?' Ben asked, seeing the strange woman approaching and probably fearing he would be laughed at by yet another person he'd never met.

'My friend, Rosa. Don't worry, she's lovely. We'll give you some water and work out the best plan of action, but we really do need to call an ambulance urgently,' Effy responded, looking at him with concern. 'Oh, please don't, I'm begging you not to. I hate hospitals . . .' Ben said. He was sweating now, and had gone a little pale. She started to see a larger trail of blood, seeping from the region of his torso and onto the decking. Thoughts of internal bleeding popped into her mind, and her heart started to race with fear.

'Shit, Ben, we need to get you to hospital. You're bleeding a lot now,' Effy gasped, feeling a little cold, the initial hilarity of the situation seeping away like his blood.

'Bollocks,' Ben said, a frown creeping over his face as he tilted his head towards the pool of red stuff.

'Hi, I'm Rosa.'

Rosa bent down and squeezed this strange man's hand softly, in an attempt to shake it.

He squeezed back gently and laughed, somewhat shakily. 'Lovely to meet you, Rosa. I'm Ben, from Ossa PR – that's how I know your lovely friend here. Oh, and by the way, I've fallen, quite spectacularly, over a skateboard and onto

124

another one. Bit ridiculous, really,' he said, matter-of-factly, making Rosa laugh suddenly before she apologised.

'He's bleeding, quite badly.' Effy looked up at her friend in alarm, amazed at how useless she was in this situation. 'Rosa, what do we do? You're a GP's receptionist.' Effy realised that all her initial negativity towards Ben had long gone, because he did seem to be in fairly serious trouble.

Ben looked up and grinned at her again, despite his predicament. There was mischief in his features, and he was wearing the smile she'd noticed when she first met him.

'OK, you've got a good point, Eff,' Rosa said, walking around and seeing the ever-growing trail of blood.

'I may be dying, and I do feel this would be an unfortunate way to go,' Ben cried jokingly.

'I'm calling an ambulance,' Rosa said calmly, taking her phone from her pocket and starting to dial.

'Really? Is that really necessary?' Ben asked in a squeaky voice, wiping his brow with his forearm. He was starting to slur his words a little. He looked as if he might pass out.

'Yes, it is. You're becoming hysterical as well, which isn't a good sign,' Rosa added bluntly.

'Hysterical? Really? Like a headless chicken? Rosa, are you a vegetarian? You look like a vegetarian . . .' he muttered, almost delirious now, his eyes starting to glaze over.

Rosa pulled a face of serious concern at Effy.

Within ten minutes an ambulance arrived, as close to the bridge as it could get. A pair of paramedics ran to the scene, clutching bags and a stretcher.

A mortified Ben Lawrence was put on the stretcher despite his well-spoken protests of 'I can walk!', more references to the hysterical chickens, and his wildly thrashing limbs. After a dramatic wrangle he was taken away, leaving Rosa and Effy in silence, only broken by the occasional giggle. It was dark by this point; the familiar buildings glittered in the distance.

'Well, that was strange . . . he's an odd man,' Effy muttered, smiling to herself, as they started to walk slowly back to the train station.

'He's lovely, Eff. Really rather lovely . . . but I suppose you already know that,' Rosa said, turning towards her friend and giving her a wink.

Effy was genuinely shocked. She had thought he was so horrible at that charity partnership do, and she certainly didn't think he was the type of guy Rosa would like. 'What do you mean? OK, obviously he's good-looking, but personality wise, he couldn't be further from my type!' Effy protested.

'Oh, come on, Eff. It's written all over your face . . .' And, laughing, Rosa dodged out of the way of the wine cork her friend launched at her head.

Fourteen

So this must be what it feels like to be worry-free

Friday 19 September 2014
Canary Wharf, London

Ben was back in the office, high on strong painkillers. Given the severity of his injuries, he knew he should have stayed at home and got some rest but, being the workaholic he was, he had brought his tender self into Tower 100 for another busy day.

He'd got the bus in to work to avoid all the steps in the underground because his stomach still hurt. He had found that travelling by bus was actually a lot of fun. Despite his pain, he'd been quietly chuckling to himself at the back after seeing two commuters momentarily caught together by their backpacks: one frantically keen to dash off the bus, the other totally unwilling to let go of the pole he was holding. It was a fantastic example of how people seemed to lose their minds when getting from A to B in London. In high spirits, the sight of them irritably

127

trying to go their separate ways had proved too much for him, and he'd been fighting tears of laughter for a long time afterwards as he sat wedged between an elderly man in a flat cap and a scowling schoolgirl frantically tapping away on her smartphone. The cocktail of drugs he'd taken just an hour before he left the house made the world around him a softer place. A lot less scary. The edges were less sharp.

He'd floated into work, into the lift, and then into his office, a giant grin on his face. His reaction to the drugs had been so strong, he wondered if he wasn't a little intolerant to something he'd been given, but he was enjoying his high all the while. Without the medication, he couldn't even move around without crying out in pain. In addition, his usual fears had migrated to a place very far away . . .

So this must be what it feels like to be worry-free, Ben thought now, savouring the moment. He felt strong, brave, and even good about himself . . .

He boldly picked up the phone, swinging a little in his chair. Effy answered quickly, which surprised him a bit because he had got the impression she was the kind of girl who was too busy to open her own post, let alone answer the phone within a couple of rings.

'Twenty-five stitches . . . *twenty five*,' Ben said, before she had even had the chance to speak, smiling as he did so. 'The doctors told me I could have bled to death,' he continued, wickedly. She gasped down the line, a kind of faux-shock that he instantly picked up on despite his drugged-up hysteria. He carried on regardless. 'The board cut a rather impressive hole in my stomach and I broke three ribs . . . What with that and the bruises, well, I'm a broken man,' he continued proudly, like a soldier back from battle. A particularly brash confidence was seeping through his veins. Partnered with the co-codamol, the pair were doing the tango around his body and he felt invincible.

'Oh, hello. How lovely to hear from you . . . and wow, that is a lot of needlework,' Effy replied.

Ben detected a little awkwardness in her voice. He imagined her running a hand through her wild curls, unable to shift the gross image of his patchwork stomach, and suddenly felt a little bad for being so graphic. The whole episode had been embarrassing, for both of them, he realised. He needed to patch up the situation for the sake of their professional relationship.

Ben could hear the faint sound of the radio in the background of her office. 'What are you listening to?' he questioned.

'Oh, er, LBC – two angry women rowing about the rocketing price of school uniform, I think. I'm not really listening to it,'

'Oh, right, OK. Well, what are you working on today?' he asked, hoping he wasn't being too nosy, too familiar or too chit-chatty. He realised, as he was speaking to her, that he felt even more anxious than usual. This was weird. He put it down to the medication.

Effy paused a little before speaking. *Does she sound a bit put out?* Ben suddenly thought.

'Are you sure you should be back at work?' Effy asked.

'Probably not, but, as always, I have a lot on. I'll have to soldier through . . . they can't do anything much with ribs, anyway,' he replied, spinning round in his chair and looking at the city view he knew so well. Ben wondered if he could see North London, where Effy had casually mentioned that she lived during a phone call. He pictured her hunched over a laptop, making good things happen. It filled him with warmth.

He was curious about her, but he put that down to the nature of her work. What was this feeling washing over him? Why did he care so much?

There were a few more moments of quiet on the line, and Ben figured that Effy was probably very busy and just wanted him to get to the point.

'Listen, Effy. I do feel rather bad that I spoiled your night with your friend . . . er, Sarah, was it?'

'Rosa.'

'Right, of course, Rosa. It can't have been much fun for you, having to deal with some bumbling fool falling over a skateboard,' he said, more calmly now.

'Oh, it's OK, don't worry at all,' Effy replied. 'If that's all you were calling about, I need to be getting on with my work now,' she said in a sudden rush.

Ben felt a little sting of embarrassment. All of a sudden, his drug-induced courage was slipping out of the office door and abandoning him when he most required it. His palms became sweaty. Why did she make him feel so embarrassed? He was never usually like this.

For a split second Ben wondered if he should ask what he'd planned to ask. He had so little time to make up his mind, and so few other 'reasons' to call. He scanned the buildings near Tower 100 for inspiration, and wished there was an easy, immediate answer.

'Right, sorry, well, just quickly, if you don't mind . . .' he said. 'I wanted to ask if it would be OK for me to take you out for dinner. To say sorry?' he continued, feeling the fear come rushing back.

In the next moment's silence, Ben wondered how she was interpreting his offer of dinner. He was used to creeping around London's most elegant eateries, wining and dining clients and partners, and he hoped she didn't think he was being too forward. He hoped she'd understand that he was just trying to develop their working relationship – despite the strange feelings that were creeping in around the edges.

In the almost total silence, Ben could hear his heart beating in his ears, while the painkillers' buoying effect continued to disappear from his bloodstream, leaving him feeling really quite exposed.

He suddenly felt annoyed at himself for bothering. It wasn't like him at all.

'Erm, right, well,' Effy said, and he guessed she was quickly trying to think of a way out of the situation, scanning her mind for all the imaginary things she could be doing for the next, well, forever.

There's no need for us to go to dinner, Ben thought. Another meeting, if necessary, in his office, would have been fine.

Oh goodness, do I like her? Do I actually like her? What's going on? he questioned himself, spinning back around in his chair and starting to draw random shapes on a notepad in front of him as he waited for the verdict.

That smile of hers had appeared in his mind too often recently. Those chiselled features . . . She was sexy . . . classy, though, too. Ben had no idea where these feelings, whatever they were, had suddenly come from. He didn't know if she was married, or single, or in a relationship, or if she'd even look twice at a man like him – but he knew she was out of bounds anyway. It would be outrageous for him to go chasing after a person involved in the year's corporate charity partnership. And what would happen if he succeeded, anyway? If she got past his shallow lifestyle and actually agreed to date him, what would she think of his past? *She would be disgusted. She would get hurt*, he thought, feeling that familiar coldness creep into his tummy once again.

'I guess so,' she said after some time, with very little enthusiasm in her voice.

Ben cringed. Visibly. It resembled a man ducking from a golf ball that was soaring towards his head. His stomach stung dully beneath the painkillers.

'Great, that's wonderful. Are you free next Thursday evening?' Ben asked, seemingly ignoring the fact that she hadn't actually said yes.

'Yes, yes, OK . . . Thursday sounds good,' she said, the tone of her voice still not perking up.

He guessed that she was probably already planning to develop food poisoning or another debilitating-but-non-deadly ailment. A grumbling appendix would probably be ideal, he considered.

'I'll, er, email you the details,' Ben muttered. It was a disaster, and he wished he'd never bloody well picked up the phone. He was usually excellent at getting what he wanted, and he felt more than a little surprised that she was being so surly with him.

But it only made her more interesting.

'OK,' she replied. Short and blunt.

Ben tried to save the situation by sounding casual. 'Have yourself a lovely day, Miss Jones. I'll see you next week,' he added, before hanging up and dropping his face into his hands.

Fifteen

Because he was dying

Sunday 21 September 2014
Dalston, London
The painkillers were wearing thin and the agony had returned: searing pain, as if he'd been beaten with a pole. Ben was having his family round for a late lunch and they were due to arrive very soon. He hobbled around his kitchen wearing a faded Tasmanian Devil apron, taking sharp inward breaths to deal with the pain radiating from his torso. Against the advice on the painkillers' packaging, he took the odd sip of wine in a bid to dull the ache.

Don't think your little run in with the "yoof" will get you out of this one, Benny boy, his sister had texted him the night before, clearly looking forward to a family gathering at his flat. They didn't happen very often, but when they did, they were always drunken affairs, with plenty of delicious food and passionate debate over the table. Conversation was often heated, to say the least.

Ben's mother had called a few days before and in sympathetic tones had asked if he was well enough. He had pictured her by the phone in the kitchen, twiddling her hair and staring at the calendar pinned to the wall. He hadn't wanted to let her down. Having been so rubbish at calling her recently, he had felt it was important that today went ahead, regardless of his pain.

He'd ordered the food online, and a heavy-set, grunting delivery guy had hauled the goodies into the kitchen, great beads of sweat dripping down his face. Ben didn't do things by halves: there were fine wines, a selection of cheese that would have made Henry VIII blush, and enough caviar and other luxuries to sink a small fishing boat. He'd thrown a chicken in the oven and sliced up some vegetables. *The rest can look after itself*, he thought now, assessing the selection of luxury meats and dips spread out before him like a delicatessen burglary haul.

When the oven's alarm sounded two minutes later, Ben knew that the chicken was finally ready. Forgetting about his stomach for a moment, he pulled it from the oven, the sudden pain making tears well in his eyes. He plonked it down on the table with a pained sigh and a great thump, the metal container clanging loudly against the surface.

'Fuckety shit,' he gasped to himself in sheer agony, reaching for the wine again, and taking a deep breath.

When he relaxed a little, he noticed that the chicken looked and smelt good, sitting in a pool of gravy, onion and herbs. He arranged things on the table. It took a while, but he got there in the end. *After a few candles have been lit, the place will look all right*, Ben thought, feeling a strange calm wash over him. He didn't normally bother with candles but he knew his mother loved them.

He thought of Effy again, for the tenth time that day, wondering if he had done the right thing by calling her and asking her for dinner. He was still a little embarrassed by her reaction. He wondered if he would ever be able to really get to know her . . . Then, he wondered if he would ever feel good enough about himself to be with someone like her.

And the coldness returned. Anxiety. What was done was done, and he couldn't change it.

Ben was torn from his thoughts by the sound of familiar and energetic knocking at the door. He hobbled towards it, hearing Gina chattering away on the other side.

'Benny, you ugly bastard!' she yelled the moment he opened the door, flinging her arms around her brother, just like she had since they were little. She was followed by Marcus, their parents' eight-year-old terrier, who pushed his way between several pairs of legs before hurtling into the kitchen and gleefully helping himself to a tray of salami.

'Ben, old chap, how are you?' Dan, his sister's husband, asked in mock warmth before leaning into Ben and slapping him heartily on the back, looking like a fish out of water. *He's a funny one, Dan*, Ben thought. He always seemed so awkward and uncomfortable, even coming to Ben's place, which he had been doing for years now. But he was a good bloke, just a little socially awkward.

'Yes, fine, thanks. Apart from the injuries, of course,' Ben replied nervously, hoping Gina wouldn't punch him in the stomach just to be funny. She might actually finish him off if she did that.

Gina and Dan shuffled past him and into the kitchen, flinging their coats into his room on the way. Behind them were their mum and dad, dressed in their Sunday best, with the usual concerned smiles on their faces.

They always looked concerned when it came to Ben. He never saw them look at Gina like that.

'How is it, son?' Ben's father asked, hugging him gently and grimacing in sympathy.

135

'Fucking hurts, actually, but anyhow,' Ben replied, starting to laugh.

'Ben! Don't swear!'

'Sorry, Mum,' he replied, pulling her into a warm but reluctant embrace, and wondering why she still toed the no-swearing line, even though Gina and Ben were adults and swore like troopers. It was a losing battle, really.

When the cold-meat theft was discovered, a small pretend trial was carried out near the fridge. Naturally, the only culprit was Marcus, who was banished to the terrace garden, and finally they began their meal. The wine started to flow, as it undoubtedly would until the stars glittered somewhere beyond the smog above Ben's Dalston flat, overlooking what seemed like the whole city in panorama.

'So, what's new, Ben?' his mother asked, biting on an asparagus spear soaked in garlic butter. The table went suddenly quiet. Ben guessed that word about the drunken phone call to Gina had spread, and all the niceties of this gathering were something of a mask for all the questions his family really wanted to ask.

They would probably have liked to have said things like, 'We're worried for your future'. Ben knew that that was what they really felt, and thought. But, of course, this was a typically British family, where people attempted to dig out clues amongst small talk and political banter rather than actually saying them out loud.

What's new? Ben thought, pondering the question. All he could think about was Effy. He certainly didn't want to talk about Effy. It was pointless, and so strange to him – so strange for him to be feeling like this when he never really felt anything for women beyond the physical, lusty element of things.

'There's a girl, isn't there?' his mother asked, sitting up

straight in her chair and smiling widely, her short, greying hair tickling the tops of her shoulders as she spoke.

She may as well be slapping her hands together like a seal, Ben thought, bracing himself for her questioning.

'Oh, calm down, Claire,' Ben's father said, laughing to himself as if the suggestion were ludicrous, one hand clutching a vat of wine, the other perched on his rotund stomach.

A girl . . . Effy flashed before his eyes again: that wild curly hair, the cheeky smile, the freckles and the dimples, her sparkling eyes. Beauty. *She* is *beauty*, he thought, feeling something fold in his stomach.

'No. No girl. Sorry, guys,' Ben responded, not looking up from his plate as he sawed away at a piece of meat. He was tiring of the Spanish Inquisition when it came to his love life. He sometimes wondered if it was because his family didn't know what else to talk to him about. They were dodging reality. The fact that they couldn't really relate to him, or understand his life.

Eventually, the family continued with other conversations, moving on from the moment like dancers recovering from a slip amid the harsh gaze of a critical audience. Talk of the recent flooding, the latest topics covered by the *Guardian* and *The Times*, and why his father was switching golf courses. It turned out the nine-iron tampering had gone down rather badly and he had been banished from the local golfing community.

They passed the time pleasantly enough. There was laughter, and joy, and all the things that should happen when families are together. That was until his mother, fuelled by her third large glass of rosé, decided to raise it.

That day.

'I saw Alex's mother, Leanne, at the supermarket, Ben,'

she said, pushing her plate gently to the centre of the table, her soft, wrinkled hands trembling slightly. She leant back slowly in her chair, the wood creaking.

There was deathly silence, disturbed only by the yapping of Marcus beyond the double-glazed windows.

Ben felt his top lip twitch slightly and his eyes narrowed, almost confrontationally. He couldn't control it. He felt utter disbelief. He couldn't believe she had brought this up, and so publicly.

Ben stared into his mother's eyes, feeling the warm salt water rushing to pool in his lower lids. He swallowed, hard, trying to suppress the waves of emotion. He saw the swan, gliding around the lake. *Her majesty.*

'I'm, er, just going to, erm, check on the dog,' Dan said, rising to his feet sharply and walking quickly to the terrace, opening the door and shutting it behind him.

'And how is she?' Ben asked carefully. The terror was lapping at his toes again, like the sea rapidly and hungrily approaching someone so frightened of waves they could scream at the moon until they drowned in fear.

'Still alive. Which is a miracle, really,' his mother responded, calmly taking a sip of wine.

Gina instantly reached her hand out and gripped onto Ben's arm, gently squeezing it in a silent show of solidarity. Their father bowed his head towards his lap.

No one had ever recovered since that day, as far as Ben was aware. He'd imagined how things were for Leanne – or Mrs Taylor, as he used to call her, an ex-accountant and Alex's mother. He pictured her going silently mad in her five-bedroom semi-detached home in wealthy suburbia. The place where tragedy like that was never expected. A place where everyone floated around in Land Rovers and a bubble of naive comfort. He knew for a fact she'd attempted suicide some years before, and when that hadn't worked, she had turned to God. The rest was all hearsay, rumours of her life spent in the local church hall, no doubt selling slabs of dry Madeira cake for charity with a face that said it all. In his mind, the tragedy was in the huge bags beneath her eyes; it was probably written into the wrinkles on the greying skin of her face. A story that told how she'd lost everything, and this was all that was left. Futile attempts to make flowers grow where everything else had died.

Ben's top lip trembled. He placed his glass down gently and rubbed his eyes with the inside of his forearm, a fist gripped tight. He hated showing this level of emotion in front of people, his family, and he felt a look of pure grit spread across his features. The same look a child adopts when it falls over in the playground and doesn't want to cry in front of classmates. *I cannot crumble. Not here. Not here*, Ben thought, so angry that his mother had brought this up, but desperate to hear her answers.

'Did you speak to her?' he asked, with a wavering voice, dreading what he might hear, the image of Leanne's pale face and slim frame filling his mind. Her tortured self, floating around the wine section of Waitrose like a ghost.

'I did. I did,' his mother said quietly, saying it twice, just to confirm.

Ben turned towards the balcony and spotted Dan, who was pacing, stiffly, round the tiny rooftop garden, peering through the glass for a moment, gauging to see if he could return, but Ben assumed that their body language said it all. *Not now*.

'She likes you, Ben. She's probably missed you – well, of course she has,' their mother said, thick tears gathering in her eyes.

Ben sighed and felt a warmth crash over him, but all he wanted to do was push it away.

He hadn't seen Leanne since the funeral, when her thin body had curled itself around Alex's coffin, her back rising and falling in agony.

Ben had always imagined that she hated him. That she would never forgive him for what happened, like he never forgave himself. No matter what anyone said, he didn't believe them. He felt it was all an act, kindly put on by his loved ones, so he could see past today and onwards to tomorrow, somehow.

'You do know, Ben, that there is no hostility towards you back home. You are missed. Everyone misses you . . . I think Mrs Taylor would probably like to speak with you about Alex. I'm quite sure you would have lovely stories to share. Things that could bring her comfort,' Ben's mother continued. There was something steely in the way she spoke, as if she wasn't going to back down this time. She wasn't going to let her son live and die in a pool of guilt. She wasn't going to stay quiet. She wasn't going to be silenced by Ben's protests of 'I'm OK,' when he clearly was not.

Despite Ben's youth, money, designer clothes and the flat, he wasn't really living. Something inside him had passed away. He knew that.

'I'm sorry, I've got to go,' Ben said, rising suddenly in his chair, wincing in pain, still clutching his glass of wine, wondering exactly where it was a person could go when wanting to escape their own home.

There was an emptiness inside him. It was like he was tired of it all. Too tired to fight any more. His initial aggression had seeped from his body, crept down the hallway and slid away through the letterbox until there was nothing left in him.

Ben shuffled painfully towards the back door, his sister's hand still stretched out in the air where it had previously clutched his arm.

'Ben!' she called, half in her seat, half out of it, unsure of what to do.

When he got to the terrace door and opened it slowly, Dan slid quietly past him and they swapped places. The door was once again closed, separating the kitchen from him and the outside world.

Ben walked to the edge of the terrace, looking at the London skyline soaked in sunset. The colours were overwhelming, streaky cirrus clouds that looked as if they had been torn by careless aeroplanes. Tears filled his eyes and he felt that hopelessness come back, starting to flow down his cheeks as he shakily reached into his trouser pocket and pulled out a packet of cigarettes. He would do anything to turn back time and change things. He would trade his life, his money, *everything*, to go back and make it different.

I just want to be alone, forever, Ben thought. *I don't deserve to be loved, by anyone . . . I don't deserve to love because I cause destruction.*

The warm patch on his arm where Gina's hand had rested was by then as cold as the evening air. Ben pushed a cigarette between his wobbling lips and lit it, taking a deep drag and flinging his head back as he breathed out. He wondered what would become of him. The smoke curled into the air around him, sloping off to join aggression, wherever it had chosen to hang out . . .

To his sister, his face must have been just a silhouette in the sunset. Gina had crept outside so quietly he didn't immediately notice her.

'Ben,' she said softly. He could hear her pull her shawl

around her shoulders and shiver a little. He ignored her, and continued staring into the distance. Towards North London . . .

'Ben,' Gina said again, walking slowly towards her brother until she was standing at his side. He stayed silent, not even acknowledging her presence. 'The thing is, Ben, you try to be brave, don't you?' she asked sweetly, even though she knew she wouldn't get a reply. 'You hide all this stuff inside, and it's destroying you, really.'

There was silence, only disturbed by the sound of a police car tearing past, and a bubble of a stranger's laughter from the street below.

'It wasn't your fault, Ben. What happened was not your fault. And, anyhow, there is nothing – I repeat, nothing – you can do to change it . . . You are a good person.'

Ben suddenly felt like he had to speak. 'That's the problem, Gina. If I could change it I would, I'd give every inch of my being to go back in time. To have done things differently. I will always, always blame myself,' he said, before taking another silent drag on his Marlboro Gold.

Gina took a deep breath. He imagined she was thinking for a moment about what to say. He wondered if she would sugar-coat it, step softly around this unexploded mine.

'Ben. I'm going to say this now. If you are not careful, this will define you . . . for the rest of your life.'

Sixteen
Alone again

Thursday 25 September 2014
Sloane Square, London

Ben sat at the table, which was dripping in white linen and fine silverware, looking at Effy beyond the flame of a single candle. It made him smile. She was clearly in awe of the place because her mouth was hanging open slightly.

When she saw him grinning, she cleared her throat and gently closed her lips before taking a deep breath inwards and slowly exhaling, causing the flame to flicker slightly.

'Like it?' Ben asked, feeling very concerned that this stunt of his screamed of his growing feelings for her. His stomach still hurt, but his adrenaline was helping a little.

'Yes, of course, sorry. I've been lost in my work for the past few days; it's something of a shock to be out of the office – well, my kitchen – let alone in such a beautiful restaurant. After working for so many hours I find it diffi-cult to operate a kettle, let alone come and sit down and have a proper face-to-face chat, so please be patient with me. Where is everyone?' she asked, with a smile at the corner of her mouth.

Ben looked around the room. There were eight tables in all, and not a single soul apart from Effy and himself. Ben felt – another – flurry of nerves tickle his stomach before his mind drifted back to her question. 'No idea, actually. I guess people are just elsewhere at the moment. It's a lovely place,' he lied, thinking that his actions were now a little obvious. He didn't know why he had done it, really – he had just wanted to do something special for her so she could enjoy herself.

The icing-sugar white walls were covered in original photographs of celebrities from years gone by: Monroe, Presley and Sinatra stared back at him with glints of trouble in their eyes, when they had their youth and their health, and everything was limitless.

Effy looks stunning, Ben thought. Granted, he could tell she'd been working solidly for a few days: she had that glaze in her eyes that people get when they've been glued to a screen for too long, but that did nothing to detract from how beautiful she was. Her green eyes were a little darker than they usually appeared in the daytime, and that fascinated him. Her thick auburn curls were piled together in a loose up-do, a few tendrils falling down beside her face, which drove him wild. She was wearing a black camisole made out of some indeterminate shiny fabric with some grey tailored trousers, which – he hadn't been able to help noticing – made her bum look incredible. The finishing touches were a pair of dainty black heels, and a large silver necklace that trickled over her collarbones like a waterfall. She was so classy it hurt. Ben had felt intimidated the moment she walked into the foyer of the restaurant and removed her coat, a long, fitted thing. He had given her a soft kiss on the cheek and offered to take said coat, and a waft of her perfume had drifted past his nose as she moved.

She was breathtaking, and Ben found himself trying to decode her. Had she made such a spectacular effort for him, or was she one of those women who just always pulled out the stops for nights out? He had no idea, but he also knew it was unlikely that a woman like her would be interested in him.

The plus side was that she seemed a lot warmer tonight than she had been on the phone and in previous encounters, much to Ben's relief.

He had struggled to know what to wear that night, his nerves and injury pain making basic decisions a lot more difficult, and had eventually decided on a pair of black trousers, a grey shirt and a blazer he'd picked up at a vintage shop with an ex-lover. He'd not really understood what was so amazing about it, but she had cooed and sighed as he tried it on. That was the decision made.

Effy surveyed the cutlery before her as if she were wondering which bit was for which part of the meal.

There was a slightly awkward stillness, which she filled by starting to fiddle nervously with a fork, turning it over and over in her delicate fingers. Ben couldn't fathom whether she was nervous, tired or just a little quirky.

'You look lovely, Effy, did I tell you that at the start? I'm not sure if I did, but if I didn't, you do . . . Um, did that make sense?' he bumbled, scratching his head and filling the silence with his way-too-honest stream of consciousness, and going red. Again.

Ben was baffled at how he just fell to pieces around her.

'Thank you,' she said simply, smiling, before glancing down at the cutlery again.

Cringe.

'Benjamin!' a booming voice yelled, making them both jump a little.

Thank God, Ben thought. It came from his friend, Archie, a large, red-haired man who stood at the entrance, arms outstretched, before charging towards the table like a tiger released back into the wild. Ben couldn't help noticing how Effy physically braced herself by gently holding on to the table as Archie began his launch in their direction. Typically for Archie – who, although not more than twenty-seven, dressed like an old-fashioned member of the upper classes – he was wearing yellow cords and a loud shirt (his almost permanent attire, with the occasional variant in trouser colour, extending to the green end of the spectrum if he was feeling particularly flamboyant, and often paired with winkle-pickers), and he made his way across the room with all the elegance of a lame cow. Ben loved him, though. They had gone to school together, and he had taught Ben how to smoke and talk to girls.

Effy looked as if she'd never felt more out of place, but amused all the same.

'Benny, you actual fuckedy fuckwit,' Archie said in a terribly posh voice, lunging down to him with such force that everything on the table rattled. He threw his arms around Ben, a great mass of ginger curls enveloping the view he had previously had of Effy. Ben choked on a few strands of hair before he was released from the vicelike embrace, by his friend probably who had re-broken some of Ben's delicate, slowly recovering ribs.

'Ahhh, Archibald, it's so good of you to have us here tonight,' Ben said, slightly embarrassed by the way they both sounded. Their strange in-jokes and banter were perfectly normal in his eyes, but he appreciated that it could be a bit odd for a newcomer.

'Yeah, well, it's no problem closing the restaurant for you after all you've done for me, chappy,' Archie announced.

Ben suddenly turned a dark purple, feeling a little light-headed. A kind of instant-humiliation sweat arrived to cover his whole body in a microsecond.

Effy raised an eyebrow at Archie's words and, taking a sip of her wine, looked as if she was struggling to mask a wide smile.

Ben tried to change the subject, becoming increasingly flustered. *God knows what Archie will say next*, he thought. He might tell her about the time he drunkenly curled up and fell asleep in a men's urinal in Barcelona, or the time he got his head stuck between the bars of a hotel balcony on a stag do and had to be freed by the fire brigade. The stories were endless.

Archie's restaurant was brand new. He had promised to reserve it for Ben as it was a quiet time, and he owed him a few favours after Ben had sorted him out with some PR that had ensured him a few spectacular reviews in the national press. He had only been opening for special guests on week-nights recently anyway, and was due to open the kitchen properly in a fortnight or so. It had all been very exclusive so far and, Ben was pleased to say, a great success. Food critics had applauded the interior design and delicious menu, splashing their thoughts all over the weekend pages of the *Guardian* and the *Evening Standard*.

It was a shame Archie himself hadn't quite managed to keep things as subtle . . .

'So, how's the venture going?' Ben asked, hoping they could swerve away from his simmering humiliation. He was only just cooling down.

'Bloody fantastic, thanks, after all those spangly reviews,' Archie shouted, rubbing his hammy palms together in satisfaction. Suddenly, he span 45 degrees on the heel of his vintage brogues and fixed his gaze on Effy, as if he'd only just noticed her.

Ben's heart sank. Typically, Archie was going to make this dramatic, as if he'd just discovered, in his restaurant a rare type of bird, of which there was only one left in the world . . .

Effy sat up, clearly a little uncomfortable with the unexpected level of attention, a look of alarm flashing across her features, which made Ben smile to himself. Archibald dramatically slid to his knees and held her left hand, like a bashful Prince Charming, a halo of curls wobbling around his head. She started to giggle.

'And who, Ben, just *who*, is this shockingly beautiful lady who joins you this evening?' Archie said, still clutching Effy's hand and turning to beam at Ben as if they were getting married or something. It was totally over the top. Almost panto. 'She looks like Julia bloody Roberts, doesn't she?' he yodelled, before either of them had the chance to answer. *He's got a point*, Ben thought. She did look a little like Julia in her youth, probably the *Pretty Woman* days, minus the hooker wig and heels . . . Still, this wasn't supposed to be a date – he had just wanted to do something nice for her.

Ben buried his face in his hands, before managing to compose himself. 'Erm, well, this is Effy Jones. She is a business contact of mine. Effy runs her own charity, Dafina Kampala,' he said, genuinely proud to be dining out with her, and still confused by the feelings he was having for this girl; this beautiful woman who he thought would never look twice at a man like him. 'She is the new charity partner for Ossa PR,' Ben added, before Archie had the chance to start jumping to more wild conclusions.

'But you're so young!' Archie shrieked, making Ben wince, and kissing Effy's hand in awe, prompting her to laugh with embarrassment.

Effy didn't know what to say, so muttered an awkward 'Thank you!' through her laughter.

'Well, many congratulations on your incredible achievements, Effy. I know you wouldn't have attracted Ossa's attention if you weren't an amazing person. Your selflessness is quite the inspiration,' Archie said, before giving Ben a knowing wink and waltzing out of the room as dramatically as he'd arrived.

They were alone again. Ben was just pouring Effy some wine when some mushy, romantic music came on, as if from nowhere, and the lights suddenly dimmed – even more. *Thanks a lot, Archie, you absolute penis*, Ben thought, as he continued pouring her drink with one hand. He suddenly feared two accordion-playing fools might appear, playing 'Bella Notte' from *Lady and the Tramp*.

The atmosphere had now moved from cringe to one of utter embarrassment.

'Your friend seems nice,' Effy said, raising her glass to her lips and giggling.

'Yes, well, he's a little gregarious but he has a heart of gold. And please ignore this whole display of his – I think he's got the wrong end of the stick,' Ben replied, managing to laugh as Effy nodded kindly.

A sharply dressed waiter arrived and took their orders, putting a red rose on Effy's side of the table and attributing it to Ben. Ben quite simply wanted to curl up and die. When this mortifying display was over, he could finally get down to asking her questions – all the things he'd been desperate to know, hopefully escaping all the humiliating gestures. 'So, tell me a little more about how you decided to start Dafina Kampala. I know you and Dermot touched on this when you came to the office the first time, but I'd like to know the full story,' Ben said, leaning forward, keen to know all about it. He suddenly wished he'd actually done the research Dermot had asked him to do when he had first told him about the charity job.

Effy took a deep breath, giving him the impression that she wondered where to start. 'Well, believe it or not, I worked in fashion once,' Effy began, gesturing towards her outfit and grinning, 'though I'm pretty out of touch with things now, as you can see.'

Ben shook his head in disagreement.

'I used to work in the industry,' Effy continued, 'when I was young and silly.'

'What did you do?'

'I used to deal with accessories – we picked and supplied them for magazine shoots and stuff like that. But then, one year, right in the midst of it all, I went to Uganda on a trip organised by my aunt. She was living there for a while for work, and asked me to come and see her.'

'You must have been really young when you went,' he commented, imagining himself at that age, and how hopeless he would have been in a foreign country.

'Well, I was in my early twenties . . . anyway, I casually accepted her invitation, and booked the flights, without even thinking what Uganda would really be like. On the flight out there I pictured it being a certain way, but it was just totally different,' she said, laughing to herself as she remembered. 'I thought it would be a beautiful place, full of happy, smiling people . . . It's horrendous for me to admit all this, but I thought things in Africa were so much better.' She shook her head ruefully, and took a sip of wine. 'I guess my aunt wanted me to see the reality of it all for myself, because she certainly never corrected me when I piped on about how delightful it was going to be,' she continued, clearly ashamed at her own youthful ignorance.

There's something so honest about her, Ben thought, admiring the soft freckles on her nose. He liked that. And them.

'But when I got there, the things I saw . . . the poverty, the challenges they faced. It was a massive shock. I don't know what I can have been doing when the news came on all my life. God, I was preoccupied . . .' She trailed off.

Ben suddenly thought about his own life. Did he really know what was going on in the world beyond his office, beyond London? How often did he think about it? London was so all-consuming at times it seemed as if city dwellers forgot there was any other kind of existence beyond their own postcode . . . *There's a certain arrogance about Londoners*, Ben thought, knowing he was very much a part of it all. His sister even poked fun at it when they talked about life in the country, saying things along the lines of 'Yes, Ben, there are trains, and cars and roads out here,' and 'Yes, Ben, the supermarkets do open on Sundays.'

Ben felt a little ashamed and he could also suddenly feel the anxiety creeping in – it was just starting, a sad trickle at the bottom of his stomach. He worked hard to push it to one side.

Thankfully Effy was still in full flow: 'Now, don't get me wrong, Uganda isn't a place dominated by misery. There's something very uplifting about it. Its economy stabilised in 2012 and slow growth is expected. It's rich with culture and beauty. On the other hand Uganda's poverty levels are still among the worst in the world, and there is an average life expectancy of just fifty-two, I think, for men, and a few years older for women. Sorry, I'm really going on, aren't I?' she laughed.

Ben shook his head to say no, and urged her to continue.

'The people are amazing; a lot of it is truly inspirational. I was fascinated by the place, I fell madly in love with it and I didn't want to leave. Something was pulling me back, keeping me there . . . So I moved my flight back, and explored Kampala. I told work I would be away for a while, and somehow they were OK with it. I think they had to be, really . . . I was past the point of caring.'

Ben sat back in his seat as their starters arrived: two perfectly polished white plates. His had pâté on it, and she had chosen a seafood dish. The food was beautifully presented, but he could hardly pay any attention to it.

'What would you say was the crunch moment? I guess we can all go somewhere and be moved by it, but most people have forgotten what they saw by the time they've gone through duty-free at Heathrow. What you did was somewhat beyond the usual response, if you don't mind me saying . . .' Ben commented, eager to hear more.

Effy seemed surprised by his genuine interest.

'Well, that's the thing. This situation – it found me, not the other way round,' she said, spearing what looked like a mussel with a tiny fork. 'There was a particular day, and something life-changing happened. My aunt was working so I went out on my own. I was walking away from the centre of the city. It was a hot day, and children were running past me on the way to school . . . And I heard something – I heard a whimpering and it was coming from a tree.'

Ben nodded at her, encouraging her to continue. Her words were taking his mind off his ever-growing panic just enough for him to be able to concentrate.

'It was a little girl. She was crying in a way I'd never heard back home. There's a kind of crying that comes from a child; it doesn't mean, "I want that toy" or "I'm a bit hungry". It means, "I'm in pain", "I'm desperate". It's a sickening sound, actually; it makes you feel nauseous to the core, when you hear a child suffering like that . . . And I couldn't ignore it. I started to walk past it, unsure of what to do, but I couldn't, so I turned back.' Effy paused, pushing a few rogue curls behind her left ear. The volume of her voice had dropped a little. 'So, yes, I walked back towards the tree and bent down a little so I could crawl beneath the branches, and there she was, a little girl in a beige dress. She looked at me like I had saved her life and reached her arms out to me. So you see, she chose me, rather than the other way round. And I still didn't know what to do . . . I was so young. I just shuffled down and sat next to her. I asked, unsure if she would understand me, I asked her what was wrong and she pulled up her dress, a little above the knee, and there was the nastiest injury I'd ever seen, Ben.'

As Effy told the story, there was a light in her eyes, as if she could see the little girl like it was happening right there and then.

'The cut, it was this huge, deep laceration. I think her uncle had accidentally hit her with a machete, when she got in the way at the wrong moment. He was working at a farm. At least that was what I could work out from what she was saying, anyway . . . It was badly infected, and someone had made an awful attempt to treat it. She was in agony. And all she could say to me was simply, "I can't

153

go to school. I want to go to school. I have an exam today."
I asked her where her mother or father was, she said she
didn't have parents. And her uncle was nowhere to be seen.'

'What did you do?' Ben asked, by now enthralled by this
story – the story of a young girl who had been pushed into
something wonderful by a very bad experience.

'I didn't really think, I guess. I scooped her up, flagged
down a taxi and took her to a private hospital in the city.
It was mainly used by expats and wealthy locals. I paid
for her treatment, and made sure she was looked after
because I couldn't bear to just drop her off somewhere and
leave her to it. I made sure she stayed in the hospital until
she was well enough to leave. Then we found her family.
Her uncle had lost her and was so relieved to have her
back, and, well, the rest is history – she went back to school
when she was fully recovered. Even though she's still so
young, she hopes to go to university one day – she says
she wants to be a doctor. I still get letters from her, though
they can be very hard to read, but her English gets better
every time,' Effy said, smiling, looking down at the
tablecloth.

'Would she have died, if it wasn't for you?' Ben asked,
suddenly feeling all the hairs on his arms stand to attention.
He thought about his past, and felt a sickness rise in his
throat. *If it wasn't for you . . .*

'Ohh, I don't know, to be honest. It's possible; the infection
was getting very serious and she was showing signs of
complications. Had it been left much longer, she may well
have died, but who knows what would have happened. I
mean, obviously I took her to a good hospital, but that
kind of care just isn't available all the time. The hospitals
are of course stretched, and sometimes patients don't stay
for any real recovery time because they need to work or

help their families, and they don't get better. Things are more challenging in the rural areas too, healthcare is harder to access . . .' Effy nodded, as if to herself. 'But this isn't about me. I did what any person with a heart would have done. And I just realised there was a need for more health-care that could support the whole family through difficult times. When the children and young people got hurt, they often ended up in the same position as the little girl I helped, just getting worse and worse but still having to work, or support their families because of a lack of money. I wanted to put a stop to that, and I really hope one day I can expand the number of healthcare facilities I set up across the country to support what already exists. I want to be able to go out to rural Uganda too, and take injured children to our health centre, look after them properly for as long as it takes, and then drop them back home with their families,' Effy said, looking at Ben now and smiling widely.

'It's incredible, Effy,' he responded, folding the white serviette in his lap reflectively before looking up at her.

'Well, it's scary if I'm totally truthful,' she said, finishing her starter and putting her cutlery side by side on the plate to confirm this.

Neat and tidy. Polite.

'I've got a long way to go – the charity is in its very early stages, as I'm sure you know. I haven't set up my first centre yet, though Ossa PR will be a huge help. There's been an awful lot of research to do, gathering funds, applying for permissions. It's a huge task, so of course I am more than a little daunted.

'It's not just individual incidents, either – there's also natural, or environmental disasters, things like that. I'm sure you heard about what happened with that disgusting oil company in Africa, didn't you? The Ropek Oil disaster? Well, children still need help as a result of that, believe it or not. What happened out there was absolutely horrific. They make me sick,' she finished, a look of disgust flashing across her face, as if she'd tasted something revolting.

Ben's stomach dropped and suddenly he felt like he couldn't eat. She worked with victims of the Ropek disaster?

'There are people, and of course children, who suffered such horrendous burns they died months later, in agony. Those who didn't – well, various organisations are trying to help, and mine will, too. Ropek Oil has handled the situation horrendously, too – they've hardly offered any real support, apart from token, minimum contributions that far from rectify anything . . . They make me so angry, Ben, I can't even describe it,' she added finally, unable to finish her own sentence for all her bitterness.

Ben saw a flicker in her eyes; it was hatred: real, genuine hatred. It scared him. It wasn't often, if at all, in his working or personal life that he saw such passion about anything, and something about it frightened him.

Time seemed to slow down for him. He hadn't known that she was working to deal with the fallout of the disaster. He'd had no idea. And wouldn't she have researched Ossa PR enough to know about their working relationship? She couldn't have done – she had become so full of rage talking about Ropek Oil, and yet she had taken the help of a company working for them. He couldn't believe she didn't know, and the way she was putting it . . . it was far worse than the disgust from his relatives.

He suddenly felt sick, and guilty. Fear washed over him, and he felt unwell as panic rose in his throat. He couldn't be in this restaurant, with this wonderful woman who sat across from him. *It's a farce*, he thought, feeling that familiar wave of low self-worth come crashing down over his shoulders. He had to get out of there. He had to escape.

'Effy, I'm terribly sorry. I'm not feeling well,' he bumbled, rising to his feet just as the main course came, nearly knocking his plate from the waiter's hands, fear controlling his body. 'I'll take care of the bill, but I'm going to have to go. I'm terribly, awfully sorry,' Ben said, before walking quickly out of the room.

Effy sat alone at the table – well, alone in the whole restaurant – baffled by what had just happened. The night had been going so well, despite her previous dread of tearing herself away from her work and spending time with Ben, and then he'd just disappeared. He said he was ill, but there had been no clear build-up to that: he hadn't been massaging his temples or wincing in the way people do when they are secretly battling a sickening headache. He hadn't looked pale, or hot, or cold, or anything like that. Nor had he been dashing off to the toilet, or mopping a sweaty brow with a tissue. None of the obvious signs had been there. She was so confused.

Did I say something? she wondered, sipping her wine in the peaceful room and staring at the wreckage of Ben's side of the table: a half-full glass of red, a plate still full of food, and a white napkin, sadly crumpled on the table beside it. And that's how she felt. Deflated, confused, and a little lost.

She wondered if she hadn't been too graphic with the story of the little girl in Africa, and how she had been inspired to set up the charity, looking down at her own meal and suddenly feeling like eating was the last thing she wanted to do. She glanced at the rose guiltily. She guessed sometimes she took for granted how disturbing it all was because she was used to it . . . maybe it had been too much for him to cope with? But she would find that surprising. Surely he hadn't experienced that much of a sheltered upbringing?

Effy was disappointed. That was the predominant feeling, and it surprised her. When she had first met him, she'd thought he was one of those horrible 'lad' types. Ben's mere presence had scared her in the wake of her break-up with Frank, because he had reminded her of all the horrible guys she'd dated before her most recent relationship: men who 'couldn't commit', men who had 'trust issues' and all that bullshit; which, in her opinion, was just code for, 'I want to shag everyone and not be challenged', and the whole thing had made her a bit depressed about what might lie ahead.

Then, when Effy had seen him on the bridge, partially impaled on a skateboard, she had felt that little element of amusement, because he still just seemed such a . . . well . . . *idiot*. There really was no other word for it. She was sorry to even think it, but this was her honest truth. All this was to her was a mutually beneficial relationship that made Ossa PR look good, and provided her charity with much-needed funding. Even when he had called to invite her out for dinner she had just wanted to get him off the phone: his voice had annoyed her. She had so much work to do and couldn't help but feel that dinner was a little unnecessary. But she knew she would have to go for the benefit of the partnership – she had even made an effort in the end, accepting the situation and telling herself that she may as well enjoy it.

For Effy, the biggest shock of the night was the effort Ben had gone to: the restaurant stunt, which his friend so unfortunately ruined for him, was sweet. She almost wondered if it wasn't a little . . . suspicious, but she guessed he did have great contacts, and he probably did stuff like this all the time to impress people. The rose thing looked like it had been initiated by Archie. Effy figured that Ben was just that kind of guy: everything was larger than life. Armani. Gold. Private restaurant.

People surprise you in life and Ben surprised me tonight, she thought. When she had seen him she had been bowled over by how good he looked. He was astonishingly handsome. Not only that, but he was intelligent, great to talk to and an utter gentleman. He had totally excelled in the situation . . . well, before he'd disappeared, and had seemed like a totally different man.

She felt a little rush of excitement in her stomach. She hadn't wanted it to end. And then it dawned on her. *Holy shit, I like Ben Lawrence . . . I definitely do.*

I didn't want or plan for this to happen. And then: *This is not good.*

Seventeen

She was so beautiful she turned him into custard

Thursday 25 September 2014
Dalston, London

Ben knew that most men would label him an utter lunatic, leaving a woman like Effy in an incredible restaurant they were lucky enough to be sharing, alone. He thought about this as he fled the building's lobby, richly decorated with thick, red carpet and various sculptures in the shape of mischievous cherubs: all curls, fat dimples and chubby cheeks.

Archie caught up with him on the way out, probably tipped off by the waiter who, no doubt, witnessed his sudden departure. Archie was out of breath, his jacket flapping as he attempted to run after his friend, his neat, polished brown shoes sinking deeply into the carpet beneath his ample weight.

'Buddy, what's up? Was it the rose? Was it too much?' he asked Ben as he was about to leave, concern etched on his face, his giant monobrow all crinkled in the middle.

Ben didn't know what to say, so he lied to him too, as he stood there, Archie's pink, heavy hand on his shoulder. 'No, no, it's OK. I'm really not well, mate. I'm sorry. I'll call tomorrow about the bill and I'll pay it straight away,' Ben muttered, flashing him an apologetic smile.

'Oh Christ, it isn't the fucking food, is it?' Archie gasped, panic written all over him now, his worst nightmare materialising before his very eyes. Ben could almost see his blood pressure rising.

'God, no, Archie, the food was incredible, thank you,' Ben replied, trying to calm him.

Archie patted Ben's back, still looking confused as Ben buttoned up his coat. Ben thanked him once more and started walking down the set of marble steps that led up to the entrance, taking a deep gulp of the warm evening air, his heart hammering in his chest. He was so glad to be outside.

Ben reached into his coat pocket and pulled out a packet of cigarettes before lighting one and taking huge lungfuls of smoke to calm himself down. He wished he could bloody well stop smoking, but that was the least of his problems at the moment.

The sun had only recently set, casting London in a warm, purple haze. The streetlights had just come on, painting the pavements below in orange. A few people were clattering out of bars and heading to other venues that would no doubt be open later. They would probably continue their evenings with music, huge glasses of wine and pointless chatter that would dance them into the small hours, and it would all pass by in a four-hour timeframe that would feel like five minutes.

That should have been how this night ended for Effy and me, he thought, though he was quietly relieved it hadn't, given how fearful he was of his feelings towards her . . . *well, towards anyone*, he considered, as he started walking in the direction of the underground.

He walked past all the designer shops: dresses that had been placed on mannequins, probably pinned at the back so they would hang right; diamonds reflecting the light of halogen displays behind thick panes of glass, reminding people all the time that they 'needed stuff' – *material crap that they're led to believe will make them happy*, Ben thought. It was a constant tap on the shoulder wherever anyone went; a subtle reminder of the merry-go-round of consumerism that would never be satisfied. He was tired of it all, he hated that he was a part of it, and he wanted to escape.

His heart was still thumping hard in his chest as he stubbed his cigarette out on the top of a bin before throwing the butt inside and heading down to the District line. He felt dizzy with fear, concerned that he was going to end up having a panic attack on the tube, before being calmed down by a drunken tramp with a paper bag for him to breathe into.

Ben had never worried about the contract with Ropek Oil before, despite the warnings from his family. He certainly hadn't worried about the charity work with Dafina Kampala. He just let it all happen. But something about Effy's vitriol, her fury, had instantly planted guilt in his mind, but he couldn't work out why.

I mean, technically, it isn't bad, is it?

As I've explained so many times before to my family, working for Ropek Oil is just one of my many projects. It doesn't mean I support them personally, or think they can just get away with what happened.

It doesn't mean I endorse what happened. I, like everyone else, totally agree that it was, and still is, horrific.

And surely it's a good thing, to then help the situation by giving money to a charity like Effy's?

So why am I feeling so horrendous?

The thoughts rattled around Ben's mind. They were noise, and he couldn't work out if he was being a little neurotic or not. He was still amazed Effy didn't know already, but the truth had not volunteered itself at the dinner table despite the fact that she had been talking about Ropek Oil. Now he felt bad that he hadn't said something, he realised, picking away at the shabby cloth of the seat he had chosen on the tube. *And what was all the stuff about Ropek Oil not helping the people of Uganda?* Ben thought. As far as he was aware, they had done a lot . . .

Ben was so deep in thought that he missed his stop, and had to take a rather convoluted journey home. As he changed tube trains he was struck, almost fused to the spot, by a huge poster advertising the Wildlife Photographer of the Year exhibition 2014. It featured a swan – a huge, ivory bird, gliding on a picturesque lake – and he felt even worse. The reminders were everywhere, it seemed, and his new-found problems with Ropek Oil and the charity contract seemed overwhelming.

He wouldn't normally even care that much, but there was something about her . . .

When Ben finally emerged from the tube station near his home, he lit yet another cigarette. He had a feeling this would be another one of those nights lost at home in a haze of whisky and nervous smoking. It never made anything better, though: just a short-term calming of the nerves, but all the issues would still be there. He couldn't drink or smoke them away.

Ben unlocked his front door and slumped his weight against it to push it open, partially stumbling into the hallway, only just realising that he was fairly drunk already.

There was no scruffy dog or nonchalant cat to greet him: no frantically wagging tail; no look of disdain from a feline face. No children clattering down the stairs to say they'd had a bad dream. No partner curled up on the sofa watching a film, ready to greet him. No family. No pets. Just whisky and fags. It was depressing, and he was deeply confused.

Ben walked into the living room, grabbed a remote and turned the lights to a relaxing glow, before sticking on some classical music in an attempt to clear his mind. There was so much noise in his head he wanted to dull it with violins and cellos. Within minutes, the whisky was poured and he was in his space, alone with his thoughts.

Ben played the night back in his head. The moment he had seen Effy he had felt that crash in the pit of his stomach. She was so beautiful she turned him into custard. Just this mass of sweet, sugary, excitement where there was normally scepticism and excuses.

And he hated it, because he *couldn't get close to her.*

He'd only had strong feelings for someone once, a long time ago. It had been love, despite how young he'd been, and he certainly didn't discount it now that he was twenty-eight. He knew it was real. With Effy, for the first time in a long time, he was beginning to realise he was starting to feel something. Those first, nervous feelings were creeping in. Despite it all. Despite that day . . . despite the agonising pain, which haunted his existence.

Of course he had fancied women over the years, and he'd been attracted to them – that wasn't an issue. But *feelings* were what he feared might be happening here. This thing with Effy – well, this non-thing, really, had reminded him of what that felt like. He didn't just want to sleep with her, he wanted to get to know her; he wanted to know everything, yet he was also terrified.

Ben had never really understood the whole love-at-first-sight thing. It seemed impossible for him to 'fall' for someone, let alone someone he hardly knew, but here he was, starting to fall, to tumble, out of control. He had already imagined what it might be like to introduce her to his friends. How proud he would be to have her with him.

It was all coming back to him now . . . how it felt to really care about somebody, to one day maybe even love somebody. It was a very specific and different thing, he realised. You almost never noticed your heart when you took it for granted, beating away beneath the rib cage, quietly keeping things going. But when you tried to thwart it, to deny its true feelings – then you were suddenly so painfully aware of it.

All those feelings were coming back . . . He looked back to when he was younger and was able to remember how love felt. He had been fourteen when he'd first seen the girl who would turn out to be his first girlfriend, riding around on a luminous green bike. He had run up beside her as she made her way over a field, desperately trying to ignore him, her long brown hair furling out in the breeze, her pale face clenched in irritation. She had made no attempt to slow down when Ben had asked her where she was from, all puffed out from running next to her. He had been delighted when she had said she lived a few streets away. Absolutely made up. And, from that moment on, he had dedicated himself to making her his girlfriend, despite her initial disdain and the way she looked at him like he was a fly hovering near her food. He was Romeo back then.

For quite a long time he had worried that he might be annoying her, until one summer evening after school when she kissed him, and it seemed like all the stars swooped from the sky and spiralled around his head. He was fit for nothing after that, just lolloping around the house working out which garden he hadn't yet stolen flowers from, and which part of the park was most secret so that he could take her there for kissing sessions.

Her parents hadn't been massively keen on him. He had been a scruffy kid whose body was growing too fast, making him clumsy and always knocking things over in their huge, sprawling home, dropping knives covered in peanut butter onto the carpet. They hadn't liked how much time they had spent together, worrying about her grades. But she and Ben hadn't cared. The world was against them, but everything was fine as long as they had credit on their mobiles for late-night texting and their hiding place for letters was still a secret. That was love . . .

Now he wanted someone, wanted Effy, in a way he thought would never be possible again. But he knew that because of his past, this would never be a reality for him. Not only that, but this situation with Effy's charity and Ropek Oil was compounding the whole mess.

After an hour or so of drinking and thinking, Ben made his way to bed. His room was immaculately tidy – the cleaner had been in that day – and his bed looked like that of a hotel's, all clean, fresh and tucked in at the sides. He hurriedly took off his clothes, unable to muster the enthusiasm to hang them up, before climbing between the sheets.

Lying there in the dark, he realised he had to say

something to Effy about his sudden departure. She probably knew he wasn't being truthful and it was bad form.

Ben grabbed his phone and tapped in a message to her, saying how sorry he was for his sudden 'illness'. Then he made a vow to himself that he wouldn't speak to her again unless work dictated it.

There was absolutely no way she would be OK with his work for Ropek Oil. But he was in too deep already, and he was frightened.

Eighteen

It's nice to be reminded from time to time how insignificant we are

Saturday 27 September 2014
The Natural History Museum, London

Effy had arranged to meet Rosa by Dippy – the 26-metre-long replica dinosaur skeleton. While she was waiting for her friend, she stared up at its huge rib cage, imagining a time when dinosaurs existed, and a natural skeletal framework much like this one would have been covered in flesh and thick, puckered skin. A time when the world was not afflicted with Facebook, internet trolls, reality TV and *The X Factor*. A time when this creature – the Diplodocus – took giant steps across a dry, crumbling land, concentrating only on survival. Effy wondered if the dinosaur species ever knew it would eventually die out, only to be remembered in models and text books, and gawped at by people like her.

The dinosaur made her feel small. *But I like that*, Effy thought, looking up at the intricate components of its feet, giant mottled 'ankle joints' connecting to huge 'leg bones', that looked so old and brittle now it was a wonder it was still standing. *It's nice to be reminded from time to time how insignificant we are*, she thought. How our problems are not always so great as they seem. We are part of something, but we are not the be all and end all. It's a great comfort, in a very strange way, she considered.

Rosa was ten minutes late, but Effy was thankful for that time away from her laptop. She felt like a small drop in the ocean; putting everything into perspective. Children ran excitedly around the entrance to the museum, holding hands and pointing at things, emitting the odd, ear-piercing shriek. Mothers and fathers huddled around the ticket desk before finding their children again, dishing out tickets and telling them to calm down and stop screaming. A baby lay in a light blue pram, staring up at the huge glass ceiling with impassive blue eyes. His dilated pupils were trying to comprehend surroundings that for him, might or might not be genuine – something possibly man-made and suspended from a mobile, or something in the real world. He was too young to know. Effy longed for simplicity at that moment. She longed for that feeling she'd had when she was a child and was so carefree that she could lose herself in anything. When a box of glitter, glue, pom poms and brightly coloured card could be her everything on a rainy Saturday afternoon . . .

When Rosa arrived, Effy was so deep in thought that she shocked her a little, her cute face materialising before Effy's like a vision, in kohl eyeliner and retro red lipstick.

Effy was so surprised she jumped back.

'Bloody hell, Effy, are you OK?' Rosa said, pulling her friend into a hug. Effy noticed her familiar smell: a fruity perfume by Lacoste that she always asked her to buy for her when she went through duty-free.

'Sorry, yes, of course. I was just thinking,' Effy responded, pulling herself together and straightening up, wondering if she would be in a socially sharp enough place to even make it through the day.

'You're always thinking, Effy Jones. I'm surprised you haven't totally lost yourself in that huge, muddled brain of yours yet,' Rosa quipped affectionately, a half-compliment delivered with a teasing smile.

Rosa was wearing a knitted grey dress, over which was casually draped a cool, black leather bomber jacket with maroon sleeves. A vintage satchel hung casually over her shoulder, and she'd finished off her outfit with a nice pair of black boots. She was heavily made-up.

Effy glanced down at her own, slightly half-hearted ensemble – a pair of skinny jeans and a fluffy jumper – wishing she'd made time to deliver her monstrous pile of washing to the dry cleaners. Rosa appeared to just glance at her wardrobe and end up looking great. It all seemed like much more of a struggle for Effy.

'I can't wait for this exhibition,' Rosa said, clutching their tickets in her hand and waving them around frantically. She had already picked them up, and Effy hadn't even noticed her doing so while she was people-watching.

They were going to the Wildlife Photographer of the Year exhibition, which promised to be a 'moving, delightful and sometimes shocking' collection of images of the natural world. The papers had been raving about it and there were posters all over the London Underground featuring, funnily enough, a swan on a lake. Effy thought that was why it called out to her so strongly, since she was so fond of making paper swans. But there was so much on her mind she was concerned that she wouldn't be able to focus on the photos. Her encounter with Ben had been rattling around her head like a metal ball in a pinball machine, and she was desperate to tell Rosa about it. She seemed to have gone from one extreme to the other when it came to Ben, and she didn't like it too much . . . It was all a little too teenage for her, and not like her at all.

Luckily, as they made their way into the exhibition – past all the stuffed animals in various states of interrupted death – it was clear that it was going to be a chatty environment, so they would be able to talk. In reality, Effy wanted to grab Rosa, cry into her hair and get her to tell her that everything would be OK. She was really going to have to toughen up if she was back in the dating game, she realised.

'So how are things? You look troubled,' Rosa said, as they looked at the first image, displayed on a backlit screen. She crossed her arms and stared at the photograph: a huge tiger glancing threateningly into the lens of a camera operated by a photographer who was, no doubt, shitting his boxer shorts at the time. It made the hairs on Effy's arms stand on end, it was so shockingly beautiful.

'Yeah, well, things are a bit weird,' she muttered, unsure of where to start with this one.

'What's up?'

'Well, you know Ben, the skateboard guy?'

Rosa nodded and smiled to herself, as if she were still highly amused by the whole memory. Just then, a young boy who must have been about five, barged his way past them and planted a chocolate and probably snot-coated hand right on the image in front of them, covering the tiger's face with a smeary glaze. His mother went into meltdown, frantically scrubbing the screen with a wipe that seemed to just materialise in her hand.

Rosa and Effy moved on awkwardly, not wanting to fuel the woman's embarrassment.

'Well, he called and asked me for dinner. I didn't really want to go – I wasn't sure what the point of it was – he just insisted on it because he said he felt sorry that he'd ruined my night with you.'

'OK, and did you go?' Rosa asked, turning towards her friend and raising an eyebrow as they approached an image of a badger. It was sitting in thick undergrowth with what Effy wanted to assume was his badger wife, girlfriend or lover.

'I did, yes . . . And it was funny, because we went to this incredible place in Chelsea. Ben had basically got it closed to everyone but us – his friend owns it,' Effy said, still confused by that.

'Jesus fucking Christ, Effy! That's amazing, isn't it?' Rosa spluttered, and was instantly shot an evil glance by an elderly woman who stood nearby.

They hushed their voices a little before stepping away from the star-crossed badgers and on to a picture of a rather bedraggled-looking bird, covered in a film of oil. It had one scraggly foot entangled in a rusty beer can.

'Yeah it is nice; anyway, things were going well and then I told him all about how I started Dafina Kampala. We got onto the subject of Ropek Oil and all that, and then he suddenly said he didn't feel well and that he had to go. And that was it. He disappeared before the main course came.'

Rosa turned to look at Effy with an expression on her face that simply said 'gutted'. But there was almost a level of mocking to it, and Effy felt her hackles rise a little.

'What did you say to him, Effy?' Rosa joked, gently elbowing her in the side, picking up on Effy's irritation. It hurt a little.

'Nothing, nothing – I was just talking about my work.

I don't really think he was ill; I think it was an excuse.' Effy sighed, looking at the yellows and pinks in the oil, wishing she could reach into the photograph and save the bird.

'Hmm, well, if I'm totally honest, it does seem a little odd that he just went like that,' Rosa said, her profile gently illuminated by the light coming from the screen in front of them. 'It's very rare that people are so ill they just have to disappear like that. Unless they have the shits, which is unlikely if it was a posh restaurant,' Rosa continued, matter-of-factly.

Talking to Rosa was scary because she was honest, Effy remembered. She was the kind of friend who didn't just tell you what you wanted to hear and, as a result, Effy very much trusted her opinion. She told the truth, and that was something that was difficult to take sometimes.

By now they had slowly shuffled towards the next photograph: a penguin on an iceberg significantly far away from any of the others. It looked confused, lost and momentarily stranded.

'I love this one,' Effy said, explaining to Rosa that it very much reflected her own feelings. Feelings of turmoil, being lost – lost and alone.

'You're terribly dramatic today, Effy,' was Rosa's reply. 'Why are you so bothered about him leaving, anyway? I thought you always felt he was, well, a bit of a knob, really.' She shrugged her shoulders at Effy. Her eyes glittered in the low light and there was her knowing smile.

Effy loved the way she spoke so beautifully and then dropped such base descriptive words into her sentences.

'Well, yes, you're right . . . The thing is . . . I think, *I think I like him*,' she whispered, as if she were concerned he might be around. That he might hear.

'Well, yeah, that seems pretty obvious,' Rosa said flatly, before laughing softly beneath her breath.

Effy felt a little hot and flustered. She pulled a hair band from her wrist, piled her hair into a bun, and secured it.

'I didn't like him much before, despite what you say, Rosa. But things have changed now . . . I know it's a bit cringy,' Effy went on, looking down at the shiny floor. Rosa rolled her eyes. 'He's kind of different to how I thought he was . . . He's really quite something,' she added.

'But he walked out on you in a restaurant and left you all alone? Are you sure you aren't having some delayed Frank crisis? Maybe these are rebound emotions?'

'Nope. I'm totally over Frank, and I really like Ben. I do. It kind of dawned on me when I was left alone, actually. You see, the thing is, when I first met Ben I felt a bit of a flutter of something, but I quickly ignored it when I saw him in front of his colleagues and I just put him in a box, really. But he seems to be two different people – Ben at work and Ben out of work, and I kind of understand why . . . It's a pretty weird job he has, very high pressure.'

Rosa gently grabbed Effy's hand and led her friend along to the next photograph. Effy's was a little sweaty, and she was embarrassed.

'Look, this one's for you,' Rosa said, almost changing the subject deliberately. She smiled as she spoke and gently released her grip on her friend.

Effy's eyes were greeted by a swan's own tiny button ones, buried in a pale, elegant face. It was the image on the adverts, plastered all over London on billboards, bus stops and transport networks. It was beautiful, peaceful, the bird so self-assured about where it belonged. Graceful and majestic.

174

Effy loved it. It was a far cry from the paper versions she made.

'To be honest, I don't know what to say,' Rosa told her, switching back to the previous topic as Effy stared so hard she started to get double vision, the swan turning into two beautiful birds with chalk-white wings.

They whiled away another half-hour in the exhibition, but came no closer to answers. Eventually Effy walked away from the images of the world, no clearer about her own.

As they left the museum, Rosa turned and faced Effy. 'Listen, I think you're a little stressed. This thing with Ben – yes, it's confusing, but it's no big deal. You hardly know each other and I've never seen you so bothered about a guy so quickly . . . And about him leaving the restaurant so suddenly? People are odd sometimes – don't let it get to you. I know you like him, but if it's right, it will work out. You have to trust me on that. So don't waste your time and energy worrying about this – you've got enough on your plate anyway, right? Just focus on you.' When she had finished, there was a lovely expression of serenity on her features and Effy realised she'd done her usual professional job of calming her down.

Effy made her way home by bus, curled up on the back seat, watching London pass her by in the gorgeous autumnal sunshine with a kind of contentment haze all around her. Rosa was right. She was getting carried away. As much as she liked Ben, it just wasn't that big a deal. In fact, she felt a little embarrassed that she had been so bothered about the whole thing. They hardly knew each other.

There was, however, a strange surprise for Effy when she arrived home. Having let herself into her painfully empty flat, she made a cup of tea and sat down to her laptop ready to check for any emails.

She had just expected the usual stuff: charity applications' progress, staff recruitment updates, and forwards of cute animals from her old school friend, Georgia, so it was a huge shock to see Frank's name pop up. He had sent her an email.

Effy felt a little shiver run down her spine, and wondered for a moment if she should open it. She had come so far; she had no idea how this message would make her feel, or what it would say. The subject line simply said 'Thank you'. It worried her a little. It could be a 'Thank you for the good times' or it could be a 'Thanks for ruining my life' kind of message.

Effy took a deep breath and opened it.

Effy,

I'm sorry I haven't been in touch sooner and I hope this email doesn't come out of the blue as a shock or a source of upset.

It has been a difficult couple of months for me, but I finally feel ready to speak to you and say how I feel.

When I first left our flat I was devastated. I spent weeks feeling horrendous. I couldn't eat, or sleep, or even dress myself properly to be honest! I don't know about you – and I'm not sure I want to know, really – but I was totally broken.

Anyway, enough sadness. I feel like I have come a long way since then, and I now know we made the right choice. I apologise if this email comes across badly, I am in no way intending to be rude and hope this message is a comfort to us both.

What I am trying to say is that this was the best thing for us, and I hope you agree. I hope you are OK, Effy. I still think about you a lot, of course, but I'm glad to say that we set each other free. Our relationship was, in the end, hugely dysfunctional, and I'm glad we stepped away to get the perspective we needed.

Having had some perspective, I would like to first of all say sorry. Sorry for being a bit of a thorn in your side whilst you worked so hard on something brilliant. I loved you, Effy, and it was hard to see you love something more than me. I hope the whole experience has taught me something, that I must be more supportive of people in future, less selfish, and more proactive in my own life and dreams. I'm just sorry this lesson came after the loss of us.

I would also like to say thank you. Thanks for all the great memories we shared. Thank you for putting up with me for so long! Thank you for making me happy for the first few years of our relationship. The problems we experienced towards the end do not detract from that, and I will always remember those wonderful times.

Effy, life is probably better now for both of us and I pray to God you feel the same. I'm sure you are coming on leaps and bounds – you are a star and I admire you, if only from far away now, with my memories.

I'm feeling happier now. I've got more work on, because I'm more open to it. I'm spending more time with my friends, life is good again. It all now makes sense.

I hope we can still be friends, and I hope you are now as happy as I am.

All my heart,

Frank

X

Tears trickled down her face as she read the final line of Frank's email. It was a bittersweet message to read. Really, she couldn't have wished for more: the peaceful, mutual ending of a relationship between two people. Two people who had loved each other wholeheartedly once, but no longer fitted together as beautifully as the final pieces of a jigsaw puzzle.

No bitterness. No anger. No regret. Nothing but time, space and mutual admiration, written into words and sent across cyberspace and into her inbox. But it was still hard. As much as she'd moved on from him, it was painful, in a strange way, to know that he was over her . . .

Effy was moved to tears by his account of the weeks after their break-up and how accurately they mirrored her own. She was strangely pleased to know that he'd suffered as she had. Yet she was relieved that he was happy, that he was moving on with his life. She almost wanted to shout 'I knew it!' at the screen, that she knew he was capable of more than the person he'd been in the final months of their love story. Effy was grateful that he now, finally, saw everything she'd wanted him to see during those long frustrating nights, listening to him sighing himself to sleep as she frantically tapped away at her laptop.

But it was hard to read those words.

It was the end of a chapter. However, sad though it was, it meant a new one could finally begin.

Nineteen

He wasn't arrogant, but he also wasn't stupid

Wednesday 1 October 2014
Canary Wharf, London

It was 2.30 p.m. and Ben was back in his office after a long, wine-fuelled lunch with a client. A client who may as well have put a large funnel in his mouth and enthusiastically filled it with Chablis, had they skipped all the formal niceties of the occasion.

Ben was struggling to concentrate, weighed down by what felt like a ton of sushi, yet disastrously light-headed due to all the alcohol he'd consumed. He had just managed to get back into a report he was now very poorly writing – peppering the document with drunken spelling mistakes – when his phone beeped loudly.

It was a message from Effy Jones, the first line of which had appeared as a banner on the screen of his iPhone. Because he could see most of it already, he instantly knew it wasn't related to the charity partnership, the progress of which was gaining huge momentum. Everyone in the office was raising money for Dafina Kampala by signing up to marathons, triathlons, three-legged races, bike rides, tandem skydives, and various humiliating fancy-dress excursions to raise as much cash as possible. There was also a charity ball in the planning, which was expected to raise at least £40,000, where London's wealthiest and glossiest would gather in a Kensington hotel and casually bid thousands on things they had never known they wanted. And, of course, the inevitable lump sum that Dermot would drop into the pot, like it was nothing. This was great, of course, but it all seemed to have been built on top of recent events and his fear of hurting Effy, and he felt like there was no escape. It was far too late to rock the boat now . . .

The charity partnership also served as a constant reminder of her. Every time a sponsorship form landed on Ben's desk he saw those green eyes and wished everything was different, so he could just kiss her. He wished he didn't fear getting close to someone.

Now, as Ben stared at his phone, he felt his heart jump into his mouth. *Jesus*, he thought to himself, suddenly wishing that she'd leave him alone. He hadn't heard from her since the dinner, which had happened nearly a week ago, apart from a text back saying that she hoped he'd feel better soon from his illness. He hadn't replied to it, and hadn't sent her any other messages. Now here she was, back in touch again, for something that didn't involve work: Hi, Ben. I hope you are OK. Do you fancy coming to the cinema some time this week? Thought it would be nice to hang out again. Let me know. Effy x

His heart sank and danced all at the same time, a confusing cocktail of emotions. He realised that she must like him if she was sending him a message like that, but he didn't know why, because he had behaved like such a child at dinner. A woman normally so nonchalant and casual was now sending him a text, asking him to 'hang out' with her outside their formal working relationship.

He wasn't arrogant, but he also wasn't stupid. Before, he would have leapt at the chance: he would have probably bloody well run to the cinema that very moment, popcorn in one hand, a bunch of roses in the other and his heart casually pinned to his jacket, beating away outside his clothes.

But now things were different. No matter how much he liked her, Ben had made a vow to himself to stay away from her. He couldn't face getting close to her. He knew he was still a long way from battling his own problems, and he also knew the saying about not being able to love someone until you are comfortable with yourself: he was still lying awake at night thinking about the past, and how much he would do to change it. He still noticed youngsters on the tube sometimes, and wished he could step into their shoes and go back. Start his own time again . . . he felt so fucked up, he couldn't think straight any more.

Ben read the message a couple of times, before placing the phone down gently on his desk and putting his face in his hands. This was a disaster: he was now battling the fact that he had feelings for a girl who seemed to like him, too – if he wasn't being utterly delusional about the reality of the situation.

Effy had been on his mind all week. He couldn't shake the image of her sitting across the table from him, looking like she did and speaking like she did, with that gorgeous accent of hers, a mixture of middle-class elegance and the occasional lick of that gorgeous London twang she had . . .

Then another thought struck him. The Ropek situation
. . . *Will she get angry and withdraw from the partnership?*
It would reflect very badly on him. Dermot would be furious,
naturally, and would probably say that Ben should have told
her in the first place. He never did his research properly, and
his mind flashed back to that meeting with Dermot where
he'd been asked to research Dafina Kampala . . .

Ben turned his phone off and threw it in his leather
satchel. He had to focus on other things. He had a date
later on, with a girl called Tarcia, who he had met ages
ago through some mutual friends. He had decided it would
be better to just slip back into his old ways, those easy
romantic liaisons that didn't require commitment and
promises. He knew it was bad, but it was all he knew.

Twenty
'I'm otherwise taken, I'm afraid'

Sunday 5 October 2014
Finsbury Park, London

The bar was heaving with people; a huge dining area at the back sprawled out before Theo and Ben, all mismatched lampshades and huge leather sofas customers could get lost in. Pictures were hung on the walls in a cluttered fashion, some frames traditional and gold; others probably from Ikea or similar, with sharp, modern lines. It was 8.30 p.m. and an Annie Mac compilation was pumping out from the speakers, giving the room the level of cool the owners were clearly working towards – and with great success, too.

Ben and Theo were sitting at a small wooden table near the fire, totally different chairs beneath them: Ben's was a white dishevelled thing that gave him the impression it might collapse at any moment; Theo's was a purple plastic contraption that looked as if it had been found in the corner of a charity shop, a throwback from the eighties that no longer worked in anyone's home any more. Beyond the windows, which were lightly covered in a film of condensation, the night-time shaded the outdoors in an inky blueness, interrupted occasionally by clouds of cigarette smoke.

The Half Full Bar, which was more of a confused pub, did one of the best Sunday roasts Theo and Ben had ever had, so they often trekked up to North London to make the most of it. They had, by now, been drinking since midday, and both of them were bathed in the comforting glow of alcohol and pub grub. Well, *drenched* might be a more appropriate word, Ben considered, having visited The Greyhound Inn and The Horseshoe as well, to try out their finest wines.

Finsbury Park had that beautiful buzz it often has in the autumn. *It's a part of London that does the season justice*, Ben thought. There was always a level of excitement in the air, a kind of tension that he loved about the north of the city, and he had no idea why it existed. What caused it? Why did he feel particularly alive when he was there?

He had been trying to work this out while watching a group of giggling women who looked to be in their mid-twenties and who were commanding the attention of the room every now and then with their enthusiastic laughter. It would rise and fall, infiltrating the consciousness of fellow customers whenever it got louder. It was . . . almost irritating, but interesting, too. They were very attractive young women, with glossy hair in various shades, lengths and styles. They were clad in trendy clothes – skinny jeans, leather-look leggings and Converse trainers – giving them the aura of a girl band having a catch-up between shows.

Ben couldn't help but glance over every now and then

– well, a lot, actually. They were kind of entrancing. He noticed a few other guys were doing the same thing, their wives or girlfriends irritably stabbing at their roast-dinner-filled plates, and rolling their eyes.

'I like the ginger one,' Theo said, raising an eyebrow cheekily over his pint glass.

She was gorgeous. *They all are*, Ben thought, quietly amused by how many men were so distracted by their presence.

'I love a redhead,' Theo continued, as he polished off the last bit of roast potato on his plate.

'Yeah, me too, although the brunette's the hottest, I think,' Ben replied.

She glanced over as they spoke, her thick curls tumbling over her shoulders, smiling very specifically at Ben, which took him aback. She reminded him a little of Effy. Ben cleared his throat, went a little red and looked at Theo again, hoping he could rescue him from the situation, which had become slightly embarrassing.

'Spotted perving, were you?' Theo said through his laughter.

'Pretty much,' Ben replied, finishing his own dinner now and washing it down with a huge gulp of cider.

The atmosphere was great and, for the first time in a long time, Ben was feeling quite carefree. He and Theo continued chatting away about various topics, from irritating colleagues to why Theo's dog had started urinating on furniture (Ben came up with a theory about insecurity due to Theo's girl-friend moving in), so it was quite a surprise when the attractive brunette got up from her seat and walked over to their table, a confident swagger in the movement of her deer-slim limbs.

Ben instantly panicked a bit. And that wasn't like him

at all. Things were different now, since he'd met Effy. She had really unnerved him. He was just about to take another sip of his drink when the mystery woman pulled up a stool and sat at their table. *Goodness, she's forward*, Ben thought, almost choking on his drink. She looked about twenty-five at the most, and she was even more attractive close up, Ben realised.

'Hey there,' she said, matter-of-factly.

Theo started grinning like a fool but sat back in his seat, using his body language to count himself out of the situation, though still keen to watch for the sheer entertainment of it all.

'Hi,' Ben squeaked, still a little shocked at his sudden lack of control in situations like this. This was normally his 'thing'.

'I couldn't help but notice you. What's your name?' she asked Ben, her eyes narrowing a little.

'Ben,' he said, reaching out and shaking her ring-adorned hand. The gesture just looked odd, and seemed a little business-like. She giggled. Had he lost his touch?

Theo seemed to be thinking the same thing, as he started to laugh so violently, Ben was concerned he was about to spray his beer all over the table.

'I'm Lauren.' She looked at Ben. 'Fancy going for a drink some time? I would get you guys to come and join me and the girls for a drink, but I'm told they're frightening . . .' she trailed off, a mischievous glint in her eyes.

They look bloody frightening, Ben thought, glancing over at the group again. He feared that if he went over there he would be overwhelmed by his new-found nerves, and might start filling conversational pauses with panic-fuelled phrases like, 'So, you like pubs?' He couldn't cope with it. He just wasn't in the right place mentally, he realised.

'Er, actually, Lauren . . . while you are obviously absolutely gorgeous,' Ben started, pulling himself together and leaning towards her a little bit as he spoke, 'I'm otherwise taken, I'm afraid,' he continued, giving his best bullshitting face.

She looked a little shocked, but not at all embarrassed, and Ben liked that. She was clearly pretty cool. The whole dating game: getting numbers, talking to the opposite sex, all that jazz, involved a lot of brazenness, and being genuinely tough-skinned. Ben respected people who put themselves out there and didn't start panicking when things didn't quite go as they'd hoped. It was life.

'Ahh, OK. Well, she's a very lucky girl,' Ben's beautiful stranger said, before he wished her the best. She walked confidently back to her table and then carried on with her evening as if nothing had happened.

Theo, however, looked as if he'd been floored once Ben had peeled his eyes away from her and met his gaze once again.

'What. The. Fuck. Was. That?' he muttered, pausing after each word for added emphasis. He looked genuinely angry.

'What the fuck was what?' Ben chimed happily, putting his hands across his chest.

'Are you ill? She was bloody gorgeous!' Theo groaned, running a hand through his hair.

'Well, yes, I know she was. It's just—' Ben said, hoping to change the subject.

'We need to talk, young man,' Theo interrupted, getting up and going to the bar for more booze, despite the fact that it was Ben's round. It was almost as if he considered his friend utterly ridiculous, and felt more alcohol was the only way to knock any sense into him.

When Theo returned, managing to put the pints on the

table without spilling them all over the place, which was probably a record for him, the interrogation truly began.

'Is something wrong with you, Ben?' he asked, a very serious expression clouding his features. His wild curls seemed to be unravelling the more they drank, although Ben wondered if it wasn't just his vision.

'No, nothing at all,' Ben replied, bluntly.

'Well, what just happened there? That wasn't the Ben I know.'

There was a small silence as they looked at each other. Even Ben was a little surprised. Normally he would have jumped at the chance, probably falling over a few tables on the way. The old him would have, anyway. What had changed?

'Have you fallen in love or something?' Theo asked mockingly, though he'd had a startling insight that genuinely shocked Ben. Theo didn't know anything about Effy, apart from Ben's casual mention of her some time ago, after she'd come for the charity partnership drinks at his office, and even then it had just been his usual spiel about how hot she was.

Moments like this were rare in Ben's life. He was particularly bad at sharing his innermost thoughts and feelings with people, and the only person he really did talk to was paid £250 for 50 minutes for listening to it. Ben just assumed that people a) weren't that bothered and b) had enough to worry about in their own lives to care about his random thoughts on love, life and everything in between. Though Theo was a close friend of Ben's, he didn't know him that well . . . or so he had thought.

'Why would you say that?' Ben asked.

'Well, first of all, mate, you've got a funny look in your eyes. Like you are ever so slightly elsewhere. Second of all, you keep checking your phone, as in a lot. It's a bit annoying, actually – I'm surprised you aren't charging it behind the bar yet. Thirdly, there's been very little chatter from you about your usual adventures, and fourthly – is that even a word? – anyway, *fourthly*, *that* just happened, with *that* hot girl over there.'

Ben wasn't sure of what to say. Normally he would have shut like a clam and just moved the subject on, but he had consumed enough alcohol that it seemed the truth was about to come out.

'OK . . . well, you may almost be right,' Ben said, looking miserably at his friend – who fist pumped the air and yelled 'Yessss!'

'Calm down, mate. It's not as good as it sounds,' Ben whispered, wincing a little at the attention Theo was drawing with his reaction.

Theo did pause suddenly, and looked disappointed. Ben was sad not to give him a happy ending to his story, but he and Effy hadn't spoken after he'd ignored her message.

'Why? Who is it?'

'Well.' Ben took a deep breath. 'I don't know if you remember me telling you about Effy?' he asked.

He watched with amusement as Theo almost visibly scanned his brain for one of the many women's names Ben had dropped into conversation over the years, unstitching all the drunken discussions in pubs from the rather more sober ones in coffee shops and breakfast bars. It looked painful, so he put him out of his misery.

'Effy from Dafina Kampala, as in charity-partnership Effy,' Ben muttered. He glanced out of the window and wondered what she was doing. He pictured her, holed up in her office with a big sweater on, typing away and forgetting that she probably hadn't eaten for the past eight hours.

'Yep, yep, yep. Hot auburn curls girl,' Theo replied, impressing Ben with his memory.

'Yeah, well . . . erm . . . I kind of started to really like her,' Ben said, dramatically toning down the reality of the situation, when really he had managed to trip, slip and fall into a tangle of love – which he had quickly extracted himself from due to plain, simple fear.

'*Love* her?' Theo prompted, reminding Ben of what an utter romantic he was: desperate for a happy ending, coveting liaisons of the heart at all times like a romantic fiction novelist.

Ben shook his head from side to side, and carried on drinking.

'Oh. OK.' Theo sighed theatrically. 'Well, what happened?' he begged, squeezing everything out of his friend – a reluctant orange being lowered into a juicing machine.

Ben caved in and told him the whole thing. How he'd met her, liked her but never quite got the chance to . . . the whole Ropek Oil story. Everything. Well . . . apart from one big thing.

That day.

Theo was a man of many words normally, but he just listened throughout the whole story. By the time Ben finished, the women had left, and both of their glasses were empty again.

The bell for last food orders rang, shaking them from their little bubble.

Ben winced a little as he prepared to deliver his verdict, his body language indicating that it was coming: a straightened back, both hands flat, palms down on the table; the positioning of his facial features. Frankness. Honesty.

But he was thwarted by a sudden explosion. 'What on earth were you thinking, boy?' Theo yelled, exploding into animation once more and turning them into the male version of the noisy women. 'There's absolutely nothing to worry about!' Theo spluttered, his face softening, his line taking a totally different angle to the one Ben had initially imagined.

Ben couldn't speak, so he just looked at him.

'You've done absolutely nothing wrong! A job's a job. You took it on and, not only that, but you're supporting the victims of the Ropek Oil disaster thingy by doing this. There's nothing cold or calculating in it at all,' he continued.

Ben took a deep breath. 'Well . . . yeah, I guess I knew that deep down. I'm just worried—'

'You're a tad neurotic these days, Benjy, that's what you are.' Theo took a gulp from his empty glass, banging it back down on the table distractedly. 'You should go for it. Start seeing her again, and just tell her. She'll understand – it's clearly been a bit of a mix-up, and if she doesn't understand, then quite frankly, she's not for you then, is she?' he said, putting it all quite simply and logically, and successfully stripping away all the bullshit.

Ben felt relief wash over him.

The two friends eventually prised themselves away from the pub at 11.30 p.m., bidding each other a noisy and back-slapping good night. Ben strode off feeling better than he'd felt in a long while. But, as he made his way home, the same old cloak of negativity started to swoop down on him. It followed him as he shuffled along the street, covering him in fear and dread.

He knew he hadn't told Theo about the biggest thing: the fact that he didn't feel like he could love someone for fear of hurting them.

So, really, the problem hadn't been solved at all.

The flashbacks returned. The swan, gliding across the lake. A cold day.

Those awful moments he could not forgive himself for. He didn't deserve a girl like Effy. He didn't deserve love. He was going to shut her out. It was easier.

Twenty-one

I wish you all the very best for the future . . .

Monday 6 October 2014
Angel, London

'I got you a coffee,' Lily said, almost tripping over her green faux-leather bag as she entered the room. Effy nodded, looking up from her laptop just for a second, a raised eyebrow doing all the talking. A dull London morning was filtering through the blinds with a kind of grey dampness that made Effy's skin feel cold and clammy, even when she was indoors. It created a slick of sadness all over the streets of the city.

Dafina Kampala had been loaned a small room in a printing office based in Angel, for a year. It was a gift from a business, and Effy had only found out at the end of the previous week. She was delighted, imagining a large, trendy work area with posh chairs and lights. Things had happened suddenly, quickly, as was so often the way in the charity world. But she'd had no issue with packing up her messy kitchen office and moving it to this new space, however meagre it had turned out to be . . .

A strip light had been flickering from the moment Effy had switched it on, driving her mad. She'd decided to turn off the lights and work from the harsh glare coming from her laptop. It really wasn't a healthy working atmosphere, so she made a note to buy some second-hand lamps with mismatching shades to give the office not only light, but also just a sliver of the upmarket cool it was surrounded by.

'Wow, it's pretty sick in here, isn't it?' Lily exclaimed, looking around at the fading grey walls and the peeling health and safety posters. She had an expression of desperate positivity smeared all over her face. She could find the best in everything, even this room, but even her look was slightly transparent. It was as if she were perched on the edge of a sinking ship, making daisy chains and exclaiming what a lovely day it was.

'It's a very good start,' Effy said, smiling, and grateful, but trying to mask an undercurrent of unhappiness and irritability. However much this room needed a lick of paint, it was hers, for a while anyway. It may not have been the modern, sprawling space she had first envisaged, but it was a step in the right direction.

Lily had been doing a great job in her first few months as an intern for Dafina Kampala, with her major coup being the partnership with Ossa PR. There had, of course, been some teething problems and it would have been unfair to expect otherwise: Effy had ended up teaching Lily a lot of things from scratch, and sometimes she was easily distracted, but she was eager and keen to learn. Her inevitably middle-class background was allowing her to work for Effy for free, though Effy wished that young people from less privileged backgrounds would have the chance to gain such good experience. She wished she could be the one to provide it, but the money just wasn't there. Lily had some great skills, however much she distracted her new boss with a constant trickle of chatter, sentences peppered with 'like' and 'yah', and constant updates concerning the goings on in *LA Sisters*, a hideous, fifteen-part reality show that followed a gaggle of rich, vacuous American women and their useless boyfriends in and out of nail bars and sushi joints. It both amused and exasperated Effy, but it was help, and she needed as much as she could get.

'Have you, like, heard from Ben?' Lily asked, flinging herself down in a blue chair with stuffing overflowing from a small hole at the top of it.

Effy wished she hadn't told her so much, in a moment of caffeine-fuelled weakness. Lily kept asking about it: she had seized it as an opportunity for the two of them to bond.

'No, no, I haven't,' Effy responded, feeling a heat rise from her chest. An angry heat. She didn't care to be reminded of it all, and she could feel tears pricking at her eyes. She noticed that she felt a little hormonal – but there was no time for hormones when she was running an international charity.

'Oh, OK, that's a shame . . . So, Effy, the other night I was, like, definitely thinking about space.'

'Space?'

'Yah, as in outer space.'

'Oh, right.'

'I figured it's a great way of knowing what kind of person someone is if you ask them this simple question, "If you were offered the chance to spend six months on the International Space Station, for free and with, like, training of course, would you go?"' Lily asked.

'Erm, well. How can I put it? I think I would manage to experience both claustrophobia and agoraphobia at the same time before having a massive panic attack and ejecting myself into space in an ill-thought-out bid to make it back home. I'm guessing I'd then either float around and slowly starve to death, or meet a fast, painful end upon re-entry into the Earth's atmosphere. Does that help?' Effy responded, feeling quite irritable.

Lily nodded and cleared her throat awkwardly. 'Well, technically, yah, you might not re-enter, it depends on which direction—'

'What are you doing today, Lily?' Effy asked midway through her sentence, changing the subject and shuffling her chair a little closer to her eager volunteer.

'Er, not a lot, actually. I've kind of run out of things to do,' Lily said as she set up her laptop with one hand and composed an email to her friends – probably – on her smartphone with the other, Effy guessed.

'OK, well there is a lot of stuff I need help with. Can you proofread these five grant applications I'm just emailing you now?' Effy asked, pinging the files off as she spoke.

Lily nodded.

'And then can you come up with our Facebook and Twitter plan for the next month?'

'Yah.'

'And this afternoon I've got a meeting with a data analyst, who's willing to offer us mates' rates. Do you want to come to see how it goes?' Effy asked.

'Deffo,' Lily said, finishing what she had been doing on her phone and dropping it into her bag.

'Well, I'd better let you get on then, Lily – that's great. And thank you for the coffee.'

As she spoke, Effy hit 'Refresh' on her emails and that was when it arrived. A message from Ben Lawrence. The radio silence had been broken. Finally.

Despite how much Effy had talked herself out of her feelings for Ben, she suddenly felt her stomach tighten. *For fuck's sake*, she thought, a coldness washing over her, the hairs on her arms and the back of her neck standing on end. But that could be down to the broken heater, she considered, vowing to buy a temporary one.

She started to read the message.

From: Ben Lawrence, Ossa PR
To: Effy Jones
CC: Noah Jacobs
Subject: Your new charity contact

Effy,

I hope all is good with you and Dafina Kampala.

I'm sorry I have dropped off the radar recently. I wanted to let you know that I am moving to a different role within the executive team at Ossa PR. This means I will no longer be looking after the charity partnership.

Your new contact will be Noah Jacobs (ccd into this email). He is very excited to start working with you. He has a bundle of great ideas, so it might be a good start for you two to set up a meeting. I know he is very keen to meet you.

The fundraising here is coming along in leaps and bounds. The admin team dressed as cartoon characters and spent Saturday and Sunday running around London with collection boxes (I'm not kidding). They raised about £3,000 in two days.

Noah should be able to give you an overall running total. Anyway, I'll leave you in Noah's capable hands.

I wish you all the very best for the future, Effy.

Ben

I wish you all the very best for the future . . . Effy read the line again. It was so final. He could have put 'See you around' or 'Catch up soon' – something like that. 'I wish you all the very best for the future' had implications. It had goodbyes. It had closure. It had all the characteristics of someone who was running away . . . *But why?* Effy felt tears start to rise. But she couldn't crumble now. Not here, in this musty office with her lovely volunteer who would, no doubt, make her cry more with her sympathy. Yet how had this happened? What was going on?

The email could be read in one of two ways, she decided. Anyone external to the situation would scan the words and glean nothing suspicious or untoward from them. It was an innocent message for a corporate purpose – but Effy had a different viewpoint. She had, at one point, started to fall for this man. This handsome, slightly silly guy who had grown on her in the most unexpected way. She still couldn't get his face out of her mind: the face of a man who had gone from being an irritant to a crush. She often wondered what he was doing on a Saturday afternoon while she was stuck in front of her laptop, wearing a baggy jumper and black leggings. When she did make it out to a bar for a few drinks, she always secretly hoped that by some strange coincidence he would walk into the room. He was running away, she just knew it . . . But what was he running *from*? What was going on? What had she done? She felt embarrassed. Embarrassed that she'd started to like him. It had shown. *That text message*, she thought, *it was inappropriate*. She shouldn't have sent it. She had humiliated herself, and she wondered if Ben had any idea how she felt right now, that she was teetering on the edge of a total meltdown. Eyes brimming with sloppy tears. Had he ever really cared about her at all, or was she just another . . . The tears. She tried to fight them but they were coming regardless. They started to flow down her cheeks, followed by the inevitable nose-trail of snot. *Tissues, tissues, where are the fucking tissues?* Effy thought.

'Oh, babe.' Lily sighed, looking at her from over the lid of her silver laptop and biting her bottom lip.

'It's OK, it's OK, don't worry. I'm being a vile cow today. I'm sorry,' Effy said, flapping her arms, mortified at the display of emotion she was seemingly unable to prevent.

Lily awkwardly twitched in her chair, her right arm sort of stabbing the air a couple of times before she got up and shuffled over to Effy. 'What's happened, chicken wing?'

'It's nothing, really,' Effy said again, cringing at the pet name and wiping the tears away from beneath her eyes. 'God, I'm so sorry, this is so embarrassing,' she continued.

As she did so, Lily gave her a huge cuddle. The kind that squeezes emotion out like toothpaste from a tube and there is nothing the recipient can do to stop it. Effy started to cry hard. It was flowing from her, and she hated it.

After an awkward cuddle, Lily eventually prised herself away and walked towards the window. 'Absolute *bastards*, aren't they? As Audrey Hepburn said in *Breakfast at Tiffany's*: *super rats . . .*' she said, those normally huge, innocent eyes squinting almost evilly, scanning the street below.

Effy wondered if this cute-looking girl might suddenly sprout a pair of horns. It was quite frightening, but funny, too. 'How did you know it was about a guy?' she asked, laughing through her tears.

'I can just tell. Those were man-induced tears for sure. Whoever he is, forget about him. You deserve better. I'm going to go and do some photocopying – you know, give you some space for half an hour or so, babe,' Lily said, before quietly letting herself out of the room.

Effy nodded, smiling now. She was grateful for the space, and amazed at the intuition of the young girl. How had she known it was guy related? Was it so obvious? Effy wheeled her chair towards the window and looked out at the lowering day. It was starting to rain. Office workers in black and grey suits scuttled below, clutching coffees, newspapers and umbrellas.

Effy was going to Uganda for several months soon. She thought about this now, as she watched the world go by. Dafina Kampala was, of course, the most important thing now. As much as this situation with Ben had left her feeling like a prize pumpkin at the village fair, she had to concentrate on her charity work. It had to be her everything. It always had been, but she'd found herself easily distracted of late.

Any potential relationship with anyone, be it Ben or someone else as yet unknown, would never survive her up-and-coming commitments anyway, she convinced herself.

Effy dabbed at her face with a tissue. 'Buck up and buy a vibrator,' she whispered to herself and, just as she did so, a bright beam of sunshine fought its way through a cloud, bathing the pavements below in a glittering light.

Sloane Square, London

'How are you feeling?' Sally Whittaker asked, as she always did, perched behind her desk in her usual pose of understated intelligence. One knee was delicately crossed over the other, while an expensive pen was wedged between two long, slender fingers. Sally looked at Ben, who was lying back in the chair, his eyes nervously studying the brushed plasterwork on the ceiling. Ben imagined that in her quietest moments – perhaps when she was driving home from work, the windscreen wipers batting away the raindrops – she probably thought she'd never 'fix' him. He figured she probably considered him a hopeless case. It frightened him a little, however imaginary it all was.

'I'm still not good. I totally cut myself off from Effy,' he blurted out, a wave of shame sweeping over him.

'How so? And why?' Sally asked, leaning forward a little. The light of the lamp cast a long, almost spider-like shadow of her eyelashes across her cheeks.

'I spoke to a friend in the pub about it. He said I hadn't done anything wrong, and that I should go for it with her. I agreed, but then on the way home that feeling came back. That I didn't deserve it – well, her. Someone like her . . . That whole feeling that I will hurt her, and that I don't deserve to be very close to anyone . . . I mean, Christ, if she found out about my work with Ropek Oil she'd likely be a bit shocked, and I would have hurt her already. So I told her, by email earlier today, I wasn't going to be her contact for the charity partnership any more,' Ben muttered.

The hopelessness of it all seemed to him to be now washing around the room, seeping into the spaces between leather-bound books, slinking down in the gaps between a chair and its cushion, making everything sad and restless.

He pictured Effy in Africa. He had imagined it so many times, although he'd never been there – it wasn't the sort of place he had any interest in visiting. He pictured her wearing denim shorts and a white vest top to be able to cope with the heat. She was so beautiful to him, he melted inside.

'Do you think we should talk, specifically, about the events of that day again?' Sally questioned.

Ben flinched a little as she suggested it. Going back there. It was like taking the saddest walk back in time, back to a nightmare that he couldn't wake up from because it was real, and it had happened.

'Talk to me, Ben. Tell me what unfolded that morning. Describe it all, imagine you're telling Effy about it . . .' Sally whispered now, trying to be as gentle as she could, but firm, too.

There were forty minutes left of the session – could he do it? Ben wondered if he had it in him to revisit it all as he glanced at the second hand of the clock. To describe again those moments was the hardest thing he could do. But he had to trust this woman; he had to do what he was told.

So Ben started to speak and, as he did so, the familiar flashbacks returned.

The swan. White feathers. Water. Drowning.

He told the story as if it were the first time the words had leaked from his lips. Normally it was a disconnected series of events in his mind; images and memories that flashed around in his nightmares. Dreams so hideous he had to turn on the light and drink milky tea until he slipped away into the uncertain world of sleep once more. Sometimes he woke up drenched in sweat at 3 a.m. He heard the sound of dripping water too, sometimes, and he could never work out where it was coming from. He'd even called in a plumber, but the man had been unable to find anything that could be causing the noise.

'It was a very cold day. Bitterly cold. The kind of cold that seeps into your bones. I had gone to knock for Alex that morning, and Leanne asked us to take the dog for a walk,' Ben started. As he spoke, he was taken back to a time when he was seventeen years old and his body was growing at lightning speed. A time when he lived on cigarettes and McDonald's double cheeseburgers. A time when his moral fabric was questionable, to say the least. Life was just a series of experiences, thrills, and it was vital that he knew where the next one was coming from, and that it was bigger and better than the last.

He continued, intertwining his fingers as he spoke, 'Anyway, we took the dog, Betty. Betty was a fat dog, really, a Staff that was given too many scraps. She had this kind of barrel-like stomach, and she struggled to breathe when she walked. Alex and I went down to the lake slowly, so the dog could keep up, but it was really frustrating because we just wanted to go haring off.'

Ben took a pause and looked down at his hands, which were clasped together on his chest.

'We had been warned not to go there – by everyone, all the time, ever since we were both really young. It was just part and parcel of growing up where we did – all parents warned their kids against it. "Don't go to the lake," parents would say, but, of course, that only made it more tempting. Me and my mates had been going there for years anyway, and by the time Alex and I were seventeen, it was just something we did. It was a quiet place where we could do what we wanted without being seen.'

As Ben spoke, he felt himself slip into his teenage shoes: a pair of scuffed Adidas high tops. His attire was usually the same: a hoodie and some tracksuit bottoms with hot-rock burns in the crotch where he had been cotched up somewhere, smoking weed in the darkness. He was so different back then to the man he had grown up to be. He had been 'lucky' in many ways: there was something about the middle-class village where he had grown up that somehow made it a little dead-end . . . high-powered executive parents had been so focused on their work that they didn't really know what their kids were up to. It had been, in Ben's opinion, a recipe for disaster. Some of the boys who grew up in his village were now in prison, or dead-end jobs. *My past really was a hovel*, he thought to himself as he spoke, glad he had got out of it, but aware that, in many ways, he was as much of a 'victim' as they.

'Alex and I made it down there and sat by the water. I was happy there, Alex was my best mate. I was happy despite the cold, and it was so fucking cold I could feel it seeping through my tracksuit bottoms. The water . . . I remember clearly, had a layer of ice on it.'

Ben stopped again, as if he were summoning the courage to continue.

'As usual I was up to no good, and Alex was starting to tire of it. I was the more rebellious of the two of us, and it was starting to tear us apart. I'd managed to get hold of some weed, and as we sat there I rolled a joint. Alex just sat next to me, not wanting to get involved,' Ben said, feeling the all-too-familiar waves of shame start to ripple from his toes and rise up his body.

'Anyway, I lit this roll-up and started to smoke it, coughing and choking, of course, because I was shit at it all. And . . . I must have let the lead go during my choking fit because Betty got up, waddled over to the edge of the lake and started sniffing at something, her lead trailing along the grass behind her.'

Ben paused as he said this, and swallowed hard. He could feel his heart rate building up, faster and faster. The panic was returning.

'Alex tutted as Betty walked away from us. I couldn't be bothered to get up, of course, because I was selfish. We just sat there, looking at her skinny hind legs quivering in the cold. Alex asked me to go and get her. I said no. I was much more interested in my joint.' Ben choked as he said this, looking down at his hands. The tears were forming now, pricking at his eyes.

'"She'll be fine, anyway," Alex eventually said to me. "There's thick ice on there, and she's never bothered about the water." I nodded in agreement. There *was* no way Betty would go in the water. So Alex and I sat there, thinking about stuff, talking about stuff, being young. Then, out of nowhere, this swan—' Ben stopped again and ran his hands down his face.

Sally had a look on her face that implied she could tell this hurt every day as much as it had all those years ago. 'Carry on when you feel ready,' she said, gently prompting him to continue.

Ben took a deep breath. 'So, this . . . this swan just landed on the ice. It was so weird. It hit the surface so hard it made us jump. The swan was huge – I've genuinely never seen one so majestic and beautiful, but maybe that was because I was stoned. It had these eyes like hot coals against snow, and it looked at me. I picture that day in black and white most of the time. It knew . . . but I didn't . . . As it landed, the ice cracked. It split and separated in all different directions. The ice wasn't as thick as we'd thought . . . It spread its wings and flapped, and I don't know why I did this, but I threw a stick at it. There was this huge stick next to me, and I just had to throw it, because I was a teenage boy and I was stupid . . . I wanted to hit it on the head. I guess I thought it would be funny or something.'

Sally interrupted. 'OK, obviously it wasn't a very nice thing to do, but isn't that the normal kind of stuff teenagers do? Don't they throw sticks and balls, and not think of the consequences? Don't teenagers constantly make mistakes?' she challenged.

'Yes, they do, you're right. But I made an awful mistake. The next thing we knew, Betty had jumped to chase after the stick. She jumped onto the lake, the frozen lake, and the ice just split beneath her weight.' Ben swallowed. 'It was so strange and unlike her – she was normally too lazy to bother with sticks, and nonplussed when it came to chasing around the living room after toys, or whatever. I still don't understand to this day why she decided to chase the stick . . . Anyway, the water was deep, and very cold, and she immediately started to struggle. Her face said it all. Terror and total confusion.'

Ben could see it all playing out in his mind. His body felt cold at the mere thought of it. He could see Alex's face even now, and the look of horror plastered across it. He remembered the beads of sweat rising on his face as the events unfolded, despite the cold.

'Betty was white, with some brown spots on her face, so at least we could see her clearly in the water. For a moment I hoped her lead might be floating near the edge of the lake and we might be able to pull her back out, but it was obviously sinking to the bottom because there was no trace of it on the surface, or at least on the bits that weren't covered in ice. Alex was horrified, understandably. Then . . . then the argument began. About how we shouldn't have come to the lake anyway, about how Leanne would kill us if anything happened to Betty, about how stupid I was to throw the stick . . . It all just kept coming,' Ben continued, now running both hands through his hair. He always felt nauseous at this point, and wondered if he was going to have to run out of the room. He managed to continue.

'We stood up quickly, both of us just open-mouthed in disbelief. I started calling Betty in some pathetic attempt to coax her to the edge, but she just struggled, frustratingly moving in the opposite direction to us.'

The swan had not been remotely bothered, Ben remembered, as he sat in the deep chair of his therapist's consulting room. It made him angry even now – but how could he be angry at such a beautiful creature, a creature that was just going about its business? It had been all his fault, and there was no one and nothing else to blame.

'It suddenly dawned on me that this was really serious. My teenage brain seemed to safeguard me from stuff until the shit really hit the fan, and then I was just a wobbly, useless wreck. We ran towards the water's edge, and Betty was now whimpering desperately. I'd never faced a make-or-break situation before. I just remember that bloody swan in the distance and thinking how furious I was that it had ever arrived, and how much I hated myself for letting go of the lead, and for throwing the stick at the lake. While I was thinking all this, I was looking for a long branch on the ground but there was nothing around but damp twigs coated in slippery green stuff.'

Ben remembered afresh the way his teenage brain had operated: he had wondered, for a second, if he could save the day. That somehow he might be a hero, jump in after the dog, rescue her and come home soaked and full of laughter, and Alex would think he was really cool. He had wondered if he could manage to hook something to Betty's collar before pulling her back and wrapping her in his jumper.

But it hadn't worked out that way.

'That was when Alex and I started to really argue. Alex screamed at me, started to shout, told me that we were going to be in so much trouble, that everything was all my fault, that I was irresponsible, reckless and stupid. Of course, being a teenager, I had rage inside, too. It was there all the time, just bubbling beneath the surface, and it wasn't hard to disturb it. Alex's words made me incandescent with rage. I glanced over at Betty; she was still desperately struggling to stay above the water. There was this expression of utter panic and fear on her face. But then I just lost it. I started shouting . . . And then Alex pushed me, kept pushing me, hard. I didn't want to push back, I desperately didn't – I was summoning every inch of control in my body to stop myself pushing back. Then Alex hit me round the face and I shouted things back – awful things, nasty things.'

Ben could feel that thump like it had only just happened. He remembered looking into Alex's eyes and feeling a burning hatred, a hatred for someone he cared for so deeply.

The consulting room was silent except for the sound of Ben's sobs.

'Can you go on?' Sally asked calmly. She put her pen down on the table softly.

'I can't, I'm sorry,' Ben said, trying to collect himself. Life felt hopeless to him. There was more to say, more to tell, but he couldn't face it. Not today.

'OK, that's fine. Well done for getting as far as you did. Next time we'll continue from where you stopped. How does that sound?'

Ben nodded. He noticed that the session was about to come to an end: there were only a few minutes left.

'Listen, Ben. I want to say something to you quickly, and I'm not sure how you'll feel about it. We've talked a lot about Effy . . . Don't you think it's time to let go, and have you considered that just maybe this situation with the oil company might not bother her as much as you think?'

Ben smiled a little, and then the barrier came down again.

No. I'll only hurt her . . .

Twenty-two

'My God, she's gorgeous!'

Thursday 9 October 2014
Covent Garden, London

It was 2.44 p.m. Noah Jacobs sat in the corner of an over-priced French brasserie sipping a frothy cappuccino. He checked his watch before glancing out of the window, noticing a woman bumbling past with her skirt wedged into her knickers. Obviously, because this was London, no one had told her. *You just never know when someone's making a fashion statement*, he thought.

Effy Jones was fifteen minutes late, a long time in his world. He drummed the fingers of his left hand on the wooden tabletop impatiently, drawing an evil glance from a waitress standing nearby, which prompted him to still his irritable digits immediately and instead fiddle with the serviette beside his cup.

At exactly the same time, Effy was scuttling out of Covent Garden tube station, instantly intimidated by the number of people she was going to have to negotiate to get from A to B in one piece. A stiflingly hot summer had melted into autumn like an ice cream dropped onto the pavement. The air had a layer of cold combined with the humidity of the past few months which was still clinging on hopelessly, before it would be enveloped by another wet and freezing British winter. She clattered across the cobbles in a pair of high heels she had been struggling to walk in, let alone run in. She didn't normally bother with heels these days, but she had felt that if she made an effort to look good, she might feel more confident on the outside. She had reluctantly slipped them on before she left the flat, instantly regretting it as she wobbled to the bus stop – more ostrich on roller skates than Beyoncé in the 'Crazy in Love' video.

'Shit. Shit. Shit!' she wailed, desperately trying to weave her way between the tourists, the elderly, the waddlers and the chuggers: 'Hey hey, lovely lady, do you have five minutes spare to sign up to . . . ?'

'Oh, go away,' she whispered under her breath, noticing the irony but too breathless from her pursuit of time, which always seemed to be several paces ahead of her, turning around and poking its tongue out at her like an insolent child.

Effy had just seven weeks to go until she was due to board her flight to Uganda and start the main projects she had been building up to for so long. It was a crucial time, and things were getting really stressful. She didn't have time for disruption, for complications, and she didn't have time to be meeting her new charity contact from Ossa PR and explaining everything all over again, however grateful she was for the connection in the first place. She hoped this guy had done his homework. She also didn't have time to still be thinking about *him*. OK, so he was no longer dominating her every waking moment, but she remembered him at least ten times a day . . .

She wondered what this new bloke would be like, and how on earth he was going to match up to Ben Lawrence. She had, to her dismay, felt a childish resentment of the change – an instant, unfounded negativity about the whole thing.

'Er, excuse me, please,' Effy squeaked, as she shoehorned herself into a gaggle of American college students who were walking slowly, half of them tripping each other up and punching each other's arms, and the other half gawping at something sparkly in the window of Kurt Geiger. One of them managed to twat himself in the face with a football he had been bouncing, which was pretty funny to Effy, who had to work hard to stop herself bursting into uncontrolled laughter.

Eventually she made it through and pushed her way into the brasserie, nearly slipping on a stray serviette that had fallen onto the floor and made itself into a fabric-based hazard, like a banana with a thread count. She looked around the room quickly, catching sight of herself in a mirror. Her hair, which had been styled into a pretty up-do just an hour earlier, was now all dishevelled and uneven from the effort of her run. Two great curly tendrils hung by her face in a bedraggled-dog kind of way, rather than an actress-off-set-in-LA-catching-a-smoothie kind of way. Effy worried about how she came across sometimes . . . She was so busy with her work that she often turned up looking a little messy and confused.

There was a very handsome guy in the corner who looked like a film star scanning his lines, an elderly couple lovingly sharing a newspaper, and a grumpy woman who looked like she worked for a train company due to the navy blue uniform she wore.

Nope. He must be late, she thought, starting to root irritably through her bag for her phone so she could call Ossa PR and give someone an earful. As she rifled through the papers, keys, books and the remains of paper swans she'd made and carelessly shoved in her bag, she heard someone calling.

'Sorry, are you Effy? Effy Jones?' the movie star half yelled from the far corner, partially getting up from his seat and waving at her. He seemed unwilling to abandon his coffee and briefcase – no one trusted each other in this city.

Holy fuck, Effy thought, smiling at him and starting to walk towards this good-looking stranger, who was blessed enough to be a cross between Ryan Reynolds and Ben Affleck. He was horrendously handsome, but in the kind of way that turned Effy off. He had short, brownish-blond hair, tanned skin and blue eyes, and looked as if he had a muscular build beneath his expensive clothes – the kind of guy who was a member of a rowing club and a rugby club, and perhaps partial to a spot of polo, too, while she was in the process of shamefully judging him at first glance.

She preferred alternative, rugged-looking men. She liked well-crafted tattoos by reputable artists, and beards – she loved beards . . . She liked quirks, and marks and mistakes. *This guy is too perfect – the teeth are too straight, too white, and there's no depth*, she thought. It was all just there on a plate, like a hot-man buffet.

He looked like the kind of guy you were supposed to fall in love with at first sight, and therefore she was going to rebel. He was like a living Ken doll.

'Oh, hi there, I didn't spot you!' Effy exclaimed, lying through her teeth as she made her way over to his table.

'Yeah, you kind of glanced in this direction but looked straight through me,' he said, smiling and standing up fully to shake her hand, revealing a beautifully fitting shirt and totally crease-free trousers. *How?*

Effy shook his hand firmly before sliding unceremoniously into the chair opposite him. She tucked the hanks of hair behind her ears, mentally sighing. She had been suspicious enough of the situation as it was, and now Ben had sent some film-star wannabe to come in and look after the partnership . . .

'I'm so sorry I'm late,' she murmured, suddenly feeling a little embarrassed.

'Oh, it's OK. The longer I can get out of the office the better, to be honest,' he responded politely, in a voice that matched his exterior. Deep but not too deep. Sexy, smooth and *yada yada yaaawwnnn.*

Effy ordered a strong coffee from a nervous, twitchy waiter and the two of them spoke intently about how the partnership was going. Ben was right: Noah did have some fantastic ideas, and he was keen on his new role. *Maybe this could be a really good thing,* she thought, finally coming round. The staff had already raised more than £50,000, which blew her mind a little. Effy pictured them humiliating themselves for a fantastic cause, running around Tesco in fancy dress, annoying commuters as they left train stations and running for miles with a wedgie. She was delighted, and as much as the man sitting opposite her should have been making her heart flutter, the only excitement she felt was about the fundraising so far, and how spectacularly well it was going. She started to make calculations again, thinking about the amazing things she could do with the money.

The only real distraction was *him*. Ben Lawrence. This guy worked with Ben, and Effy wondered if he knew about what had happened. Had Ben pulled this guy into a meeting room and asked him to take over because she was making him feel uncomfortable? Was he being genuine? How embarrassing! She considered all this as Noah spoke. It all seemed to blur into slow motion, his beautiful, kissable lips moving but no sound coming out.

'How's Ben?' Effy asked.

There. She had said it. The question had just spilled from her lips, and she hadn't wanted it to come out. She raised her hand to her mouth, but then pulled it back down to pick up her coffee, realising how weird it looked.

It was a valid question. She was allowed to ask how Ben was doing.

'Oh, yeah, Ben. He's fine. Still working like an absolute lunatic,' Noah responded, pulling a face. It confirmed Ben's claims about his workload, about changes in his responsibilities. 'He's been a bit of a pain lately, though,' Noah said, chuckling to himself.

'How so?' Effy asked, slowly putting her mug on the table.

'Ah, I don't know. I think he's met someone. He's all loved up and weird; but you know him, he's always a little, erm, out there,' Noah said, his face suddenly warming as a hint of regret kicked in to his features. He was young, very inexperienced in the working world, Effy realised, remembering her own workplace gaffes of the past. Too much information. He wasn't meant to have said that, and it showed.

Effy felt something in her stomach. A sick feeling.

'My God, she's gorgeous!' Noah enthused as he pushed his way into Ben's office without knocking, his briefcase landing on the floor with a thud. Ben watched Noah run a hand through his blond hair in joyous disbelief, as if he'd just seen a star fly from the night sky and land in his recycling bin. His blue eyes were glittering the way they do in cartoons when people fall in love. It was all rather . . . *sugary*.

'Who?' Ben asked, sitting up straight, slightly put out by the sudden intrusion into his illicit game of Bejeweled. *Can't I even have a five-minute break?*

'Effy, for fuck's sake!' Noah yelled, as if he were talking to a senile old man. He leant back against the door, his stance like that of a bashful teenager. No one ever saw Noah like this. Normally it was the other way round.

'Oh, yeah. Yeah, she's nice, isn't she?' Ben responded, feeling his stomach sink and the pain of jealousy nipping at him like a terrier at his ankles.

'Nice? *Nice?* That's the word you use to describe a pretty walk in the countryside, or a homemade cake from your gran. Ben, come on!' Noah said, pulling up a chair in front of his esteemed colleague. He took a quick glance at the beautiful view of the city that was sprawled out behind Ben like a painting. The buildings were breathtaking. It was all just so *wonderful*. He didn't have a view like this from his office. He was junior level, wedged between a break-out area that always smelt mysteriously of sick, and an old filing cabinet.

Ben noticed that Noah was sweating, his forehead shining a little beneath the harsh office lighting. *It's almost funny, the effect that Effy Jones has on people*, Ben thought for a moment, closing the game on his screen and replacing it with a complex-looking spreadsheet. It was a protective measure, just in case Noah decided to move over to the glass behind him and gaze longingly at the cityscape he loved to view when he popped by for a chat. Ben thought about the beauty that seemed to emanate from the core of her and made grown men silly. Ben knew he was not the only guy in a suit, dancing around on the inside as he sat stolidly in tube trains and taxis, just giddy with the thought of her. In a way, he was glad he wasn't alone. In another way, he was filthy jealous, and kicking himself for the fact that he had sent the most good-looking bloke in the whole of Tower 100 to meet the girl he liked.

However much he'd vowed to deliberately push her away.

Effy would almost certainly like Noah, Ben reckoned, a sense of hopelessness crawling inside his body, pushing its way to his toes and fingertips. It rumbled around in his stomach and made him feel sick.

He studied the man in front of him. Noah was four years younger than he was. He was part of a rowing club and won trophies at the weekend. He never got ill and he ran five miles every night. He was a pain in the arse. An alcohol-free, well-brought-up, virtuous nightmare. With an expensive skincare regime.

'I'm going to ask her on a date,' Noah said.

'No. No, you most certainly bloody well can't, all right?' Ben said, suddenly leaning across the desk and shouting. He was all puffed up like a cockerel.

'Holy shit, man. Calm down,' Noah said, looking a little embarrassed all of a sudden.

Ben, shocked by how aggressive he had been, shrunk down in his chair a little and cleared his throat. Awkward . . .

'God, I'm sorry, Noah. I'm just a little stressed, I think. What I am trying to say is that it's just not a good idea . . . Let me explain.' He put his hands together at his mouth and leant back in his chair again. 'It's an important relationship, you know, the one between our major charity of the year and yourself. You just can't jeopardise that, OK? It's too risky. Stuff goes wrong and then we are in all sorts of trouble.' Ben trailed off. *All sorts of trouble?* I'm *in all sorts of trouble*, he thought. Mad about a girl he couldn't be with. Not able to trust himself to ever be close to a woman like her.

'Ben, you make total sense. I understand. Hey, she probably wouldn't look twice at me, anyway. She's one of those girls who can only hang out with the gods and I, my friend, am a mere mortal.' Noah laughed, getting up and turning round to pick up his briefcase. He had the tone of someone who wanted to move on from something because he was embarrassed.

But she would, Ben thought. *I bet she would.*

Thursday 9 October 2014
East London
The bar was buzzing. Thursday nights had long been the new Friday and it was a part of London's identity now, like a fingerprint. It was a fact: great Thursday nights had become part of the unspoken code of the city, like not standing on the left-hand side of the escalators, and avoiding the end seats on the tube in case someone elderly or pregnant got on, making you inadvertently look like a selfish bastard if your book was engrossing enough.

Bass-y music pumped out from the speakers, and bartenders threw bottles of brightly coloured spirits in the air before pouring them skilfully into long, slender glasses. Rosa sat in front of Effy wearing a dark green racer-back dress. She was smiling widely because there was good news. Effy had just delivered it over the loud music, flapping her arms around in excitement.

'That's bloody amazing, Effy!' Rosa shrieked, jumping up and down in her seat before proposing a toast.

The two friends had little money, but Effy's news – which

had come just two hours before – was so spectacular it had prompted her to book herself a precious night away from the computer and out on the tiles in East London, sticking a bottle of fine champagne onto her personal credit card. Rosa had been more than happy to accept the last-minute invitation.

The voicemail had been waiting for Effy when she got off the train following her meeting with Noah; a notification had been flashing temptingly on her phone. She had decided to listen to it when she got back to the office and could make herself a cup of tea. It was from Connect, a small but rapidly emerging UK telecommunications company. They had announced a high-profile charity awards scheme that Effy had entered Dafina Kampala into one late, stormy night, hunched over her computer, her eyes tired, while Frank had been lying next door drowning in his own discontent. The caller had told her that while she had entered the charity as a whole, the judges were so impressed by her they had decided to present Effy with a 'Leading Light' award, for new charity founders who were inspiring the sector and needed funding to progress with their goals. They had looked in detail at her accounts and plans, and felt it was time to give her the boost she needed.

It was incredible. Effy had felt tears come to her eyes as she listened to the message. When she called her contact back, more details had emerged. By getting the award, she had secured a £100,000 prize for Dafina Kampala and a bundle of media coverage, which would soon follow. There would be an awards ceremony soon, and she had been advised to wear a 'posh dress' by the smiley-sounding woman at the end of the line. The invitation would be sent to her by post, and she had been told to prepare for some media calls over the coming days from the national newspapers.

She had been totally overwhelmed, and by the time she had got off the phone, she had cried salty tears of joy while Lily danced around the tiny office space, whooping and cheering for joy.

After that, Lily got straight to work on a press release about the award.

'Effy, I'm so proud of you,' Rosa said now, taking delicate sips of her champagne.

Effy smiled at her friend. 'I just can't believe how well this is going. I mean it's hard, really hard – you know how tired and worried I get – but this news, it's just incredible, on top of Ossa PR as well.'

Rosa nodded enthusiastically, and looked genuinely happy for her friend.

'But there is one thing I've been thinking about, Rosa, and I know you aren't going to be massively keen on it,' Effy said, broaching her subject nervously, placing her glass down on the random-but-typically-East-London table: it was see-through, and had a car tyre and a stuffed bird inside it.

'What's that?' Rosa asked suspiciously.

'I'm going to ask Frank to come to the ceremony.'

'You what?'

'No, wait, hear me out. Do you remember when we went to that exhibition a few weeks ago? The nature photography one?'

Rosa nodded, her face a little more serious now.

'Well, when I got home, I had this email from Frank. It was really nice, Rosa. He said that he'd had a hard time over our break-up, just like I had, but the essence of it was that he was happy now. He told me, tactfully somehow, that he was over it all . . . and he said sorry.'

Rosa's eyebrows shot up, and she looked surprised.

Break-ups are never normally this, well, lovely, Effy had thought. People always vowed to remain friends and keep some kind of perfect distance where they would still be a part of each other's lives but, inevitably time would pass, resentment and blame would build, and they would soon be snubbing each other at the awkward parties of mutual friends.

'Well, that's nice, isn't it? I'm really glad you've been able to find some peace in it all,' Rosa said.

'It really is. I know I'm over him and I'm OK about it all now. He said he was working more, and seeing friends. I think he's changed his life and, you know what? I still want to be a part of it, as a friend,' Effy said, smiling to herself and looking down at her lap. She flexed her ring-adorned fingers, her dark red nail polish glinting. 'I, well, I want to see him again. I want to say thank you to him for being a part of Dafina Kampala. However difficult it all was, he was a part of it.'

Rosa smiled warmly at her friend. 'You're so kind, Effy Jones, and that's why I think you are the cat's pyjamas,' she said, squeezing her friend's arm.

Effy was pleased and relieved that Rosa hadn't burst into an angry lecture. She understood. It was a big decision to make, but Effy felt like it was the right one.

Suddenly, the girls' conversation was interrupted by two men. They had been hanging around and sporadically glancing at them from over the tops of their beers, obviously trying to find an opportune moment to slide over to them amid all the emotional conversation that was clearly taking place.

'Hi, girls.'

Effy and Rosa looked up at the men. One was a tall,

dark-haired guy with dimples and brown eyes; the other was a little shorter, blond and skinny. The women glanced at each other and shared a message in the way that only women can with no words, and just split seconds in which to communicate. It said: '*Oh, sod it, let's chat to them. We can always disappear if it gets embarrassing.*'

'Hi,' Effy said, smiling pleasantly, suddenly a little nervous. Rosa started fiddling with her hair. Effy instantly knew that she didn't feel particularly attracted to either of them, but she realised how the situation was developing . . . She was in a bar with her hair all done nicely; a black plunge-neck dress sloping down her chest; and a pair of glittery earrings glinting in the light. A slick of pillar-box-red lipstick completed her look. She was oozing singleness, but she wasn't sure if she was ready for all of this after Ben.

She knew what would happen. The small talk. The flirting. The dodging of the truth. The packaging of oneself to be the very best version you could be, before embarking on a relationship and, six months later, peeling off the mask and revealing the real you, which inevitably he wouldn't like . . . Urgh, she was being such a cynic about the dating stuff. It made her shudder; she wished she didn't feel this way. And relationships? That was a whole other problem.

Despite all her fear, Effy was hiding it well. The men looked delighted that they hadn't been sent away like a pair of skulking dogs, and some kind of conversation ensued. But after twenty minutes or so, Effy zoned out. Because she still couldn't stop thinking about him.

Nothing and no one matched up to Ben, and this was becoming painfully, unavoidably clear.

Twenty-three
'He still loves you'

Thursday 23 October 2014
Mayfair, London

Effy Jones stood in the Ladies in front of a full-length mirror, a little shocked by what she saw. Or more specifically, *who* she saw. Rosa had transformed Effy's usually tired skin by buffing, polishing and scrubbing at her best friend's face earlier that evening. Various potions and lotions had been deployed until Effy glowed. Effy's hair, those curls that normally sprang out in a mop of red corkscrew chaos, had been styled by a professional hairdresser into an almost Roman-inspired up-do with plaits running down the side of it, meeting in a gorgeous curly bun. Effy had slicked some tinted moisturiser into her skin, which gave her arms and chest a beautiful sheen, as though she'd been on holiday. And the dress she'd borrowed from a friend . . . It was a one-shouldered, black, slinky thing that hugged her body as if every stitch had been designed with her in mind. It was long, trailing softly along the floor behind her, only broken by a sharp slit that stopped just above the knee. She was wearing a pair of delicate silver high heels that she could just about totter around in, providing she held her dress out before her a little. It was a red carpet look, and Effy, for the first time in a long time, looked at her reflection and felt beautiful. She had almost forgotten what it was like to feel this way about herself – it was a stark reminder that she had abandoned her own needs for a long time.

No one would ever have guessed that this young woman had spent the last few months, years even, hunched over a laptop so late into the night that a pair of threatening dark circles beneath her eyes had become almost permanent; the only thing that could combat them was the daily use of expensive cover-up in a peachy gold tube. No one would ever have imagined, looking at her now, all the sweat and tears that had gone into setting up Dafina Kampala alone. Onlookers could never imagine how something so wonderful had driven a wedge between Effy and the man she had loved for years. The man she had asked to marry her near St Paul's Cathedral, one dizzy afternoon, when she was too young to know what she really wanted. *It just looks so easy*, she thought now, gazing at the woman who was reflected back at her. The woman whose arms moved when she moved them. *It's me!*

Frank had looked a little shocked when he met her outside the venue earlier on. It was a posh hotel in Mayfair with an old-fashioned porch that reeked of romance. It would have been the ideal setting for some doe-eyed perfume advert: a stunning dame leaning against a balustrade, verging on orgasm while pressing a glass bottle to her clavicle.

Frank had stepped out of a bashed-up minicab, wearing a sharp suit. *Quite the juxtaposition*, she had thought. Effy had noticed his eyes widen as he saw her. In fact, he had looked a little as if he'd been punched in the stomach, she realised, however fleetingly arrogant that thought seemed to her. Effy had smiled at him, coyly playing with her handbag, not keen to move forwards in case she tripped over herself and clattered down the steps. Instead, she had tilted her head to one side and smiled.

'Fucking hell, Effy, you look beautiful,' Frank had muttered, walking towards her and planting a soft, almost worryingly tender kiss on her cheek. He had clearly tidied up his beard, and his suit was typical of him: a nicely cut designer creation with a faint, ironic 'old-man' pattern that made him stand out as a trendy, fashionable kind of guy.

Studying him covertly, Effy had realised his face was slightly slimmer than it used to be, and his sharp cheekbones stood out a little more. *Chiselled and still handsome*, Effy had thought, immediately berating herself. She knew this wouldn't be a walk in the park, as he was still the devastatingly good-looking man she had fallen in love with all those years ago. What else did she expect of an ex-model who had lost his way and found it again? He was now a better version of himself. He was the old Frank. The Frank who had whispered filthy things in her ear in tequila bars, while his arm snaked passionately round her waist. The Frank she'd wanted to sleep with. All the time. Before everything broke.

But things are different now, she had told herself as she stared at him. *Things are different now.*

'Effy, I'm so proud of you for all this,' Frank had said, gesturing at the space around him with one arm. It was an unclear movement, but Effy interpreted 'this' as her award, and perhaps the way she had managed to transform herself from a scraggly nervous wreck into this shimmery, glittering girl Rosa had helped her to become.

Frank had taken his ex-girlfriend's hand and led her into the foyer, where they were immediately given glasses of champagne. Effy was so nervous about the evening it had been a struggle to hold the glass. She had felt self-conscious and uncomfortable, despite her decadent dress and all the work that had gone into her appearance. She had made small talk with Frank for a while, before feeling overwhelmingly intimidated by it all, and excusing herself to visit the Ladies for a moment.

And that was where she was standing now, looking in the mirror and telling herself to pull it together. 'This is a big night, Effy. Don't fuck it up, OK?' she whispered loudly to herself. Turning around, she realised to her embarrassment that as she did so, an elderly woman had come very quietly into the room and probably heard every word.

The woman was sharp and sophisticated looking. She wore a red, fitted suit; her short, grey hair shining silver in the light. She reeked of money; Effy noticed that it smelt like Chanel N° 5.

'Nervous, are you?' the woman asked, very directly, the words like darts hurled across the room. So she had heard her. There was a hard, ball-busting expression on her long, thin face. It reminded Effy of the moon when it is a mere sliver, dangling in the sky. She stood there for a few moments, staring at Effy, completely intimidating her, before she swaggered over to the mirror, all jutting hips and razor-like shoulder blades, clinking her glass of champagne down on the marble surface near a small pile of white, freshly laundered hand towels: this was the kind of venue where you dried your hands on your own miniature towel as opposed to some Blue Roll; the kind of venue that had gold taps, and even the toilets were beautiful.

Effy blushed a violent red as the strange woman started

applying lipstick at lightning speed. She looked as if she could do it in her sleep, and Effy suddenly pictured her own attempts at applying lipstick, which could take up to ten minutes, and involved desperate efforts with loo roll to correct the hopeless attempts at smooth, clean edges.

'I was in your shoes thirty years ago, darling,' she said, finishing her war paint and turning to smile at Effy, who was standing in her heels, knees ever-so-slightly turned inwards.

It was a strange smile. One that didn't light up the rest of her features. Isolated. Not supported by the woman's eyes or eyebrows, as if she were in conflict with herself. Either that or she'd overdone the botox, Effy suspected, cocking her head to one side, her mouth open a little.

'Oh, really?' Effy asked, at the same time wondering why this woman had freaked her out so much.

'Yep, I was the founder of an emerging charity, too. You're Effy Jones, right?' the woman said, finally starting to soften, and reaching a thin, slender hand out into the space between them.

There was still a palpable tension and Effy had no idea why. Was she staring at what she would become? An over-worked, tired, frightening lady? Effy reached out to shake her hand, embarrassed that she didn't know who this person was. A woman who looked like she would be more suited to the front row of London Fashion Week, sharing a tray of macaroons with Anna Wintour . . .

'I'm Imelda Reeves,' she announced. Effy's stomach immediately went cold. She knew that name. 'I founded Reach UP UK, and I was on the judging panel this year. I was blown away by what you've done, Effy, especially on your own,' the woman added, trying to smile again, and her face once more failing her.

Reach UP UK? Effy was shocked. She'd been inspired by this charity. It provided opportunities to young people from disadvantaged backgrounds, but she had researched little about the founder or how it had started, though she had certainly heard Imelda Reeves's name before. She suddenly felt even more nervous: the evening seemed so daunting as she considered again all the important people she would be expected to stand before and deliver some kind of coherent speech.

'Wow, Imelda, that's amazing. It's so nice to meet you and thank you, for, well all of this,' Effy continued, gushing a little, to her embarrassment.

'Now, listen, a little word of advice. Who is that guy with you?' Imelda said, packing her lipstick in her bag and snapping it shut with a sharp click.

The sudden change of subject was almost alarming. Effy raised an eyebrow, and glanced in the direction of the lobby. She was amazed that this woman had even noticed her, let alone Frank. She hoped she'd heard nothing of their brief, difficult conversation about life after love.

'Erm, he's my ex-boyfriend. It's kind of, er, complica—'

'Wait, wait, wait,' the woman said suddenly, raising a finger in the air, which Effy stared at in shock. Then a small smile curled from the left side of her mouth. That was all she could manage. 'He still loves you. It's written all over his face,' Imelda added, before raising an eyebrow knowledgeably, grabbing her bag and striding out of the room as quickly as she had arrived.

The door swung wildly behind her, slamming shut hard. It was so dramatic.

Effy picked up her award in a haze of champagne bubbles and nerves – the kind of nerves that rattle around the body like marbles and make you feel nauseous, so she decided that the only way to get rid of them quickly was to drown them in alcohol. By the time her category was announced she had already consumed four glasses of Moët, and was clutching her fifth when Imelda took to the stage to say a few words, her face still uncooperative. Effy was sweating all over, but managed to keep a nervous smile on at all times.

When her name was called out, Frank squeezed her arm before she stepped up carefully and made her way to the podium, trying to hide the amount of booze she had consumed with a stiff, certain walk up to the platform where she would speak.

The function room was huge and, as Effy looked out at the audience, she found herself baffled as to how she had reached this point in her life. There were about twenty large tables, seating around sixteen people each. The tables were draped in blindingly white cloths cluttered with bottles of wine and huge bunches of flowers. This was her moment, but why was it so frightening? Imposter syndrome? Why was she so afraid to accept any kind of recognition? Why did she always bat it off with comments like, 'Oh, no, it's been OK, really'? Everyone was looking at her; thankfully the majority of them were smiling widely. Before Effy spoke she looked over to Frank for help and noticed that he was wiping a tear from his cheek. He never usually cried and she realised then how much he must still care for her. It was a bittersweet moment, but she hoped the night would bring the closure she needed with her ex-boyfriend. A thank you to him. Just to the right of Frank were Lily and Rosa, who were holding hands and blubbing, quietly. She'd invited her mother and father from France, but they had already had plans – which had slightly upset her . . . She swallowed, hard, before looking around at the sea of people before her.

'Hi, everyone,' Effy started, a little shaky, and somewhat surprised that her voice was now leaking out of several huge speakers dotted all over the room.

Silence. A few people cleared their throats and the occasional sound of a glass being set down on a table could be heard coming from mysterious places in the far end of the room, shrouded in inky darkness.

Effy could feel her heart beating in her ears and neck. She ran her sweaty hand down the side of the glass award, which was made to look like a statuesque woman with a long, billowing robe. It was beautiful.

All of a sudden, something washed over her, and she felt *ready*. Ready to accept some praise, the kind of thing she usually shied away from. Ready to step up to the podium for the cause she cared about.

'I am so thankful for this award, the Leading Light award,' she started, but quickly realised that she didn't have the strength or desire to read the speech she had prepared on a set of little note cards. It suddenly felt awkward and forced, so she pushed them to the top of the podium, took a deep breath, and decided she would see what would come out.

'I am thankful that my efforts have been recognised in this way but, most of all, I am thankful that Dafina Kampala has been recognised. I am making a promise, tonight, in front of all of you, that I will help these children. They will benefit so much from this, so each and every one of you here in this room is a part of that.'

Calm continued to flow through her veins, and finally she was enjoying her moment. She glanced over at Frank again, who was still wiping tears away with his paw-like hands. It was so strange, to see him reacting like this.

'I don't know how many of you know how Dafina

Kampala started. It's all down to one little girl. Her name is Gimbya. I was in Uganda, visiting my aunt five years ago. I was walking along one day when I heard crying.' Effy broke off for a moment as she said this, noticing the captivated faces before her. She was so glad she could tell her story to so many people. People who were willing to listen for once, rather than her usual pleas down the phone to some potential corporate sponsor with no time to even take a basic message. 'The crying was coming from some bushes at the side of the road. There were so many distressing things I saw and heard on that trip, but something about this cry was impossible to walk away from . . . I ducked down into the bush and that was when I found Gimbya. She had a horrendous cut, it was badly infected, and she had no one to help her. Gimbya was having to work to help support her family and so the wound couldn't heal. She would have died from blood poisoning had she been left. So many children die in these circumstances, not just in Africa of course, but all over the world. That was when I knew I had to do something. And so, here we are, four years later, and I am due to go to Kampala soon to set up my project. I have been incredibly blessed to have not only a wonderful corporate partnership with Ossa PR, but also the proceeds of this incredible award. I cannot thank you all enough.'

As Effy said this, the room broke into loud applause. She blushed and looked down at her award. *This isn't about me*, she thought. She was just an ordinary person in extraordinary circumstances. She was a human being who fucked up just like everyone else. She had fears, and regrets, and sometimes she wished she'd done things differently, but *this wasn't about her*. This was about Gimbya, and all the children she wanted to help in the future.

The rapturous cheering settled down as Effy prepared to finish her speech.

'I can tell you that Gimbya is already planning to go university when she's older. She wants to be a doctor, so she is working hard towards that goal. So there we have it. I will spend this prize money wisely, and I will make more success stories like Gimbya's. Thank you.'

The applause began again. She had done it. It was over.

As Effy started to walk back to her table full of supporters, she noticed that everyone in the room had now stood up, and was clapping and cheering. As she walked towards Frank, she could still see tears in his eyes. Lily was at the table, standing next to Rosa, both of whom were also wiping emotional, drunken tears from their faces. *Had it been that moving?* she thought. Or were they just empathising with her nerves?

As the room settled down again, Effy took her place next to Frank and passed him the award without saying a word. She had started to feel emotional. He held it in his hands for a moment or two, turning it round and running his fingers over the woman's carefully crafted face, gently biting his bottom lip. Then he leant in to Effy, pulled a ringlet away from her ear and said quietly, 'I'm sorry I ever doubted you.'

Effy Jones stared straight ahead, Imelda's words rattling around in her mind.

Effy and Frank were back outside, standing in the romantic portico, looking out at the London streets and all their late-night chaos. Taxi drivers buzzed around with the same aggression found in winged insects, the occasional angry beep ringing in their ears – a symphony of the city. The evening had cooled down somewhat, and Effy wished she had brought a jacket with her. She had been so flustered on her way to the event she had bundled into a taxi in a haze of confusion, her cheeks and shoulders hot with nerves. She had left her coat indoors.

Effy shivered a little, and Frank removed his blazer and put it around her. To her surprise, she felt a shiver of something else as he did this. Attraction maybe. Or was it just the cold? It was as if the old Frank was back. They had stepped back in time, and here they were, both at their very best at the end of a wonderful night. *Perfect.*

Or it should have been perfect, Effy thought. *Things between us could have been perfect had we not lost our way.* The words rattled around in her mind as she looked at him. She realised how drunk she was, his handsome face moving around a little in front of her . . .

There was a moment of strange silence between them as they looked into each other's eyes, the glittering lights of the hotel porch reflecting back at them. What was going on? What were the unspoken things passing between them? Effy thought about Frank and how tempting it suddenly was to patch things up. He was just like he had been before. Ashamedly, she also needed some attention, even though she knew that he was the wrong person to provide this for her. *And yet* . . . she thought, looking into his eyes and wondering what the right answer was. If they were both 'over' each other, as they had claimed to be, maybe they could just share one last passionate night. It would be a kind of send-off. Effy knew she was trying to justify it to herself, wondering if this thought process was simply happening because she hadn't had sex with anyone in a long, long while. And there Frank was before her, handsome, tempting and yet somewhat worryingly vulnerable.

'Effy Jones!' came a shout from the drunken Rosa, who tottered down the steps in her heels, arm-in-arm with Lily. The pair hadn't met before, but seemed now to be the very best of friends thanks to the fine wines at the event and a shared love for baked camembert and Paloma Faith.

Frank and Effy both jumped a little, guilty looks plastered all over their faces.

'I bloody love this girl!' Rosa yelled, looking at Lily like she was a toy she'd won at the funfair. Lily's cheeks were a drunken shade of cherry. Everyone was so happy.

'Effy, can I have a word please, young lady?' Rosa asked mischievously. It clearly wasn't really a question, though, as she pulled her best friend by the arm and yanked her down the final steps and away from Lily and Frank, who were now preparing to light, and smoke, a celebratory cigar.

'What the *friggin hell* are you doing?' Rosa said urgently, her face suddenly melting into a look of angry concern. The long, silk skirt of her blue dress was flapping behind her in the breeze.

'What are you talking about?' Effy said, playing dumb.

'Oh, come on. You and Frank looked like you were just about to kiss, for God's sake!' Rosa whispered, with real anger now. Rage was dancing all over her face, like a thousand little imps manipulating her features. Rosa's angry honesty was always amplified by alcohol.

Effy looked down at the ground.

'Listen, I know he's turned up tonight looking and smelling all nice and saying all the right stuff, babe, and I know it probably seems like he's changed, but Effy, please, you've come so far, don't make the same mistake again . . . God, you're so selfish sometimes.' Rosa glared at her, then looked suddenly amused as she clocked Lily coughing and spluttering after accidentally inhaling the cigar smoke.

It's like watching a teenager tackle their first cigarette, Effy thought hazily, turning around herself and catching sight of it, too. But Rosa had said something, hadn't she . . . ? 'Excuse me! I'm not going to do anything with Frank! I know what you mean, Rosa, I know you are making sense . . . but – selfish? That's a bit much!' Effy felt angry now too, but tried to brush it off a little as just being the result of Rosa's drinking.

She knew her thoughts about Frank were wrong, but she was so desperate for some passion. To be touched and held by someone familiar. By someone who knew how . . . The romantic-film buff in her had already imagined how it might go. They would bundle back to her flat, have romantic, amazing I-miss-you-but-can't-have-you sex, and then that would be it, they would continue with their lives. And she wouldn't need to hunt down some bumbling idiot in a bar and have fiddly, crappy sex with him, and end up feeling even more frustrated than she already was . . . Frank would somehow become a model again and he would be happy. And, as for Effy, well, she would ride off into the Ugandan sunset with someone . . . someone she really cared about . . .

But she knew that wasn't how it would really turn out. She knew that she'd probably end up despising Frank Rhodes all over again, and he might feel the same about her, too.

'You know what you should be doing tonight, Effy, and that's going home ALONE. Watch a fucking blue movie, eat a pizza, drink more wine – I don't care what you do, Effy, but do it *alone*!' Rosa continued her verbal assault, with added vitriol in the word 'alone', anger still etched all over her delicate features. As Rosa spoke she blinked a lot, probably because of the booze, revealing thick smears of black, glittery eye shadow.

Effy hadn't seen this side to her friend for some time, and it reminded her how much she cared, however aggressive she was being. 'I know, I know,' she said quietly.

As she did so, a taxi pulled up beside them.

'Lily, that's us!' Rosa yelled, ushering her friend away from Frank and giving Effy a hug, and a kiss on the cheek. 'Don't forget what he put you through, Effy, and don't be a dick,' Rosa whispered, just before she pulled away and got into the taxi with her new best friend. Effy watched with concern as the taxi screeched down the street.

As Effy pulled Frank's blazer tighter around her body and stared at the space where the taxi had been, she felt a pair of arms snake around her from behind. They were Frank's. She knew it was wrong, and she regretted it already but, before she knew it, she had spun around. In a haze of twinkling lights and car beams, she and Frank were kissing.

It was a stolen moment she shouldn't be having. *Nothing good will come of this*, she thought, as she traced her lips over his. *It doesn't feel right*.

'Effy, we need to talk,' Frank said eventually, his lips against her forehead. His warmth was radiating through her, and the coldness that had previously crept between the folds of her dress and chilled her bones had fled to the cracks of someone else's coat.

'We certainly do,' she responded, regret filling her tummy in the way regret does. She didn't want to talk, she didn't want to tread over old ground, she didn't want to get involved with Frank and then watch him slip away into a shell of his former self again. Effy feared that Frank wasn't the kind of person who could keep his own identity when he fell in love. She was terrified it would all happen again, but it was too late now; she'd kissed him, she'd opened the box . . .

The pair jumped into a taxi, Effy sitting close to the back window, the glass shunted down a little so a cool breeze could tickle her face and prevent her from feeling carsick. Frank sat right next to her, holding her hand and undoing his tie. She could sense his anticipation, that maybe he'd been hoping they could patch things up all along, and this was his moment . . . She was surprised, genuinely surprised, especially given the email he'd sent her.

Oh God, what am I doing? Effy thought, the city skidding past her. Lights, late-night newsagents and the homeless – displaced, a mess, a blur. She pictured Rosa, yelling at her, angrily wagging a finger. She cringed inside. The evening had been so magical, so special, and now she was about to ruin it, she just knew it.

'Effy, there's so much I want to say to you,' Frank declared, as the taxi pulled into her street.

'I know, I know. I'm sorry, I just don't feel too well. I drank too much . . . Give me a minute please, Frank,' Effy said calmly, turning towards him and displaying a fake smile.

He must have read her like a book: 'I'm scared' was the opening line. The first words. She felt ashamed of herself before anything had even happened. A coldness filled her tummy and she contemplated the prospect of letting him back into the home they used to share; the home she'd worked so hard to feel warm and comfortable in once more.

And now she was about to open the door and fill it with cold air. With Frank's presence.

Frank paid the taxi driver with a crumpled, sweaty £20

note. Effy's heart started to race. She climbed out of the taxi, Frank lagging behind her a little. She walked towards her front door slowly. A huge bush she had made a vow to herself to cut at the weekend obscured the blue door. She felt worried, giddy . . . dizzy. And as she turned the corner, around the overgrown border and to her home, she saw him.

A handsome man, standing under a single light bulb in the porch, wearing a suit and holding an enormous bunch of roses.

Twenty-four
He was here

Thursday 23 October 2014
Muswell Hill, London

'Fuck. *Ben*. What, what are you doing here?' Effy gasped, stopping in her tracks so suddenly that the heavy fabric of her dress swung around her ankles before eventually swishing to a soft standstill. There was silence, apart from what sounded like a fox tearing a bin bag to shreds a few doors down. Just audible, the hungry and urgent noises of the animal scattering empty tins and discarded packaging around some poor sod's front garden.

Effy's eyes scanned the man standing at her doorstep. His lower body was partially pointed towards the door; his upper body was twisted around a little. His stance was relaxed, despite the events unfolding. It was so typically Ben. Effy's heart started to race. Faster. She couldn't believe he was there. She wanted to run towards him: it was instant; instinctive. The man she had been pining for for such a long time. The man who had caused her such confusion. He was here. Finally. *Why is he here?* Questions crowded her mind as her eyes slid down to the roses, a giant splash of crimson exploding from the lush green stems.

Ben ran his free hand through his hair, his face dropping as he saw Frank walk around the corner behind her. As Frank came to a halt himself, he put his hands in his pockets and leant back a little on his heels as if to say, '*Well, what do we have here then?*' It was amazing, the volumes that the body could speak, she realised, looking from one man to the other, mortified.

'Er, gosh, Effy, sorry. I didn't realise you . . . erm . . .' Ben said, his polite tone sharpened.

Effy turned back to look at Frank, his features now shadowed by low light and disappointment. It curled at the edges of his mouth, adding to his almost eccentric moustache. It had replaced the previous twinkle in his eye.

'Guys, I'm so, so sorry. I'm going to leave,' Ben said, his cool exterior finally breaking down to be replaced with utter embarrassment. Even he couldn't hide that.

Ben walked down the steps and towards Effy and Frank, but just before he left properly he turned to Frank. His body language seemed to have not quite caught up – it was as if his legs wanted to continue on at great speed, but his mind and his upper body were keeping him back.

'Listen, mate. I'm sorry. There's nothing going on with Effy and me, she's a friend. I just came to congratulate her . . . It was stupid,' he continued, patting Frank on the back and smiling stiffly.

Effy knew exactly what he was doing. It was what he did at work every day, and he knew how to do it. PR. He wanted to protect her. He didn't know who Frank was, and he didn't want to land her in trouble with him. He could have been anyone for all the time that had passed

since they'd last spoken: a lover, a friend, a boyfriend . . .
Ben wouldn't have had a clue and, in fact, he didn't have
any kind of claim over her, she realised.

Frank didn't return Ben's warmth, however, and stared
at the stranger who had surprised them so much. He looked
aggressive. Frightening. Like a dog preparing to snap. Effy
hated it. She had no idea what to say. She couldn't just
let Ben disappear, not after everything she had been
through. How could she watch him just walk away?

Both of Frank's hands remained in his pockets, but the
look on his face did nothing to quell Ben's obvious embarrassment. Tiny muscles in his jaw twitched.

Ben let his hand slide idly from Frank's shoulder, and
then started to walk away, his head down. The roses hung
limply from between his fingers. Sadly. A romantic gesture
gone awry.

Effy imagined the petals ageing and dying, falling away
from the centre where they had been gathered by nature,
because nothing would hold them together. She felt tears
rising to her eyes. Ben was who she really wanted. He
was all she'd ever wanted since she'd found him, face
down on the bridge at the South Bank. She hadn't known
it then but she knew it now. She smarted inside at how
fickle she seemed but she knew the situation wasn't simple.
She turned to look at Frank. She had seconds to make a
decision.

'Frank, I need you to leave,' she said firmly, business-like,
trying to be calm. Her left eyebrow was raised ever so slightly.

'What? You've got to be kidding, Effy,' Frank said, hot
anger rising in his tone.

It only confirmed to her that she was making the right
choice.

'We were going to talk, Eff, for fuck's sake!' Frank said,

curling both hands around the back of his head and pacing about a little. The fury.

Toys and a pram.

'I'm sorry, Frank. I'm really sorry,' Effy said, as she realised what she was going to have to do.

She looked down the road again. Ben was just a small outline now; he'd walked quickly. The streetlights cast his silhouette in an orange glow. She knew she wanted him. Needed him. It was as if the choice had been taken away from her when it came to Ben. She had tried to forget about him, to move on, but she just couldn't.

'What are you doing, Effy, you absolute lunatic? You're drunk, you've lost it, there's been too much pressure . . . You need some sleep! I've always worried about this with you, how it's going to affect you,' Frank said, as he watched his ex-girlfriend lean down and start to frantically untie the straps of her delicate shoes as if her life depended on it.

'Frank, I won't say this again. Please go,' Effy replied, quietly. She hated what she was having to do, but she also hated his aggression. Oh, how quickly the façade had melted. When she had finally untangled the mass of delicate leather strapping on her shoes and stood up once more, Frank was gone. He'd clearly turned around and walked off in the other direction. *Probably punching at bushes and grabbing chunks of leaves in a classic, Frank-style fury*, Effy thought. She'd seen him do it once before from her bedroom window after a particularly heated row: she had leant out of the thin space into the cold, winter air, and witnessed him kicking a bush like a drunken Basil Fawlty.

Suddenly energised, Effy tore her shoes and Frank's blazer off and flung them at the door behind her. They clattered against the letterbox before landing in a heap on the top step.

And that was when she did it. That was when Effy Jones hitched up her dress and *ran*. She ran so fast it felt as if she had taken off into the cold air and soared down the street, but she knew the cold, numb soles of her feet were pounding the pavements. There was a rhythm as she ran, chilly air rushing in and out of her lungs. *Come on, come on, I can't lose you again*, she thought. He had disappeared at the bottom of the road and she didn't know which direction he had taken.

Effy fled past it all, past the bins, and the front doors. Past sleeping babies in cots, past elderly couples holding hands side by side on the sofa watching late-night films: love stories of yesteryear in black and white. Her dress spread out in the air and flapped behind her.

After what seemed like an age, Effy stumbled to a halt at the bottom of the street, out of breath and holding on to a postbox as she scanned around her with nervous, darting eyes, desperately looking for him. Left. Right. Left. Right.

Her heart was pounding in her chest. Where was he? She couldn't make him out in either direction. *Maybe he got on a bus*, she thought. Maybe he had ordered a taxi. 'Damn you, London, and your half-decent transport links,' Effy muttered to herself. And then: 'Fuck. Ben! Ben! Where are you?' she yelled, both arms outstretched beside her. Her voice boomed from her chest, splitting a little from the cold and the effort. Effy felt huge tears rise to her eyes as her hands sailed back down through the air and landed softly and hopelessly on her thighs. She was tired.

An elderly lady who was well known locally for wandering the streets late at night, always pushing a trolley with her, walked past. 'Move on, love, he's an arsehole,' the lady said, casually imparting her hoarse words of ill-informed wisdom.

'He's not! He's not an arsehole, OK! You don't even know him!' Effy shouted back when she would never normally bother, watching the lady hobble off with her empty trolley, its wheels rattling loudly as she switched from road to pavement. *He's amazing*, she thought to herself.

'Shit,' Effy said, walking backwards and sinking down onto a wall. She pulled her knees up beneath her and stared for a few moments at a kebab shop across the road. A group of youngsters were hovering in the doorway, throwing chips at each other.

Hope. There had to be some in all the madness and darkness of London . . . She looked to her right one more time, and that was when she saw him. Ben Lawrence, a hardly recognisable speck in the distance, bar the giant blooms in his hand. It was the only way she knew it was him.

He had turned around, probably in reaction to her shouting. With a squint, she could just about make out that he had one hand propped against his forehead, as if he was trying to double-check that it was her.

He started to walk, tentatively, in her direction. Effy smiled as his form got bigger. She slowly rose to her feet, the fabric of her dress trickling off the wall. She turned to face him and, as he made out her slim figure, she saw a huge smile spread across his face. That was when he started running, too.

Ben ran the last few metres towards her. And there he was. Butterflies filled her stomach again. How had she developed such strong feelings for this guy? This handsome man who had initially completely unimpressed her?

'Effy!' Ben cried, softly and happily. 'You've got no shoes,' he started to say, but he was interrupted.

'I don't care, Ben. I don't care about the shoes. Why, why are you here?' Effy asked, still a little breathless. Her drunkenness had fled now, and here she was, feeling stone-cold sober, staring at a man who looked so good she wanted to kiss him right then and there.

'I, well, I found out about your award – I heard Noah talking about it. It's amazing, Effy, I'm blown away. I know it's bad, but we had your address at work . . . God, this sounds terrible. I wanted to surprise you with these flowers here and tell you something, but God, it was so ill thought out, I'm so sorry,' he said, raising the flowers in his hand as he spoke, before dropping them down to his leg in frustration. A few petals slipped out and fluttered to the ground.

Effy looked at him. His stubble had grown a little, temptingly – she wanted to run her fingers over his cheeks and pull his face towards hers. His twinkling blue eyes were still so colourful, despite the darkness of the October night. His black suit looked brand new, beneath it a light grey shirt. He was tall. The kind of tall that made him instantly attractive anyway.

'What happened to that guy? Who is he? Do I need to speak to him again to explain? Effy, I'm so sorry if I got you into trouble.'

'Listen, don't worry about him. He's just a friend . . . well, it's a long story,' Effy responded, not knowing whether she should explain everything yet. 'What did you want to tell me?' she added, hoping it wouldn't be another bloody update about the charity partnership, delivered in some misleading and flamboyant way. She found men so confusing nowadays, she just didn't know what to expect any more.

'OK, right . . . well, I don't know if I should say now,' Ben said, nervousness all over his face.

Effy studied him again. She wondered what on earth he was about to say. 'Tell me, please,' she whispered, tucking

245

some curls that had released themselves from her plaits behind her ears. She couldn't take the tension any more; the cold was starting to nip at her. It really didn't help that she was standing barefoot on the freezing pavement.

Ben looked down at her toes and frowned. 'Well, first of all, Effy, if I'm going to tell you this, I don't want you to catch a cold, so . . .' he started, walking away from her for a moment and placing the roses on the wall she had been sitting on. He took the four steps back to her, and snaked an arm around her waist confidently. She breathed in sharply as he did so, feeling all the hairs on her arms stand to attention.

The simple feeling of his arm around her sent electricity all over her body. It was the sexiest thing that had happened to her in ages . . .

Then, as she gawped up at him, confused, he slid his shoes close to her toes and lifted her up a little so her feet were on top of them, and off the cold pavement. Then he took her hand in his own and pulled her close to him.

It was the oddest sight. Effy Jones and Ben Lawrence. She in a dress, he in a suit. Had they not been surrounded by fast-food joints, bins and orange streetlights . . . had they been cut out from the scene and isolated, one would be forgiven for thinking they were in a ballroom, dancing. Together.

And with that, Ben Lawrence slid his face against Effy's. Cheek to cheek. He whispered in her ear. 'This has got to be one of the most frightening things I have done in a long while, Effy . . . I came to tell you that I like you. I really, really like you. Is that OK?' he asked, looking beyond her at what was now a full-blown food fight in the kebab shop and saying a little prayer.

And with that she smiled, and she kissed him.

Twenty-five
'I make them sometimes'

Saturday 8 November 2014
Sloane Square, London

It was less than three weeks until Effy was due to fly to Uganda for six months. For some reason, this fact still came as a shock to Ben. It didn't feel real. He feared he would become like other guys probably had – insecure, difficult and frightened to lose her. Especially after he'd come so far to even tell her how he felt.

That was difficult for most people, let alone someone who intrinsically feared hurting others.

So, he did what many people would do in his position and ignored it. He skipped the words of articles about her in the paper and just focused on her picture. He just had to make the most of the next few days and weeks and take it from there. If she really was someone special, six months would be nothing in the grand scheme of their lives.

Ever since that fateful night when Ben had decided to

turn up at Effy's front door with a bunch of roses and unspoken words dancing at his lips, he had been walking on air. It had only been two weeks, but it was the best fortnight he'd ever experienced. Nothing was as good as kissing her: not the money he earned and all the lavish possibilities it provided; the meals he could afford; the clothes; the experiences. He would trade it all for her and he knew this already.

It was amazing to Ben that he'd plucked up the courage to tell her that he liked her. It was also incredibly frightening. It seemed that months of therapy with Sally Whittaker, a woman who would look at him calmly from beyond her heavy consulting desk and tell him that he deserved everything he put his mind and heart to, had done some good. That, and the supportive words from Theo; the enthusiasm of an office junior who had met her just once and saw stars; and the heavy emptiness of his £1million flat in Dalston.

He had realised that he was going to have to just go for it, in spite of himself. In spite of his fears. He would have to challenge the things that frightened him.

He had been in his flat alone on the evening of Effy's award ceremony when he had received the text message that had tipped him over the edge. I hope you've contacted Effy. I can't bear the fact that you are wasting an opportunity to be with her, you absolute dickhead. Theo

That's so typically Theo, Ben had thought, as he gazed at his iPhone in one hand, a glass of New Zealand sauvignon blanc in the other.

Another night alone with a box set. Sigh.

He had calmly put the phone down and glanced at his giant, towering television. He was watching old episodes of *Homeland*. A takeaway was on its way to him. Did it all amount to this?

He had lost his appetite for other women in the same way a person can go off food when they feel unwell. His previous insatiable desire had disappeared. All he wanted was her.

Lovesick.

Girls still texted and called his phone. They asked him if he fancied a drink, or dinner, or they just came out with it and asked him to 'pop round for coffee'. But the messages went unanswered. Effy had changed him already. And how strange it was to him that the woman who made him feel this way was a woman he hardly knew. He had always thought that if this ever happened to him, it would be someone he had been sleeping with for a long time. Someone who had grown on him.

And for the first time in a very long time, he thought about that day. Properly. The day in his past that had scarred him. And he realised that he wasn't going to be able to move on unless he tried.

It wasn't a lightning-bolt moment. He knew there was no quick fix, but it was a final, dawning realisation that in order for him to unlock himself from his own prison, he must *try. We all make mistakes*, he thought, as he watched Claire Danes run around crying and screaming into a mobile for the umpteenth time. *Give me a man who hasn't made mistakes and I will give you a lie.* He thought about all his friends and their mistakes. It comforted him, in a strange, selfish kind of way. A way he was almost ashamed of. He thought about Tony Wilcox from his first job. Tony, who had managed to lose a client worth £3million a year because he had bumped into the CEO in a bar and drunkenly imparted information he wasn't meant to discuss. He thought about Michael Rise, an old friend and policeman who had repeatedly tasered the wrong person when he got an ID mixed up during a routine call-out. He thought about Caroline East, his sister's friend, who cheated on her husband with a handsome waiter from a new local restaurant and then realised she'd made a mistake, but by then it was too late. Then, he thought about Rachel Tompkins, a girl from his school who had hit an old woman with her car when she'd slipped off the pavement and into her path. She would probably have been able to brake in time had she not been fiddling with the CD player . . . Everyone made mistakes on varying scales. Even Theo. Theo who popped his wallet into a letterbox instead of a love letter. Slushy, hopeless Theo.

Ben just had to find a way to forgive his own mistakes, and he hoped that maybe telling Effy how he felt about her would be the first step to confronting his worries.

He was also going to have to tell her about Ropek Oil. Soon. When the time was right. He hoped she would be rational enough to understand how the situation had come about, and that it certainly wasn't a result of maliciousness on his part. He was also going to donate his £40,000 from the contract bonus to Dafina Kampala. A gesture to reinforce how sincere he was about the success of her charity, and that he didn't find it appropriate to hang on to the money now he knew about her charity and all it was planning to achieve.

It's early days, still, he had thought, trying to calm his spiralling feelings when he sat opposite her in a bright blue coffee shop in Chelsea on a sunny afternoon a few days prior. But it was hard to stop himself falling for someone so effervescent, someone who injected beauty into everything they did. In his eyes, she was perfect, although he knew that wasn't realistic. It was both wonderful and frightening in equal measure.

He hadn't told her that he was falling for her. He vowed that he wouldn't . . . not until things were more solid. It seemed foolish to him, to say it so soon. Almost teenage. He was pretty sure he would put her off if he did – make her cringe – and he was still scared, too, despite the courage he'd summoned to make his feelings known. His fears still existed, but he was desperately trying to push through them.

He would wait and, if things worked out, he would tell her just how much he felt for her. But for now he had to be calm. Keep it all inside, keep his cards close to his chest, he vowed to himself. Effy was special and he didn't want to make more mistakes in his life. He didn't want to rush things, or jump into bed with her too soon. Everything had to be perfect.

It was 4 p.m. on a chilly Saturday afternoon in November when Ben walked up the King's Road, his hands in his pockets, to meet Effy for their fourth date. With Lily working for her, she had a little time to go out and enjoy herself, but he always had to work around her diary as she had so much on.

He and Effy had planned to spend an afternoon (and evening, he hoped) on the tiles, and it would all start soon, in a nautically themed pub down a winding side street with its own beautiful London postbox outside. The sun was out, giving the kind of sharp, brilliant sunshine that only blessed the city in the autumn. The trees were just starting to tire of a summer dressed in the season's hot trend of vibrant green. The leaves had started to turn brown and die, twisting and tumbling helplessly to the ground whenever there was a gust of wind. Ben wore a pair of dark denim jeans, a chunky maroon jumper and a dark grey duffle coat. He looked effortlessly stylish, and women glanced at him when he walked past them. It was ridiculous sometimes, and it amused the people around him, who noticed it with a secret jealousy. Theo always found it particularly funny, labelling it, 'The Ben Effect'. In fact, Theo had even been able to tailor a range of amusing anecdotes around the types of injuries women had sustained while staring at Ben and not focusing on their driving/walking/cycling.

The side street came up, and Ben took it, his heart starting to race at the prospect of seeing her.

Effy was already in the pub, curled up in the corner of a huge leather sofa, reading *White Teeth* by Zadie Smith – probably for the fifteenth time now because, she had told him, her mind was always too crowded with work for her to read things properly, and to actually engage with the words.

'Hello, beautiful,' Ben said. He had crept up to her quietly, swooping down to whisper his greeting in her ear.

She jumped a little, before looking relieved that it was him.

Ben looked at her with amusement. 'Were you about to punch me, then?'

'Yeah, for a second! You scared me!' Effy said, sliding the book onto the wooden table and giving him a kiss.

She had already bought a bottle of white wine and it sat there temptingly, the flickering flames of the fire magnified in the glass. Two slender wine glasses were neatly placed on the table. Side by side and touching.

Ben sunk down into the sofa beside her as she poured the wine and passed him a glass.

He felt an animal desire to just kiss her. The kind of feeling where he didn't care about the people in the pub: the miserable, wrinkly old gits propping up the bar and the giggling women, bubbling with gossip and laughter. He just wanted to take her in his arms and kiss her until the hours slipped away into the night-time, in what would feel like thirty seconds.

Effy was wearing a fluffy grey jumper, a pair of black jeans and some high-top trainers. Her curly mop was down, tumbling over her shoulders. Ben noticed that she smelt delicious.

He felt giddy with it all. A little sick, even – in the nicest, happiest kind of way. He was aware that he had had a flashback to 'that day' when he was on his way to see her, and he had wondered how she would react if he told her – but had then decided against talking about it. It was his biggest fear. When he was with Effy, Ben could almost pretend to be a better version of himself. Someone who didn't feel responsible for a tragedy so devastating, it had left a huge, permanent mark on the image of his life, of himself and of the world around him. Sometimes, it was nice to act like it had never happened . . .

'How are you?' Ben asked, a grin on his face the size of the Thames. She was smiling too, he noticed.

'Well, I'm great, if a little nervous,' she said, taking a deep breath in a kind of outward 'I'm trying to be calm' gesture.

Ben noticed that each of Effy's nails was painted a different colour, a look usually worn by clueless schoolgirls with frills around their socks and a penchant for neon scrunchies. But she had the kind of whimsical cool required to carry it off and still look classy. He almost wanted to take the piss out of her for it, but he felt it might be a little too soon for all that.

'Why are you nervous?' Ben asked, leaning back into the sofa and wondering what could be troubling this girl, who seemed so strong.

He was starting to realise that everyone was scared. Every single person walking the streets of his city and beyond was frightened of something.

'Just about going away. I'm excited about it, don't get me wrong . . . But it's just so daunting, too, and there's a lot to do. And, well, what do you want to do about, well, *us*?' she finished in a rush, a look of genuine concern across her face, tinted with a flash of embarrassment.

Ben raised an eyebrow. 'Well, erm, it's early for us, of course, but we could stay close despite the distance . . . if we try . . . Of course, if you want to, that is? What do you think? I totally understand if you just want some space,' he said, feeling nervous himself now. He was garbling, and hoping against hope that she wasn't about to break it off, after everything that had happened.

After everything he'd battled to get to this point.

'No, I totally agree that we can still make it work . . . I just wanted to see what you were thinking. I didn't know if you wanted to break things off while I'm away or not. I don't want to be selfish and just leave you here in London, stuck in something long distance you don't want. I know it's really early days – too soon to be having this conversation, really.' She looked up and smiled at him. 'I know we're just dating, but we're kind of forced into having this chat, aren't we?' she asked, giving no indication of pressure either way.

'I know exactly what you mean, but I'm happy to stay seeing each other while you are away if it's what you want? Of course, if it isn't . . . I totally understand.'

He watched as Effy's face lit up.

You should tell her now, a little voice went off in his head. *Tell her about Ropek Oil. Come on. Before it's too late.* He ignored it. There would be another time.

A better time to talk about Ropek Oil. Now was *not* that time.

'No, I would love that, Ben,' she said, looking a little more relaxed now. She had clearly been building up to asking him, and now her body calmed, her shoulders lowering. Ben buried his relieved smile in his glass.

The afternoon went by in a blur, the two of them tucked up by the fire in the corner of the nautical drinking hole. By 9 p.m. they had polished off a second bottle of wine and had moved on to spirits.

'Effy, I hope you don't mind me asking, and I don't want to pry, but who was that guy at the doorstep that Thursday night?' Ben asked, desperate to know what he had interrupted that night.

There were a few moments of difficult silence as Effy considered what she would say. 'OK, well, his name is Frank. He is my ex-boyfriend,' she said, looking embarrassed and ever so slightly ashamed.

Ben felt a little nervous about this all of a sudden. There was something more worrying about an ex: it was more threatening than a guy she was seeing, or a date. An ex had been a part of the past, but he had come back into her present – maybe her future? A bundle of questions flooded his mind. Was this guy a threat? Why had he been there? Did he have a whole load of mutual friends in tow who wished they would get back together?

'OK. Don't worry, you don't have to tell me. I just wondered,' Ben said.

'No, I'm going to explain this to you. I think we should both be as honest as possible – it's important. Frank and I split up a while ago now, although, to be honest, the relationship had been over long before that.'

Ben sat up as she explained, hoping this wouldn't be a

problem for him. For them. He also felt a flicker of guilt that she was ready to be honest and he wasn't, not just yet.

'We were living together, in fact we were together for years. Frank and I, well, we fell out of love. Being with me can be hard, Ben. As you know, my career takes a lot of my time and effort. He couldn't really cope with it all and so our relationship collapsed,' she finished, sadness in her eyes.

'Can you tell me why he was coming back with you that night? I'm sorry to pry, it's just . . . well,' Ben said, leaning towards her a little now.

'Yes, of course. I appreciate that it probably doesn't sound great. I invited Frank to the awards night because we had made peace with each other – we were both totally over things, and I wanted him to come as a thank you. He was a big part of my life when I set up Dafina Kampala, however difficult things were, and so I felt it would be a nice thing for him to come and share my success. Anyway, it was a mistake . . . We kissed. I don't know why. It was crazy and I instantly regretted it. He wanted to come back to mine to talk, but I was so worried about it. I was so glad you were there, I really was,' Effy responded, staring at the fire as she spoke.

Ben blew out a puff of air. 'Listen, Effy, it's fine. I understand. I actually saw your face as you came round the corner, before you realised I was there. You didn't look happy . . . well, you looked fucking miserable, actually . . .' Ben trailed off, grimacing a little as he said it.

And Ben genuinely did understand and relate to what had happened to Effy that night. He had experienced similar things himself. He knew that things weren't always simple. There were straggly ends. Lonely nights when you thought that *Maybe, just maybe . . . No.*

'Yes, exactly. Nothing would have happened, but I think he did want to patch things up between us. I haven't spoken to him since, if that helps,' she continued, still gazing at the fire.

She chose me, Ben thought. Smiling inside.

It was 11.30 p.m. Suitably drunk, Ben and Effy tumbled into his flat in Dalston, a buzz of laughter and kisses. It had taken them at least five minutes to get to the front door, their journey interrupted by kissing and the passionate removal of jackets and jumpers.

'Yeah, yeah, your flat is all right, I guess,' Effy said sarcastically as he turned on the light, revealing his sprawling home that wouldn't have been at all out of place splashed across the pages of some pretentious home-furnishings catalogue.

Ben leant against the hallway wall by the switch as he watched her gazing at his flat: a huge, open kitchen decked out in marble, leading to a huge living room full of leather and clean edges. The walls, peppered with artwork, caught her attention for a few moments. There was a strange silence.

'Holy shit, Ben, you've done well,' she finally said, turning around and smiling at him. In a nice way. There was no jealousy. No bitterness. No comments that tried to mask a secret resentment. She just thought it was cool.

'Are you going to make me a coffee or what?' she asked, starting to laugh.

Ben clicked the door shut and led her by the hand into the living room.

'I was thinking cocktails, actually,' he said, naughtily.

'Right, well, let me think . . . if I drink any more, tomorrow will almost certainly be hell . . . Yep, let's have those cocktails,' Effy said, throwing herself on his giant sofa.

Ben made his way to the kitchen and arranged a few bottles of spirits on the countertop. Effy watched him from the edge of her seat, her wild hair spilling over her shoulders. Her eyes had a warm, drunken glaze to them. Suddenly, all Ben could think about was what it might be like to take her to bed. To slip between the sheets with a woman he was desperately attracted to, and had been ever since he first met her. It was all he wanted to do.

'Any preferences?' he asked, trying to get the thought of her naked body out of his mind. It was becoming very distracting.

'I love Cointreau . . . but surprise me,' she said, her smile turning into something else. Something sexy . . .

Shit! Shit! Shit! Ben thought. It was their fourth date. They had known each other for a fair amount of time. Tonight would be a perfectly 'acceptable' time for it to happen, if there were even silly rules like that nowadays. Sex. He had not waited this long to sleep with someone for . . . well . . . he couldn't even remember – waiting hadn't really been a part of any of his recent romantic liaisons. But he'd made a promise to himself. To her. A promise she didn't know about. He tried to remind himself of this as he thought about her body. The body she dressed so well. So classy but tempting at the same time. It drove him wild.

You don't deserve her. You'll hurt her.

And there it was again, out of the blue. The voice. Despite the alcohol and the laughter, and all the magic of their fourth date. The voice was back. It wasn't a foreign sound, an unidentified noise. It was his voice, and it was back.

He tried to ignore it.

Don't forget what you did. What about Alex?

Fuck. Help me, Ben thought, pouring the drinks and plastering a smile on his face. He felt the emotion start to rise at the bottom of his throat. He didn't want to break down here. Not now.

She should know what you did.

He pictured it as he stared at Effy's face: the swan, sitting in the icy water.

Loss. A mistake.

'Are you OK? Come over here,' Effy said, a beautiful warmth in her voice. She ran her right hand over the leather of the sofa and pulled a joke sexy face.

'Yup, yup, I'm fine,' Ben said, deliberately pulling back his shoulders and trying to look happy. He took the drinks over and slid down next to her once more, just like he had done at the pub.

The swan was still there, in his mind.

But before they'd even had the chance to take a sip of their drinks, Effy leant forward and pushed him back against the sofa, forcefully, but gently too, a difficult thing to achieve. His heart started to race.

Slowly, she pushed her face towards his, their lips meeting. A mischievous look appeared on her usually innocent, smiling features, and it made the whole thing even sexier. Ben felt a heat rising as he kissed her back. She was so attractive it hurt. He felt instantly turned on.

Effy started to undo the buttons of his shirt. Slowly.

You don't deserve her. The voice – his own – said again.

Effy sat up, and in one fluid movement, slid her top off. She was wearing a black lace bra. She was slim and curvaceous. She started to kiss him again, so softly it tickled. She pushed her top lip against his. She smelt delicious.

She should know.

Ben winced at the thoughts in his head. The voice that said such nasty things about who he was. He blinked a few times to try and get rid of it, which seemed ridiculous in retrospect, but it was a strange thing he did to try and clear his mind.

She'll find out who you really are.

He started to feel sick with panic. The anxiety was rising up to the base of his throat, making it hard for him to breathe. He was trying so hard to focus on her, on this beautiful woman he had *finally* been able to care about . . . He looked at Effy's body, at her soft skin, her cleavage. She was so sexy.

You are scum.

And then he lost it.

'Effy, Effy . . . I'm sorry,' Ben said, sitting up suddenly and pulling himself away a little. His heart was pounding as if he'd awoken from a bad dream.

Effy sank back down again quickly, a look of disappointment and worry across her features: that beautiful nose of hers, the eyes . . .

'Did I do something wrong? Too soon?' she asked, looking a little shocked. And surprised.

'No! God, no, not at all, Effy. I'm so attracted to you. You're gorgeous . . . I just want to wait. Is that OK?'

Effy looked at him, still surprised. 'No, of course – sorry. It's just . . . can I ask why, though? Do you mind if I ask why?' she said again. Genuine. Honest. Just a question. She was biting her bottom lip gently, looking genuinely concerned.

'No, of course you can,' Ben said, wrapping his arms around her naked waist and pulling her close to him so his face was against her cheek once more. He swept a swathe of her hair away from her face, revealing her left ear. 'I just really like you. I don't want to rush things.'

Effy pulled away, grinning like an idiot. She looked touched and flattered. 'Of course. I totally understand,' she said. As she did so, her handbag fell off the sofa, the contents spilling all over the floor.

Ben looked down, hoping she hadn't noticed his utter panic, and spotted a weird paper structure amongst the pens, keys and cards. It looked like origami. 'What's that, Eff? It looks interesting,' he asked.

Effy bent down and picked it up. She held it just so, and pushed it through the air and into the light.

As she did so, Ben saw what it was. A swan.

'It's a paper swan. I make them sometimes. Weird, I know.'

Ben felt a shiver down his spine.

Twenty-six
'No, I'm not . . .
nobody is'

Monday 10 November 2014
Angel, London

'God, you look happy, Eff,' Lily said as she charged into the room, bursting Effy's daydream as abruptly as a pin to a balloon.

Effy had been staring over the top of her laptop screen and out of the window, an expression of sheer joy on her face. In her eyes, there were rainbows where the rain used to be . . . it was ridiculous! Even she quietly mocked the airy-fairy existence she now lived, floating from one daydream to another.

She was in the first throes of love. Everything was magical and beautiful and coated with sugar. Even her morning commute failed to get her down. No, not even a smelly armpit or a farting schoolboy was going to knock her mood that day, or tomorrow, or ever, as long as she had Ben Lawrence in her life.

Effy was managing to irritate even herself.

'Ha ha, thank you, Lily. I am happy indeed.' Effy smiled, looking at her young apprentice and her snagged knitwear. She wanted to give her a hug and ruffle her wiry locks like a big sister and tell her wisely that 'the right one will come along one day', all the while staring off knowingly into the middle distance.

Dating Ben Lawrence had made her see the world in a different light. Everything was bright and beautiful. And everything made sense now. His change of charity contact, his silence. He had been thinking about everything. He had been confused and he had needed some time to make a decision. And Effy knew he had made the right one. *Everything works out for the best*, she thought.

'How are *you*, Lily?' Effy asked, vowing to herself that she would take her out to lunch soon – do something as a thank you for all the help she was giving Dafina Kampala. Something bigger than Effy's occasional stifled grunts of gratitude from beneath a pile of paperwork. Her happy state of mind recently had seen her wanting to share that joy, thinking of ways she could thank the people in her life for their unending support, planning things and writing letters when she had the time. Perhaps she could even put some brightly coloured paper hearts in the envelopes so that when people opened them they would all float out? *That's absolutely bloody ridiculous. Get a grip*, she had thought to herself.

'Yah, babe, I'm fine. Weekend was totes amaze. Went to a friend's house in the country and ate pheasant,' Lily said, still breathless with her own happy memories of the weekend.

'Wow, well, that sounds great!' Effy said, turning back to her laptop and quietly gagging at the thought of eating pheasant. Silence descended for a time.

The pair were soon interrupted by a knock at the door, however. A tall, slim lady in a skirt suit popped her head around the doorframe, her lips pursed together as if she had picked up a bad smell.

'I've got a delivery for Miss Jones?' she asked, looking at the two women, who were eyeing her expectantly. There was a kind of flatness in her voice usually only associated with a six-day-old can of Coke.

'Yes, that's me,' Effy said, expecting it to be a box of printed leaflets, or some new donation boxes that she was expecting.

The woman disappeared out of view for a moment before opening the door wide and producing the biggest bunch of flowers Effy had ever seen.

They were ridiculous. 'Holy shit, they're as big as me!' Effy said, leaping to her feet as the flowery tower was wheeled in. Yes, *wheeled* in.

'Indeed. It was so big we needed to use the mini tow,' the woman muttered. 'They were difficult to get into the lift. He must have really screwed up,' she said sharply before disappearing, click-clacking her way down the corridor, the sound growing ever quieter until she could no longer be heard.

Lily rolled her eyes in a 'Oh, sod her, she's a bitter cow' kind of way and walked towards the arrangement, pushing her face into a particularly bulbous rose, the arrangement of her face reminding Effy of an excitable and slightly bashful animal in an animated Disney film. 'Oh, they're beauts! Jesus, Effy, I think he loves you . . . as in properly "I love you" loves you, know what I mean?' she asked, her hands clasped together with glee.

Effy went bright red and sighed as she walked around the flowers, wondering how on earth she was going to get them home without scratching someone's eye out, or accidentally suffocating someone. 'Wow, they really are quite gorgeous.' She sighed, reaching down for the envelope and plucking it from the centre of the bunch.

*For you, Effy Jones. London's most beautiful lady . . .
There's a taxi coming to yours tonight at 7.30 p.m. I know
you are busy, but I want to see you as much as I can before
you go. Please, hop in? Ben xxx*

Effy feared she might end up as a sloppy puddle on the floor of the office. Tonight . . . tonight, what could be happening tonight? She wheeled the flowers to the corner of the room, their sweet scent drifting around the tiny, previously rather drab space.

'Well, isn't that lovely?' Effy said, all too aware that there was a lot to be done until she went away. In three weeks' time.

Effy quickly thought about her to-do list. It was pretty intense . . . could she spare another night? Probably not . . . No, she would have to turn him down . . .

It was a strange time for Effy. She was falling head over heels in love, which was significant, but even more significant was the fact that she was about to make her dreams come true. Soon, she would be flying out to Kampala to set up her charity. Properly. The thought of it all filled her with so much joy and fear it was overwhelming. And how the two emotions danced together. Every now and then she would feel physically sick at the thought of it all and have to scramble to the Ladies and splash her face with cold water. How would it go? Would the centre be ready by the end of her six months in Uganda? Would she and Ben be OK? There were so many questions.

She thought back to the weekend, and how peculiar Saturday night had been. In the least arrogant way possible – though she cringed to think of it this way – she had genuinely never experienced a man who didn't want to sleep with her in a situation like that, and after four dates? It all seemed so ridiculous.

Of course, she had wondered if he wasn't attracted to her, but that seemed implausible given the whole situation. His romantic gesture that Thursday night, their amazing dates, the kissing, the flowers . . . *No. There's something else*, she thought, quietly intrigued by the whole thing. She wanted to get inside his head, to really understand him. He was being mysterious and it was driving her crazy, in the best way possible. Ben was such a happy, funny man, and yet there was a palpable sadness about him too. She wondered why.

'Maybe you've just found a good one,' Rosa had said on the phone the night before, when Effy had recounted 'the night of no sex'. They had spent twenty minutes decoding things but then Effy had been forced to get back to work, tapping away at her laptop until 2 a.m. to make up for time after her blissful Saturday spent gallivanting with Ben.

It was rare for people not to jump into bed with one another. *Certainly nowadays and certainly in London, with all its instant pleasure and take-me-now thrills*, Effy thought. Well, the message in the flowers seemed to ring loud and clear. Tonight, it seemed, could be the night.

'Are you going to go?' Lily asked, an expectant grin on her face as she twiddled around on her chair.

'No, no I can't . . . I've got the newsletter to do,' Effy said, biting her bottom lip and starting to go through some schedules on the screen of her laptop.

'No, you don't. I'm doing it,' Lily said firmly.

'No, that's too much, Lily,' Effy replied.

'I'm doing it, and that's the end of it. You work too much, you need to have more fun. Go, go, go!' Lily said, pointing Effy in the direction of the door.

Effy practically dived into the bath as soon as she got home. Various body parts were shaved, plucked and waxed in a hurried frenzy and scented by bath foam and creams in differing pots and tubes. She only had an hour to get ready by the time she had battled with the flowers on the train and dragged them home.

'Rosa, I think it's going to happen tonight,' Effy yelled down the phone breathlessly as she paced around her room, stepping backwards and accidentally slamming the ball of her foot into a huge pot of Body Shop moisturiser. 'Fuck!' she yelled, feeling the greasy cream squidge between her toes.

'What?' Rosa asked, hearing the commotion, crisp and loud, down the line.

'Oh, nothing . . . Well, apart from sex. He sent flowers today. A huge bunch of flowers, Rosa, you should see them. It was a nightmare getting them home, and a card, there was a card,' she said breathlessly, extracting her foot from the blueberry-scented slop and hopping to her bed on one foot. 'And in the card it said there was a taxi coming. Tonight!' Effy yelped, while wiping the cream off her feet and frantically rubbing it into her legs.

'OK, OK, calm down – it's not like you're losing your bloody virginity,' Rosa said, starting to laugh.

'I know, I know, but it feels like it. It's probably come back, for all I know, it's been so long. What if I've forgotten how to do it? What if I bite him, or head-butt him or something?' Effy cried, wincing now.

'Just calm down and enjoy it, OK?' Rosa spoke in a tone of voice that implied she was rolling her eyes.

When the phone call ended, it was just Effy and her fears. She put on her sexiest underwear, found a long, black maxi dress in a thick material, and slicked on a little make-up. Some statement jewellery comprising a mass of white ivory triangles, and a spritz of perfume later, and she was ready.

As promised, there was a beep from a car outside at exactly 7.30 p.m. Effy flung on a leather jacket before leaving the house, and hopped into the shiny black cab. It was starting to get dark.

'Hi. Where are we going?' Effy asked, the second she sank down into the soft seats in the back of the taxi, hoping the driver would put her out of her misery.

He turned and smiled at her, giving her a knowing look. The expression of a man who had probably seen and heard it all. 'Hi. My name's Warren. And sorry, but I can't tell you,' he said, a slight teasing tone in his voice.

It was so exciting, knowing that she was about to be driven to an unknown destination, and knowing that Ben would be there. He made her feel so alive. She hadn't felt this way for a long time. It was so sweet of Lily to offer to take on the newsletter . . . Effy felt very lucky to have her.

'Please . . . can you please, please, *please* tell me where we are going?' she begged once more, desperate to break the silence that had developed between her and this Warren bloke. Effy crossed her legs, her thighs sticking together uncomfortably as a result of all the moisturiser she'd had to put all over her legs. It wasn't helping her nerves, which kept rising and falling in her chest.

'I really can't help you there, love, sorry. Ben's orders,'

he said in a gravelly voice, before turning back towards the steering wheel and pulling away from the kerb outside Effy's house.

'Really? It's just it would be so good to know,' Effy pleaded, hoping she could switch on the persuasive tone she had to use almost every day to work miracles for her charity and make things happen.

The driver flashed her another toothy smile in the rear-view mirror.

'A postcode, can you give me a postcode?' Effy begged.

'Oh, I wish I could, sweetheart . . . but I have to do what the customer asks,' he said, turning right at the bottom of her street and driving past the spot where Ben had declared his feelings for her. It brought back a flood of lovely memories.

'Ben's a top bloke, a real one-of-a-kind guy,' Warren said, clearing his throat after he spoke and glancing back at her in the rear-view mirror again with a reassuring smile.

'I know. Do you pick him up often, then?' Effy asked, wondering how this taxi driver knew him so well. She had imagined that she would be picked up just by a random taxi, with a random driver – someone she would probably never see again.

'Yeah, I've known him since he was a pipsqueak. Twenty-two years of age he was – he'd just started his first PR job and I used to do private pick-ups for his old work-place. I used to think he was a right pain in the arse, if I'm honest . . . Cocky thing he was, and he was a little puker when he was in his early twenties. I was always having to stop the cab because he'd had too much to drink, and he was always bloody well lighting up in the taxi. Anyway, despite all that, we got on very well in the end, and he calls me a lot now on my mobile to pick him up from various places, parties, work dos . . . you know the kind of thing. He's sick less often nowadays, you'll be glad to know,' said Warren, breaking into a hacking laugh that seemed to spiral quickly out of control. It took him some time to calm it down.

It interested Effy that Ben had been able to make friends with a taxi driver in a city as cold and anonymous as London. A place so faceless at times – especially as Ben often came across as cool and closed. It was a huge comfort to Effy that Ben was viewed fondly by people like Warren, a taxi driver who could now add a secret, romantic journey to a mystery destination to his probably endless list of places he's been.

She studied the road signs as they snaked their way to central London, moving in and out of thick bands of traffic, like milkshake clogging a straw. The roads grew more clean and beautiful as they neared the core of the city: endless streets of kebab shops, estate agents and launderettes soon melted into expensive homeware shops with telephones shaped like aubergines in the windows, and softly lit art galleries.

Effy wished that she had paid more attention to the geography of the city she lived in: she was embarrassingly clueless about where things were, and had been living in a little Muswell-Hill bubble for too long a time. The only familiar place to her was the area's central roundabout and the shop-lined roads that forked off it: the yellow-fronted newsagent and the branch of Whistles, where she would spend the odd ten minutes gawping at the cut of the beautiful clothes but avoiding looking at the price tags. She knew Crouch End and Finsbury Park well too, but, after that, everything became quite alien, only the odd restaurant or tourist hotspot providing any real familiar feeling of comfort – places like the South Bank or Covent Garden.

The driver seemed to be going towards Waterloo, she noticed, trying to put together a patchwork map in her mind of the things they could be doing in that area . . . the theatre? The ballet? It seemed too late for all of that, she realised, looking at the clock at the front of the taxi, which now read 7.55 p.m. Shows usually started at 7.30 p.m., didn't they?

Eventually the taxi stopped on a road near the river, somewhere near Waterloo Station, but she couldn't be totally sure. There were a few restaurants around, and some offices, but it was surprisingly quiet.

'There you are, love. We have reached your destination,' the driver said, mocking the tone of a sat-nav device, looking mightily pleased with himself while pulling up the handbrake and reclining in his seat. He looked as if he was trying to stretch out his back and shoulders a little.

'Thank you. How much do I owe you?' Effy asked politely, one hand on the door handle.

'Ben's got it, don't worry, love. Have yourself a magical night,' he said, with another of his warm smiles, and more than a little Dick-Van-Dyke-style sense of fun about him.

Effy thanked him and made her way out of the cab, into the evening air. It wasn't a cold night, but it wasn't particularly warm, either. She pulled her leather jacket round herself and scanned the streets around her as the driver sped away, thankful that her dress was made from a thick fabric.

Ben wasn't anywhere to be seen. Effy suddenly felt worried. Should she call him? What was he up to?

Then, all of a sudden, she heard her name being shouted from a distance away.

'Effy! Effy!' Ben yelled.

She turned around and saw him running towards her, now clutching a single red rose between his teeth and grinning. It was so silly, so cheesy, a typical romantic gesture from Ben – half joking, but half serious, too.

He was handsome, young and beautifully dressed in a faint houndstooth-patterned suit with a white shirt and a thin black tie. His dark hair looked like it had been recently cut – short at the sides and a little longer on top – and was styled in a slick, throwback way that made him look like a gentleman from a time long ago. Effy had grown jaded about modern-day relationships in recent years, but this man was restoring her faith in humanity. He was extravagant, but not in a way that alienated her or made her cringe. *He's classy – he always gets it right*, she thought.

He always played the fool, too, but he did it so well, Effy realised, as he ran the final steps towards her and pulled her into his arms. He smelt so good. She remembered that aroma he had, unique to him, a mixture of his spicy aftershave and the scent of his skin.

Ben held on to her shoulders and gawped at her, as she took the rose from his mouth.

'Thanks, yeah, a few bloody thorns on that one,' he said, laughing to himself before kissing her softly on the lips.

Effy felt her stomach flip as he kissed her. All of a sudden she felt warm, not just outside, but inside, in the pit of her stomach, in her heart. She really liked this man – as in *really* liked him. She feared she was going to be unable to stop herself from falling in love with him; she felt like a ball rolling furiously and uncontrollably down a slope, and there was nothing there to stop her.

She felt a flash of guilt about spending time with him and not working, and she briefly wondered if she would have done this for Frank had she cared about him enough . . .

Suddenly, it put a whole new light on their situation. She felt a surge of apprehension at this realisation, paired with the fact that she would soon be in Uganda for a considerable length of time . . . She quickly swept this away, pushing it back to another day, another time. *Think positive, Effy,* she told herself.

'Where are we going?' she asked, feeling like she was going to explode into a thousand pieces if the secret was maintained for a moment longer.

'Come with me, Eff,' Ben said, confident as anyone she'd ever seen. He put an arm around her shoulder and led her through a small street that brought them out near the Thames.

Dozens of people were milling around, some friends and some lovers, some taking a stroll with their dog on a pleasant autumn evening in London. She still had no idea what they were doing there.

'Do you like heights, Effy?' Ben asked, facing her now, a gorgeous smile written across his face.

'I don't mind them,' she responded, nervously.

'And do you like wheels?' he continued.

'Ha ha, yes, I think wheels are great – very useful things,' Effy responded, bursting into laughter and realising what they were about to do.

'Look up,' Ben whispered, as Effy craned her neck to take in the London Eye, tall and glittering in the night sky.

'This is amazing, thank you,' she said, smiling to herself as Ben stood behind her, wrapped his arms around her and kissed her neck.

Muswell Hill, London

The next day, Effy was exhausted, but *not* in an 'I-stayed-up-all-night-shagging' kind of way.

She sat up in her bed and pulled the black and white spotted duvet up to her face. It still smelt of Ben, that delicious scent of him still danced on the threads as if he were still there with her. She took a huge, deep breath before adjusting the pillows behind her back so she could be more comfortable. She leant over to her dresser and picked up a large cup of coffee, trying to bring back the happiness she had felt in the last few hours before another working day began.

It was 9 a.m. and Ben had got up and left for work an hour before.

They'd had an amazing night on the London Eye, drinking champagne and looking out over the city, their pod all lit up in the night sky with twinkling lights and romance. Then they had gone for dinner at another one of Ben's swanky restaurants, with all the silver cutlery and starched linen. They had both ordered the seafood, and it had arrived balanced precariously on leafy structures that looked as if they'd been crafted using a toothpick and a magnifying glass.

Drunkenly, she had asked him – no, begged him, play-fully – to come back to hers as they had embraced outside the restaurant, the cool river breeze ruffling their clothes.

She'd wanted him so much, and she'd had no doubt that this would be 'the night', but things had turned out unex-pectedly again, though not in a particularly bad way. In an unusual way.

Effy smiled to herself as she played back the evening's events in her mind. They had stumbled drunkenly into her flat, dodging all the clothes and various tubs of beauty products Effy had left all over her room while she had been hurriedly getting ready to go and meet Ben. There had been a lot of laughter and a lot of kissing. They had climbed into bed at 1.30 a.m., both of them in their underwear, and, skin to skin, they had spent the next five hours just talking, and kissing, then talking some more, and kissing some more.

But *it* hadn't happened . . .

It was the most interesting situation . . .

The night was passionate, almost more intimate than it might have been had they just done away with it all and slept together. No one had ever showed her before how special it was to just be together; to just take some time, not rush things, and respect each other.

It was amazing, Effy thought, so attracted to Ben now that she could just explode. It felt like they were teasing each other in some way, holding out on it so it would be really special when it happened. Effy wasn't disappointed, or upset – more *intrigued* by Ben, and the reasons why he was holding out on her.

When they talked, she discovered that they had so much in common: not in the structure or events of their lives, but more in the way they viewed the world, life and everything in it. He really was her kind of guy, and there seemed to be so many layers of him for her to discover.

He had also talked to her a little about his youth. He told her that he had been a bit of a rebel – well, a lot of a rebel, and she just couldn't imagine it. She pictured him being studious and impeccably behaved when he was young, always working hard towards his vision of this great adult life he now had, a far cry from the smoking, drinking bad-boy he'd described himself as being.

She'd told him about her past too, naturally; cherry-picking the best bits and weeding out the sad, shameful moments – they were, after all, in the twilight zone, and it was too magical, too beautiful to be talking about their deepest fears and insecurities yet. They were just trying to be the very best versions of themselves, and it was lovely. But tiring, too.

'You seem so perfect, Effy, it kind of intimidates me,' Ben had whispered into her ear at 6.30 a.m.

Effy took another sip of her coffee as she thought of those last few words he had said sleepily, before they'd drifted off.

'No, I'm not . . . nobody is,' Effy had whispered back, quietly, but he was asleep.

Now, she wondered what he'd meant by that. Why was he intimidated by her? All she knew was that she'd met someone very special, and that he was different, respectful. She'd finally found a gentleman in a world full of rogues.

Twenty-seven

How was she going to manage without him?

Tuesday 25 November 2014
Dalston, London

After a working day that had started at 6 a.m. and ended at 8 p.m., Effy allowed herself to spend another evening with Ben, eating food at his place.

Classical music seeped softly from his Bose sound system and filled every corner of the room, which was full of softly glowing candles.

Ben had cooked this time: sea bass with black pepper and garlic. It was beautiful, but there was more than just a hint of sadness about the night.

So many things were unsaid, phrases and questions stalling on the tongue, leaving great question marks bobbing in the air between them like giant balloons.

Ben Lawrence was still a mystery, too. In just a few weeks she had fallen madly in love with him, but she hadn't told him exactly how she felt . . . Something was holding her back. And he, while romantic and extravagant, hadn't really told her how he felt. For all she knew, this could be a fairly casual thing in his eyes.

He had the money to be flashy, and she was trying not to be blinded by it.

Effy was leaving for Africa in just two days. On 27 November she would be boarding a plane to get things going with Dafina Kampala, and with a good amount of money behind her, too. It was terrifying, one of the biggest moments of her life, the goal she had been working towards for years now, and something she had sacrificed so much for.

Previously she had always been held back by a lack of funding – the only reason why she hadn't been able to purchase a centre, hire staff and open the whole project; but now she had the money to get things going, she felt even more scared, because now it would really begin.

She was so daunted by it all. Daunted by leaving the UK for so long; missing Rosa, her very best friend; missing her family; facing some of the biggest challenges she would ever face . . . And, of course, leaving Ben.

She watched him as he carefully topped up her glass with champagne and put the finishing touches to the meal, and she felt her eyes sting with tears. How was she going to manage without him? She'd grown so attached to him, and now she would have to go, for six months. Six whole months without Ben Lawrence. She almost hated herself for thinking about it this way. What had happened to the previous version of herself: the woman who, while warm and kind to those around her, held most people and things away from her a little with a kind of sharp mistrust and disdain.

Ben seemed so cool – about it, about everything. He

seemed like the kind of person who wasn't fazed by anything. She almost felt angry with him for it, and angry for putting herself in this position, blindly falling in love with a man she hardly knew, when it would all be so painful in the end anyway . . . What else was she expecting?

Ben had asked her the obligatory questions: how was she feeling about the future, the trip away, and the amazing things she was about to do. She had given all the usual answers: that she was overwhelmed and nervous, but she was positive too. He'd also asked her about the centre she had bought, and how she hoped it would look.

The way she was feeling, it now made total sense to her that Ben had been holding off on the physical side of their relationship. This was all very painful, and she guessed that he had been trying to protect himself. She totally understood what he had been doing, as she felt a pang of fear in her heart as they spent one of their last nights together before she boarded a plane for Uganda.

Now Ben discussed the future as Effy listened, sitting on his sofa in a pair of skinny blue jeans and a light grey silk top, carefully sipping a glass of Prosecco. He referred to the things they would eventually do together when she got back. He talked about Skyping her regularly, sending letters and text messages . . . He certainly didn't seem to want to end it, but she was still so worried.

The more insecure side of her was terrified he'd meet someone else. He was so gorgeous to her, so irresistible . . . other women would surely look at him and feel the same, and what if he got fed up with waiting? She hated feeling like this . . . Her imagination started whirring. She pictured some beautiful leggy blonde arriving as a new recruit at his workplace, snaking her way into his life with her long, long legs and sweeping eyelashes, a flash of cleavage and the distance between her and Ben proving to be too much. Too far . . .

Her mind flashed back to Frank, and how much he had hated her being so tied up with Dafina Kampala. How could another man be so understanding? It would take a really amazing person to stand by her through all of this, and while she was mad about Ben, she'd hardly known him long enough to be really sure about what he was capable of.

Effy going away was the thing they both feared, but it was happening and it was going to happen very soon . . .

Ben begged her to stay that night but she declined, and climbed into a taxi at 2 a.m., her eyes full of giant tears that splashed onto her cheeks as the car pulled away from his flat and drove off in the direction of Muswell Hill.

She needed to be at home: she had so much work to do, and she was terrified of being reduced to a blubbering, snotty wreck at his house. She'd told him that she had to have an eye-wateringly early start in order to get everything ready for going away for such a long time. He had been understanding, but the departure had been melancholy: a quick kiss before she left, full of sadness and fear.

Painful and quick, like ripping off a plaster.

Suddenly, Effy really wasn't sure of the status of their relationship. Ben had told her that he certainly wasn't planning to see anyone else; she wouldn't be dating other men; and the time they had spent together had been incredible. But she didn't really know where they stood. They hadn't had 'the chat' yet. There was no label. They seemed to be engaging in a very strange undefined situation, their actions and gestures clearly showing their serious feelings for each other, yet the lack of physical intimacy and the avoidance of putting a label on their relationship smacked of fear.

At 3 a.m. she climbed into bed, alone, picking her laptop up from the floor and turning it on. She had a couple of emails she needed to reply to about a media volunteer who would be joining her for a while, and what felt like a thousand other things to sort out.

As she logged into her email, she was dismayed to find another message from Frank, waiting there in her inbox like an unblinking monster in the darkness beneath the bed.

Effy sighed loudly as she saw the message, highlighted in a thick, black font because it was yet to be read. A message from Frank was the last thing she wanted to see now – she almost found it irritating, to see his name glowing there at the top of her inbox. It was an intrusion.

Effy imagined that he was probably hoping to talk to her about that embarrassing evening: the night when he had planned to rekindle their relationship and then they found Ben on the doorstep. She looked back to that night for a moment, and cringed at the way he had reacted. She guessed he wanted to discuss it before she disappeared. But any hope of friendship with Frank had been destroyed after that. She didn't want to read the message; a message that she guessed would be full of apologies for his furious reaction, or full of anger and vitriol towards her. Frank's behaviour that night had been so strange, so desperate, that she didn't know what to expect from him any more.

Effy took a deep breath, her finger hovering over the trackpad on her laptop. She decided not to read it – she simply had too much on her mind to be reading a guilt-inducing email from her ex-boyfriend.

She eventually curled into a ball to try and sleep, but she couldn't. All she could think about was Ben, his face, his smile – and how desperately she hoped their relationship would survive.

She'd had coffee with Rosa the day before. Rosa had imparted some of her usual wise words as she cradled a cappuccino with her delicate fingers, nails painted jet black: 'Effy, if Ben is the right guy for you, if this is meant to be, he will wait for you.'

The words span round in Effy's head as she lay in a state of sleeplessness, the numbers on her digital clock blinking slowly in the darkness.

Twenty-eight
But she had to have faith

Thursday 27 November 2014
Muswell Hill, London

Effy and Ben spent the morning at her flat in a murk of tearful kisses and tight cuddles, a sad breathy feeling, the sorest farewell. Ben had come round at 8 a.m., taking a half-day of his holiday allowance, his boss half nodding in acknowledgement while he yelled at someone down the phone.

Effy's flight was at 7 p.m., and the hours, minutes and seconds were floating away from them like balloons released into the sky on a summer's day.

They climbed into bed and cuddled and kissed as if their lives depended on it. Effy's phone kept ringing all the while: various relatives and friends wishing her all the very best in voicemail messages that she knew would inevitably drive her to more salty tears when she listened to them at the airport later. Her mother and father promised to come and visit her in Africa, and she was already excited to see them.

'Effy, the last few weeks with you have been incredible,' Ben said, as he held her face gently and stared into her eyes. It was raining outside and the droplets were teeming against her bedroom window, before sliding down the glass and onto the cold, hard pavement below.

Effy nodded as he spoke, more tears arriving to chase the ones before them as she stroked the stubble on his cheek. She felt sad and angry: she had finally met someone amazing, and fallen in love, and she was going away. She looked back at her whole life so far, all the years she had been living and working in London, all the time she had spent revolving around the same place, more or less. That would have been the perfect time, so why now? Why, when she was flying off to try and perform what she felt would be a thousand tiny miracles? Which now, when she thought of them, seemed so far beyond her she was just filled with terror.

'Listen, I know it's still kind of early days for us, but I'm mad about you, Effy. I've honestly never felt this way before, about anyone. You have changed me,' Ben said, a tinge of embarrassment on his face as he said this. His top lip curled a little, in the way it always did. Effy had noticed this when she first met him, but she hardly noticed it these days.

The way he came across, and the way he had been when she first knew him . . . she got the impression that it had been a long time since he had spoken to a woman like this. But, at the same time, she still felt a flicker of worry that he was a player, and that maybe he *did* say things like this to women all the time, misleading them and confusing them.

But she had to have faith.

Despite the doubt, they were the most beautiful words Effy had ever heard. She didn't know how she had changed him; she didn't know enough about his previous life. He seemed to be so together, so successful – what had she changed that could be beneficial to his already very blessed and privileged existence?

She wondered all this as she stared into his eyes, and it felt as if she were looking in a mirror. She had grown so close to him it was as if he were an extension of her – she'd never experienced that before. Not even with Frank. Frank had always seemed a little obtuse, and she'd realised in recent weeks that she'd never felt entirely comfortable around him. Even when they had lain in bed, his body had never quite fitted hers properly: he'd been all jutting bones, his cuddles a little too stifling.

'Effy Jones. What you are about to do is incredible, so admirable . . . You are an inspiration to me and I know you are going to make a success of this. I will be with you every step of the way, in the only way I can be, which will be thinking of you, every day,' Ben continued, through what sounded like giant lumps of emotion in his throat.

Despite his words, fear continued to thread its way through Effy's legs and arms, tingling at her fingertips and toes. She felt sick.

'I'm so scared, Ben . . . what if I fuck this up? This is such a huge responsibility, and it's dangerous out there, too. What if something goes wrong with the centre I bought? I think, I'm just wondering . . . if I've made a really big mistake.' Effy gulped. 'I feel like a kid still! I know I'm closer to thirty than I am to twenty – but I still feel like a kid, a child who shouldn't be meddling with this stuff,' she continued, so scared now it was starting to really alarm her.

'Listen, if there is anyone out there to do this, it's you. You are going to be amazing, I just know it. You've worked so hard on this, you know your stuff, and you're so well prepared . . . It's all going to be fine . . . This is your *dream*, Effy. Go and make it happen,' Ben said, soothingly, as he pulled her a little closer, her slender frame sliding across the sheets, closer to him. The man she was falling in love with.

'And what *is* going to happen with us?' she asked again, needing reassurance. She needed to hear it again.

'We'll be together still,' Ben said simply. 'That's what I want. Is that what you want?'

Effy nodded quickly.

'I'll talk to you every day, and I will be waiting for you at the airport when you come back and we will celebrate because I know you will make a success of your dreams . . . Just focus on that. But please, Effy, stay safe. That's all I ask of you,' Ben said.

It was all she needed to know: that Ben felt as much for her as she did for him. That he was committed to her.

He'd said it now and she was so relieved.

Ben left at midday. He had a client meeting that afternoon that he couldn't miss. He also had a business trip to New York coming up soon, and there was, as always, so much to do.

He apologised for not being able to spend every last second with her before she flew off to Africa. Effy told him that she understood, of course she did: he was a dedicated businessman in the same way that she was dedicated to her charity. Life was a constant merry-go-round of juggling, recognising the meetings and events you had to attend, and the ones you could skip, spending the right amount of time with friends, family and loved ones, and making sure you did all the work you could in a limited amount of time. It was hard, but so rewarding. She knew what it was all about for him . . .

The final kiss was the sweetest and most painful thing she had ever experienced. Sugar and salt, at the same time.

After he left, Effy shakily made herself a cup of tea and sat down to her computer. She felt like the hardest part was already behind her. If she could get through saying goodbye to Ben, then she could get through anything.

The email from Frank was still playing on her mind. She'd ignored it, but it was tickling away at the back of her consciousness. At least she was going to Africa now, so if she didn't like what it said she could just forget about it, safe in the knowledge that she would be far away from him.

She took a few sips of her tea and opened the window a little for some fresh air. The rain had finally taken a short break. She opened her emails and clicked on Frank's unopened message.

To: Jones, Effy
From: Rhodes, Frank

Effy,

I'm so sorry to be sending you this message.

I swore to myself that I would leave you well alone after the events following the awards evening. It all hurt so much, but I understand that you really like this guy so I told myself to back off and leave you alone.

Essentially, at the heart of all this, I want you to be happy, but I need to confess something to you. I've done a bad thing, Effy, but I think you need to know about it.

I miss you, every day, and I know that I still love you. I did what every crazy person in love does. I'm going to lay it all out here in this email for you to see. I'm not proud of what I did, but it led me to some information that I cannot hold back from you, because I still care about you.

I went on your Facebook one night in a drunken fit of jealous rage. I'd had a lot to drink at the pub with my friends and all I could think of was you. I got home and switched on my computer and I searched your friends list to find him. I wanted to find out more about the guy who had swept you off your feet in this way – what this man had that was so much better than me. It was a kind of morbid curiosity that I simply wasn't able to hold back from . . . I knew his name was Ben, after that utterly embarrassing display on your doorstep. You only have three friends named Ben, one of whom I know from when we were together; the other I don't know of, but I guess you must know him from school or uni; and the final Ben was Ben Lawrence. His profile picture gave it away too, of course – that smug know-it-all smile, that bloody ridiculous shirt he's wearing, the eternal glass of champagne in his left hand. That guy. The one you care about more than me. I know this makes me sound like a psycho, but I'm just trying to be honest with you here.

After a few minutes of looking at his photos and morphing into even more of a slimy, jealous monster than I already am, I decided to Google him. Yes, I know, it's pretty shameful.

After a little research I found out that Ben was a successful PR guru. Oh joy. He seemed to have it all. The looks, the job, the girl. My girl. I have to be truthful here . . . I hate him for it.

Anyway, a few search pages in I found this webpage, the link to which is pasted below. I want you to click on it and just think about what this means for you, for you and him, and not only whether morally you can be involved with this man, but also how it will affect your reputation as the founder of Dafina Kampala.

I miss you, Effy. I'm sorry for my disgusting behaviour, but this is something you need to know. I am sure you will thank me for it.

Always yours,

Frank

www.hyperprglobal.com/newbusinessrelationships-ben-lawrence-oil

As Effy read the email, a sick feeling washed over her, and her stomach felt as if it were folding in on itself. Aside from the fact that Frank was coming across as desperately creepy – almost frighteningly so – there seemed to be some big revelation waiting in that link about the man she had fallen so quickly and helplessly in love with.

But what on earth was it going to be?

She picked up her phone, and there was a message from Ben displayed on the screen. What are you doing to me, Effy?! I will miss you so much . . . Ben xxx She felt a huge lump catch in her throat.

This had to be a mistake, a mix-up – maybe Frank had totally lost his mind. But doubt kept creeping in as she stared at the link, too frightened to click on it. What on earth would this webpage reveal?

She started to wonder about Ben, his unusual behaviour, and the way he had held back from sleeping with her; the cryptic things he said about her being 'perfect' and how that scared him. The weird gut feeling she had dismissed a few weeks ago was back, like a trick-or-treater at Halloween, repeatedly knocking on the door and peering through the letterbox. She had ignored this feeling in the past, just as she had done where it concerned Ben, but she had always been proved right in the end. Was this about to happen again? she wondered. Was this all now about to fall into place in the most terrible way?

Effy took a deep breath and clicked on the link. She was instantly greeted with a headline: 'PR 'genius' to save stricken oil company'. And there was a photo of Ben, standing with a man who was also wearing a suit. She had no idea who the man was that Ben was with. She vaguely recognised him, and guessed he must be some big-shot businessman. Unable to hold back her curiosity, she read on:

PR 'GENIUS' TO SAVE STRICKEN OIL COMPANY

A young star of the PR world has pledged to salvage the reputation of an oil company responsible for one of the worst man-made disasters of the 21st century.

Ben Lawrence of Ossa PR has just signed a contract to work with Ropek Oil, the multi-million-dollar company responsible for the tragedy in 2012. The major explosion and subsequent fires at Ropek Oil's HQ in Uganda killed 900 people, injuring and displacing 8,000 locals. It was dubbed one of the most significant killers of innocent people in the developing world after an investigation revealed a catalogue of safety errors by Ropek Oil that led to the fire, started accidentally by an employee. It also emerged that the company had been warned about safety at its HQ on three occasions, but had ignored the advice of inspectors.

Lawrence, who was awarded the title of 'Young PR Executive of the Year 2013' has taken on the controversial role, which aims to turn around the reputation of Ropek Oil in just twelve months.

Lawrence is one of the highest-earning PR executives in London, after cutting his teeth on a variety of high-value contracts working for a range of clients, from telecommunications companies to electricity giants.

CEO of Ossa PR, Dermot Frances, said: 'I am delighted that Ben has taken on this highly responsible role on behalf of Ossa PR. Ben has a natural, and very special talent for public relations which verges on genius, and I know that he will do a great job for Ropek Oil. The 2012 natural disaster was a shocking accident that changed thousands of lives. Ropek Oil has taken responsibility for its errors and is now facing up to its future as an institution, which includes pouring money into the rehabilitation of lives in Africa and trying to help the families affected. Ben will be a great help for them at this time.'

Mr Lawrence was not available for comment. It is rumoured that the contract is worth £10million for Ossa PR.

Effy felt giddy as she finished reading the story, but not in a good way.

Whilst she'd done no more than a bit of drunken ogling at Ben's Facebook, she felt so stupid that she hadn't done more research on Ossa PR.

She felt waves of disappointment and rage pulse through her body. She ran both hands through her curly hair, trying to get some air to her face, which had flushed an angry crimson.

How could he have done this to her? Why didn't he tell her? She felt disgusted that he had agreed to work for this company, the company that was too sloppy to put in any up-to-date fire regulations or guidelines at its premises in Africa, probably as a way of saving money; the company that had ignored warnings and killed so many innocent people. It had caused the mess that she was partially trying to help clean up as part of her work with Dafina Kampala.

She knew the human impact of the Ropek disaster well: she'd seen the photos of the horrific injuries, read the stories, carried out her research.

It might have been vaguely forgivable for her, had Ropek Oil not cheated its way round the rules to save money, had it been a genuine accident. But, to her mind, they had greedily cut corners, which had led to terrible consequences. She felt fury as she reread the lines about Ropek Oil owning up to its mistakes and stepping up to its responsibilities: she knew that wasn't the case. She'd heard the stories about the promises Ropek had made to so many people that they had failed to deliver on, but the working people of Uganda didn't have a loud enough voice to shout out about it, to highlight the fact that Ropek Oil wasn't stepping up to its responsibilities. She knew that they just wanted to start bringing in the money again, as quickly as they could, and they had fallen drastically short in their promises when it had come to cleaning up the mess the company had made.

Ropek Oil had adopted a new logo recently, and there were rumours that it was changing its name. *Ben was probably behind that*, she thought, suddenly seeing him in a whole different light. Their shares had drastically risen recently. She felt sick that she had been dining out on money that Ben had earned in what she considered to be such a filthy endeavour. *No wonder he has so much money*, she fumed, thinking back to his stunning flat, and all the designer things inside it. Everything was top of the range, the latest gadgets and gizmos; a television so big it had startled her and made her own look like a joke when she had got home and stared at it, sitting on top of a kitchen surface, looking pathetic in comparison.

As she sat in front of the computer, stewing on all of this, her mobile started to ring. It was Ben. She hung up on him, angrily slamming her fist down in the region of the end call button. Immediately he tried to call again. Effy wanted to pick up her phone and throw it across the room. She had known it was too good to be true. She had known that those worried feelings she'd had about him were right. She had known that the perfect man couldn't exist.

Her fairytale was broken, smashed into a million pieces, and she would never be able to trust him again.

She must be taking an important call on the landline, Ben thought, as Effy hung up his tenth call to her mobile. It was 3.30 p.m. and his meeting with Ropek Oil had finished early; he was now pacing his office, desperately trying to get hold of her. He and the CEO of Ropek Oil were finally homing in on a new name for the business, but the discussion had ended much sooner than he had expected, as his client had been rushed away to something urgent. This meant that he would be able to surprise Effy by meeting her at the airport, just to be with her for those final moments before she'd board the plane. He just needed a little more information about which flight she was getting, and from which terminal, before he'd be able to make his way there. He was going to try and casually glean the details from her in a phone call, but it was looking like she wasn't available.

He left it ten minutes before trying her again, but the

call was ended once more. Ben felt a sudden feeling of intense worry wash over him. This was so unlike her. Normally she would answer the phone, and she replied to messages quickly – the beauty of their relationship was that there weren't any games. All his insecurities came flooding back, about himself, about the world around him, and he felt himself break out into a cold sweat.

'Ben, what the fuck are you doing?' asked David, who had spotted his colleague pacing the floor in some kind of strange, agitated display as he walked past to chat to Dermot about a new contract. He leant around the door, half in, half out of Ben's office, his red tie dangling in the air where it had freed itself from his suit jacket. His belly hung heavily over his waistband, filling the fabric of his shirt like a bulging water balloon.

Ben looked up at his colleague, both hands behind his head, his jacket splayed out around his torso.

'Argh, it's nothing, mate,' Ben said, irritably, hoping David would go away, and quickly, so he could continue panicking in solitude.

'Oh, come on, bud, talk to me,' David said, as if he were talking to a child indulging in a post-birthday-party strop.

'Sorry, David.' Ben was tight-lipped. 'I'm really sorry to say this, but can you just piss off a minute? I'm having a bit of a crisis here,' he said, shocked by the words coming from his own mouth.

David looked a little taken aback, his eyebrows raised and his mouth open. 'Oh, right. OK, mate, see you later,' he said politely, before tiptoeing out into the corridor and going on with his day.

'Shit, I shouldn't have done that,' Ben whispered to himself, instantly feeling guilty. He wondered if he wasn't overreacting: there had to be a reasonable explanation for this . . . He thought back to all the times he had panicked before and there had never been any actual problem at all. His sister once didn't answer her phone for a whole afternoon and he was absolutely convinced she'd had a car accident. In actuality, the battery had just died on her mobile, and he was left feeling like a fool after leaving her umpteen panicked messages, which she then laughed about, playing them over and over again to a group of friends at a party. It had taken a long time for him to live it down.

Ben shut the door to his office, sat down and took some deep breaths. He tried to use some techniques his therapist had taught him when he was struggling with the memories of the past, hearing her voice in his head: 'Breathe in for five, and out for five, and in for five and out for five. Think of your worries as clouds, observe them but let them drift away. Imagine your worries are being put into boxes, and you are throwing those boxes away . . .'

And blah blah blah. It all sounded so fucking simple.

Suddenly, a text message came through. It was from Effy.

Ben frantically grabbed his phone, knocking a cold cup of coffee all over some important paperwork as he did so.

Ben. I know about you and Ropek Oil. You disgust me. Don't contact me again.

And that was it.

Ben's world fell apart. She knew.

He berated himself once more for not telling her about the contract sooner. Had he told her, he would have been able to explain it better, and he was sure she would have understood . . . Not telling her had made it all worse. But he just hadn't been able to bring himself to do it – he had been trying to prove to himself that he could love her, that he could love. He'd come so far that it became too difficult for him to then potentially jeopardise things.

He wondered how she had found out.

And he was disappointed. So disappointed that she had not spoken to him properly, so he could explain . . . But it did look bad. He knew that.

He thought back to the warnings his sister and mother had given him, about taking on the controversial work, and how he had just brushed them aside. Threatening glares behind a pair of delicate glasses, or a thick, blonde fringe. Maybe they were right. *But no*, he thought, *they weren't right. Effy isn't right*. He thought about the conversation he had had with his therapist and Theo: they had understood him and reassured him that he hadn't done anything wrong, and that she *would* understand . . .

But he realised the mistake he'd made. He'd withheld the information, and for selfish reasons, too. By doing that he'd made a choice. He'd lied to her in some way . . . *Had I just told her at the start, maybe none of this would have happened*, he thought, emotions sweeping over him. He couldn't get the image of Effy out of his mind: her mess of gorgeous curly hair, her beautiful lips, the way she moved and the way she spoke.

Effy had made him happier than he had probably ever been. His suffering, his constant ruminations about that day at the lake were still painful, but he had felt a little better with her. Love was the most powerful and therapeutic drug, he'd learned in recent weeks. She had made him want to be a better man. He knew that, one day, he would tell her about the tragedy of his past, and how much it haunted him. She was the first person who had made him feel like that was possible. But the bad feelings were returning now. The thoughts of 'You don't deserve her' or 'You don't deserve love' . . . He felt that it was God's way of punishing him for his past: he would live a life of financial and material luxury but, like a sad, twisted fairytale, this was how he would pay for what he did – he would never truly be loved, or be able to love someone. These were the thoughts that his therapist had been trying to knock out of him, but they were back now, with a vengeance, clouding his mind.

Ben knew he had to do whatever he could to explain this to her. He had to fix this mess.

Shaking with adrenaline and nerves, he frantically typed, 'Flight, Kampala, Uganda, 27 November, 7 p.m.' into Google. He was so upset that he couldn't see or think straight, the white screen and the letters swirling before his eyes. He had to blink several times to see the search results properly. He was eventually led to a tracking service provided by her airline, and he could see the missing details he needed: the terminal and flight number. He just hoped he'd remembered the name of the airline correctly, and that there wasn't more than one flight going to the same place . . .

Dave reappeared, and opened the door to Ben's office softly. 'Mate, we need you in a meeting. Are you OK to come through to room 1B now?' He looked a little nervous as he delivered his request.

'No, I'm sorry. I can't come to the meeting. I'm not well, I have to go,' Ben muttered, as he memorised the details on the screen and quickly gathered his things. He took a brief glance for luck at the dramatic London scene behind him as he called Warren, desperately hoping he was free.

Twenty-nine
'I need to explain this whole mess'

Thursday 27 November 2014
Somewhere on the M4, London

It was 5.30 p.m. Ben was in the back of Warren's taxi, his palms sweating and his pulse racing. It was raining. Again. While Warren usually wore a kind, warm smile, his face was now screwed up in concentration as they had hit long tailbacks of traffic.

'Fuck! Warren, is there any other way of getting to the airport quicker?' Ben shrieked as he sat in the back of the taxi, his bum at the very edge of the seat and his head resting in his hands, which were cupped together at his chin. Everything about his body language oozed panic.

'I'm sorry, mate, I'm trying. What the hell has happened, anyway? I thought your business trip to New York wasn't for a few weeks? I thought I'd put it in the bloody diary!' Warren replied, sounding tense himself now, which was unusual for him. He was a laidback kind of guy by default, like his factory setting was constant nonchalant happiness.

'No, you are right, it's not for a fortnight yet, but I'm going to the airport for a different reason. I need to see someone . . . I desperately need to . . .' Ben trailed off, unable to finish his sentence, looking out of the window at the hard shoulder of the M4 and wondering if it would be illegal to jump out of the cab and run to the airport.

'Ben, you aren't making much sense, mate. What's happened?' Warren asked, shifting his attention from the front windscreen and turning round to look at his friend. His wrinkled face held a look of genuine concern.

'You know that girl?' Ben asked, the image of Effy filling his mind now. He imagined her sitting in this same seat just days before, on her way to meet him for another incredible night together. He wished she were there with him at that very moment, holding his hand and looking at him in that way she always did.

'Oh, what, the sort I picked up the other day?' Warren asked, glancing forward again – only to see the same huge lorry in front of them, stationary and imposing. He turned back.

'Yes, her,' Ben said.

'Ah, well, whatever's happened with her, I'm sure you'll fix it. She really likes you, Ben. We were talking about you in the taxi on the way to the London Eye,' he said, smiling bashfully.

'No, no, Warren, this is bad. I've really fucked up. I lied to her about something, and now she's found out. Well, I didn't lie, I just failed to tell her something, but I suppose technically that's just as bad. She's about to fly to Uganda and that's why I'm going to the airport. I need to tell her how I feel about her . . . truly. I need to explain this whole mess,' Ben said, rambling now, and banging his fist against the window in pure, unadulterated frustration.

He looked out at the long line of traffic in the lane to his right. A small child in the car next to them was pushing his face against the window of the car he was in and pulling taunting faces at Ben, which included the occasional yanking of both ears.

'Oh, piss off, will you!' Ben shouted, flying into a rage and gesticulating at the child, who, of course, was only spurred on by this, continuing to contort his facial features into new, advanced varieties of mocking, squashed-up expressions.

'Ben, fucking hell, calm down, will you? He's just a kid!' Warren said.

Ben felt ashamed of himself, but so desperately frustrated by the situation.

'Do you love her or something?' Warren asked, matter-of-factly now. The traffic still had not moved an inch.

'Yes, I do, of course . . . I love her! But I'm helpless here, stuck in this sodding traffic jam! We haven't moved so far as a midge's dick in the past twenty minutes!' Ben was shouting loudly now.

Warren sighed knowingly and lit a cigarette. 'Want one?' he asked.

'Yes, of course I bloody do,' Ben said, grabbing the one that was passed back to him and lighting it with shaking hands. He was coming undone, both mentally and physically. His blazer and trousers were creased, and the top of his shirt splayed open crookedly where he had undone some buttons so he could get some air. His hair, which had been carefully styled and sculpted with wax earlier on that day, was now ruffled and messy.

'Do you want to hear a story? I think it might help you,' Warren said kindly, still staring at the back of the lorry which, on closer inspection, had been decorated with a variety of crude cartoons, drawn on by the skilled method of dragging a finger through the layer of filth on it.

'Yeah, sure, go on,' Ben responded, despite feeling not massively positive that this would help. He liked Warren, but he had nothing in common with him, and he wondered how on earth he could help him at a time like this, in a situation so complex and messy.

'I used to be an alcoholic, mate. I met the wife, Linda, when we were nineteen . . . I developed a drinking problem after we had our second little girl, Chloe. I don't know why, Ben, I don't know why it happened. I guess the pressure was too much. I was doing the taxis seven days a week, providing for my family, and I couldn't cope in the end,' Warren said, looking out of the windscreen beyond the lorry and its 'artwork', and into the far distance.

'But I'm not an alcoholic!' Ben said sharply, hating himself for the way he was talking to his friend, all angry and sullen. At the same time, he thought back to all the drunken nights he'd had in recent years, drowning the sorrows of his past and having meaningless sex with various women. He wondered if maybe he *had* been drinking too much in the past few years. It was very much a part of his lifestyle, and that of his friends, like David and Theo.

'I know you ain't. But that's not the point. I'm talking about me, not you,' Warren said firmly, a wry smile on his face.

Ben blushed.

'So, anyway, I was doing a lot of sneaky things. I was drinking behind her back – I knew she didn't like it, so I went out of my way to hide it. Naturally, things got worse.

I was drinking so much that I ended up not going home some nights – you know, kipping on a mate's sofa and all that, just so I could get out-of-my-mind drunk. Anyway, one morning, I was still pissed and I went out to work . . . It's terrible, Ben, what I did,' Warren continued, looking ashamed.

Ben nodded distractedly, thinking about the time that was slipping away and imagining Effy checking in and entering the departure lounge and the parts of the airport that he wouldn't be able to get to . . .

'This one particular morning I was working and I had a little crash – nothing major, and the police turned up. I got breathalysed, and, well, you can imagine what happened. I got hauled up before the courts and I lost my driving licence for a while. I put my whole family in jeopardy, Ben, because I was the sole breadwinner. But Linda was there. She was there in court, she was there for my recovery, she was there for me while I worked at Tesco, packing shelves during my driving ban, and she will always be there for me . . . If this Effy girl, if she truly loves you, you will overcome anything. That's what I'm trying to say. If a man like me can be forgiven by a woman as wonderful as my wife, Linda, then anything can happen.' Warren finished by stubbing out his cigarette in a mug that was filled with previous fag butts from what looked like dozens of sneaky smoking breaks.

The pair sat in silence for a while, processing things. Ben was still a little embarrassed at how rude he'd been to Warren. And while he felt calmer, he still felt no hope that Effy would see this all in the right way.

Suddenly, the lorry ahead of their car started to move. 'Oh, look, the traffic's going again,' Warren said cautiously, starting up his engine.

'Thank God,' Ben said, bobbing up and down in the back of the taxi like a meerkat, trying to work out if they would grind to a halt again.

Miraculously the queues quickly dispersed and they began to pick up speed.

'We're actually pretty close to the airport now. I think you're going to make it,' Warren said, positively.

Ben felt sick. It was 6.05 p.m. If he was lucky, he might be able to find Effy, but he wasn't hopeful. She may well have already checked in by now.

They pulled up to the pick-up and drop-off point at the terminal at 6.15. Ben clambered out of the taxi, Warren shouting at him to give him a ring when he was done.

Ben ran quickly into the terminal, desperately scanning the crowds to try and find Effy. The place was packed. It all felt so hopeless. There were hundreds of people there, milling around, chatting, grabbing snacks and talking on their mobile phones.

He suddenly caught sight of a huge pile of curly red hair. *That must be her*, he thought, his heart rate picking up, but as he started to walk towards the woman, she turned around and revealed an old, haggard face decorated with sweeping fake lashes and baby pink lipstick.

'Shit, shit, shit,' Ben muttered under his breath, scanning all the signs to try and work out where she could be.

He started jogging, squeezing through families swamped by seas of luggage and restless children fiddling around on iPads and moaning at their parents. He weaved in and out of businessmen and women – thin, waif-like suited obstacles – many of them clutching the lethal wheelie cases that he so often cursed when he nearly tripped over them on the London Underground.

But there was no sign of her.

That's it, Ben thought. *Effy will have six months in Uganda thinking I'm an absolute wanker*. Suddenly, Effy appeared, coming out of the ladies' toilets. Her eyes were red and her cheeks were puffy.

'Effy!' Ben shouted instantly. She didn't hear him.

'Excuse me,' he cried, over and over again, as he made his way through what felt like a thick wall of people and suitcases, until he finally caught up with her.

'Effy!' Ben said once more, touching her arm to get her attention.

Effy whipped around, her eyes narrowed like a cat on the defensive. She looked surprised, and also horrified.

She didn't look at all pleased that he was there.

'Ben, for God's sake! Will you just leave me alone? You've done enough!' she yelled loudly, causing a few heads to turn.

'Effy, please,' Ben begged her. 'I just want to talk to you.' He ran a hand through his hair and looked around him, slightly self-consciously. He really didn't want there to be a scene.

All of Effy's rage, frustration and disappointment erupted. 'How on earth did you think it would be OK to work for Ropek Oil and be with me? You know how I feel about those fuckers!' Effy hissed.

She's still beautiful, even when she's fiercely angry, Ben thought, despite being slightly frightened by her fury. 'I can explain, Effy. Please, just sit down with me – I have so much I need to explain.'

Ben just wanted to have a quiet chat with her. Shouting wasn't going to achieve anything. It wasn't his style, and he knew that it wasn't Effy's.

'I don't want to hear your explanations. You covered

this up, Ben, and by doing so, you were dishonest. You knew I wouldn't like it, didn't you? Didn't you!' she cried, her chest heaving visibly. By this point, at least half of the people in the waiting area were staring at them, open-mouthed. One slightly dumpy woman wearing beige shorts and a pair of Birkenstock-style sandals took a nearby seat, opening up what looked like a pre-packed ham sandwich and smiling with glee as the row continued.

Ben didn't know what to say. Yes, he had known that she wouldn't like it . . . but it was such a big thing for him to tell her, especially when he knew he still needed to tell her about Alex . . . And there was another thing – how he felt about her. Thanks to Effy, Ben had achieved something he had never thought possible: he loved her in spite of his fears and the everyday battle against them.

'Effy, I have to tell you how I feel about you.'

'Go on then!' she yelled once more, frantically fishing through her bag to find what Ben assumed was her passport and documents. As she did so, one of her paper swans flicked up in the air and sailed towards the floor, landing softly on the floor. It made him feel sick with nerves.

He'd never seen her so angry; in fact, he'd never seen anyone so angry.

'I love you, Effy. I love you more than anything in the world. I need to be with you,' he said, shouting himself now.

He couldn't believe he'd said it.

A few people in the crowd made 'ahhh' noises and sniggered, which deeply irritated him. He looked at them, flashing them a look of warning that their audience commentary was not appreciated. 'This isn't an episode of *Friends*, you know!' he yelled, throwing his arms out as if he were trying to usher them away. Only a couple of people obeyed his gesture; the rest remained transfixed. He half expected their row to be live tweeted by some guffawing fool with a smartphone.

He gave up on them and turned back to Effy, who had located her passport and was holding it tight in her hands, her knuckles white.

'Well, you know what?' Effy said, calming down a little now, giving Ben some hope that she might be able to talk to him properly.

A few people moved closer so that they could hear.

'You are just like all the rest. You can take that love, and you can have it back, because I don't want anything to do with you. Ever!' she suddenly screamed again, grabbing her bag and storming off into the crowd, completely disappearing.

Ben was left alone, his audience slowly losing interest and starting to go about their business. He stared at the polished floor, at the paper swan just lying there, battered from being in her handbag.

Ben bent down and picked it up. Staring at it for a while, he ran his fingers over the paper, noticing how beautifully made it was.

He felt his heart break.

Effy boarded the plane, hot tears still wet on her face. Her complexion was blotchy, and there was a lot of sniffing and snivelling. Her usually bright and sparkling eyes were red and puffy, and she noticed they were starting to feel sore. Ben's appearance at the airport had made her fly into a rage that had shocked even her. She wasn't usually the type of person to indulge in screaming public rows, it just wasn't her style. She always tutted and rolled her eyes when she saw people yelling at each other in the street – it made her cringe. But Ben had not only compromised her heart, he had also compromised her morals.

She had tried to remain as composed as possible as she had walked down the shaky corridor to the aircraft entrance, their short-lived relationship playing out as a series of images in her mind: the luxurious meals where she would look at him across the table, baffled by how handsome he was; the kisses, the cuddles, the way he smelt; how insanely attracted to him she was. She couldn't believe the level of his deception. It was, to her, unforgivable.

But at least now things made sense.

The occasional person stared at her as she walked past. A middle-aged American man in a flamboyant mustard-yellow suit and tartan shoes asked her if she was scared of flying and offered her a diazepam. She declined, one tissue to her nose, and thanked him all the while, the thought flashing through her mind that she would develop a migraine if she spent any more time looking directly at his outfit.

She told him that her emotional fragility was down to just that – a fear of flying. At least she could pretend her way out of the situation. *I, Effy Jones, am afraid of flying. I am not at all heartbroken*, she told herself over and over again, and she found herself playing a role, slipping into someone else's shoes. She pretended she was worried about the mechanics of the plane, concerned about the chances of a lightning strike, unsure that the emergency doors wouldn't just fly off their hinges mid-flight, the typical kind of stuff. In actuality, she wasn't remotely bothered about flying, she'd done it so many times before.

Effy told herself a few things as she slid down into her window seat and did up her seatbelt, tight across her lap, giving herself a few home truths in the way that her mother always would, or Rosa. She told herself that men didn't mean anything to her, particularly Ben Lawrence. She told herself that she could achieve her dreams. She also told herself that she had to be her own best friend from here on in. She was struggling with feelings of guilt, too: for being so flighty and going on those dates with Ben when she'd had so much work to do. But she also knew that that wasn't entirely rational, and that at some point she'd have to have a life. She knew that her working life was going to catch up with her some day and she hated how guilty she felt if she ever allowed herself a break.

Effy needed something to take her mind off things, something to help her stop thinking. She rooted around in her bag, looking for a book Rosa had lent her, wondering what had happened to the paper swan that had fallen out of her bag at the airport. She pictured it being swept up by a cleaner and chucked away amongst banana skins and coffee cups.

Effy opened the book, a copy of John Green's *The Fault in Our Stars* – and out fell a strange, paper structure, which had been flattened between the pages. *What's this?* she thought. She held it up in front of her face as more and more people filed onto the plane, faffing around with their bags and buckling their seatbelts with a satisfying click.

She pulled at the edges of the paper and eventually it folded out. It was a swan . . . Effy smiled. It had been slightly clumsily made, the edges not quite as sharp as they would be had she made them, the dimensions of each fold not quite right, but it was recognisable all the same. And beautiful, too. It had been crafted from a light pink paper with red roses printed onto it.

Effy pictured Rosa making it, possibly lying in bed with a stack of magazines on her lap, her tongue poking out as she concentrated on it while the Pixies played in the background. Rosa had given the book to her just before she left, telling her to take it with her on the plane. Effy had had no idea there was something hiding inside.

She carefully and instinctively unfolded the swan, the paper crunching softly at her fingertips. As she did so, she could see some writing, in thick, black biro:

Believe with all of your heart that you will do what you were made to do - Orison Swett Marden

And that was it – a few simple words, attributed to a writer of the past but penned by her very best friend in the world.

Thirty
'Ben, are you listening to me?'

Friday 28 November 2014
Sloane Square, London

'I think you might have obsessive compulsive disorder, Ben,' Sally Whittaker said calmly, as she assessed the shadow of a man before her. He had never needed an 'emergency appointment' before, and she was very concerned about him.

Ben was lying in the chair, fiddling with the buttons on the left sleeve of his jacket. He noticed he'd become almost childlike in his level of unhappiness, his body language regressing several years – he felt like a kid trying on his father's suit, the legs trailing round his ankles. He could feel anxiety and despair crawling over his body like a million tiny ants, and he felt uncomfortable no matter what he did, or where he was. There was no safe place any more. Even his own home felt unwelcoming and alien, the expensive coffee maker imposing, the paintings now meaningless, the bed akin to lying on a granite floor.

A miasma of sadness had crept up on him since the row at the airport, and it seemed as if it had stepped inside his body like a ghost, tinting his every movement with despair and aching pain. He sat now, staring at the paper swan Effy had dropped, feeling like it was the only way he could be close to her.

Sally had been taking notes as he spoke about his continuing feelings of guilt surrounding that day, so many years ago.

As she reached her conclusion, she put down her pen and stared into his eyes.

'What? I don't have OCD. I don't go checking doors, turning lights on and off and stuff like that,' Ben said, wondering if his therapist had gone a bit mad herself. To him it seemed like a ridiculous thing to say, based on his knowledge of OCD – which he had gleaned from the media and jokes at the pub.

'It's not as simple as that, Ben,' she said, calmly and firmly.

Ben looked up at the ceiling as she spoke, wondering if he should tune her out and just focus on replaying the events of that cold winter's day again in his head, to try and look for a new angle on it all. He always hoped that one day he would recall the events differently, and realise that he hadn't in fact done the terrible things he thought he had. That he'd somehow remembered it all incorrectly.

'Ben, are you listening to me?' Sally asked.

'Yes, I am.'

'OCD does not always show itself as obsessions and compulsions in the way you are describing them, like going back to check things like switches and sockets over and over again. The examples you have given *are* OCD symptoms, the kind you've probably seen on TV or in the movies,

but there is such a thing as 'pure O' OCD – purely obses-
sional, which is a rumination form of obsessive-compulsive
disorder. I know it's not my place to say it, but I think you
should explore the option of seeing someone for diagnosis.
I've been seeing you for some time now, and I've started
wondering if perhaps this is an affliction you suffer from.
I know, I'm not meant to say this . . . but it's very difficult
watching you suffer, and for so long, and I think you
might need some extra help,' she said, and more softly
now.

Her hair had grown a little longer, beyond shoulder
length now. It was thick and bristly at the ends, hanging
over her snug-looking green cardigan. The winter cold had
arrived, and people all over London had dug out their thick
padded coats and scarves.

'Can you explain it in more detail? I don't quite understand,' Ben said, still wondering what on earth she could
be talking about. *Pure O*, he thought, *sounds a little bizarre*.

'Well, you've been seeing me for quite some time now.
We've discussed the events of that day, back in your youth,
which are causing you frequent and increasing distress in
your adulthood. You tell me that you are unable to stop
thinking about it, and that thinking about it causes you a
lot of hurt and, I think, depressive tendencies.'

Ben nodded as she spoke. As he did so, he pictured Alex's
face, the last smile he could remember before it all went
so horribly sour.

'I think it's possible that this situation, this awful thing
that happened to you, has resulted in a rumination OCD.
This means that you are unable to stop thinking about it.
Your thought processes surrounding it are not entirely
rational in that you are extremely cruel to yourself about
it, so the situation has taken on a whole new slant – and it

seems to be worsening. Ben, I am very concerned about your future if you don't take the step to seek diagnosis from a psychiatrist and get the right treatment. If it turns out that you do suffer from this type of OCD, as I suspect you do, you may be able to get some medication to work alongside the cognitive behavioural therapy we are working on here . . . I just think you need some extra help.' She paused and looked at him kindly. 'And it might benefit or comfort you to know that you are not alone in this, and that a lot of people have similar problems to you, about a whole range of different things. It's just, well, you seem very depressed. I'm really concerned about you,' Sally finished.

Ben noticed she looked a little nervous, her eyes ever so slightly narrowed as she looked at him. He guessed it was in anticipation of how he would react.

'Wow . . . seeing a psychiatrist, eh? Sounds bad,' Ben said, feeling a little despair rising in his chest. He pictured men in white coats wheeling him off into a quiet room, hidden away from the world, where he would spend hours playing Fruit Ninja on his iPhone and fiddling with bubble wrap.

'Lots of people have to see psychiatric doctors, Ben. Mental health problems are very common, and it's up to you whether or not you wish to ignore the stigma. But I suggest you do, for your own welfare,' Sally said bluntly. She obviously felt passionate about all this. She almost seemed a little irritated by his attitude.

'I don't know, Sally. I think I "ruminate" on this day over and over again quite simply because the way I handled it was bad. I feel responsible for something terrible that I did, and I think I'm suffering the inevitable guilt that I deserve,' Ben said, matter-of-factly, seemingly unwilling to accept the suggestion that he may be suffering from something that was skewing his perception of events.

Sally took a deep sigh and made some more notes in her book, the sound of the pen scratching against the paper loud in the room.

'Well, Ben, just have a think about it. Does this issue tend to get worse during stressful times, or changes in your life? For example, you seem to be suffering a lot at the moment. Has anything happened to you recently?' she asked, putting her pen down again and taking a sip of what smelt like herbal tea. Ben could just about pick up the notes, floating across the room: pond water mixed with grass.

Ben wondered if he should tell her about the recent events with Effy. He felt so ashamed of it all. And he knew it was a bad sign when he couldn't even be honest with his own therapist.

'Er, no, nothing's happened. I've got a business trip to New York coming up, but I'm not worried about that, I've done that before,' he said softly, snapping shut and folding in on himself as he stared up at the bumpy texture of the plasterwork on the ceiling.

'Are you sure? How are things with Effy Jones?' Sally probed, shuffling a little in her chair.

'Well, pretty terrible, actually,' he started, realising that he wasn't going to be able to dodge this.

'Right, OK. Can you tell me what happened?' Sally asked, a master of pulling stubborn words from reluctant mouths; a good-looking, highly paid extractor of information.

'Well, we had that discussion recently about her, and how I was concerned she would be angry about my work with Ropek Oil, didn't we? And we came to the conclusion that it was just a part of my job, and that I didn't necessarily need to fear her reaction,' Ben started, relaying it all.

'Yes, and you said that when the time was right you were going to tell her, didn't you?' Sally asked.

'Yes.'

'Did you tell her?'

'No.'

'Right, OK,' Sally said, with no emotion whatsoever in her voice. It was her job to stay neutral. The people who saw her needed to say what they felt without any kind of external influence or fear of judgment.

'The thing is, she found out about the Ropek Oil contract. I don't know how, but she did. She was furious, absolutely incandescent. She reacted exactly how I'd feared she would. We'd had the most incredible few weeks together, after I told her how I felt about her.'

'Well, that's amazing progress, Ben. For you, that's incredible, for a man who was terrified of intimacy beyond sex with women you couldn't attach yourself to in any real way . . . You must be proud of that, and recognise what you did there . . .' She paused. 'Did you tell her about what happened in your past?'

'No, I didn't. I felt I needed to really know her well before I could talk about that. But there's no way I'll get the chance to now – she hates me,' Ben said, glancing down at the floor and examining the strange pattern on the carpet: sporadic black dots embedded in a thick cream shagpile.

He wondered how Effy was doing in Africa; he hoped and prayed that everything was OK, that she had somewhere safe to sleep at night, with the guard she had been promised, and that all the volunteers and support workers would keep their word and fly out to support her.

'Do you think she's overreacting, Ben?'

'Yes, yes, I absolutely do, to be honest.' Ben looked at

Sally, hard. 'But of course I understand that it looks bad. I don't think it helped that I held it back from her. But I wonder if there is something she knows that I don't about Ropek Oil. I remember, when we had dinner ages ago, she made some comment about the fact that the oil company wasn't doing as much to help people as it had promised. I just brushed that aside at the time, and I feel I really need to talk to her,' he said, his brain exploring all the different things that could be going on behind the scenes, things he perhaps didn't know about.

'Do you love her, Ben?' Sally asked, her face once again totally straight and devoid of any kind of expression.

'Yes, I love Effy madly. I'm crazy about her. But I don't deserve her.'

There was a short silence.

'You do, Ben. Listen – on top of potentially going to see someone for a diagnosis, do you think perhaps it's time to go back to the events of that day?' Sally asked, one eyebrow raised a little.

'Oh, Sally, I don't know. We've talked about it so many times, and I never feel better.'

'No, I don't mean talking about it with me. I mean talking about it with someone else.'

Thirty-one

'You must do your best to be happy at all times'

Friday 28 November 2014
Entebbe International Airport, Uganda
The plane landed at Entebbe airport, with a hard thump, at around 4.30 a.m. local time. It hadn't been a smooth flight. It was the kind that prompted people to grind their teeth uncomfortably and think of their loved ones, wherever they were in the world, and just how much they cared for them. Then, they would feel a short rush of relief upon landing at the fact that they had survived, followed quickly by embarrassment at how much they had panicked . . . Effy was glad to be off the plane.

The sun was just starting to rise on a new day in Africa, a colour wheel of reds, pinks and streaky yellows. The average temperatures for the month of November in the capital city, Kampala, were always pretty warm, ranging from 18 to 24 degrees at times. *It's a far cry from the drab, wet streets of London*, Effy thought as she got off the plane, her heart lifting despite itself. She could feel humidity wreathing her. She had layered up for the flight, and now removed her thick jumper.

She went through passport control – always a very serious and intimidating affair – and when she came out on the other side of the barrier, there was chaos.

Despite the fact that it was early in the morning, the airport's arrivals area was packed with taxi drivers and of passengers' relatives, all vying for a space. She tried to read all the signs that were being held up: 'BOB', 'KIGONGO', 'VERONIKA', 'MUSOKE', 'WESESA', 'RICHARD', 'LISA' – the list just went on and on, but none of them said her name.

Nerves flooded Effy's stomach. Lily had arranged for a driver to pick her up and, as she scanned all the signs but didn't see her name, she started to worry that he had got the wrong day.

This is it. I am here. This is it, she thought to herself as she tried to see straight, taking a few deep breaths to calm herself down. But it seemed like the first disaster was already happening, in the long list of disasters Effy had imagined unfolding during her six-month stint in Africa. As the passengers united with their various drivers, or friends and family members, the area started to empty. Soon there were only a few drivers left, clutching signs and starting to look vaguely concerned themselves.

Effy put her backpack down and sat on it, her head between her hands, trying to stay calm. The whole episode with Ben had made her a lot less able to cope with things that wouldn't normally bother her too much, she realised.

'Ifiii? Is anyone here called Ifiiii?' a man started calling out in the near distance.

Effy continued to stare at the floor, hoping her team of

volunteers had made it on time for their flights. She thought about Lily back in the London office, and told herself that she must have faith in her to have organised everything as she promised. Lily had calmed down considerably after realising just how much work had to be done, and she'd flourished into a vital member of the team. Effy had even been able to start paying her a modest wage, asking her to work full-time for the charity from their Angel office.

'I'm looking for a woman. Her name is Ifiii,' she heard again, coming from the right of her. 'She has red, curly hair, and it is the same colour as the sun as it sets. That's what I was told.'

As she heard this, Effy smiled, and slowly pulled her head up from her hands. She imagined Lily trying to have a conversation with the Ugandan chauffeur company, and describing Effy whimsically in this way as she juggled a million other things at the same time.

'She is the founder of a charity and she is here to do good work . . . She is a very important person, a VIP, and I fear I have lost her,' the man continued. He was talking to another driver, his arms waving around nervously. He looked like he was about to cry himself.

It was her driver.

Effy sprang up and walked over to him. He was clutching a sign, which had the letters 'IFI' written in red felt-tip pen in shaky writing.

'Hey, that's me! I'm Effy,' she said, accentuating the 'E' and reaching a hand out to the man, who was now trying to hide the sign, embarrassment written across his face.

'Oh, I'm sorry. I'm Simon, and I will take you to your new house, Eefeeee,' he said, trying to pronounce her name a little better.

'Brilliant – thank you, Simon. It is so nice to meet you,' Effy said, feeling pure relief wash over her.

Simon's hand was dry and bony as she shook it; it was a long handshake, as he didn't seem to want to let go, and he looked as if he were in awe of her.

'Eefeee, you are a hero, or is it heroine you say?' Simon finally said, letting go of her slender hand, his own slapping against a pair of dark grey chinos. He was wearing a smart shirt with black stripes. He looked about twenty-one, with an astonishingly bright and reassuring smile set against his smooth-looking skin. 'Come with me,' he said, as he grabbed her backpack and slung it over his shoulder as if it weighed nothing. Effy was astonished: she'd struggled to drag it from the taxi to the airport check-in area.

As they walked out of the airport, Effy smiled as she recognised the familiar smell of Kampala. It was an unusual scent but she loved it: it smelt a little of dust, diesel fuel and bonfires.

She was back.

A million memories returned to her from the visit to her aunt. The first time she had come to the city she had had the biggest culture shock of her life: the food, the smells and the sights. Kampala was so alien compared to London, but as Effy had experienced it all before, she knew how it worked, and she loved it. Her aunt now lived in New York, and Effy wished she was still around. *But it won't be too long until I see Mum and Dad*, Effy thought, comforted.

They made their way to Simon's car: a beat-up Ford Fiesta covered in dents and great scratches, as if he'd been in a few scrapes on the roads. Effy wasn't remotely surprised: the traffic systems of the city were unbelievable to watch sometimes. The rules of the road seemed as if they had been discarded long ago, and now it was every man for himself, with hundreds of cars negotiating huge roads with broken traffic lights and no real crossing rules. It felt as if there had been some kind of formal system in place a long time ago, but the people of the area had done things their own way, weaving in and out of each other, the occasional dink and bump an inevitable part of everyday life.

Effy always thought London felt imposing and high pressured, but at least there was a kind of system of rules to it all. For example, you would never find cows or chickens in the city roads back home; the traffic lights generally worked; and people vaguely stuck to the conventions of pedestrian crossings and the like. But none of these things applied here in Kampala, a city she had fallen in love with years ago and still did love, now she was back. It was like seeing an old friend.

Effy sat in the front next to Simon and, as they made their way into the centre of Kampala, they talked about what she was hoping to do. Simon was amazed, and continuously told her that she was an inspiration. She listened to him talk about his family – he had a wife and three children. His work as a private taxi driver meant he was on call seven days a week. Finally, they talked about his attitude to life: 'Effy, life is beautiful and short. You must do your very best to be the most happiest you can be all of the times,' he said, as he wiped beads of sweat from his brow.

Effy loved that about Uganda. How people always spoke to you and casually imparted words of wisdom with no sense of the embarrassment or self-consciousness that seemed to prevent people in London from speaking to each other, or often even acknowledging each other's presence on a bus or a train.

As they neared the centre of Kampala, the huge palm trees that had lined the clean streets by the airport had melted into something much more chaotic. As they got closer, the number of people on the pavements and roads increased dramatically. Effy glimpsed the familiar sight of children standing by shanty-like huts, dust and mud covering their feet as they held up coconuts and toys for sale. Even though it was so early in the morning, there were already so many people around. It made central London look calm. People stared at her with interest as they drove along. It wasn't too often that they saw white people in the city, and it prompted comments and general interest, particularly from the children, who were fascinated by the sight of her. So often they had shouted the word *mzungu* at her, a reference to the colour of her skin. It wasn't usually an insult, or an intrusion, just a statement that she was unusual to them and an attempt by them to get her attention.

They had to stop frequently when there was a cow or a few chickens in the road. All the while, men on motorbikes and pushbikes zoomed past them, or weaved around them at breakneck speed.

Eventually they pulled up outside the place where she would be living for six months. It was a tiny flat in a secure development, inhabited by expats and charity workers just like Effy. It certainly wasn't luxurious, but it looked tidily kept and clean, and Effy knew she would be able to make it more homely.

'There you are, Effy – welcome to your home for the next few months. You have my mobile number?' Simon asked, waving his phone around, an old Nokia 6210 with some kind of home-applied metallic coating peeling off.

'I do, thank you, Simon,' she replied, as they got out of the car and Simon pulled her bag off the back seat.

'You can call me whenever you want. I will drive for you as much as I possibly can, unless I am going to the airport, for example, which will make it difficult for me to be with you quickly. But you can pretty much count on me to drive for you all the time,' he repeated, as Effy paid him for the journey. 'So, are you gonna be OK here?' he asked, as he buttoned the cash into the pocket of his shirt. 'When does your guard arrive?' he quizzed, looking around him as if he were trying to fend off trouble.

'I believe he gets here in a couple of hours,' Effy said, calmly.

'OK, well, look after yourself,' Simon replied, before shaking her hand again and gazing at her as if she were a celebrity.

As soon as Effy got inside, she surveyed the place that she would call home for the next half a year. It was exactly as she had expected: lots of white tiles, basic wooden furniture, a newly fitted kitchen that may or may not function fully, thick white curtains, and bars over all the windows. It reminded her of a retirement bungalow, but a little smaller, and less decorative.

Effy locked herself in and pulled her laptop from her bag, setting it up on the kitchen table. The adrenaline was making her hands tremble. Her new office staff had already been to the flat and set up her internet, though the service had been unpredictable at times when she had tried to use the net on previous visits. She logged in and signed on to her emails, preparing to send a message to her friends and family to let them know she had arrived safely. Her support workers and volunteers were due to arrive today and tomorrow, so she was hoping she could catch up on some sleep beforehand.

As she opened her emails, however, she saw she had one

from Ben. Her heart skipped a beat. He'd flickered through her mind once as she'd panicked about where her driver was, but she'd firmly closed that avenue down. And, when she was venturing into the city with Simon, watching all the magical chaos around her, she had managed that fine.

The subject simply read 'Sorry'.

Effy shut the lid of her laptop angrily and crawled into bed, exhausted with fear and excitement, slipping into a light sleep as a brand-new day started in the wonderful city of Kampala.

Thirty-two

'I just read, and . . . get lost in the words'

Tuesday 9 December 2014
Heathrow Airport, London
'Oh fuck, oh fuck, oh fuck-a-duck. I hate flying,' she said, flapping a hand in front of her face, trying to cool herself down.

Ben wasn't brilliant on planes himself, though he rarely gave in to these fears and allowed them to consume him whole. He'd grown rather good at keeping them at arm's length, tickling away at the bottom of his stomach, on all his previous business trips for Ossa PR. Travelling to far-flung destinations, ranging from Hong Kong to Sydney, was a fairly regular part of his job, and this flight wouldn't be much different.

He was prone to being wound up by others, though, so the worst thing that could happen was this – an emotional co-passenger sitting next to him, spiralling into a full-blown panic attack and stretching his already frayed nerves like a child bashing a triangle next to his ear.

'Want a paper bag?' Ben asked, desperately rustling through the pile of magazines and general advertising matter stored in the pocket of the seat in front.

He could have been seated next to anyone: a scientist, a student, someone carrying out a fascinating research project. He could have been discussing something interesting, something that would open his eyes to a whole new part of life he'd never known about but, no, he was stuck next to the world's most neurotic air passenger.

He turned and looked at the woman – though she seemed more of a girl thanks to the fear and vulnerability written all over her face. She must be in her mid-twenties, he guessed. She had thick blonde hair that looked as if it hadn't been brushed once in the past decade, and she was slightly chubby, pale and spotty. She spoke with an East London accent. Her demeanour was making him feel unsettled.

'Yes, please,' she said, grabbing the sick bag Ben had discovered and starting to breathe in and out of it, her eyes wide with fear. He struggled not to laugh out loud at the sight of her.

'Listen, you know that statistically, flying is the safest method of travel?' Ben said, trying to comfort both her and himself.

'I know, I know. I just don't get it, the whole flying thing. I'd feel a little better if, perhaps, the wings flapped, you know?' she said, making large up and down movements with her right hand, almost knocking over a man's coffee across the aisle from her. He tutted and moved it, before going back to reading a copy of *The Times*.

'What? You mean the plane wings? You'd feel better if they flapped up and down?' Ben asked, starting to laugh and flinging his head back, sliding both hands down his face and picturing said plane with giant aluminium wings and moving parts, gliding through the air and dodging the clouds.

'Yes, exactly. I feel very uncomfortable with the fact that they are just stuck there, unmoving,' she said, starting to breathe into the bag again. 'Like, if something goes wrong, you know that we are screwed, right? Because the wings can't flap . . . If, for example, the plane decides to just tilt to one side, we can't flap our way out of it like a bird could,' she continued, waving her free arm around again, more fear flooding her eyes.

'So what brings you on this flight?' Ben asked, changing the subject while looking at the girl and wondering what she was off to do. She was wearing a navy blue suit. It was probably supposed to be smart, but something about the way she wore it made it look shabby and unkempt. He was warming to her, though – there was something so hopeless about her, he just wanted to make her feel better. She was certainly cheering him up with all her talk of planes and flapping wings.

'Business, of course,' she said, between breaths, her glasses sliding helplessly down her nose.

She didn't ask him anything about himself – she was clearly too busy. He couldn't picture her as a businesswoman: it seemed at odds with the person he was speaking to now. He could imagine her stumbling in late for meetings, her skirt tucked into her tights and several snotty tissues wedged into the sleeve of her blazer.

'Would it help if you borrowed my book? It might help take your mind off things?' Ben asked, thrusting a dog-eared copy of *On the Road* by Jack Kerouac in her direction. 'It really helps me when I'm freaking out. I just read, and you know, I get lost in the words,' Ben said, realising that he was lying through his teeth and that it sounded like a cheesy pick-up line. He wasn't able to focus on anything when he was down, let alone a novel, and he was surprised he'd just lied to her like that. He had no need to, except for a desire to make her feel better and distract her from her terror.

'I can't concentrate, I'm sorry,' she said, swapping the bag for a tissue for a few moments as she blew her nose violently, causing a few people to turn around and eyeball her.

The chief cabin steward asked everyone on board to make sure their seatbelts were done up, and Ben couldn't help noticing that she kept checking and double-checking hers.

'It's locked – you don't need to keep checking,' he said flatly as he watched her fiddling frantically with the metal connectors in the middle, the snotty tissue now balancing precariously on her knee.

'The seatbelts are irrelevant, anyway, you know,' she said, her eyes welling with tears. 'If we crashed, we'd all be fucked, regardless,' she continued, her breath speeding up. 'Conspiracy theorists claim the only reason they make you adopt the brace position is so they can identify your dental records more easily!' she shrieked, prompting more evil looks from fellow passengers.

Ben cringed, but was finding the whole thing very funny.

An air hostess was checking the row of seats further down the plane, a wide smile on her face, lipstick in classic red painted on her lips. Luckily she didn't seem to have heard the comment about the brace position. She walked past Ben and his nervous new friend, acknowledging her with a knowing raised eyebrow and an attempt at a reassuring smile, which was somewhat disguised by the amount of foundation she was wearing.

'Well, I think seatbelts are probably relevant – very relevant, in fact. And as for the dental records, I wouldn't get too bogged down in all of that,' Ben said, challenging her.

She looked up at him and smiled a little. Well, as much as he could make out beyond the paper bag which was filled with air and obscuring a lot of her face.

'Look, it'll be OK. Calm down,' he said, awkwardly putting an arm on her shoulder. 'What's your name anyway?'

'Fran,' she said, crossing her legs awkwardly and kicking the seat in front of her hard as she did so. 'Sorry,' she said, to no one in particular.

They felt the plane move as it made its way to its take-off point.

Fran kept huffing and puffing into the bag, her breaths getting even faster now, the paper crunching loudly with each in and out movement.

Ben looked out of the window, watching the runway tarmac blur beneath them.

He thought about Warren and their conversation on the way to the airport. He had been so supportive, so positive about Ben's future, but Ben was still struggling with it all.

As the plane took off, Fran seemed to wind herself up even more, so Ben chatted to her about this and that: the news, politics. When they reached 30,000 feet, she finally started to calm down, though she was still jittery enough to stand out from the other passengers, some of whom were already gearing up for sleep like professional nappers, all kitted out as they were with thick eye-masks, high-tech earplugs and fancy, inflatable neck pillows.

'Hey, let's have some champagne,' Ben said, turning towards her with a mischievous grin on his face.

It was the first time he had offered a woman champagne without the intention of getting her into bed almost immediately afterwards – well, apart from Effy . . . *I really have changed*, he thought to himself.

'What? That's ridiculous!' Fran said, looking at him as if he were casually offering her crack cocaine.

'No, it's not. We're stuck here on this long, boring flight; you are clearly still shitting yourself; champagne rocks, so come on. It makes sense. It's on me,' Ben said, both hands open, his shoulders in the shrug position.

Fran looked around her, as if she were carrying out one final mental check on the plane and its safety features before she could allow herself to have any fun. 'Yeah, OK, sod it – you only live once,' she said, immediately coming across as a woman who certainly didn't live by that kind of theory usually. She looked like the kind of woman who had been thinking about pensions in her late teens, probably had the suggested three months' worth of savings stashed away in the bank and a back-up plan for almost every scenario possible, ranging from being mugged to tripping over a loose paving slab. Her attempt at being carefree didn't sit well with her. Her face and body looked at odds with it – it reminded Ben a little of his father's attempts to dance at weddings.

Ben ordered a bottle of champagne and, within a few moments, it was sitting between them, two glasses full of the stuff, bubbles fizzing frantically all the way to the rim.

'This is kind of you, thank you,' Fran said, as she took a sip of her drink, visibly relaxing as she did so.

'No probs,' Ben said, looking out of the window, only to see inky blue darkness. He pulled the shutter down.

'So, you must have a girlfriend, right?' Fran said, after she had downed her first glass and necked half of the second, giggling away behind her glass as she spoke.

Ben had the feeling that Fran and alcohol did not frequently mix, and feared she may be coming on to him.

'Well, er, I kind of did until recently,' Ben said, feeling his stomach sink. He didn't want to talk too much about this – he could scarcely get Effy off his mind as it was. Sitting next to this strange, startling woman had temporarily steered his thoughts elsewhere. Helping someone else . . . he'd enjoyed it.

'Oh, that's sad. What happened?' she asked, staring at him with barn-owl-like eyes full of curiosity.

'Oh God, well . . .'

'You don't have to tell me.' Fran hiccupped not-so-discreetly. Ben ignored it.

'No, it's OK. She isn't talking to me at the moment. We only met recently, and we'd been dating for a short time, but I really fell for her and I'm, er, not really the type to fall in love,' Ben said. As he did so, he noticed that Fran was drunkenly leaning to one side, twiddling a big clump of matted hair in her fingers. Chipped nail varnish. She had drunk eyes already, unfocused and slightly glazed.

At least she was relaxed now.

'Yeah, you look like the type,' she said, rolling her eyes with a little spurt of alcohol-fuelled attitude.

'Oh, yeah?'

'Yeah, I mean, look at you. You're very good-looking – I mean like, wow, bloody-hell-look-at-that-man-over-there good-looking,' she started, the sentences snapping between each word like twigs. Ben smiled awkwardly and shuffled uncomfortably in his seat as she continued, waving her glass around a little as she spoke. 'You dress well, clearly. I bet you've broken a few hearts,' she said, looking him up and down, surveying his Aztec print shirt and expensive jeans with a knowing look.

Ben felt a flash of guilt and the faces of several women played through his mind, most particularly Marina's. He wondered how she was doing now.

'You look like the kind of guy who has women falling at his feet. I bet you just have fun, you know? You come across like that kind of guy, not wanting to commit, just doing your thing,' she finished, biting her bottom lip.

Ben couldn't tell if she was trying to flirt with him, or whether she was badly masking an utter disdain for 'guys like him'. He was half expecting an ill-thought-out lunge of a kiss one moment, and a giant slap across the chops, from womankind to mankind, the next a grand narrative.

'Well, you seem to have me all boxed up,' Ben said, starting to laugh to himself, only slightly offended but more than a little startled by her.

But she's right, he thought. *That's exactly how I was before Effy.* Before Effy Jones walked into the forty-fifth floor of Tower 100 and subsequently turned his life upside down. Was that how everyone viewed him? The instant impression he gave to so many people without even realising it? It made him shudder. Was that how Effy had thought he was, when they'd first laid eyes on each other? He hoped not. How little people knew the real reason why he was unavailable.

'So, I was going to ask you . . . You don't look like the kind of person I usually see on the flight,' she said, leaning towards him now and pouring them another glass of Moët.

Ben looked around him. She had a point. The plane was full of what looked like medical students in brown linen trousers and hippie sandals; retired couples wearing Bermuda shorts and clutching sun hats; and families wearing brightly coloured robes and shirts. 'What brings a man like you to Uganda?' she asked, eyebrows raised quizzically.

Thirty-three

He wondered if this wasn't an utterly crazy thing to be doing

Wednesday 10 December 2014
Kampala, Uganda

Ben had been to a few places in his time: America – New York, Las Vegas and Los Angeles, business and pleasure; Australia – the East Coast backpackers' route when he was eighteen; Hong Kong, for business; and lots of European cities for weekends away with friends. But he had never been to Africa.

To describe him as a fish out of water would be putting it kindly. He was a sorry sight walking through Customs: tired, grumpy and a little hung-over, having said goodbye to Fran on the plane. She'd grown very fond of him during the flight thanks to his kind words and champagne, so she'd decided to take a risk and give him a nervous kiss on the cheek before she departed, walking backwards while waving goodbye and bashing into someone as she did so.

Ben was touched by the whole encounter and, once again,

he felt that meeting Effy had changed him in more ways than he had originally imagined. He was more inclined to help people now, even the kind of people he would usually ignore or find irritating, and this had shown on the flight and how he had reacted to Fran. He was a little bit more of an open book, despite his constant struggle with his thoughts and the way he felt about himself. The biggest thing was that Ben now realised he'd become shut off without even being aware of it. He would just walk past people in need in London without a second thought because it was somebody else's problem, and had always failed to even make eye contact with anyone he encountered in his day-to-day life who wasn't a friend or colleague. Simple transactions with supermarket or corner-shop staff had been carried out with his head down, with him barely managing to get out a muffled 'Thank you' (if he could be bothered) as he was given his change. It was a shock to him that he'd been so keen to make Fran happy – he was almost uncomfortable with it.

But this isn't easy – none of this is easy, he thought, his mind turning back to the task at hand. Not only did he have to find Effy in a city so alien to him, but he also had to convince her that he wasn't the human version of Cyril Sneer from The Raccoons.

A particularly worrying thing about this trip, for Ben, was that it wouldn't hold all the usual comforts of a business excursion. He wouldn't be picked up at the airport by a friendly driver in a nice, clean car. He wouldn't then be taken to a five-star hotel/retreat where he could quietly work his way through the mini bar and stick it on expenses. He wouldn't be spending evenings after meetings in posh bars with a seemingly endless tab, making mundane chatter with people he'd probably never see again. Despite the blandness of business trips, there was a certain comfort in them, and he felt intimidated by the thought of being in such a different place, alone, without any kind of support.

He was out in Kampala to find Effy Jones, and he didn't have a clue where she was. In addition to that, he didn't know where he would be spending the night. He didn't even know how he would find somewhere decent to stay.

His decision to go to Uganda had all been very off the cuff. He couldn't face another lonely night in his Dalston flat, thinking of this beautiful woman and all that could have been. The simple fact of the matter was that Effy was the first woman who had made him feel like he could possibly love someone, despite his long-held belief that he was dangerous and couldn't be trusted with women's hearts. That was huge. Ben Lawrence loved Effy Jones, he knew this for sure, and if she wasn't going to come to him, then this was what he had to do. He felt like he had too long a list of regrets in his life already, and he didn't want to add letting the woman he loved slip through his fingers to the top of it.

Talking Dermot round had been the first major obstacle. Ben had shuffled into his office nervously – half expecting to be screamed at – and had told him that something bad had happened 'at home', and that he needed some time off, citing 'personal problems' as the reason – a vague, gluey kind of phrase that brought about images of some kind of serious and sensitive situation outside the office that must be addressed. Dermot had looked down at his desk for a few moments, his hands clasped tightly together, grinding his bony jaw, before looking up and telling Ben that he was his most precious member of staff. He had said that his wellbeing was vital, and immediately honoured Ben with two weeks last-minute annual leave, which was good of him, Ben had to acknowledge. In fact, Ben had been surprised at how understanding he was. But he also knew that Dermot wouldn't have been so kind if it wasn't for Ben's expertise and all the money he was bringing in. Dermot was playing his cards well.

Now that Ben was in Kampala, he wondered if this wasn't an utterly crazy thing to be doing. He'd Googled the city of Kampala a few times as he booked his flight – his only knowledge of it having previously come from long chats with Effy, the flame of a candle usually flickering between them. He'd glanced at images on the web and it had all seemed rather chaotic: lots of dirty, busy roads and rubbish. But he hadn't wanted to judge the place before he arrived.

He had brought hope with him, squeezed somewhere in his luggage between the last-minute guidebooks he'd purchased and a few pairs of shorts. He truly hoped that if Effy knew that he would do this for her – fly all the way to Uganda – then maybe she'd realise how serious he was about her. He just had to find her . . .

'Oh wow, oh wow, oh *fuck*! Do you think you could possibly slow down a little?' Ben shrieked, his legs curled tightly around the body of a *boda boda* – a motorbike taxi. He'd read about them vaguely before he left, but little did he know that this form of transport was not for the faint-hearted.

The driver, a painfully thin man who looked to be about eighteen years old was seemingly oblivious to his pleas as they weaved violently between the traffic, Ben's leg occasionally catching on the side of a car or van. He suddenly imagined calling his family from Kampala to tell them that he'd lost a limb in a collision just an hour into his time in the city.

It would be the ultimate fail.

'Listen, mate, can you just slow down?' Ben shouted now, directly into his driver's ear. His hair was flapping in the breeze. Neither of them were wearing helmets – that idea seemed to have been discarded, along with the rules of the road or any kind of speed limit, though there wasn't much of an opportunity for speeding, with all the traffic piled up on every street and narrow alley he could see. Plus there were the chickens, which would dart out into the road at any given moment as if they were already headless.

'Are you new here, *mzungu*?' the boy asked, turning around as he ploughed forwards, only just missing a scruffy cat that had triumphantly stepped out into the road only to leap back onto the pavement in panic.

Ben glanced around him at what seemed like a million stalls selling fruit and vegetables, all blurring before his eyes. 'Yeah, I am . . . can you slow down a bit, or at least be . . . WOAH!' Ben shouted, as the driver slipped suddenly between two moving vehicles, only just making it out the other side unscathed.

It felt nice for Ben to finally feel something real, to have the blood pump through his veins for a reason other than his continual imagined fears. He had never thought the simple notion of transport could be so frightening.

'Sorry, I forget about you boys and girls from London – you don't like the roads out here,' the boy laughed as he started to slow down a little; but it wasn't much of a consolation to Ben. He was very aware he was at the mercy of a teenage boy, raging with hormones and possessing unbridled access to a motorbike. He should have chosen one of the older guys.

'Well, it's not the roads, really, it's more the driving. And what's a *mzungu*?' Ben asked, irritably. He had already noticed people in the street shouting it as they had driven past.

'It means you are white,' the driver said, as they swung heavily into an alleyway and proceeded to bounce uncomfortably over a load of uneven slabs and bricks.

Ben could feel his balls shrivelling quickly.

'Oh, right, OK. Well, I am aware of that, thank you,' Ben said, slightly affronted by the term. 'And my name is Ben, actually, so you can call me that.'

'But I will never see you again, *mzungu*. There are 20,000, or maybe 100,000 of us in the city – I don't know, I'm not good with the numbers. But the odds of me picking you up again are slim,' the boy said flatly, as he drove past a gang of his friends and high-fived each and every one of them, whooping and shouting as he did so, causing the bike to swerve violently from side to side.

Ben scrunched his face up in pure, unadulterated fear. He could feel a tension headache coming on. 'Right. OK then. So you won't happen to know who Effy Jones is, then?' Ben asked, holding onto the bike even more tightly now.

'No, I have never heard of her. Can you loosen your grip on me a bit, Benjamin? I'm concerned you are about to break some of my ribs,' the driver said, before yelling out to a middle-aged man and shrieking with delight.

Ben released his grip, unaware of how tightly he had been clinging on to the boy. All of a sudden the bike stopped violently, skidding to a halt outside what looked like a huge tower block, though some of the walls were missing altogether, exposing whole rooms to the elements. Great thick hunks of torn material were flapping from rickety washing lines, and the entrance was surrounded by rubbish, mainly cardboard boxes and metal wiring. A depressed-looking dog with shabby fur was skulking around, his ribs sticking out like a xylophone.

'This is the best hotel for miles,' the boy said, kicking down the bike stand and jumping off with ease. There was a kind of playful sparkle in his eyes and Ben had no idea if he was being serious or not. Ben realised that the boy was remarkably tall. His gangly, thin legs hosted a pair of exceptionally knobbly knees.

'Pardon?'

'Yeah, this is the one I usually take people to,' the boy said, looking up at it and smiling as if it were a Ritz Carlton.

Ben paid his driver, his hands still shaking from the adrenaline of the ride, before walking towards the entrance of the hotel. Just outside, a guard with a huge gun was sitting astride a chair, asleep.

Brilliant, very bloody safe, Ben thought, carefully picking his way past the rubble outside and going into the reception. He couldn't believe the state of the place. He decided he would stay there for one night, before trying to find something nicer. At least he could lock his stuff away and focus on finding Effy. He quietly cursed himself for not preparing beforehand. He had just assumed it would all be relatively easy.

Ben checked in with the help of a smiley, rotund lady at the reception desk, who moved slowly with a great swing in her hips. After five minutes or so, Ben couldn't believe how long it was taking. He instinctively started to tap his fingers in restless rhythm against the wooden desktop.

'Are you in a rush?' the lady eventually asked, stopping suddenly in her relaxed routine – the effect attention-grabbing, like an unexpected punctuation mark in a meandering sentence. Her previously mellow smile had transformed into a piercing and critical stare. One hand on her curvaceous waist and a sharp, raised eyebrow said it all. She looked wise, teacher-like. She knew his type: pushy, twitchy London folk who shoved their way around the city, and wanted everything done straight away. Ben gulped, suddenly feeling a little scared of her. 'God no, goodness gracious me, no, I've got aaaalllll the time in the world,' he responded, a little sarcastically. He pulled his antsy fingers away from the wooden surface and placed them awkwardly by his side. He tried to make himself look relaxed but it was difficult, his body refused to cooperate. This place, this city, this hotel even, was so far from what he knew . . . 'Oh goooood, I will continue then,' she said with a kind smile and a wink, before casually chucking his passport on the side and disappearing into an unknown room beyond the check-in desk. She audibly larked around with a colleague for a few minutes before coming back and finishing the process. After another ten minutes that felt like an hour, she seemed to be done.

'Your room, it is on the second floor at the left,' she said, flinging him some keys before turning around and wandering off without any explanation of where she was going, or if she'd be back. Ben wondered if anyone was going to come and get his bags . . . *Awks*, he thought. He stood there for a moment or two and realised how ridiculous this was. *Probably not*, he thought, grabbing them and thudding up the cracked marble stairway.

After getting through his rather frustrating check-in experience, he stood outside the door of his room to catch his breath. His heart was pounding and a few beads of sweat trickled slowly down his forehead. Because he wasn't sure how much more he could take, he counted to ten as he slipped the key into the lock to give himself some time to calm down. The lock wobbled mysteriously as he turned it. He waited a few more seconds before opening the door to reveal the room.

'*Holy shit*,' Ben whispered to himself, standing in the doorway and dropping his bag on the floor with a soft thud. He scratched his head as he surveyed the room, his mouth wide open in horror.

It was a bit of a dump to say the very least. The double bed was half collapsed, and stood at a jaunty angle. On closer inspection one leg was snapped in two, wooden splinters protruding from the break. He imagined that one would have to clutch onto one side of the mattress, and try desperately hard not to slip off. The shower was somehow within the room itself, a flimsy curtain separating it from the rest of the space. A dirty drain in the corner was clogged with hair and deceased flies.

He flung his bags on the bed with a loud sigh and walked over to the wardrobe. Both doors were hanging open. Ben pushed them gently to shut them, but they swung out again, creaking sharply as they did so. It made him jump.

A buzzing sound drew his attention to the corner of the room and away from the dodgy-looking furniture. He glanced over to see a large, unidentified – moth-like – bug dying a slow and dramatic death on the tiles. '*Fuck me*,' he whispered to himself, wondering what he should do – he didn't have the energy to go searching for a different hotel, plus, there was something else he had to do more urgently. Eventually, Ben shut the door behind him and walked over to the window. He pushed the thick, dusty fabric of a torn, makeshift curtain to one side, and looked down at the chaos of the street below. He'd never missed the dullness of his life at home so much . . .

Once Ben had got over the horror of his room, he reminded himself why he was there and this gave him a second wind of energy. He got changed into a pair of long denim shorts, a navy T-shirt and some white high-top Converse All Stars before making his way out into the street and taking a deep breath. *He had to find Effy.*

Effy hadn't registered any details of her office on the internet, and he'd tried to contact Rosa for information but she'd simply ignored his Facebook messages. He'd considered trying to contact one of her staff or volunteers in the UK, but he guessed they'd probably have been told to put the phone down on him or something. And as heartbreaking as this all was, he felt that he had to fight for her, and if fighting meant finding the woman he loved in an unknown city, then that was what he would do.

Ben started his hunt by going into every shop, stall and stand, and asking people if they knew who Effy Jones was. He was met with a range of responses from looks of confusion and disdain, to wide, warm smiles and sympathetic nods. But nobody could help. On the way, he managed to accrue a basket of eggs, some bananas and a few handmade tourist souvenirs including a giraffe made of wire, but he was no closer to knowing where he could find her. At one point he thought he'd got close, with an elderly man who seemed to know who she was. Ben had felt his stomach flip over in excitement, until the man had pulled out a magazine cutting of Victoria Beckham and asked if she was who he was looking for, before hobbling off, talking to himself.

After an hour or two of wandering around aimlessly, getting a mixed reception from the locals and irritating a few people as he tried to work out how much money he needed to pay for a Diet Coke, Ben slunk into a tiny café and decided he would have to draw up some kind of plan. The city was so much bigger than he'd imagined, and much more complex. He'd been ignorant, and he was angry at himself for this. He realised that wandering around Kampala asking people if they knew Effy Jones was probably as daft as doing the same in London or Paris.

Ben ordered a tea and sat down. He pulled out a range of maps he'd picked up at the airport, wondering what on earth he was going to do next. He wiped a thin layer of sweat from his forehead, feeling nerves flicker in his chest.

'Hey there, you look like you are all lost at sea,' came a voice, as he was deep in concentration. *Thank God*, Ben thought, turning around with a giant smile.

Sitting on the table next to him was a pale, blond man with a scruffy beard. 'I'm Finn, nice to meet you,' the man said with an Irish accent, reaching out a bony hand and shaking Ben's enthusiastically. It almost hurt.

Finn was wearing a faded green T-shirt, a pair of cargo trousers and some sandals. They made Ben shudder a little bit – he couldn't stand sandals on men – but still, he was so glad to see a friendly face.

'I'm Ben, and yes, I am a little lost,' Ben said, shuffling the maps around for a moment before throwing his arms up into the air dramatically.

'Is this your first time in Uganda?' Finn asked, leaning back in his chair, one arm slung casually over the back of the chair next to him.

He looks totally relaxed, Ben thought, noticing how his own shoulders were so high and tight they may as well have been stapled to his earlobes. 'Yeah,' he said, suddenly feeling a lump in his throat. He thought of London and its nice, smooth pavements, the way cars actually adhered to traffic lights and other conventions, and he wished so badly that he was back there.

'Thought so. Well, you'll bloody love this city before you know it, Ben. Give it twenty-four hours and you'll be totally loved up,' Finn said, grinning and looking at the messy room around him.

Ben wondered if this would actually happen. He feared it might not.

'The people are feckin' awesome here, Ben – amazing. The place is just fantastic. Why are you here?' Finn asked, pouring rather a lot of sugar into what looked like a mug of dirty dishwater.

'I'm here to find Effy Jones. Do you know who she is? Have you met her?' Ben asked, suddenly rising up in his seat, hope etched all over his face. He felt like a fool.

'Effy Jones . . . Effy Jones,' Finn said, repeating her name over and over again.

As he did so, Ben saw Effy in front of him, an imaginary slide show with automatic Instagram-style filters. Beauty. Love. And it was then that he gained a little strength, because he remembered why he was there, and what he had to do, and how much it all meant to him.

'Does she work for World of Difference, the Vodafone programme? I feel like I've heard of her, but I can't place it . . .' Finn said, drumming the fingers of his right hand on the table now.

'No . . . no, she doesn't,' Ben said, crestfallen. 'But she does work for a chari—'

'Where are you staying?' Finn interrupted him.

Ben leant over a little and pointed towards the huge tower block with gaping holes just down the street.

'Oh Jesus, that's not the place you should be. The worst

in the city I reckon! The place is pretty much a building site at the moment anyway. Room number?'

'Of course, of course, just my bloody luck. It's 28. Why?' Ben asked, hoping this guy wasn't some kind of nutcase. He looked a little wild – there was something about his eyes.

'Good to know,' Finn replied, enigmatically. 'You'll find somewhere much nicer to stay, you were unlucky there . . . And what does she look like?' he asked then, taking a sip of his drink.

'She's, erm, very beautiful. I only say that because it's glaringly obvious and I think people would remember her . . . She has this great load of red curls, she's quite pale, a little freckly, very slim, petite . . .' Ben responded, aching inside.

Suddenly he was interrupted by a voice. 'Curls as red as the sun when it sets?' the man asked.

Ben turned around and looked at the guy who had spoken. He was sitting at a table that was lit up by the sunlight filtering through the makeshift curtains. His skin had a sweaty sheen to it. He looked young and fit, and was wearing a nice shirt and tie.

Finn had turned round now, too.

'I'm sorry, I couldn't help but listen to your conversation. Is her hair as red as the sun when it sets?' the man asked again, leaning forward, the table creaking a little under his weight. His elbows were sharp.

'Er, well, yes, I guess so. Maybe not in London, because our sunsets are usually a bit shit, but possibly here, yes,' Ben said, glancing out of the window of the café and looking at the start of his first African sunset. Already it had trumped London's anorexic-looking clouds and puffs of smog and general exhaust-fume crap. 'Sorry, who are you?' Ben then asked, totally confused by the intrusion.

'I'm a taxi driver. I felt I had to say something when I heard you talk about red hair, because I don't see red hair that much. I picked up a woman recently, she had big red curls, just like you say, and before I picked her up she was described to me by a lady in London. The lady said she had hair as red as the sun when it sets.'

Ben was amused by this romanticised description. It was really rather lovely. He was also delighted by this possible lead: 'Well, yes, I'd say that could well be her! When did you pick her up?'

'A few days ago. I don't know – I lost track of time,' the man said hopelessly, shrugging his shoulders a little.

'Can you tell me where she is?' Ben asked, pulling his chair across the linoleum floor to be close to the man, feeling a little frustrated by how vague he was.

'No, I'm sorry. I know she was staying at a house nearby but the security wasn't good enough so she left and went somewhere else. She hired another driver, as I was on another job, and I haven't heard from her.' The man trailed off, looking a little sad.

'Balls,' the Irish man said, looking at Ben with concern.
So close, but yet so far.

'Iffeee is a hero,' the man said, stirring his drink and looking down at the whirls of brown liquid as they span.

'Did you say Iffy?' Ben said, suddenly whispering.

'Yes, that was her name, though I can't spell it, I never could . . .' the young man responded, smiling now at the thought of her. She seemed to have mesmerised him, too. *Join the queue*, Ben thought.

'She is here to do great work for children,' the taxi driver added.

'Yes, yes, bloody hell, that's her!' Ben yelled, causing the few remaining people in the café to look at him, interested

347

in what the commotion was all about. 'Oh God, please, can you just tell me something, anything?' he begged, his stomach in knots.

While the conversation in the café had been useful, it had not brought Ben any closer to Effy's whereabouts; in fact, it all felt rather hopeless. Despite this, he seemed to have made firm friends with Finn, a cameraman working for the BBC. He'd also had an enthusiastic and kind embrace from the young man in the café, who had wished him all the very best on his hunt for Effy.

Later on, Finn had chatted to him about the secret rules of the city, primarily the dos: do eat a 'Rolex' (a rolled chapatti filled with eggs and onion) from a street stand; do visit a local film club screening and get to know the locals, who 'are awesome', according to Finn; and do visit as many landmarks as you can – 'Soak it all up'. And the don'ts: don't ride *boda boda*s – they were responsible for a third of the city's road deaths; don't eat grey eggs; and don't leave your stuff in your hotel room without a chain lock. They swapped details as they shook hands to say goodbye – Finn had to leave to do some filming.

By 9 p.m. Ben decided the only thing he could do was go and get a drink, or five, alone. He had to try and make sense of the mess he was in.

He walked a few streets away from his hotel, and found a bar. It had lively signs outside: the lit-up names of various beers and soft drinks. Again, the side of it was completely open and exposed to the street, except for some flapping, ragged plastic sheets hanging from a metal framework. There were a few expats in there, as well as local people, winding down during some post-work drinks.

It looked so shabby compared to his favourite bars, but Ben hadn't the energy to go hunting for something else. Dispirited and weary, he stepped through the entrance and looked around at the dark interior of the room, which was softly lit with a few candles and garish product signs.

And that was when he saw her.

He wondered if he was imagining it, like a mirage in the desert. But no, it was definitely her. Effy Jones was in the corner of the bar, alone, clutching onto a bit of paper, probably another one of those origami swans . . .

Well, that was easy, he thought, feeling instant tears coming to his eyes.

Thirty-four
Effy was being unreasonable

Wednesday 10 December 2014
Kampala, Uganda

Effy sat in the bar in solitary sadness. Her co-workers had offered to take her out, but tonight she had just wanted to be alone with her thoughts. She was perched on a tall, rickety stool, staring at the crumpled swan, teasing it with her fingers a little and turning it around in her sweaty hands. The paper was totally ruined from where she had angrily scrunched it into a tight ball and thrown it into the wastepaper bin, later retrieving it tearfully, desperate to hold on to something of her best friend.

Rosa had emailed Effy and had not been pleasant, the words like daggers to her heart. The message was a response to a self-pitying email from Effy, which had clearly prompted some withheld feelings that had been bubbling beneath the surface. The words had moved her to angry tears as they spooled before her eyes. Rosa, while telling Effy that she cared for her and loved her, had delivered some home truths, the way she always did.

She told Effy that she was 'unimpressed' with the way she had 'led Frank on so cruelly' at the awards bash, that there was no excuse for it, and added that Effy had to choose between Frank and Ben, and stop 'faffing around'.

The words were painful, each and every one of them, amazing Effy at how language could be used to both heal and hurt.

> You are your own worst enemy sometimes, Effy. I cannot understand how a woman like you, someone so smart, resourceful and intelligent, fails to see the love standing before her. Ben hasn't actually done anything wrong – I'm sure if you would hear him out, you might finally learn something because, dammit, you can be so stubborn sometimes, so quick to jump to the conclusions that work for you.

Effy felt frustrated after reading the message. She had only been able to fill Rosa in vaguely on the events surrounding Ropek Oil, and she hadn't been able to give Rosa enough background about Ben's deception. Rosa had simply said that Ben was the best thing that had happened to her for a long time, and that she thought Effy was being unreasonable.

Effy strongly disagreed with this, and she felt angry that Rosa wasn't on her side this time. It really hurt her. She felt like the only person in the world who truly understood how wicked Ben had been, by holding back the information about his work with Ropek Oil in such a way. But she was still unable to get him out of her mind.

He's probably in New York now, she thought,

remembering him mentioning an upcoming business trip, though she couldn't recall quite when it was. She'd still not read his email – she had no interest in it – and she guessed that he had probably moved on already, picturing him in some Manhattan bar, whispering into the ear of a young American girl, prompting her to giggle orgasmically and twiddle her bangs as she looked at him.

She didn't need him any more. It was over. Anyway, she figured he would be happier on his own, living his playboy lifestyle without the complications of, well, her.

Despite all this mental torture, the first few days of her project had gone remarkably well. Her volunteers and staff had turned up at the first meeting, oozing enthusiasm and brimming with promising skills and ideas. She had been in regular contact with Lily, who was managing things brilliantly in London. The building she had bought was being cleaned out before it would be redecorated, and she had an office space already, near the site. Effy had kept the address of the office secret for now, just while the project was starting. She didn't have enough security and, naturally, like any big venture, some people weren't happy with what she was doing. It was incredible, but exhausting.

She'd had a ridiculously busy day, so she'd headed to the bar to get some alone time. In recent days, Effy had been so inundated that she'd taken to smoking every now and then to try and cope with the pressure. She'd try to hide away somewhere but she was usually discovered by a volunteer, who would scuttle away awkwardly.

Now she just needed to think about how she would respond to Rosa. She knew that her friend just cared for her, but she felt like she didn't understand it, at all.

She was lost in those thoughts when she felt someone

tap her wrist softly. She looked at the hand: smooth, soft skin. She recognised it. *It couldn't be . . .* Yet when she looked up, she saw Ben Lawrence, standing before her with what looked like tears in his eyes.

'What the hell are you doing here?' Effy said, her voice wobbling a little. She couldn't believe he was standing before her. Ben Lawrence in Africa. *It's the most ridiculous combination*, she thought. He looked like a bit of a mess, she noticed, his hair pointing in all directions and a kind of dusty, sweaty sheen to his skin.

She quickly looked around her a few times to check that she wasn't going mad, or imagining him. She noted that a couple of women at the bar were looking directly at him, so he couldn't be a figment of her imagination.

'Effy, please don't fly off into a rage. I came here to talk to you,' Ben said, trying to calm her as he spoke.

He pulled up his own stool and sat opposite her, his face lit blue from a bulb in a nearby beer pump. There was determination in his eyes and, despite his scruffiness, he looked as handsome as ever, she noticed – perhaps even more so. His stubble had grown a little longer than it usually was. *He is disgustingly good-looking*, she thought. *But he isn't on the inside*, she told herself.

'I cannot believe you got the plane to Uganda and found me. Who told you I was here, in this area? Was it Rosa?' Effy said, leaning forward angrily, already thinking of the abusive email she would be sending later to her so-called 'best friend'.

'No, no, no. I contacted Rosa and she didn't get back to me. She's very protective of you . . .' Ben trailed off, looking dully at the wall before glancing back to Effy, biting his bottom lip a little nervously.

'Well, you've made a wasted trip,' Effy said, staring him

in the eyes as he looked up. An expression of sad desperation swept across his beautiful face, and for a moment she almost pitied him. He looked genuinely crushed.

'Can we just talk?' he pleaded now, his palms open on the table.

Effy stayed silent and looked down at the paper swan, her eyes brimming with tears. It was the last thing she needed, she realised.

'I take it you didn't read my email? Or perhaps you chose to ignore what it said?' Ben said, reaching across the table with one hand and trying to cling on to her fingers.

'Get off me,' Effy whispered aggressively, pulling her hand away quickly.

She felt that if he touched her, if she felt his soft fingers against hers, that she might fall in love with him again. While she partly despised him, what Ben had done was genuinely the most romantic thing she had ever experienced. She realised for a moment that if this was happening in a film, she would be shrieking at the TV: 'Just kiss him, you daft cow!' or something similar. But it all felt rather different now it was happening to her.

'Do you have any idea how much you put me at risk by doing this? Can you just imagine it? "Founder of charity in Africa, planning to heal victims of the Ropek disaster, dates the PR busybody of the company responsible"? It's a fucking joke!' she spat.

Ben stood up suddenly, pushing his stool back before moving round to be closer to her. He reached where she was sitting and put one arm on the table and one on the back of Effy's stool. They were almost face to face and she could feel the heat of him. His familiar scent was coming towards her and it made her melt, but she couldn't . . . she just couldn't . . .

'You knew what you were doing was wrong . . . and that's why you didn't tell me,' she growled.

She saw Ben swallow hard as he looked down at the dusty floor, and when he tried to speak again she interrupted him. This time she was pointing a finger angrily, jabbing it into his chest as she spoke. 'You know those so-called efforts to "clean up the mess"?' she asked, her voice dripping sarcasm.

Ben nodded, his nostrils flaring slightly. 'Yeah.'

'They aren't happening, Ben. It's all bullshit,' she said.

Ben raised his eyebrows, looking as if he didn't believe her. 'Well, that's certainly not the story I've been told. As far as I'm aware, they're doing a lot of positive work. Are you telling me my client has lied to me? To everyone?' Ben was breathing fast now, his eyes more intense than she'd ever seen them.

'Ben, do you want to do something to make this better?' she asked, her face softening a little.

But before she had the chance to tell him what that thing was, he kissed her.

And she kissed him back.

Ben put a hand gently around her face, and the other around her waist. He pulled her close and she felt the familiar rush of emotions – and tears. It was like he'd never wanted anyone so much. His soft lips against hers, that familiar feeling, it was all coming back now. The kiss she had craved all the time before he had let her down . . .

Effy put a hand on Ben's chest and shoved him backwards. He looked shocked. There were a few moments of quiet before she spoke again.

'Get up, turn around, walk out of the bar, get a flight home and don't come back,' she said calmly, before turning away from him in her chair.

Thirty-five
'He's no one'

Thursday 11 December 2014
Kampala, Uganda

Ben had already booked his flight home. With a heavy heart, he had struggled to summon the strength to use the one hotel computer, which looked like it dated back to the late eighties. The keyboard was covered in filth, and it took what felt like ten minutes to load each webpage. His new flight would leave the following day at 7 a.m.

He could have stayed in Uganda for a week or so, moved to a better hotel or something . . . he'd certainly thought about it. He could have fallen in love with the place, as Finn had promised, but he felt so low he just needed to be at home, near his friends and family. Ben could feel himself caving in, somewhere deep in his heart, and he had to be in the right place to try and recover from it.

He saw the promise of Kampala; he had already noticed it in the warm smiles and friendly gestures of local people, in the bright faces of the children as they made their way to school, and he knew he would probably end up adoring the city. But Ben had never felt such sadness in his soul, and he became frightened of it. Frightened of the way a man could grow to despise himself. His mother had always told him that he had to be his own best friend, but his personal bully was back and alive inside him. Kampala simply wasn't the right place for him to be in such a difficult frame of mind.

How brutal it had been to finally find Effy, only to be spoken to like he was something unpleasant she'd discovered on the bottom of her shoe. The worst part of it all was that he totally understood why she was angry. It did sound bad, and it would affect her reputation, and she'd worked too hard to risk it all on love . . . That was, if she had even loved him in the first place.

He doubted that now. The kind of love he felt for her could have overcome anything. She seemed to give up at the first sign of trouble. But that kiss . . . she'd taken quite some time to push him away . . .

Finn had knocked on the door of Ben's hotel room at 1 a.m., clutching a piece of paper with the address of Effy's office. He'd managed to find it out from some colleagues who had heard of her project.

Ben had wearily accepted it, but then crawled back into his slanty bed, bleary-eyed and sad to the pit of his stomach, sure he wouldn't be using it.

It wasn't until he woke up that next morning at 6 a.m. to the sound of what must have been at least 100 crowing cockerels that he remembered the cheque in his wallet. It was worth £40,000, and was made out to Dafina Kampala. He'd had it ready to give to her when he told her about his work with Ropek Oil, when the time felt right . . . How he wished now he'd broached it sooner.

He still loved Effy, despite all her disdain for him, but

he also knew when to stop. If he continued to declare his feelings for her after today, after this trip, he would be plain creepy, desperate even . . . some might actually label him that already, he realised for blindly booking a flight to Uganda to find her.

He knew that you could never force someone to love you, just in the way Marina had known the exact moment she should give up on him, and walk out of the door, leaving him in his room amongst crumpled sheets and guilt. Finally he knew how it felt to experience this, rather than being the one telling others 'No'. It was painful, and new feelings of remorse lanced through him as he thought of all the women who had walked out of his life with tears in their eyes and shattered hopes. He finally knew how they must have felt.

There was a saying he saw every time he went back to his parents' house, hanging on a slate in the kitchen. It was written in thick blue chalk. It had never meant anything to him before, but now each and every word seemed to ring true:

> *God, grant me the serenity to accept the things I cannot change, the courage to change the things I can, and wisdom to know the difference.*

It was from the Serenity Prayer. Ben had previously stared at it, usually hung-over, wondering what the mumbo jumbo meant and quietly amused by how sentimental his mother was. Now he knew and understood, because in the last few weeks Ben had grown up. *This is one of those moments*, he thought. He had to accept that he could not change Effy's mind.

Being in Africa had also given Ben some clarity on the events of *that* day, from so many years ago, which dogged him.

Sally had made quite a remarkable suggestion to him: a way he might perhaps be able to face up to the past and find a way to accept it. It hadn't been until he was thousands of miles away from London that he had finally felt he might just be able to do it. That it might be the right thing . . .

Before he left to go to London, he had just one thing to do. Ben wanted it to be over quickly, so that it caused him as little pain as possible, before he would slip quietly out of Effy's life forever.

Despite the warnings about the *boda boda*s, Ben flagged one down in the street. He was not in the frame of mind for cautious behaviour. He didn't care about himself any more; he just wanted to get there as quickly as he could.

The driver was a little older this time, wearing grey suit trousers and a linen shirt. Ben said nothing, but simply thrust the piece of paper Finn had given to him in front of his face.

'Sure thing, man, hop on,' the man said, revving his engine.

'Hi, Effy. It's such a pleasure to meet you. I'm Damon,' the man said as he stood in the doorway of Effy's brand-new office.

Damon was tall and handsome, and had a rack of teeth so white they nearly blinded her.

'Oh, hello, Damon. Brilliant to finally meet you,' she said, squinting as she looked at him – partially due to the teeth, and also partially due to the bright sunlight behind him.

'I'm thrilled to be out here. I can't wait to get going,' he said, with so much energy and enthusiasm, he reminded her a little of Lily when they had first met in the café in Crouch End.

Effy and Damon had been exchanging emails for some months. He had offered to be a media volunteer, and he had decided to come out to Uganda for three months with his video camera, laptop and other various gadgets to film Dafina Kampala as it went from a range of muddled plans and complex funding bids to a real, live, working project.

It would be as beneficial for him as it was her: she would end up with some fantastic publicity material to float online and show at dinner talks; and he would have some brilliant experience for his CV. A lot of her volunteer relationships were like that, and she pledged to support the people who came to help her as much as she possibly could, getting the best out of all the agreements for both her charity and the individual concerned.

She was a little dazed by Damon, however: he was so tall and happy. It was lovely to have his presence in the office, but all she could think about was Ben.

Effy was thinking about the night before, shocked by how rude she had been to him, how angry. Admittedly, she had felt a flicker of sadness when Ben had in fact followed her instructions and walked out of the bar. She couldn't get that kiss out of her mind . . .

A bad night's sleep had ensued. She'd read Rosa's email over and over, wondering – for the first time – if she had perhaps been a little cruel to him. He didn't seem to know the true extent of Ropek Oil's poor efforts to make amends . . . In fact, he seemed quite clueless and misled.

Her mind had just flipped from one side of the coin to the other. She wondered where Ben was now, and how he was feeling, yet part of her still resented him so much.

'Hey, if you don't mind, can I set up in the corner of the room?' Damon said, waking her from the daydream she had become momentarily lost in.

'Sorry, yeah, of course,' she said, bending down and ushering a chicken out of the room, which had dozily ambled into the small space, before shutting the office door to keep the room cool. Effy turned back to her computer, aware of how socially inept she was being.

'Sorry, Damon,' she said, turning around to face him. 'Things are a bit stressful at the moment . . . please set up. The kitchen is next door if you want tea or coffee. Let's have dinner this evening and talk about all the exciting things we'll do,' she said, smiling. Damon's face lit up. 'Absolutely – no problem at all,' he said, delighted, already tangled up in a bunch of electrical cables.

Effy was about to turn back to her work – to answer what felt like a thousand emails – when there was a knock at the door.

'I can get it if you like,' Damon said, carefully stepping out of the mass of wires around his feet.

'Oh, thanks, that would be great,' she replied, returning to her inbox.

Damon stepped over to the office door, then went into the street outside, shutting it behind him. Effy thought this was odd, but just assumed it was one of the other volunteers who'd come to meet him.

A couple of minutes later, Damon opened the door sheepishly. 'There's some guy here to see you, Effy. His name's Ben,' he said, a look of slight confusion on his face.

Effy felt her stomach sink. As much as she was confused by the situation, and as much as she had been thinking about him, she didn't want to see him again now. She was surprised he was back.

'Let him in,' she said flatly.

With that, Damon disappeared outside for a while as

Ben passed him, stepping into the office and closing the door softly behind him.

Effy looked him up and down: he had the stance of the ashamed – shoulders slumped ever so slightly forward, his eyes wide and sad. 'Listen, Effy. I'm not here to talk about what's happened if that's what you are worried about,' he started, looking a little fed up.

He had taken the words right out of her mouth. She wasn't sure what to do or say: all she knew was that looking at him right then, she realised how much she missed him. It was touching and moving that he'd come all the way to Uganda to see her. She couldn't quite believe it.

But it still didn't change what had happened.

'What do you want?' she asked quietly. All her anger seemed to have melted away and slunk off into the distance, leaving her tired and almost devoid of any ability to make clear and informed decisions.

Effy looked at Ben as he shuffled his feet uncomfortably. While he was still the beautiful man who had made her so happy, he looked different. There was a certain turn about his features – a sadness in the way his whole frame hung from his shoulders to the tips of his fingers, that worried her. He carried a weight of melancholy with him like a heavy backpack. She'd never seen him look this bad before.

'I just wanted to give you this, Effy,' he said, holding out a small piece of paper in the space between them.

Effy could hear birds singing loudly, while one of the nurses she had hired was hanging washing on a line outside the office, humming sweet songs to herself.

Effy took the paper and opened it. A cheque, for £40,000.

'Contrary to what you probably believe, I didn't earn millions from this contract with Ropek Oil. I got a bonus, one time, from Dermot. I appreciate it's still a lot of money, but it belongs to Dafina Kampala. I was always going to give this to you – I was just hoping that at some point you'd actually care to listen to me, for once,' Ben said.

He watched Effy as she stared at the cheque. When she looked up again, she noticed a little flicker of happiness across his lips now, like this was the only thing he could do in this bizarre situation that brought any real light to the darkness of it all.

Effy didn't know what to say. It was a substantial sum in the UK, let alone in Africa. It would really help. But was it wrong to take the money? She felt like there was no time to have this argument in her head.

'Thank you, Ben,' she said, forcing a smile.

'That's OK. Good luck, Effy,' he said, before turning around and walking out of the office, the door slamming behind him.

Effy was left in silence for a few moments; the most cavernous, aching quiet she had experienced in a long time. She felt a little twitch in her legs, a feeling that maybe she should run after him, forgive him, be a little more under-standing. She really had fallen in love with him . . .

She played back their first kiss; the night on the London Eye; the hours they had spent talking in bed. *But no*, she thought. *What's done is done*. As handsome and lovely as Ben seemed, he was not to be trusted. He was dangerous.

Damon broke the quiet by carefully opening the door and creeping back into the office. 'Who was that?' he asked, a strange expression on his face. He had clearly picked up on the tension already.

'Oh, no one,' Effy said, pushing the cheque into a cashbox by her computer. 'He's no one,' she repeated, before turning back to her emails.

Thirty-six

'I thought you'd never come back'

Saturday 20 December 2014
Ambleside village, Kent

Ben drove carefully through the quiet country lanes. He looked out when he could at the rolling hills, decorated in a thin layer of frost like a dusting of icing on a cake. The trees were no longer clumped in thick, green leaves as he had remembered from the summers of his youth: they stood neatly at the edges of the fields like carefully ruled lines, from a distance. He knew that up close they were cold and uninviting. The gnarled, twisted roots gripping firmly into the ground, and thin, black branches stripped bare and slicked with rainwater. It felt almost like they were taunting him – angry people, their fists raised like a mob.

He was about to confront his biggest fear and, as he thought about it, his hands shook. It was by far the most frightening thing he'd ever done. Telling Effy Jones how he felt about her was terrifying, going to Uganda to try and patch things up was scary, but he was petrified to the core at the prospect of this.

Facing up to that day, all those years ago, when he was seventeen and the course of his life changed forever.

Sally Whittaker had suggested that he make this trip the same day she had shared the belief that he had OCD. He had quickly cast aside the suggestion of obsessive-compulsive disorder. It seemed so ridiculous to him, but the idea of the trip had stuck in his mind. He had ignored it at first. How on earth would he be welcome in Leanne's home? How could he hold his head up in the village he grew up in, where the tragedy happened? How could he stand the agony of retracing his steps that day, when he already felt so much crushing sadness it was hard to carry on?

Somewhere, and somehow, he'd found the strength to be able to try. It was a combination of continued agony, and his trip to Uganda, which had helped him to put things into perspective. He had to face up to his past in order to overcome it, and this was the only way he would be able to do it. While his heart was broken over Effy, the situation had provided a sliver of hope: that he could love, that he was capable of it. But, sadly, it had only reinforced his fear of hurting people . . . This had pushed him into a sadness so overwhelming he could almost taste it. It wrapped itself around him, thick like a duvet, weighing him down.

His mother had called Leanne for him. Ben had been sitting in the kitchen as she did so, listening carefully to the conversation and doodling on a piece of paper with a green biro. At first there were the vague hellos, the how are yous, then the request, and then proceeding umms and ahhs. He had no idea what the verdict would be until his mother got off the phone and turned to him with tears in her eyes. 'She said yes.'

Ben's sadness and guilt were driving him slowly mad, and he hoped that somehow this would help. It would make or break him, he knew that. It was his last chance – time, for him, was running out.

He considered all this as he navigated his sports car through the thin, winding road that led to the village, and Leanne's house, at the heart of it. He couldn't believe she still lived there, in a home filled with so much pain; maybe it was the only thing she had left to remember Alex by.

Ben parked outside her cottage, stopped the engine and rested his forehead gently on the steering wheel. The village was silent. He felt sick.

Christmas decorations had been strung up outside the houses: giant reindeers and sledges that would no doubt light up that night, making the place look magical and beautiful. It didn't seem right that festivities could carry on so joyfully, without Alex around any more . . . He looked to his right at the church where he used to attend Sunday school and, as he gazed at the rows of houses and the village shop, a million memories flooded back to him. Memories of his childhood, of happiness, joy and magic . . . which had then turned into something different, one of the saddest things he'd ever known.

It was now or never.

Ben walked up the steps to Leanne's front door, his legs like jelly. The door was painted in a glossy navy blue. It had never looked like that when he was a teenager, knocking on it almost every evening, desperate to see Alex. Then, it was painted green. The front garden had changed too: hard paving had made way for beds of what he imagined were beautiful flowers during the summer time. The three garden gnomes the family had owned had disappeared but he still remembered them clearly: their cheerful faces, and chubby pottery hands gripping onto fishing rods and wheelbarrows.

Ben took a deep breath and knocked on the front door. Two minutes passed before Leanne answered. They felt like an eternity to Ben, who had already started wondering if she had backed out of the whole idea. But when she opened the door and smiled at him, he felt waves of tension peel away from him and float off into the distance.

Leanne was hardly recognisable. She was much thinner than he remembered, and her once brown hair was now totally grey. It was long, and hung around her gaunt face, making her look pale and tired. But she was still Leanne . . . he could still make it out in her eyes and her smile. He had flashbacks to all those evenings he had spent in her company – her, sitting across the table, watching him with amused disdain as he shovelled bangers and mash into his mouth, spilling peas on the floor and getting the carpets dirty with his trainers.

'I thought you'd never come back,' she said, bursting into tears and pulling him into a warm embrace.

Ben couldn't believe she was being so nice to him, and he felt huge waves of emotion thread through his body as they hugged. He'd already imagined how this meeting might go, he'd already pictured her looks of hatred, the sharp, painful words she would deliver. He certainly hadn't expected this.

'Come in,' she said, before releasing him, ushering him into the hallway and shutting the door.

The house was dark, and a sadness still haunted the rooms, Ben noticed. Each and every surface was cluttered with family photos, images of a life that was once whole, because Alex was in it. This was all that was left, photos and memories.

The first thing he did was pick up a photo of Alex. He would have normally asked permission to do so, but he couldn't hold himself back.

He felt like he had been punched in the stomach as he looked at her.

She must have been around sixteen years old, so it must have been taken in the year before she died, he guessed. Ben stared at her face: those sparkling eyes he remembered so clearly, her long, thick hair, that self-assured look she always had, and felt a huge lump build in his throat. The first girl he ever loved and, before Effy Jones, the only girl he had ever loved . . . Looking at her now, she was just a young girl. It was just an old picture in a carefully polished frame, but he remembered her as if not a single day had passed. He almost felt himself melt down into a teenager once more: he looked down at his feet and instead of his expensive leather brogues, he pictured his battered trainers, tracksuit bottoms covered in holes and sporadic patches of mud.

Leanne watched him from the edge of the doorway, tears in her eyes. There was no sound but Ben's short, sharp breathing as he tried desperately hard not to break down.

'She would have been so good at life,' he said quietly, sadness consuming his features. He pictured her as a woman in her mid-twenties, perhaps a newly qualified lawyer, or a dance teacher . . . He'd imagined so many possible lives for her, and they were all wonderful.

'I know,' Leanne said, walking into the living room and taking a seat, her light frame sinking into a brown leather sofa.

Ben walked over to the sofa, carrying the picture with him, and sat down. 'I'm so sorry, Leanne. I'm so, so sorry,' he said, overwhelming swirls of emotion washing over him.

He had known this would be emotional, but he had never expected it would be this sad. But he wouldn't cry, he wouldn't allow it, he didn't feel he deserved to. He felt that in some way, it would be almost selfish of him to cry, with what he'd put Leanne through.

She moved over to him and wrapped her arms around him. It was a little unexpected, but nothing about it felt unnatural. A bereaved woman, fifty-five years old, holding on to a grown man she would never normally have associated with. The pair of them, as heartbroken as the day it happened. She was from the countryside and, from what Ben had imagined, her days consisted of church cake sales and long, silent walks. He was from the city, his life full of the demands of his career, flash cars and skyscraper buildings. They were worlds apart, but totally bound by the same tragedy.

'You've grown into quite a fine young man,' Leanne whispered.

Ben felt guilt at these words. *Why would she like me? Why?* He looked down at his shoes. Shame.

'Alex would still have loved you if she'd grown up too, I'm sure,' she continued.

'This isn't about me,' he said quietly.

'It is, Ben. It's a lot about you,' she said.

'What do you mean?' he asked, peeling himself away from her arms and looking into her bloodshot eyes. He began tracing his fingers over the glass of the photo frame.

'I've spoken to your mother a few times, Ben. She said you have never forgiven yourself. She describes you as a handsome, successful man with the whole world at his feet, except he has never been able to truly live . . . since it all . . . happened,' she said, a motherly kindness in her eyes.

Ben didn't know what to say. He hadn't realised they had spoken so much. She had somehow summed it all up in once sentence.

'She tells me you live a tortured existence, and that you won't forgive yourself for what happened . . . Is that true, Ben?' Leanne asked, her eyes narrowing, a look of true concern on her face.

Ben paused, and then nodded, still trying desperately not to break down. His mind flashed back to all the drunken nights he would roll into bed, after frantically trying to take the edge off, his wasteful behaviour, the cheap thrills, anything he could get his hands on to take the pain away.

'You see the thing is, Ben . . . The thing about guilt, and grief, is that if you don't find a way to let them go somehow, they will consume you.' She trailed off, looking down at her skirt, which she was smoothing with her wrinkled hands. Despite the creases, her thin, ageing skin still had a kind of youthful translucency to it.

'Do you still suffer?' Ben asked, instantly berating himself for such an obvious, stupid question. But she seemed so much more together than he was. He was curious. He'd always pictured her going silently mad in her suburban home, her hands by her ears, her face reminiscent of *The Scream* painting. It was just imagery he pictured in his mind, but now he had faced up to the reality it all seemed so different.

'Yes, of course I do. I have lived through some of the darkest times of my life without my little girl by my side, growing up and turning into a woman. But I have turned a corner. I found love again after Alex's dad left. I feel happiness now, every day. Alex is a fond memory and she never leaves me, but I am able to live my life now, finally, and that is what you must do,' she added, pursing her lips together at the end of her sentence.

A fat ginger cat curled itself around the doorframe as if assessing the room and checking it was safe to come in, before lolloping heavily across the carpet and lying down in front of the fire that glowed warmly in the grate.

Then Ben asked the most terrifying question he had ever posed: 'I was responsible. You must still blame me, Leanne. Do—do you?' The letters and words spilled from his lips and hung in the air. There were a few moments of silence, broken only by his own heartbeat rushing through his ears and the gentle ticking of a clock.

'No! Good heavens, no,' she said, pulling him towards her and holding him once more. 'Ben, life is beautiful. You must find a way to live it. What happened was not your fault. It was a tragic accident, an *accident*, Ben, do you hear me? You didn't know what to do. You were a kid, for goodness' sake. You must move on. We can't lose more than one life through the sad events of that day.'

More than one life. She was talking about him. His life. What did she mean? Had she picked up on the raging sadness that hung like lead in his limbs? Did she think that one day it might all become too much for him and he might try and . . . disappear . . . as he'd thought so many times when he stared at train tracks, flickering with electricity in the depths of the London Underground, and wondered what it would be like to escape the pain.

With that thought, Ben's mind darted back to a recent tube journey. He'd been waiting for a Circle line train to turn up and, while he did so, he had spotted a mouse. It scuttled up from the tracks and took a few steps towards him, before pausing for a while. Then, when it felt comfortable enough, it had taken a few steps closer. The mouse had repeated this over and over until he or she was almost touching Ben's shoe. And then a train had come roaring into the station and the mouse had disappeared. Back to square one, probably to then try and repeat the whole pointless ritual with some other fool with an Oyster card. Ben had wondered what the point of that mouse was; that silly mouse that lived in the underground. Then he had wondered what the point of anything was: the point of working, the point of money, the point of flat-screen TVs and expensive dinners. For so many years nothing had meant anything to him. But, in recent months, he'd started to feel differently, he'd started to live again.

But now Effy was gone, everything he was surrounded by, everything he was, all seemed so empty once more.

He'd never felt so hopeless.

Leanne cleared her throat softly, waking Ben from his thoughts.

'What happened to Betty?' Ben asked, remembering the dog that had started it all. The cute animal that had stupidly jumped into the water, and somehow casually climbed out. She had stood by his feet, wet and shivering as, frozen in horror, Ben had watched Alex drown.

'Oh, she lived for some time. About six years after the accident. She died peacefully in her sleep, an old and happy dog,' Leanne said, pointing towards another photo on a side table.

Ben felt a shiver run down his spine.

'Go up to her room, Ben. I've kept it exactly the same . . . And there's something in there that might help you,' she whispered.

Ben shook his head, numbly. 'I don't think I can . . . I don't think I can cope with it,' he said.

'How about I make you a cup of tea, and you can think about it. How does that sound?' she asked, squeezing his shoulder and walking slowly towards the kitchen.

An hour later, Ben slowly walked up the stairs that led to the top of the house. Now that he was alone, he wiped a few fat tears from his eyes, trying to stop the rest from flowing. Everything was exactly the same: the stairway up to it still decorated with the beige wallpaper with pink triangles printed all over it, so very trendy at the time. Now it just looked dated and tired.

Alex's room was in a loft conversion. Ben remembered it being full of posters of the lead singers of boy bands, and there had been a lot of books, but that was all he could recall. He felt nervous going up there; again, it was as if he were stepping back in time, into his teenage shoes. He remembered how exciting it was to visit her when he was younger; how he would usually come upstairs to find her sprawled out across her duvet, painting her nails black, or watching a film. There would always be a haze of perfume around her. A fragrant halo around this fallen angel. How his heart would explode with butterflies because she was his first love and there was nothing more amazing in the world to him than spending time in her room, trying to understand her, and wondering how on earth one person could need so many pots of nail varnish.

He paused at the door, which still had a huge sticker over the front of it, emblazoned with the words: 'Alex's room. Enter if you dare.' He slowly pushed the door open and walked in.

It was exactly how it had been left. Like a time capsule, a moment frozen there for more than a decade. Ben had imagined it would be a little creepy, but it wasn't at all, and he totally understood why Leanne had kept this part of the house exactly as it had been.

It was so painful to be there, but therapeutic at the same time. Ben felt his emotions rise again as he walked over to the window seat and looked out at the garden. He and Alex had sat there together so many times, and talked about what they wanted to do when they 'grew up'. It was where they had had their first kiss, before Alex's father had stormed upstairs and interrupted them, ordering Ben to leave because they 'both had school the next day and it was far too late'.

Ben walked over to the bed, which still bore the stains of spilt foundation and eye shadow, which made him laugh a little, despite it all.

In the middle of the bed was a small package, wrapped in brown paper. Written on it, in thick, black writing, was his name. He picked it up and turned it over. Leanne had written on the bottom of the box too:

For Ben. May this bring you comfort in the difficult times. Remember the happiness of your youth and only keep the best bits close to your heart. Leanne xxx

He tore away the paper, never one to carefully unpick parcels and presents in a bid to save the wrapping, unlike his mother, who stored it carefully folded in a kitchen drawer.

Inside was a notebook, with a thick, black cardboard cover. Ben turned it over in his hands, unsure of what it could be at first. There was no writing on the cover to give anything away. When he turned the book on its side he could see the layers of pages inside, wavy and slightly crinkled with age.

He opened it to the first page and instantly recognised the writing. It was Alex's. As he flipped through, he realised that this must be one of her diaries. He couldn't believe that Leanne would give such a precious thing to him – and why? he wondered. What comfort could be found in the musings of the teenage girl he'd loved when he was a boy?

Ben snapped it shut, and walked back over to the window seat, unable to take it all in.

Thirty-seven
I met a boy today

I met a boy today.

Well, actually, it's more accurate to say that he met me.

I was just going about my business, riding my bike while thinking about all the homework I have to do this week, and he came running up to me. He was kind of frantic, waving his arms around and all that. At first I thought he was about to tell me there was a fire nearby, a gas leak, or a giant manhole that I was about to ride right into. At first I thought he was trying to alert me to danger, I really did! He had this kind of wild look about him – he was a bit sweaty, scruffy, a mess really.

He came running up and asked me what my name was, and I suddenly felt nervous. So nervous in fact that I could hardly speak and I started feeling sick, so I pedalled, faster and faster until the grass was just a blur at my feet, the daisies white, unrecognisable specks as I soared along. But he just sped up, and ran beside me until we were nearly at the end of the field and then I had to stop because there wasn't any more grass to ride on, which was annoying. The park had run out.

He was fit, though. I know I shouldn't say that. But he was. He looks a bit older than he is, and has this thick brown hair and his eyes are really blue, like the sea near Nan's villa in Spain.

'I'm Ben, Ben Lawrence, I live at number 12, over the other side of the church. My mum and your mum are friends,' he said, pulling a packet of fags out of his pocket. I couldn't believe he smoked, he's the same year as me and that makes him either 14 or 15 years old, that's so young to be smoking. It's so bad. My mum said that people who smoke die. So his life span isn't looking good if he's puffing away so young. I hope he doesn't die soon though.

I instantly knew his name, the girls talk about him at school, lots of people fancy him.

I don't know why he wanted to talk to me . . . I'm a bit of a geek really, boys like him never even notice me, let alone chase me. At the disco at the community hall last month all my friends were dancing with boys, and I just leant back against the wall and stared at the colourful lights as they danced on the bricks.

He lit his cigarette and smoked away as he talked to me, and I was so overwhelmed by it all I couldn't really hear what he was saying. His mouth was moving, but it was like there was no sound coming out. I don't know why I get so nervous around boys, I'm not really used to them. I'm a late starter, so that makes sense really although I think the girls at school lie a lot when it comes to boys. Casey said she kissed one the other day behind the school bins but I don't believe it. Casey lies a lot. I'm concentrating on my future, my career. I want to be a lawyer.

Anyway, I enjoyed talking to Ben today, despite the things I say about boys being a distraction and all that. I'm really strong though, I won't be led astray. I have too much coming up for me, big dreams, ambitions. I'm going to be a success, and when I'm 23 I will fall in love with a handsome man I meet at the bank, and we will get married, have three children, two cats and a hamster called Luke, like my older cousin, so we don't forget him after he died in that car crash a couple of years ago.

I like Ben Lawrence, just as a friend. He asked me to go to the cinema with him at the weekend but I just said I was busy and rode off. When I turned around he was still looking at me, fixed to the spot, smiling. It made butterflies dance around in my stomach, and I smiled too, all the way home.

Thirty-eight

'You never stop and smell the roses – you know that, don't you?'

Sunday 18 January 2015
Kampala, Uganda

'You've done it, Effy. You realise that, right?' Damon said, his arm around her shoulder as they stood outside the brand-new Dafina Kampala centre.

It was a hot day, but a gentle breeze still threaded its way around the pair of them, causing Effy's long, black skirt to flap a little against her legs. Her hair was piled up on the top of her head in a tight bun, but a few of her thick curls had forced their way out of the gaps between the hair band, trailing in the air.

The building was on a large plot just on the outskirts of the city. It was close enough to the chaos of Kampala that you could hear it in the night-time, a familiar rumbling in the near distance, but it was also far enough away that there was peace, greenery and a little calm. If you lay on the grass in the middle of the night you could see the stars, millions of them, as if there were angels peeking from behind thick, black curtains, holding torches and fairy lights.

Effy had completed the sale two weeks ago. The site comprised the centre itself, and a small hut on the same plot, which she was using as an office. Men in vans had been arriving all day long with various supplies, medical equipment and beds. She had held several rounds of interviews with nurses and doctors, who had recently graduated from the local university after several years of intense study. She had chosen six qualified medical staff, most of whom had cried when she told them they had got the job. Almost every day was surreal, dream-like, and almost every day Effy Jones felt like she was filled to the brim with joy, because she was forever getting closer to making her dream a reality.

'Have I?' she said, laughing to herself as she looked at Damon, his six-foot-four-inch frame towering above her. She had felt a lot safer with him around, though he was a bit of a jackass, always playing pranks with his camera. The other volunteers seemed to love him to bits, and it was clear that Lisa, a recent graduate from the University of Edinburgh who had come out to help set up the building, was developing an epic crush on him.

'Yes,' he said, looking down at her and smiling.

'I still feel like there's so much that could go wrong,' Effy said, raising a hand to her mouth and surveying the building.

It was painted yellow, and had great cracks in the brickwork. Effy always saw the cracks; the things that could go wrong. It was just the way she was. All the time she was achieving, she was constantly thinking of ways she had to protect her dreams from falling apart. She lived with a constant feeling that something bad was waiting in the imminent future, and she'd grown worryingly used to it.

'We need to get someone to fill those cracks,' she said now, her brow furrowed in the middle.

'Effy, will you just take a moment to enjoy this?' Damon asked, pulling his arm away from her shoulder and walking round to face her.

She didn't know what he meant.

'You never stop and smell the roses, you know that, don't you? I haven't known you for long but I can see it. You never just take a step back and appreciate what you've done, do you?' he asked.

Effy crossed her arms. *There isn't time to be congratulating myself*, she thought, plus, she hated people who gloated. People were meant to help others, and they were meant to do so without any level of selfishness at all, without any expectation of return. Dafina Kampala was all about helping young people, not about her. She struggled enough as it was when people complimented her on her efforts at parties and meetings, trying to change the subject as quickly as possible. The awards ceremony all those months ago had been hard for her too: while she was grateful for the money and the exposure, she had wished she could skip all the extra stuff – the speech, the clapping, the recognition. It all felt very uncomfortable.

'I mean look at this, Effy! Fucking hell, will you just smile for one moment?' Damon said, leaping up in the air and punching a fist towards the clouds.

Effy laughed at this, at the sight of the tall, good-looking man leaping around and celebrating for her. 'I get what you're saying, Damon. And I am so happy, so pleased.'

'And proud? Proud of yourself?' he butted in, putting

his long, muscular arms on his hips and squinting at the building, which shone so brightly in the African sunshine.

Effy considered briefly. 'No, not really. It's been really hard, Damon . . . really fucking hard. So much has been complicated, so much has gone wrong, I'm still worried. We open to the children in two weeks, two *weeks*, and the beds aren't even screwed in properly. I have countless meetings, so many meetings I can't physically be at all of them, and inspections, inspections coming out of my ears. I'm terrified, Damon . . . The delivery guy dropped the X-ray machine this morning, *dropped* it – I mean, JESUS CHRIST,' Effy wailed, before realising that she was sounding a little hysterical.

She was pacing the dry, cracked soil, one hand on her hip, the other gesticulating. She'd gone from speaking softly to shouting, and she seemed to be taking it all out on Damon. 'I'm tired, I can't sleep . . . I can't, I feel like I'm going to break down, or have a heart attack or something . . .' she said, trailing off, her sentence slipping away from her like a snake in the grass.

Damon walked towards her and wrapped his arms around her. It was so strange, Effy realised, burying her face in this man's chest. This man she hardly knew. But she needed it. She needed this hug, more than anything else. Damon had only been around for a little while, but he had turned out to be a huge support.

'Calm down, Effy. It's going to be fine. Look, I know I'm just doing camera stuff, but I'll help with all this, yeah? I can meet inspectors, I can go to some of the meetings and stuff – whatever you want, whatever you need,' Damon said, trying to stroke her hair, his fingers getting caught in her bun. It was all rather awkward. 'I just think you need some fun, Effy.'

'I don't have time!' she protested, feeling frustrated by him for a moment. Did he not realise how much there was to do? There wasn't time to be 'having fun'.

'Listen, you are a mess. You are exhausted. You physically won't be able to get through the next few weeks if you don't give yourself some kind of break and, hell, if you can't sleep, then do something you enjoy. I know you love this project, but I mean do something different.' He brightened. 'Hey, tonight, let's go for dinner. You need some food, Eff – you're starting to look like a toothpick. A pretty one, of course, but a toothpick nonetheless,' Damon said, pulling away from their embrace for a moment, both hands on her shoulders.

He wore an enterprising smile. 'Come on,' he said.

Effy twisted her lips in thought, and started poking at the ground with a sandaled foot.

'When was the last time you had a decent meal, or a few drinks?'

She didn't know when. She had been working most evenings in her flat, one eye on her armed guard, making sure he didn't fall asleep and leave her open to a robbery, burglary or one of her many other imagined and vastly inflated fears.

'Come on, Effy, there has to be some kind of breathing time for you, otherwise you're right. This isn't going to work. So just you think about it,' he said as he walked off to meet another delivery driver, glancing back at her as he did so with a cheeky wink.

Damon and Effy had found a restaurant just a few miles away from the city. They had taken *boda boda* bikes to get there and, for the first time in several weeks, Effy felt the breeze really rush through her hair. She felt light, free.

The restaurant was situated in a wide, dusty street, nestled between two modest and crumbling houses, one painted white, one pink. A rather stringy-looking dog with patches of mange patrolled the entrance to the pink house, its hind legs all out of sync with the rest of its body.

The restaurant boasted Italian cuisine at cheap prices. It looked rather makeshift, like the pretend diners she and her childhood friends would set up when they were kids with mismatched chairs and handwritten signs. It had real character.

The two were greeted immediately by an immaculately dressed waiter in a long, red robe. They were seated in the garden, underneath a thick veil of glittering fairy lights, the wires for which were visible and tangled.

Before long, the pair had ploughed through their meal and knocked back substantial amounts of wine. And Effy had finally relaxed.

'You were right, Damon. I did need this,' she said, leaning back in her chair and cradling a large wine glass in her hands. While the restaurant and its gardens were certainly quirky, it was really beautiful.

'See, I told you,' he said.

Effy realised, at that very moment, that Damon was more than just a little bit good-looking. In this light, she noticed the structure of his face: dark brown eyes set against tanned skin and a strong jawline, and a kindness about him.

It was at that moment that it hit her. She had been so busy setting up Dafina Kampala that she hadn't had time to even look at anyone romantically. Normally, Damon was just the kind of guy she would go for. *OK*, she thought, *he's no Ben Lawrence*. But Ben had proved too good to be true – deeply flawed, a pretender of a man who had led her on into thinking that he was good. Men like Damon were the kind of guys she should be focusing on now, she realised. Nice guys. Effy considered that you always knew what you were getting with blokes like Damon – they did what they said on the tin. Getting involved with Ben Lawrence had been like a mortal playing with the gods, and it had been an incredibly painful fall back to reality.

'Effy,' Damon said, interrupting her from her thoughts.

'Sorry, yeah?' she said, realising that she was quite drunk. The wine had gone straight to her head.

'I know you might find this inappropriate, but there's something I want to say to you,' Damon began, nervousness written all over his face. He started fiddling awkwardly with a stray serviette, and stared at the table as he spoke.

'Oh God, what is it, what's wrong? Is it the project?' she asked, suddenly sitting up, her shoulders up near her ears once more.

'No, no, it's not about the project,' he said, picking up his chair and moving it next to Effy's.

Effy put her glass down and turned to look at him. The smell of his aftershave wafted across the space between them. *He smells good*, she thought, looking into his eyes.

And, as she stared at him, and wondered what on earth he had to say to her, out of nowhere he leant forward and kissed her. As he did so, Effy closed her eyes . . .

And the image of Ben popped into her mind.

'My God, I'm so sorry,' she said, pulling away, before standing up – her chair tipping backwards and hitting the patio with a loud crash – and rushing out of the restaurant.

Thirty-nine
He told me that life never goes as you plan it

Monday 19 January 2015
Dalston, London

I had a massive row with my dad today. It happened after Ben turned up at 10 p.m. with a load of flowers he'd picked from our neighbour's garden. He asked Dad to give them to me, but Dad just threw them at him and told him to leave me alone.

He hates the fact that I'm going out with Ben. He said he was a 'scallywag' and a 'cretin'. I'm not 100 per cent sure what those words mean, I think they come from the olden days, but they don't sound very nice. He said I should be focusing on my schoolwork and not running around in the evenings with him. He also said that I will 'fuck up my A-levels' if I keep on like I am.

I was really angry. I'm nearly seventeen, for goodness' sake! I'm practically a grown-up. I know what I'm doing. Sometimes I get so angry with my dad I want to scream at him and throw stuff at him until he leaves my room, but he would clout me round the ear if I did that.

I work hard at school, and I get grade As almost all the time. I know I always said I would avoid boys but I'm hopelessly, madly in love. I genuinely believe that Ben and I will be together forever. Some people achieve that. Some people meet as childhood sweethearts, and they stay holding hands all their lives, until they are old and grey, and need sticks to keep them from falling over in the supermarket. I think that will happen with Ben and me, I really do.

The plan was always that I would fall in love at 23. I told Ben this, I told him that he was disrupting the whole thing by making it happen earlier, and he told me that life never goes as you plan it, and that when you find love you must hold on to it and never let it go. He was right, and I won't be bullied into dumping him by my dad. Ben says really deep things sometimes. He's a bit like an old soul in a tracksuit, a poet in Adidas . . . he's bloody clever too.

Ben's really respectful. He just tells me that he loves me a lot. All the time actually. He leaves me notes behind a wall by the church, we discovered that you can pull a brick out, and when you do that you can stash things in it for the other person to find. The last note said that I was the most beautiful girl in the world. I never thought I was beautiful. There are so many pretty girls at school, they wear cool shoes and they ignore the rules about what kind of skirt they can wear and how much make-up they put on, and they always look so awesome. I didn't feel beautiful until I met Ben. I hated my nose, it's quite big, but Ben said it suited me perfectly. Plus I always have to get my shoes from sensible shops like Marks and Spencer because Mum and Dad have some account card with them and they get points or something. Ben said I look like Kate Beckinsale, and that

made me smile for at least a week. I've been watching her
films a lot ever since then, trying to work out whether
or not I might look more like her as I grow up – God, I
hope so . . .

Ben makes me happier than I have ever been. He brings
colour and light where there was once darkness. Love is
the most beautiful thing I have ever felt and I'm afraid I
have fallen deep in it, never to be found again. Send out
the search party!

My English teacher said my poetry is beautiful, and said
it had 'flourished' in recent weeks. I told her it was because
I was in love. She said that was great, and that I must keep
writing about love, because not enough people write about
the happy parts of life. So, in fact, in a way, my relationship
with Ben is actually helping my schoolwork . . .

OK, so I kind of understand why my dad is worried. Ben
isn't exactly well behaved. Just recently he's started smoking
weed, and he always wants to go down to the lakes near the
village and we've never been allowed to do that. The police
are 'interested' in him, let's put it that way – they caught
him with a bag of green recently but they didn't bother doing
anything about it. They have been keeping a close eye on
him ever since. But it's just regular teenage stuff, all young
people do it. He will grow out of it, I'm sure. I love Ben
Lawrence, just how he is right now – and I'm sure, I really
am sure, that I always will.

As Ben read the final words of the entry, he snapped the
book shut and put it gently back in the kitchen drawer.
Images of his childhood flashed before his eyes: running
around with Alex, holding her hand, stealing great swigs
of whisky in the woods on Saturday nights, their first kiss
. . . He took long, deep breaths. He was twenty-nine years

old, which meant that thirty was looming over him like a wet, grey cloud. Great numbers that he should be looking forward to and celebrating but, instead, they were an indicator of more than thirteen years of sadness, suffering and guilt.

The trip to Leanne's had helped: he was glad she had found happiness, and the whole thing had been extremely cathartic, and he had quietly hoped it had been a cure-all.

Just a week or two later, the feelings had all come back.

It had been a lovely sentiment, to give him the diary. He had been reading it slowly, an entry every few days, because it was hard to hear Alex's words, so youthful, glittery and full of hope. It almost brought her back to him, he could hear her voice . . . Ben couldn't believe quite how much Alex had loved him, however clumsy and inexperienced that love was. He was quietly amused by how dramatic her descriptions of those feelings were, but it was sweet, and honest, and real . . . He understood what Leanne had tried to do: she wanted him to focus on the nice bits, the happy times, and while it did help him, tonight some of the words just seemed to ring out sadly, like off-key bells, all over his flat.

'When you find love you must hold on to it and never let it go'

Those were his own words, things he'd said when he was only a kid. But what had he become? His life felt so meaningless, a shell of work, booze and material things; he was shocked, looking back at all the pointless encounters he'd had over the years and his selfish attitude to others. Alex's death had clearly turned him from a hopeless romantic into a young man who feared the word because it caused

389

him pain. He'd just thought he'd grown up into a bit of a playboy at first; he didn't realise at the time how things had been shaping up in his mind. He'd felt that he shouldn't be responsible for someone else's heart, not after what he'd allowed to happen to the first girl who ever gave hers to him.

He had only proved himself right with the way he had hurt Effy.

The sadness was still there, and he started to wonder if Sally Whittaker was right. If there *was* something 'wrong' with him. Maybe he had depression, he wondered, pouring himself a glass of red wine and lighting a cigarette. Surely it wasn't normal to feel so hopeless for so long? Sometimes he wasn't able to eat for days he was so down, his sleep constantly broken by nasty dreams. Sometimes his anxiety would be so intense he would start to feel disconnected from reality, like nothing was genuine – and that was really frightening. But he was also worried it might be something more serious, that he might be told he had a condition that would affect him for the rest of his life. He preferred to ignore it . . . he'd almost become used to living with the depression, like it was a silent flatmate, sharing his home and filling every corner of the room with an inky blackness. Depression was the kind of housemate that never did the washing up, and came in late at night, clunking around and stopping him from sleeping. It was selfish, and closed, and did nothing for his hopes of one day contributing to the world in a positive way.

Ben's flat was painfully quiet in the night-time, apart from the odd beeping of a taxi outside, or a group of kids ambling past to go to the bowling alley down the road. He had been thinking of Effy a lot. He still loved her, despite his decision to leave her alone. The love he felt and the loneliness that came with not being able to share that was destroying him. Her face popped into his mind all the time; he could still hear her laugh, as if she were with him; and he still wished and hoped every day that she was making a fine success of her work. Sometimes he wondered if she'd already met someone else . . . he felt a stab of jealousy about the handsome chap who had opened the door of her office that day. He pictured them, falling in love. That guy, helping her with the project, being some kind of hero in funky shorts and colourful trainers. It made him feel a little sick.

But I'm certainly not going to try and win her over, no way, he thought, taking a sip of his wine. It was far too late and she thought he was scum. He just had to sit it out. He wondered how long it would take to get over her; how long it would be until he could start looking at other women with any kind of real, tangible interest.

Ben went and sat down on the sofa, the words still ringing in his ears. '*When you find love you must hold on to it and never let it go.*' The words of Ben Lawrence, sixteen, dragged from the past, into his future, and as relevant today as they had been all those years ago.

Forty
He'd never left her mind

Friday 15 May 2015
Kampala, Uganda

'You'll never understand how grateful I am for what you have done for my little girl, for our family,' Masani said, reaching out and holding Effy's hands between her own. Her daughter, Clara, was having her final check-up by the duty doctor following an intensive course of treatment on a spinal break. The five-year-old had spent some time staying in the brightly decorated ward.

Effy was dedicated to entertaining the children, putting films on for them, giving them toys and magazines, and generally making sure they were as happy as possible. She'd loved seeing Clara transform from a grizzly, teary little girl, constantly in agony, into a strong, healthy child who laughed like a drain. While it was always a good thing to wave goodbye to a child who was now healthy and well, it was hard to see them go. They all had such beautiful personalities, and they all left a mark on Effy and her volunteers, like delicate little fingerprints.

Masani's skin was beautiful, Effy noticed now. *So warm and soft*, she thought, as both of her hands remained cocooned between them. The moment moved Effy, so much that she felt a shiver down her spine. This was it. This was what she had been working towards for such a long time. She couldn't believe that she would be flying back to London on 19 June, leaving the project in the hands of two highly qualified managers for a month or two, while she took care of things with Lily from the London office and made sure lots of money was coming in to keep things going. It felt terrifying to be leaving, but she would be back later on in the year for another stint. Plus, the centre had to be in a position where it could operate without her, otherwise the situation would be useless.

'Any time, Masani. It's lovely to see Clara recovering so quickly,' Effy said, looking into the woman's eyes and noticing tears. Happy tears.

'We would never have been able to afford for her to be treated in this way privately. How long have you been here?' Masani asked, smiling now.

'Oh, only a few months. We are pretty new,' Effy said, nodding.

'People must know about you – the whole world must know about you. We will be holding a sale, in the garden, to raise money for you,' the mother said, gently releasing Effy's hands and wiping a tear away from her cheek.

Effy wondered where she lived: whether it was one of the modest homes on the outskirts of the city; or if she lived with the whole family in a makeshift hut. She couldn't remember what had been written on Clara's records.

'That's lovely, thank you. Now, will you come for a cup of tea, Masani? Clara will be out soon,' Effy said, gesturing towards the kitchen.

Masani sat down on the sofa, adjusting her red and gold *busuuti* and looking out of the window as Effy made the tea. There was something knowing about her face and her eyes. She made Effy miss her own mother, who had recently been out to visit her. The trip had been a success but it had also been tough: she couldn't help but harbour a little bitterness that they had moved to France when she needed them most. But she knew that was selfish. She had taken this on, it was her dream and her responsibility. In moments like these, all the hard work was worth it.

'You are very special, Effy. A very special lady indeed,' Masani said, in her deep, warm voice, which resonated around the room.

Effy could feel herself cringe a little. She still struggled with the gratitude that came from worried – then relieved – parents.

'Do you have a husband?' Masani asked suddenly. 'I'm sorry to pry, I would just love to know that someone is supporting you. I would be useless without my husband . . . he is my everything,' she said, reaching out and accepting her cup of tea, rocking slightly in her seat, as if the thought of him made her warm.

Effy thought of Ben, for the millionth time that day. He'd never left her mind. Not since the kiss with Damon. Damon had fled a month after it happened, his disappointment melting into anger in a way she'd often experienced when it came to men. He had ended up giving her a rather painful speech, all hot and angry, as he shouted at her while clutching onto his suitcase. He had told her that she was selfish and precious, adding that it was 'no surprise all the men you've loved are no longer around'. His words had stung. It annoyed Effy because she'd never *really* shown any romantic interest in him at all. He'd just been trying to push his agenda on her when she was at her most vulnerable. It was quite irritating really, and a reminder that she shouldn't get too close to her volunteers. She felt bad for Sophie too, who had no knowledge of the drama that had played out between them, and seemed to really miss Damon now he was gone.

Effy was disappointed in him, in the whole situation, and she found his comments about her completely out of order. More than anything she wished it had never happened. And there was still the constant wondering about how Ben was doing, and why he never left her thoughts. Why? Why had that man left such a mark on her?

'Er, no, I don't,' Effy said, starting to feel a little tearful.

'Are you OK?' Masani asked with concern, noticing Effy's eyes tearing up a little.

'Goodness, yes, sorry . . . I think I'm just a little tired,' Effy muttered, trying to smile. Embarrassed, she wanted above anything else to avoid an emotional breakdown in front of this woman, who had already been through enough to be worrying about her petty, romantic disasters.

'Come and sit down next to me,' Masani said, patting the sofa. She was such a mother. So comforting, so wise, so connected to the world around her.

Effy slouched over to her and pulled up a chair, feeling like she was a teenager again.

'What's his name?' Masani asked, smirking a little and raising an eyebrow.

'Who?'

'The man causing these teary eyes, and this droopy, droopy mouth,' she said, tapping a finger softly on Effy's

395

cheek. Effy could feel herself disintegrating like a cliff-face, slipping heavily into a sea of suppressed emotion.

'Oh, Ben. His name is Ben. We used to be together but he let me down . . . We haven't spoken since. Well, he emailed me, and he actually came out here, to Kampala. I deleted the email, I never read it, and I told him to leave Uganda, and he did just that,' Effy said, staring at the brilliant sunshine outside, just beyond the line of Masani's round cheeks.

'How sad . . . he must have done something really terrible,' Masani said gently.

'Well, he lied to me about something, that was all. And now I can't stop thinking about him,' Effy responded, unable to take a single sip of her own tea.

'You still love him, huh?' Masani asked, cradling her drink close to her chest, almost using her ample bosom as a coffee table.

'Yeah.' The word came reluctantly, but suddenly Effy felt as if some of the weight on her shoulders had lifted slightly. 'I guess I've realised that recently. I think perhaps I was too harsh on him . . . I have a feeling there's more to it, more than I thought,' Effy said, unable to shake the nagging doubt that perhaps she had been too hasty. She'd not given him the chance to speak properly, to explain himself, and the words he'd carefully constructed in an email, she'd simply deleted.

'Well, you must do something, Effy, before it's too late,' Masani said, putting a firm hand on Effy's thin wrists.

Effy looked up, feeling a kind of electricity run all over her body.

'Effy, if you love this man, you must forgive him for what he has done. Love is hard, but it's worth it,' Masani said.

As she did so, the pair were distracted by Clara, running full-pelt into the kitchen.

'Ahhh, my beautiful girl,' Masani said, as her daughter jumped into her arms and wrapped herself around her mother's neck like a vine around a tree.

As Masani and Clara embraced, Effy studied Masani's face: relief, love and happiness warmed every feature. Those emotions were painted across her, and it was beautiful.

After a few moments Clara peeled herself away from her mother, jumped down onto the lino of the kitchen floor and straightened herself up. She was wearing a bright pink dress with a little elephant embroidered on the front. Clara had chosen it from a pile of donated items Effy had brought out to Uganda from the UK for the children to wear and take home with them.

'I have gift for you,' Clara said, thrusting a piece of paper in Effy's direction.

'Ohh, what's this?' Effy asked, opening the paper to find a drawing. It was of Effy, with a stick body and giant, red curls. On her head was a tiara, all crafted from brightly coloured crayon strokes and glitter glue.

'I drew it for you, Princess Eeeefeeee,' the girl said, grinning widely, a gappy smile.

'Hmm, that's lovely,' said Masani, leaning forward and studying the childish drawing, then looking up with a knowing smile. 'Effy must find her prince,' she said, winking and looking at Effy, before pulling her into another warm embrace.

'Yes, she must,' Clara cried, waving her hands in the air. 'Eeeffeeffeeee deserves the most handsome prince in all London!' the little girl added, skipping around the kitchen now, her dress floating around her legs.

Effy's phone had vibrated twice against the scratched wooden desk in her office. Because the room was relatively empty, the walls made of poor-quality brick, it sounded far noisier than it should have, and made her jump.

She glanced around the room briefly, not realising that three hours had just slipped by without her noticing. The office was entirely dark, apart from the light leaking from the screen of her laptop. When she looked out of the window, she could see the stars, twinkling in the sky. There was very little sound, apart from the comforting and gentle mass chirping of crickets in the long grass outside. She suddenly realised how tired she was, and rubbed her eyes with her fists, great swathes of her thick hair falling over her shoulders.

Effy had been wrapped up in an email about a meeting with the Ugandan authorities. She decided it was time to sneak outside for yet another stressed-out cigarette. Picking up her phone, she made her way outside.

It was 11.45 p.m., and the centre was relatively quiet. Effy could see the soft lighting and the curtains with princesses and frogs on them from the doorway to her office. Four children were staying overnight, and there were two nurses on duty and one senior nurse keeping an eye on things. One of the children was due to see a specialist to help with possible reconstructive surgery. She had burns on her face as a result of the Ropek disaster. She was quite badly scarred, and Dafina Kampala might be able to get her the treatment she wanted. The thought that she would soon be seen by one of the best surgeons in this field made Effy glow inside . . .

All the volunteers were out and about. Some of them were exploring the nightlife of Kampala, while others had chosen to take the frightening journey to Jinja, the second largest town in Uganda. The route from Kampala to Jinja involved at least an hour of sitting in a minibus packed with passengers. The buses were usually driven by cheery men who sped along, wildly overtaking other vehicles on a winding single carriageway. To say it was terrifying was putting it mildly, but it was incredible once you arrived . . .

Effy was thinking about this as she walked some distance away from the centre, soon finding herself in her favourite secret smoking spot: a small hideaway behind an abandoned outbuilding. It faced the edge of a huge, dry field, which seemed to sprawl out for miles.

In her early twenties, she'd always smoked when she was upset, and she was now a little disappointed that this bad habit was continuing into her late twenties. But her chat with Masani earlier that day had worked to reinforce how hard the situation with Ben was, and how much it was getting to her.

Effy crouched down, so she wouldn't be spotted by anyone, and then lit up.

She took a few pulls on the cigarette, feeling the nicotine do its work, before checking the message that had arrived on her phone five minutes before.

Hi, Eff. Hope you're good. I'm not sure if you'll believe this, but Ben has given up the partnership with Ropek Oil. Well, actually, he's quit his job entirely. It's in the *Evening Standard* today. All rather unfortunate. He sent some ranty resignation email to the whole of his workplace and it's ended up going viral and even in the papers. Everyone's going mad over it. It's safe to say that Ropek Oil are fucked, but probably Ben is too . . . Google it. Laters. Rosa Xxx

Forty-one
I chipped away at it

PR 'GENIUS' IN HIDING AFTER RESIGNATION
LETTER GOES VIRAL

A PR executive once described as a 'genius' by his
boss has gone into hiding after his resignation letter
was forwarded to thousands of people.

Ben Lawrence, 29, penned a furious email to Dermot
Frances, his boss at Ossa PR, accusing Ropek Oil of
an alleged botched clean-up effort after a disaster in
Uganda three years ago. It comes as a further blow to
the multi-million-dollar oil company's reputation after
a catalogue of safety errors that led to the 2012 disaster
were revealed as the cause of the tragedy, and warnings
predicting it had been ignored.

Whether Lawrence intended to send the email to
the whole of the company he worked for is not yet
known, but within hours the email had been forwarded
to thousands of office workers across London and

beyond, giving it automatic viral status. Hundreds took to Twitter and Facebook, posing questions to Ropek Oil and sending abusive messages.

Ropek Oil have responded to the claims in the email, which is reproduced below, with a statement saying it denies the allegations and will be looking into ways to expand its rehabilitation programme for the victims of the 2012 explosion.

But Lawrence's email is the tip of the iceberg for Ropek Oil, which has already faced rumours and accusations that it has not provided enough help for the innocent people affected by the tragedy.

The Ugandan government is expected to announce that it will once again open up an inquiry into the conduct of Ropek Oil in the wake of these fresh allegations.

Lawrence was unavailable for comment at the time of going to press, but it is believed he walked out of his role at Ossa PR moments after sending the email and does not intend to return. A source close to Lawrence said he was 'in hiding' in his Dalston flat since the email went viral.

Lawrence was one of the highest-earning PR executives in London and recipient of the Young PR Executive of the Year 2013 award. The CEO of Ossa PR, Dermot Frances, said at the time: 'I am delighted that Ben has taken on this highly responsible role on behalf of Ossa PR. Ben has a natural, and very special talent for public relations which verges on genius, and I know that he will do a great job for Ropek Oil.'

Dermot,

I appreciate this email might come as a shock to you.

I am writing to inform you of my resignation, which is, by the way, effective immediately. You can stuff your notice period, quite frankly.

I loved my job, I really did. The pay was excellent, the hours (while tough) always went quickly, I had an office view that looked over the whole city from the forty-fifth floor of the reputable Tower 100 (you might want to give that to David, by the way – he's a good bloke but you never give him enough credit). So, why on earth would I leave?

Well, it's a matter of morality, I'm afraid. Yep. Morals. Those annoying things that sometimes get in the way of making huge amounts of money, but kind of niggle away at the back of the brain somewhere until it becomes difficult to concentrate at all.

I can't work with Ropek Oil any more; I can't be a part of a machine that glosses over what they are up to. They haven't been 'fixing' the mess they made, no matter what they say. They haven't, and I cannot be a part of it. I simply cannot work here any more.

A dear friend of mine told me that there might be some rather untoward things going on with Ropek Oil and its apparent attempts to help the poor people whose lives were destroyed by the disaster. So I did some research of my own to find out the truth about how Ropek Oil has *actually* responded to the incident.

It took some time. Months, in fact, to get the information I needed, but I chipped away at it. It turns out you knew anyway, Dermot. That's a bit of an issue, really . . . well, for me it is.

I'm not sure why I'm spelling it out for you because you clearly know, but it's always best to put these things in writing in situations such as these. The truth is that Ropek Oil claimed to spend £3.5million on a programme to treat the victims of the Ropek disaster, but their accounts show no such expenditure. When I raised this with the company, I was told this was due to a clerical error and a new accounts sheet would be raised soon. I decided to investigate this myself. It turns out they never spent the money, and the victims were never helped. They still struggle and suffer, and they have largely been abandoned, barring one or two rather amazing small charities that have taken on the thankless and harrowing task themselves.

I won't be a part of it, Dermot.

Good luck in the future.

Ben

Wednesday 20 May 2015
Dalston, London
Ben walked into his living room carrying two shopping bags. Inside were some pasta sauces, a couple of onions,

a packet of spaghetti and a bottle of white wine that had been on special offer.

While Ben had a little money put away for emergencies, it wasn't anywhere near enough, and so he had to cook for himself, and actually take responsibility for his spending, rather than haemorrhaging his pay cheque every month in bars and fancy restaurants.

It had been raining hard that afternoon, soaking him right through to the skin, even though he'd only popped to a branch of Sainsbury's around the corner.

Ben's sister Gina looked at him with quiet amusement as he shook his head like a dog, droplets of water spanning out around him. He felt a few beads run down his forehead, and blinked hard, twice, to stop them going in his eyes.

He dumped the bags on the nearest kitchen surface, before stomping into the living room. He sank down into the nearest chair. His heavy movements were accompanied by a loud sigh.

Gina's legs were tucked up just beneath her. Her blonde hair had grown out a little, and now just about touched her shoulders. She cradled a cup of tea, and had that familiar look of concern on her face, mixed with a little sympathy and, if Ben had it correctly, frustration.

'What are you going to do, Ben?' she asked.

'What do you mean?' he muttered, feigning ignorance.

But he knew exactly what she meant. He'd exposed the wrongdoings of one of the world's most influential and powerful companies, causing everything to go into meltdown. It was quite a big deal, really.

'Well, you don't have a job any more, and you've got this place to keep up. You've got bills to pay, and that bloody silly car of yours – in fact, why don't you sell it?' she added, cocking her head to one side.

Ben felt himself smart a little. 'Yeah, I might have to . . . But, shit, I love that car . . . Oh God, no, I can't do that. I'm sure I'll find something else,' he replied.

But he wasn't sure he'd find something else . . . he had a name for himself now, and he worried that potential employers might consider him a bit of a loose cannon. He had basically dropped his own client in the shit and, however admirable that was ethically, it probably didn't make him a particularly attractive candidate for job offers.

He had sent the email in the heat of the moment to the whole office, but he had never expected it to go viral. Now, in retrospect, it seemed obvious that his colleagues wouldn't keep it to themselves.

Ben thought about all this, staring at the huge flat-screen TV, which Gina had switched on while he went to the shops, the sound muted. He wished he had saved more for a rainy day instead of spending all his money.

Daytime TV was slowly fading out to make way for the early evening news. Daytime TV, incidentally, was dire, Ben had discovered. When he was tired at work he'd always secretly longed to be one of those people that just stayed at home and watched shitty TV all day. Now there was nothing less appealing. He wasn't sure he could take any more cooking demonstrations, or Gok Wan 'banger'-centric summer-fashion features.

'How's your holiday going?' Ben asked flatly, changing the subject. He knew exactly how her holiday was going. It had started on the M25 on the previous Friday night. Gina and her lovely family had packed into a car with suitcases, pillows and shiny tins of travel sweets, only for them to break down on the hard shoulder thousands of miles from Sussex and be towed all the way home. Now they were just trying to fill the days with perfectly pleasant things they could do on a low budget, given the outrageous bill for the car repair work.

'Oh, it's OK. Bit pissed off that we couldn't go to Cornwall, but there's always another time. Bloody car,' Gina said bitterly. 'Still, it's nice to see you,' she added, forcing a weak smile.

Ben wasn't entirely convinced that a few days with her depressed brother were quite what Gina had been looking for in an escape from the humdrum of her life, but still . . . Gina had decided to go and stay with him for a couple of days after the whole Ropek Oil episode. He had clearly been struggling following his widely publicised 'outing' of one of the world's biggest companies, which was 'quite understandable really' as she'd told him softly down the phone.

Some people considered him a hero; others thought he was a prat. His face had been splashed all over the press, and for a couple of days a few reporters had been buzzing round his flat like flies, desperate to have a chat with him. Somehow pictures from his Facebook had appeared in news articles – that just made him suspicious of his friends because he thought his profile wasn't searchable to those who weren't his friends . . .

He'd shunned it all. He'd never wanted it to end up all over the papers like it did – he just wanted out, and he wanted the truth to be known. The issue was being discussed everywhere. It had become a thoroughly modern scandal and he was at the heart of it.

It was all so *hard*. Ben had few regrets about leaving his job, but life without it was rather empty. It had only high-lighted what he had beside his work, what was left, and it turned out very much to support his previous suspicion – that there was very little . . . Not only that, but his new-found freedom during the weekdays, where he used to run in and out of meetings and frantically type reports and letters, had created some free space for his worries to inhabit. It seemed that a few more ugly gremlins had arrived at his front door, laden with baggage, to well and truly take residence in his life.

Time was not helping him. It was making him worse. And, rather than filling his days with proactive moves towards a new career, or perhaps reading some half-decent books, his anxiety had grown so overwhelming he found he spent a lot of time just staring into space, or pacing the floor and smoking.

He felt like he was coming undone.

And she hadn't contacted him. Not once. He feared she might never understand. Beautiful Effy. He wondered if she knew about everything that had happened. Ben found it hard to believe that she wouldn't. She was very much involved with the whole thing, given the nature of her work. He wondered what she would make of it. Clearly not much, he considered.

'I'm going to make you some supper, Benjy,' Gina said, getting up from the sofa with purpose.

Ben nodded, running his hands down his face. Life was starting to feel completely hopeless. He felt like such a fool. So embarrassed. He had never meant for any of this to happen.

He flicked through the TV channels as Gina cooked, lost in his own thought processes, until the smell of cooking onions and garlic filtered into his reality.

'Oh, Ben, someone rang for you when you were out,' Gina said, twirling around the kitchen holding a pan. She drained the pasta into a sieve, great swathes of steam billowing from the sink towards the ceiling. 'Sorry, I forgot to tell you earlier,' she added, giving the sieve a little shake. Ben could hear the last droplets of water fall in the metal sink.

'Oh, really?' Ben asked, uninterested, flicking now to the music channels. Jessie J was dancing around in black spandex and thrusting her pelvis towards the camera.

'Yeah. Some girl. It was a bit weird – she asked for you, and then when I tried to explain that you were out she just hung up. Probably a sales call, I guess.'

Ben felt a flicker of hope. *Perhaps . . . ?* But no. He had to stop this. He had to just give up on the whole idea.

Forty-two
It was the same woman, again

Thursday 21 May 2015
Kampala, Uganda

Effy felt her heart pounding hard in her chest. She slowly reached down to pick up the phone, abandoning the attempt halfway through before talking to herself. 'Just leave it. Just leave it alone,' she whispered to herself, biting her bottom lip and looking around the room hopelessly.

But that desire returned almost instantly. She had to know.

Effy grabbed the phone and quickly punched in a mobile number, adding a code at the start to ensure the call came through as private. She remembered the number off by heart still.

The phone rang four times, and with each ring Effy felt a little more nauseous.

'Hello?'

It was the same woman, again. The same person who

had picked up his phone the day before when she had tried his landline. Effy felt her stomach sink. She could picture it already. Ben had moved on, of course he had. This was Ben, the most handsome and charismatic man in London. And this was his new girlfriend, answering his phone, living with him . . .

'Hi, I'm sorry. I think the line's bad. Ben's asleep . . . If you can tell me who you are, I can get him to give you a call back?' she said, her voice deep and attractive. Effy was tongue-tied. She gripped the phone, her palms sweaty, wondering what she should say. She imagined the woman, a complete image already in her mind of the person who was clearly now a big part of Ben's life. Some beautiful girl with chestnut-brown curls and a teeny-tiny waist who was going out with one of the most admired men in London, if not the world . . . all for exposing Ropek Oil for what it really was. Effy guessed she was the kind of girl who wore Agent Provocateur, even on her shabbiest days . . .

'I'm sorry. I've got the wrong number,' Effy said, ever-so-slightly changing her voice so she wouldn't be recognised from her phone call just the day before.

And then she hung up.

Forty-three
'London has been utterly shite without you'

Friday 19 June 2015
Dalston, London

Ben reread the email for the tenth time before finally clicking 'Send'. He ran his hands through his hair and took a sharp inward breath as the carefully composed paragraph disappeared into the void, to be replaced by a short confirmation that the message had been sent.

His heart was racing.

Ben just hoped she would read it soon, because time was running out.

Friday 19 June 2015

'Oh my God, oh my God! I cannot wait for you to come home, Effy. London has been utterly shite without you,' Rosa said breathlessly. She could just about be heard down the tinny line, as Effy sat in the departure lounge at Entebbe International Airport, smiling widely. The room was buzzing with activity, excitement dancing in the air.

'I can't wait to see you, either,' Effy said, picturing Rosa's face, so excited to give her a hug and catch up with her. As always, they had got through their rough patch and, as always, Effy had realised what Rosa had been getting at – it had just taken a little time to sink in. *It's no big deal really*, Effy had thought once the words had stopped stinging. She and Rosa's long-standing friendship would not really feel the same without a vicious row exploding between them every now and again. Somehow they always made amends, and somehow they always seemed stronger for it.

'I'm meeting you at the airport, then we can get the tube or a taxi, or whatever. What time do you arrive again?' Rosa asked.

'I get in at 8 a.m. UK time,' Effy responded, watching people start to queue to get onto the plane.

'Amazing! I'll be there, and we are going straight to a bar to get pissed, OK?' Rosa cried.

'It'll be a little early, don't you think?' Effy gasped, starting to laugh.

'It's never too early when your best friend has been away for six whole months! We're going to get smashed, absolutely off our tits drunk! By the way, I tried to email you a few hours ago to find out when you were arriving – are you not getting emails on your phone?'

'No, I've just got this shitty pay-as-you-go thing. I packed away my laptop this morning, so there will probably be loads to catch up on when I land . . .' Effy trailed off.

'Oh, forget about that! We're going to spend the whole of Saturday having fun, going to bars and celebrating what you've achieved,' Rosa demanded.

Effy stood up slowly and made her way over to join the queue, clutching on to her passport. Her hands were a little sweaty. She was terrified of leaving her project, but she had to trust in the professionals she had hired to run things. She knew they were brilliant. She knew that everything had been handed over to a team of carefully chosen staff. But it didn't make it any easier.

'OK, OK . . . I can't wait,' Effy said.

'Listen, sorry again that I was such a cow in my email – I feel really bad about it. I still think I was right, though. I just shouldn't have worded it like that,' Rosa said, as the queue started to move forward.

'No, no, Rosa. It's OK – you made a lot of sense. Listen, I have to go,' Effy said.

'Sure thing – see you on the other side!' Rosa said, before hanging up.

Forty-four
'Are you all right, mate?'

10.30 p.m. Saturday 20 June 2015
South Bank, London

She hadn't replied. Ben had known she wouldn't. The fact that she hadn't contacted him, given the fact that he'd done what he had with Ropek Oil, really showed how much she must despise him.

She had probably hit the delete button immediately. He pictured Effy at her desk in the tiny office in Kampala, spotting his email arriving, rolling her eyes and sending it to the abyss, with billions of other unwanted messages.

By his calculations, she was due to come back to London in a week or so, though he couldn't remember the exact date. The thought of it was overwhelming. That she would be so close, but so far away. It would almost be harder, knowing she was in the same city, not wanting to see him ever again . . .

Hopelessness had arrived like a heavy suitcase dumped on his doorstep, lined up next to guilt and sadness, the luggage of his life. The black dog – ever at his heel – had even followed him all the way to the central London bar where he now sat.

He was depressed, unwell, so consumed by it all he had totally lost perspective.

He was supposed to have been meeting Theo and some other lads, but he had backed out at the last minute, standing by the doorway of the pub his friends were in, clutching onto the wet, wooden frame before turning around and walking away, favouring some time alone in another pub he knew close by.

As he did so, he was sure he heard Theo's booming laugh echoing in his ears.

Happiness seemed to be a distant memory, wrapped up in Effy, and she had taken that away to a land far away. Ben took a huge swig of whisky and turned his phone off as Theo called him, his name flashing up on the screen, only to be replaced by blackness.

Ben was alone in a room full of people; they were buzzing around him like flies, no faces or features, just blurred lines in his vision. He looked at the table before him, at his glass filled with clear brown liquid. He had ordered six whiskies, and asked for a spare pint glass. The barmaid had looked at him oddly, peering over his shoulder as she thought about it, wondering if he was alone. She had eventually obliged, assuming he was going to share it with friends. She had seemed far too busy to probe into why he needed a pint glass without anything in it.

As soon as he'd paid and the barmaid had turned around, he poured all the whiskies into the pint glass. His head bowed, he had carried the whisky through the crowd and found himself a tiny table in the corner, next to a huge window that looked out at the Thames.

It was rainy. A hot, wet, messy summer's evening in

London. It was the kind of rain that looked as if it belonged in a tropical country. People walked by clutching umbrellas, the raindrops running down the sides like overflowing gutters. The evening was a perfect match for his mood. He still couldn't get Alex off his mind, and the fact that he'd clearly hurt Effy's feelings so much that she hadn't contacted him even now . . . even after he'd done something so extreme, so unlike the man he knew himself to be . . . Effy had changed him, that was for sure, but she had only proven how poisonous he was. How all he could do was hurt people.

Ben thought of his mother and father, and Gina. He thought that maybe their lives would be more peaceful without him as a constant worry in the backs of their minds. He loved them, he knew that for sure but, right now, it wasn't enough.

As he thought about this, he took a few more swigs of whisky, swallowing it hard, his face scrunched up as he did so. His vision was blurring now, the scene dancing before his eyes like a handheld camera in a documentary.

I've made too many mistakes. There's too much pain, Ben thought, as he started to down the whisky. A table of young men near him glanced over, having noticed his hunched shoulders and the cold look of desperation all over his face, rather as if he were a sketch hanging in an art gallery, only to be viewed by people who understood what that kind of pain felt like, their heads tilted to one side.

'Are you all right, mate?' one of the men asked. Ben simply nodded his thanks, unable even to make out their faces he was so drunk. They soon turned back to their conversation, shrugging their shoulders as they did so.

For Ben there was no light any more. His life was as empty as the words in Alex's childhood diary, because she was no longer alive, and it was his fault. The love of his adult life had been disgusted by him, had shunned him, and his own friends were busy falling in love, getting married and spending Saturdays in Ikea . . .

Ben felt like he'd missed a few trains in his time. But this was no single man's pity party: this was the result of too many days, years even, lost in a murk of regret and guilt.

The music playing in the pub thumped in his ears, the chatter meaningless, clattering language and speech, a man totally alone in a city of millions.

Ben finished his drink, tipping his head back so the very last droplets of alcohol rushed down his throat. As he put his glass down on the table he drastically underestimated the space between the wooden surface and his hand, simply dropping it. The glass smashed as it hit the hard polished table. A few people looked up, and he just about spotted them in his peripheral vision.

'I'm fine, I'm fine,' he slurred, to no one in particular, waving one of his arms around clumsily. And with that he snaked his way through the crowd, and walked out of the pub.

He stood by the doorway for a few minutes, lighting a cigarette and swaying back and forth. He hadn't brought a coat. He didn't need one. He was so sad, he couldn't feel the rain as it lashed down on him. He was lost in drunken oblivion. What had he become? The only way he knew how to escape was through alcohol, but he couldn't carry on like that . . . Ben couldn't face another minute, feeling like this. His sadness was relentless, the flashbacks unbearable, the depression, almost impossible to navigate. It had got to the point where it was so overwhelming he didn't know where to be any more, how he should arrange his facial features, where he should put his hands. He couldn't imagine that anyone could understand how hard it was to feel like that.

He walked out into the rain, cupping his cigarette in his hands in a desperate attempt to keep it alight, but within seconds the butt was drenched. He threw it on the ground in frustration and started walking towards the bridge, unable to make a straight line.

But why the bridge? he thought. He had been drawn to the water. Ben found a quiet part of the South Bank, the occasional car and bus roaring past him as he made his way to some metal railings. Where there would normally be dozens of people wandering around and admiring the Thames, there was no one: the rain had forced people to duck into taxis and hop onto buses.

Ben placed his hands on the railings; they were cold to the touch. He leant over and looked down at the water, as it flowed past silently beneath his feet. He pictured Alex's face, the swan, those final moments. *It would be so easy to . . .* he thought. *So easy to jump, to not feel this pain any more.* He pictured the water and how he would sink into it. Would it hurt? It seemed so inviting now, like the kindest, quietest way to escape this world. He didn't want to inconvenience anyone, he just wanted to slip away, no fuss. No fanfare as he left this world: he didn't deserve one, he told himself. It was all just a thought process – an unexpected one – he hadn't planned it at all. But he was quickly rushing towards an end point, a decision.

It seemed like his only option. It felt urgent.

He was so wet now the raindrops were flowing through his hair and down his face. The ground wobbled, jerked and moved before his eyes, a whisky fairground ride. And that was when he decided, finally.

Ben looked up at the moon for the last time. His blurred vision had split it in two, and he had to squint to see it right. 'I'm sorry, Alex . . . I'm sorry, Effy. I'm sorry,' he whispered, as he gripped firmly onto the metal railings and began to climb.

Forty-five
No, there's definitely someone there . . .

11.30 p.m. Saturday 20 June 2015
South Bank, London

As one man was about to end his life, another walked from a nearby pub, missed his bus and failed miserably to hail a taxi. After standing in the rain for a few moments, stroking his moustache and wondering what to do, he dug his hands in his pockets to see if he had enough money to even pay a taxi driver. No cash. Shit.

Frank Rhodes shrugged to himself, warm from all the booze he had consumed, and, feeling particularly plucky, spoke to himself as the soft, warm rain spattered down on his jacket. 'Fuck it, I'll just walk across the bridge,' he muttered drunkenly, always one to talk to himself when pissed. *It's just a little rain*, he thought.

Frank zipped up his jacket and pulled his hood over his recently cut hair. The sound of the rain was now even louder against the fabric, which brushed against his ears as he moved. He walked quickly, and with purpose, across the bridge, buses roaring past and splashing his brown leather shoes with rainwater. Normally he would be annoyed by this, furious even, but Frank had been happier the past few months. He'd met someone, someone he really liked. She worked in publishing, had short blonde hair, a snub nose and she always wore red lipstick, as if it were part of her daily uniform. She had mugs with kittens on them, cushions shaped like panda bears, and there was happiness and joy in everything she did. She made him happy. The little things didn't matter so much any more, like getting wet on a summer's night in London, forgetting to put the bins out, or running out of milk. Frank thought about her as he walked quickly over the bridge, wondering if he should call her and invite her round for an impromptu night of watching films in bed and drinking more wine.

But, as he got towards the end of the bridge, he noticed something, some*one . . . ? Surely not*, he thought, wondering if he was imagining it. He carried on walking a few steps. *No, there's definitely someone there . . .* Frank stood still now, the rain starting to seep through the fabric of his jeans. He could just about make the person out. It was a man.

'Hey!' Frank shouted, from the other side of the road. The person, whoever they were, was perched at the very edge of the railings. He couldn't believe they had managed to climb over, it looked pretty difficult.

'Hey!' Frank shouted again, even louder, but it was hopeless. The traffic and the pouring rain were so noisy, he didn't stand a chance. He waited for a break in the traffic so he would be able to cross over, a million different outcomes crossing his mind. What if he failed to talk this person down, and they jumped anyway? How would he live with the fact that the last experience they ever had in life was his inane, desperate chatter? What if he handled the situation so badly, he made it worse? Nothing had prepared him for this. No training in the course of his many years on Earth had covered this kind of disaster. He'd learned about how to deal with chip-pan fires at school, when he was just a little boy, and he'd done some basic CPR when he was a Scout, but no one had ever told him what to do if he happened to stumble across someone planning to take their own life, one rainy Saturday night in London.

When Frank had made it to the other side of the road, he could see the side of the man's face. He was soaking wet, having not bothered to wear a coat or jacket, his hair thick with water, like clumps of seaweed, gathered around the backs of his ears. Frank guessed that this person didn't care very much, given the situation. He imagined there was little need for protective outdoor clothing when one was considering whether or not to jump into the Thames.

As he got closer there was a flash of recognition. 'No . . . it can't be,' he whispered to himself, suddenly feeling very sober. But yes, it was. Frank knew that face right away, even from the side. The strong nose, the handsome chiselled features: the man he had jealously Googled in a fit of drunken hysteria was perched, precariously, on the bridge railings in front of him, his legs dangling frighteningly over the water; the man who had suddenly found his own handsome face splashed all over the papers for exposing one of the most rotten corporate cover-ups the modern world had known. Frank wasn't sure if he despised or admired him, but now wasn't the time . . .

The few glasses of wine Frank had consumed just an hour or two before seemed to have disappeared from his system completely now, the warm, fuzzy haze that had seeped into his bloodstream now totally depleted. Frank suddenly felt fear in his body. The night had taken an unexpected turn, and this was one of those few moments in a person's existence where you could either make, or break, another person's life.

'Ben, Jesus Christ, what are you doing?' Frank said, unable to stop himself.

Ben stared ahead, almost in a trance, ignoring Frank as he walked closer to him. Frank didn't know what to do. He thought about Effy, and the email he had sent her about Ben. He didn't know how she had handled that. Had his revelations caused all this? He'd wondered if it had when Ben had suddenly quit his job and that email had gone viral, but he'd soon dismissed the idea. Frank suddenly felt a stab of fear that he could be responsible for this man's desperate actions, but it seemed implausible, ridiculous . . . Didn't it?

'Ben, will you just look at me?' Frank cried, his voice hoarse now.

Ben ignored him again, starting to adjust himself so that he was a little closer to being able to jump.

Frank noticed that Ben was shaking and shivering so violently it was gripping his whole body, as if he had been plugged into an electric current. But there was blankness about him, as if his mind had already fled, and all that was left was the shell of a man who had once had it all. When Frank thought back to the Ben he first met, standing on Effy's doorstep, looking like a film star, the two were hardly comparable.

Frank could hardly think straight. What should he do? Ben could drop at any time and then it would be too late. And he would have failed. So he did the only thing that came to his mind: he walked a few steps away from Ben, keeping an eye on him the whole time, pulled out his phone and shakily stabbed at the buttons. He hoped desperately that it would work in time; he hoped it would work at all.

He pressed the 'Call' button. It rang several times.

Forty-six
'Where are you, Effy?'

11.40 p.m. Saturday 20 June 2015
The Embankment, London

Effy was thinking about Ben when she got the call.

She had been drinking her fifth glass of wine and whispering into Rosa's ear so intimately, fellow pub-goers could have been forgiven for thinking they were lovers. Flashes of dark lipstick, carefully painted nails, the curves of their necks, delicate and beautiful.

It was the winding up of a long drunken day, but he was still on her mind, even as she spoke to Rosa about how hard it had all been, making her dreams come true, how bittersweet a mixture it was, to finally do it.

She had felt her stomach sink as she imagined what he was probably up to that night, somewhere else in the city of London. She pictured him, perhaps at home with his new girlfriend, the woman who had answered the phone.

Rosa and Effy had spoken about the whole situation that afternoon. Rosa was still of the opinion that Ben was in the right, though she had delivered her verdict less aggressively this time.

Effy had nodded, tearfully, knowing it was too late.

And then the call. From Frank. It was a miracle she'd answered it, but she'd had a feeling she should. A woman's gut feeling is like nothing else, and it was that feeling that drove her to answer it, rather than just hang up on him.

'Where are you, Effy?'

'Oh, hi Frank. How are you?' Effy said, shouting a little over the noise of the bar.

'Effy, don't . . . just don't . . . you need to come here now,' came the voice at the other end of the line.

Effy looked out of the window. It was pouring with rain outside. They were close to the South Bank, having planned to make their way to East London, but had found themselves so lost in conversation they had never quite made it.

Even over the sound of the pub, Frank sounded desperate, terrified. He wasn't really making sense. Where was 'here'? She rolled her eyes, wondering what kind of drama he was going to lay on tonight.

'Frank, what are you talking about?' Effy asked, as Rosa sat next to her, listening intently to only 50 per cent of the conversation and wondering what on earth could be going on.

'It's Ben. He's on the bridge near the Two Owls pub, South Bank, Thames. I think he's going to jump,' Frank whispered.

Effy wondered if this was a particularly sick joke. She would put nothing past Frank. He had shown his devious side when he'd tried to crawl back into her life, and when he'd Googled Ben and emailed her like he had; he had displayed his weaknesses as if he had nothing to hide. But would he do something this vile?

'*Pardon?*'

'You need to get here now – where are you? Fuck, Effy, please tell me you're close by,' Frank said.

Effy stood up immediately, adrenaline rushing through her body. Suddenly, something in the tone of his voice told her she should move. She'd never heard him sound like that before, and he certainly seemed to have no interest in her, in small talk.

'Oh my God, Rosa, I need to go, something's happening with Ben. I think he's going to—' Effy said, holding the phone slightly away from her ear before dropping it on the thick carpet of the bar. She felt as if she were going to pass out.

Rosa pushed herself to her feet and kept her best friend steady. Effy held on to a barstool.

'Stay calm,' Rosa whispered into Effy's ear, before bending down, picking up the phone and getting more details from Frank.

Effy and Rosa watched in shock as they stood outside the bar. Several cars, buses and taxis sped past them, whipping up sprays of rainwater, which splashed their ankles. No one would stop for them as they held their hands out urgently. Their approach clearly wasn't going to work. Effy felt helpless. The situation, growing ever more desperate, eventually prompted her to step out in front of a taxi, which ground to a violent halt, the sound of skidding tyres resonating in the air.

'Fucking hell, are you mad?' the taxi driver screamed in his cockney accent, as his window slid down, rage peppered all over his cheeks in a palette of fiery reds.

'It's an emergency!' Rosa shouted, opening the door and helping Effy into the taxi.

'Shit . . . sorry,' the driver said, looking at Effy in his rear-view mirror as they pulled away and onto the road.

Effy was soaked, shaking, tears filling her eyes. She said nothing as Rosa gave the driver directions.

They pulled up by the side of the bridge after just a few minutes.

Ben was very close by. Effy was so relieved that he was still there, clinging onto the railings, his legs dangling over the water, but equally horrified by the sight of him.

Frank was there, his hands behind his head, his body language conveying his fear.

'Do you want me to call 999?' the driver asked.

'Yes, please, I can't pay you, I'm sorry,' Effy gabbled, as she got out of the taxi.

The driver shrugged and started tapping away on his phone.

Effy approached Frank. Ben was still staring into the distance, his back to her, his whole body shaking, frozen to the spot.

'I've called 999 but they're taking fucking ages – I mean, seriously . . .' Frank said, in frustration.

'Hey, thank you. I'm glad you called me,' Effy replied.

As Effy slowly walked towards Ben, Frank turned and walked away, his shadowy figure disappearing down the road, his head down, the rain pummelling at his head.

Effy had no idea how she should handle this. The last thing she wanted was to shock him.

She walked slowly towards Ben, until she was so close she could hear his rapid breathing. He seemed to have no idea what was going on, staring across the water to another bridge in the distance, his lips shaking.

She could go with the softly-softly approach, but she

428

was still terrified he would jump, or even slip, so she made a split-second decision.

She reached her arms out and suddenly clamped them around his torso, a strength appearing in her muscles that she never knew she had. And, as she did so, she pulled him backwards, towards her, towards the wide pavement and in the direction of the nearby road. Taken by surprise, he slid heavily over the railings and into her arms. While Effy felt strong, she wasn't strong enough to bear his full weight, and the pair of them fell backwards and hit the pavement hard, Effy's arms still wrapped around him.

They lay on the wet ground, Effy's lips pressed against the back of his neck. His skin was freezing cold against her own. She started to cry, with fear, with shock and with relief that she had managed to pull him to safety.

'Ben,' she whispered into his ear.

'Effy, Effy, is that you?' he asked, moving to take hold of her hands stiffly, his fingers freezing, trembling. It was almost as if he were slowly waking up from a trance.

'Yes, yes, it's me!' she cried, pulling one of her hands away and stroking his hair. It was still raining heavily. 'What were you doing, Ben?' she asked, feeling like it was a stupid question. She knew Ben had always carried a strange kind of sadness around with him, like an imaginary dog at the end of an invisible lead, but she had eventually decided it was all through guilt over the Ropek Oil stuff.

She had certainly never thought him capable of this.

'I had to . . . I had to go,' he said, numbly.

'Go where?'

'Away,' he whispered.

She noticed he smelt strongly of alcohol, but she could still pick up the familiar scent of his aftershave against his wet skin. 'What happened? What's going on?' she asked, desperate to fit the pieces of the puzzle together.

Effy looked around: the taxi driver had gone but she could see Rosa standing nearby, awkward and unsure of what to do. Effy nodded at her friend to let her walk away. Rosa hesitated, a look of concern on her face. Effy nodded again, flashing an apologetic smile. After a moment of deliberation, Rosa reluctantly set off back down the road. Effy saw her turn back around every now and again to check they were OK.

It was just her and Ben, on the pavement in the pouring rain. It seemed so ridiculous to be lying there like that, but she just wanted to keep him still; she was terrified he'd climb up again if they stood up. She was just so glad he was alive. She buried her face into the wet hair at the back of his neck, trying to give him some warmth in any way she could.

And then suddenly Ben moved away from her, and she was terrified about what he might do. She reached out and grabbed his hand.

'It's OK, I'm not going to go anywhere,' he said. He moved, and sat with his back against the railings of the bridge. Effy joined him, sitting down so that they were side by side, watching the traffic go by, the raindrops running down their faces.

'Listen. I'm a bad person, Effy. You should stay away from me,' Ben said.

'What are you talking about, Ben? That Ropek Oil thing—?'

'No. No, not that,' Ben said, interrupting her.

'Please, Ben. Will you just tell me what's going on?' Effy pleaded, feeling a chill over her body.

Ben inhaled and breathed out a sigh that seemed to come

from the deepest part of him. 'Effy, someone died when I was a kid . . . and I can't cope with it, with the guilt. I just don't want to be here any more,' Ben started.

Effy wondered what on earth he was talking about. She reached over and held his hand. 'OK . . . what happened?' Effy asked, gently.

'My first girlfriend, Alex. The first person I ever loved . . . We were both seventeen and, one day, we went to this lake, which we weren't supposed to go to. I persuaded her. We lied to her parents about where we were going, and took her dog, Betty,' Ben said. He was still shivering violently.

'Right,' Effy whispered, prompting him to continue. She could feel the rain soaking into her skin.

'It was a cold day and the lake was covered in ice. This swan appeared, as if from nowhere and landed on the lake. I, well, I threw a stick at the swan's head because I was a stupid little git who liked to cause trouble.' Ben took a short pause. The rain seemed to get heavier but, curiously, Effy felt warm, sitting next to Ben. 'Betty went after the stick. She jumped into the water, cracking the ice. She was struggling, in the freezing cold. Alex and I, we had a big row, she was really angry at me, we thought the dog was going to die,'

'OK,' Effy said.

'When we were rowing, Alex turned around, and she hit me. I was really shocked and angry, so I started shouting at her. I shoved her back, not very hard at all, and she regained her footing, but the argument continued. Then, suddenly she slipped, backwards, on some ice. I tried to catch her but it didn't work. She fell into the water.'

Effy had started to feel nervous just listening to this story.

'Alex couldn't swim very well, and it was so cold that she went into shock, and I . . . I just stood there, useless, helpless, hopeless. I should have got help; I should have called to someone to ring 999. I should have yelled and screamed until someone came . . . but I didn't,' Ben said between great, deep breaths.

Effy stared at his handsome face. She could no longer tell the difference between raindrops and tears.

'I was frozen to the spot, frozen with fear. And you know what? You know what the ironic thing was? As Alex died, as Alex drowned, Betty got out of the lake, of her own accord, and stood by my feet, shivering and looking at me as I did nothing. *Nothing*, Effy. I will never forgive myself for it, and every day I walk around knowing that Alex never really got a chance at life because of my stupidity. I didn't jump in and save her, I didn't ask for help – I just stood there and watched, locked in fear . . .' Ben trailed off, pulling his head down to his chest.

'And you know the worst thing, Eff? I never loved again after that until you . . . I just ran around having casual, pointless encounters with women, because I was terrified of hurting them. And if any of them so much as gave me a hint that they might love me, I fled. You, Effy, you were the first person I've loved since, and I fucked that up, too . . . I wanted to tell you about Ropek Oil, but I didn't want to do anything to rock the boat. I kept telling myself I'd tell you when the time was right – and I really didn't have any idea about what they were really doing . . . I just felt like I was walking a tightrope and with one tiny step I could fall and lose it all, lose you.'

As Ben spoke, Effy started to cry. She slipped her hand in his and squeezed it gently.

'I was so scared of hurting you, I only ever hurt people

and I didn't want that for you . . . you mean the world to me. Just as I was starting to think I could give this love thing a go, I messed up and proved my fears right – I hurt you, and I couldn't live with myself any longer for doing that.'

'Ben?' Effy said, her lips close to his ear.

'Yeah?' he said, quietly.

Effy suddenly felt a stab of guilt. For being so wrapped up in herself and her anger about the oil contract that she'd never really been interested in getting to the bottom of his sadness. It had been all about her, really. She knew that now.

'Ben, I love you. I love you, I really do and I have for a long time. You were just a kid – you didn't know what to do . . . it's not your fault . . . I'm going to be the one who makes you see how wonderful you are.'

As Effy said this, two police cars pulled up, their blue flashing lights shining on the wet pavement.

Ben nodded once, then stood up, wiping the rain and tears from his face. Without looking, he reached for Effy's hand and took it.

Forty-seven
Sally was right

Saturday 12 March 2016
Ambleside village, Kent

Ben felt Effy's fingers, soft and warm, and wrapped them between his own. The perfect fit.

The spring sunshine was all around them, bright and full of hope and promise. There was finally light in Ben's life. Daisies had started to poke eagerly through the lush, green grass. Everything was growing and renewing, a hard, cold winter melting gently away before them.

There was no sound apart from their own soft footsteps and the quiet song of birds in the trees. It was a far cry from the hectic city life they loved, and the constant buzz and trill of urban living. But it was nice to be out here. To be able to breathe.

They walked together, side by side, to lay flowers on Alex's grave.

Finally, Ben felt at peace. Though he knew he would never forget Alex's death, his intense suffering at those memories had been given a name. A reason. Finally, he had been helped.

There had been some tough months since that rainy London night when Ben had come so close to jumping from the bridge. The police had arrived, perilously late, followed by an ambulance. Ben had been taken to hospital, and a psychiatric assessment had taken place.

He had resisted it at first, so angry that it was even being considered, his fists balled tightly as he stared at the pale linoleum floor of the hospital. He'd been misunderstood. Well, that was what he thought at the time. In Ben's opinion, mental health problems happened to other people. Not him. In his view, mental illness happened to the people who never went to work, and sat watching *The Jeremy Kyle Show* all day. The people who spent hours on park benches, drinking beer and chattering away to themselves. They happened to the guy who was always hanging around his local shop, mumbling things about God. The periphery he happily ignored. Ben had been a successful businessman for years; surely he couldn't have mental health problems? It just didn't fit, at first. In his mind he deserved to suffer in the way he did. To him, his torment was a natural and deserved result of his heinous mistakes.

But, given the course of events, he had little choice but to cooperate that night, as Effy gently encouraged him to go ahead with the assessment.

A grey-haired doctor had spoken to him for what felt like hours, while Ben had stared at a lamp in the corner of the room, pale and tired, the starchy hospital sheets crisp against his legs. He was diagnosed with severe depression and post traumatic stress disorder, characterised mainly by intrusive thoughts and flashbacks. *Sally was right*, he had thought, reading a sheet of jumbled words – about him, about his life and his past that felt like they were about someone else. Granted, she had been wrong about the OCD suggestion, though he had researched it and understood where she was coming from; the illnesses had some elements in common.

All of a sudden, the years of suffering he'd been through were turned on their head and Ben had some clarity. Finally.

He had taken his first batch of medication reluctantly: three pills – two orange, one yellow. 'Here goes,' he'd said as he swallowed them down, Effy beside him, her stomach a flurry of nervous butterflies, big fat tears in her eyes. She had wanted so much for him to get better.

Ben's treatment hadn't been easy. His first combination of medication had made him feel worse, and he had quickly been taken off the tablets. Thankfully, the second attempt had worked for him, but he knew it wasn't that simple. It hadn't been an instant, easy kind of miracle. It had taken time, with side effects, and patience, but eventually it was as if a great black cloud had left Ben's skyline, and drifted away.

Only in good health could Ben realise how out of hand things had become in his mind. Almost delusional. He would always regret not saving Alex, but he now understood that his reaction all those years ago was not one of malice, or deliberate complacency, but simply the shock of a lad who was losing his best friend and his first love. He had just been a kid, a very young man, rooted to the spot in horror and fear.

Bit by bit the distressing flashbacks had gone; the crushing anxiety had melted away. He finally had perspective.

In the midst of all this, Ben had somehow set up his own ethical PR company with Theo, called The Green Agency. It was his focus; something positive to concentrate on. Theo hadn't taken much persuasion. The whole conversation had revolved around a Sunday roast in the pub and by the following Monday, Theo had handed in his notice and registered the business name with Companies House.

Ben had sold a few things, including his car, to be able to put some money behind the venture, and bravely embarked on the challenge that inspired him: to work with the charitable sector and create brilliant and inspiring PR campaigns that would change the world for the better. They had just recently managed to rent their first office space in Old Street, and the business was growing.

Every day, Ben woke up excited to work with his best friend and business partner, doing the job he loved. But the thing he loved the most was Effy. She was the love of his life, his saviour – his future. The rest of Ben's life lay with Effy: years of happiness to look forward to, all there to enjoy when she looked at him. Effy had been incredible. Not just during that night on the bridge, but ever since. She still spent long periods of time in Uganda, but this time he didn't feel like they were thousands of miles apart.

As for Effy, suddenly everything made sense to her: the real reasons why Ben had held back at first; the strange cloak of secrecy he always wore. The Ropek Oil problem between them meant nothing to her in the end; she understood that he had just been doing his job and didn't have the full facts. She had cried when she'd read his exposé – something she considered to be one of the bravest things he'd ever done.

She had finally walked a mile in his shoes and she understood. He'd told her that he loved her before she rescued him on the bridge, but it had been lost in the tension of the time. He had told her that he loved her more than anything in the world in the carefully written email he had sent as she left Kampala, a message that had arrived seconds after she had shut her laptop and left the centre for the airport.

Effy felt that it was all meant to happen. She had been meant to meet Ben that day in Tower 100. They had been meant to fall out. And they were meant to come back together. In Ben she had love for life, and nothing made her happier than lying in his arms on sleepy Sunday mornings.

Ben put the flowers down softly on the grave; they had been standing there for fifteen minutes, in silence, lost in their thoughts. He would go back to Alex's grave every six months for the rest of his life. It was how he would commemorate her. It was how he would come to terms with such a life-shaping loss. It was the only way he knew how.

'OK, Eff. I'm ready to go now,' Ben said, standing behind her, his arms around her waist as she gazed at the lilies, so bright and beautiful.

'Are you sure?' she asked, uncertain if he'd had enough time there, in the village where he had grown up.

'Yes, I am,' he said, before taking a perfectly crafted paper swan from Effy's hands and gently placing it on Alex's grave.

The End

Acknowledgements

Writing my third book, Paper Swans, has been another challenging and rewarding journey.

I have a lot of people to thank . . . In my opinion novels are not, and should not be, the result of people working in solitude. They are the fruit of collaborations between writers and the people who inspire them, the people who edit them, the people who believe in them, and often all three combined. I am *so lucky* to have these people in my life.

Before I list the names of all those without whom Paper Swans may never have come into being, I want to talk a little about why I wrote this book. *Spoiler alert!*

Paper Swans explores the reality of mental illness. I feel strongly about this, partially because it has touched my life, but also because I think society has to change the way it treats mental illness. 1 in 4 people in the UK will experience a mental health problem*. That's a staggering
*Mind.

figure, but instead of working together too many people feel like they have to try and cope alone. Inevitably, this makes things worse. For me, Ben represents the people who battle daily with mental illness, keeping it wrapped beneath a cloak of secrecy and shame. He represents the people who are too embarrassed to get help, or too frightened to speak up because they don't want to be judged, or hurt. I think it's desperately sad that things are like this for so many people. Although incredible charities like Rethink, Mind and OCD UK are performing miracles each and every day, I wish people didn't have to suffer any further burden than that of mental illness itself. I can't make anything magically better by writing a book, I know that. I only hope that someone, somewhere, feels a little less alone.

I could write for a long time about this because there's so much I want to say, but there's a major risk of me rambling – infact it may have already happened! So now it's time to say thanks.

First of all, I want to thank my agent Sheila Crowley at Curtis Brown. Sheila is a ray of sunshine whenever I am struggling! I always feel so inspired when I see you. *Thank you*. Charlotte Hardman, Fiona Rose, Mark Booth and everyone at Hodder – thank you so much for your unending support and enthusiasm. I can't believe we are publishing book three already!

Jen, Louise, Jess and Linds. Not only are you the most fabulous friends a girl could hope for, you also like books (wahey)! *Thank you* for your honest opinions, your kind words and your belief in Paper Swans when I was freaking out behind a large glass of wine. I cannot express my gratitude enough . . . Lucy, thank you for inspiring me. You are like a big sister to me. Your support means more than you know, and thank you for all you have taught me.

Mum and Brenda. I am so grateful to you for being understanding when I am tired, ratty or hungry (or all three), and for helping to weed out the last few little things I could not see! What would I do without you?

Andy – you make me happy! Thank you, also, for sharing my love of space, watching hours of geeky documentaries and reading The Hitchiker's Guide to The Galaxy with me! I love you, thank you.

For my friends. You know who you are. I couldn't do this without you. Thank you for being there for me, and also for putting up with my chaos . . . I promise that soon I will buy a proper diary and actually bloody use it.

And last but certainly not least, thank you to my wonderful family. My Mum and Dad, I'm delighted that you are so content now, living in the countryside – your favourite place to be! I am eternally thankful to you for everything. Mum, please never stop sending me random articles in the post, and Dad, the only thing that should come between me and your brilliantly funny emails is a power cut (don't unplug the modem, it stops the internet working!) Helen, Angela, Greg and Richard, I cannot begin to put in words how much I admire you. My uncle Adrian, aunty Hilary, cousin Nick, my nieces and nephews and everyone else in my family – *thank you* for all your support . . .

In the best books, the ending often comes as a shock.
Not just because of that one last twist in the tale,
but because you have been so absorbed in their world,
that coming back to the harsh light of reality is a jolt.

If that describes you now, then perhaps you should track down
some new leads, and find new suspense in other worlds.

Join us at www.hodder.co.uk, or follow us on
Twitter @hodderbooks, and you can tap in to a
community of fellow thrill-seekers.

Whether you want to find out more about this book,
or a particular author, watch trailers and interviews, have
the chance to win early limited editions, or simply browse
our expert readers' selection of the very best books,
we think you'll find what you're looking for.

And if you don't, that's the place to tell us what's missing.

We love what we do, and we'd love you to be part of it.

www.hodder.co.uk

@hodderbooks

HodderBooks

HodderBooks